FO...
NOTHING WAS
FORBIDDEN . . .
NOTHING!

PANDORA ASHLEY—The Star: gorgeous, hot-blooded, totally out of control . . .

TONY HOLLAND—The Director: talented, charming, a lamb led to slaughter . . .

LUCINDA SINCLAIR—The Ingenue: wide-eyed, naive, anything but innocent . . .

ROD WARD—The Leading Man: superstud, sex-driven, Hollywood's favorite love toy . . .

MARTIN SINCLAIR—The Producer: aging, ruthless, bound by a lifelong obsession . . .

STRANGE SINS

STRANGE SINS

by

Jocelyn Christopher

A DELL BOOK

Published by
Dell Publishing Co., Inc.
a division of The Bantam Doubleday Dell Publishing Group, Inc.
1 Dag Hammarskjold Plaza
New York, New York 10017

ISBN: 0-440-20028-8

Printed in the United States of America

January 1988

10 9 8 7 6 5 4 3 2 1

KRI

I wish to thank my agent, Mel Berger, and my editor, Chuck Adams, who guided me every inch of the way with much more than professional expertise, and especially my Uncle Max, who did not live to see this book published but who made it possible.

To the man I love.

"Thou art so truthful that thoughts of thee suffice
to make dreames truthes, and fables histories."
—JOHN DONNE

PROLOGUE

"This is Gary Franklin, and, as you can see, I'm out here live in front of the Dorothy Chandler Pavilion, where the excitement is really starting to mount. You can hear the crowd going wild behind me as the nominees and many other celebrities file into the auditorium.

"We can see Al Pacino over there just getting out of his limousine . . . he's up for Best Actor this year for his performance in *Clash,* and he's a great popular favorite. But, again, he's facing very stiff competition from Dustin Hoffman, who's won before, of course, as well as Robert De Niro, Michael Caine, and Jeremy Irons.

"Now . . . oh, and you can hear the crowd behind me going crazy as this lady approaches. This lady, Jess, as you know, is—along with Sissy Spacek and Meryl Streep—a nominee for Best Actress, and I guess I'd have to say that she is perhaps *the* hottest young star in Hollywood at the moment.

"Let's see if we can't perhaps try and have a word with her . . . Lucinda Sinclair. Here she comes. She's a great popular favorite, Jess, in spite of the fact that *Moonshadows* was her very first role . . ."

1

From the windows of his office Martin Sinclair could see the marquees of half a dozen theaters—The Shubert, the Broadhurst, the St. James among them. On two of those marquees he could read his own name above the title. And although you couldn't see it from Shubert Alley, over on Fifty-first at the Mark Hellinger you could find "A Martin Sinclair Production" spelled out in the distinctive black scroll that had become, over his thirty years in the theater, a signature, almost his own logo. But no, it was more than that: It was a guarantee, Martin liked to think, of a certain standard of excellence.

In all the years, through all his sparring matches with the critics (and they had been legion, God knew), no one had ever accused a Martin Sinclair Production of shoddiness. He knew every inch of every house on Broadway, from the amenities of the star's dressing room to the faded velour upholstery of the third balcony.

Of the three productions Martin had running now in New York, one—a transfer from the Royal Shakespeare Company of their production of *Uncle Vanya*—was, as expected, a critical success, but one that would barely pay for itself despite Paul Scofield's incomparable performance.

The second, a musical adaptation of Noel Coward's *Design for Living,* had opened soft but was building. Sinclair had followed his legendary gut instinct on that one, refusing to close the show when the reviews came out, (lukewarm, except for the *Times,* the only one that counted, and *that* was scalding). Instead, as his detractors had called it, he had insisted on "throwing good money after bad" and launched one of the most expensive TV publicity campaigns ever devised for a Broadway production, the sort that specialized in audience reaction—smiling people with bad haircuts and regrettable jackets who had obviously never heard of Noel Coward, but who said the show was the greatest thing since sliced bread. It had worked. *Design* was sold out six weeks in advance, and a road company was being mounted to open in L.A. in September.

As for *Footlight Parade* over at the Hellinger, it was up for nine Tonys and looked like it would run forever. To the theater world, Martin Sinclair was truly the Emperor of New York, and, as such, his credo might well have been adapted from that of an earlier potentate, Tiberius: "Let them hate me. So long as they fear me."

And now, in his sixty-fifth year, Sinclair was to seek, for the first time in his long career, to expand the frontiers of that empire, to forsake the world of the theater with which his name was synonymous, to venture into the uncharted territories of the Hollywood barbarians. In short, he was to produce his first feature film, determined that the words "A Martin Sinclair Production" should come to have the same impact on a wide screen as they had on a theater marquee.

He had considered this movie carefully over many years. Never, it seemed to him, had he found the right vehicle—until his purchase (for a sum reportedly well in excess of one million dollars) of the film rights of the best seller, *Moonshadows.* Opinion in the film community was divided.

Some, predictably, said he would "fall on his ass." Others—
those who had watched Sinclair's rise over the years—predicted that he could come to wield a power on the West
Coast at least equal to that he had held for so long in the
East.

A red light was flashing across the rich expanse of Sinclair's mahogany desk.

"What is it, Liz?"

"I have Mr. Anthony Holland on the line from London, Mr. Sinclair."

"Put him through. Hello, Tony, my boy. Good news
this end. I've just spoken with Lou over at the Morris office
and Rod Ward not only loves the script, he's ecstatic about
the prospect of working with you. Now all we need is Pandora . . . I'm telling you, Tony, those two kids will burn
up the screen. When is your meeting with her, by the way?
What time is it over there?"

"That's great news about Rod Ward, Martin. Give Lou
the old wheeze about the feeling being mutual this end, but,
look, Martin, I want to be very frank with you. I've given a
lot of thought to this, and I can't see Pandora Ashley as
Isabel. Being notorious offscreen doesn't necessarily make
her sultry on. She's a slut, Martin, not a femme fatale."

"Tony, I'm not going to discuss this matter over the
phone now. We'll talk again after you've met with Pandora."

"Meeting her won't change the fact that she's incapable
of playing this part."

"We'll speak about this on Friday, after you've been up
to Buckinghamshire. Oh, by the way, if he's there, give my
best regards to Josh."

It was no use. The conversation was obviously at an
end as far as Sinclair was concerned. There was nothing for
Holland to do but to wheel up to Bucks and meet the

woman. "All right, Martin. It certainly can't hurt any to meet with La Ashley. I'm off tomorrow morning, then, and I'll report back to you on Friday. I'll certainly say hello to Josh if I see him."

"That's the stuff! Just keep an open mind, Tony. I've got a gut feeling about the chemistry between that pair, Ward and Ashley. Good-bye, Tony."

"Ward and Asshole," thought Anthony Holland, but all he said was, "Good-bye, talk to you Friday." He hoped to Christ that Ashley's husband, Josh Woodard, was at home. Seeing him would at least make the trek to Wandsworth House worthwhile. What a bitch his wife had been to him, if the reports were true.

Directors! thought Martin Sinclair as he replaced the receiver on its cradle. They're as bad as actors. Children, the pack of them!

The phone's red light blinked its eternal message. Mr. Sinclair, said the light, I've got a fabulous idea for a play, a musical, a film; it's a love story, costume piece, science fiction, spectacle, mystery, western; we've got money in Yugoslavia, Canada, Saudi Arabia; we can film in Bulgaria, Spain, the People's Republic of China; we have Redford, De Niro, Dustin Hoffman.

Martin Sinclair had heard it all, drivel, mostly from shysters and dreamers living on hype and hope. But once in a very rare while he would hear from artists, people with real talent like the play and film writer Josh Woodard, and, when that happened it made the rest of the bullshit worth wading through.

"Who is it, Liz?" Sinclair asked wearily.

"It's just the waiter from Sardi's with your lunch, Mr. Sinclair, and I have Merle for you on line three."

"Send the boy in, Liz, and tell Merle I'm out to lunch and I'll get back to her."

"She says it's urgent, Mr. Sinclair."

"Everything is, with Merle. Tell her I'll get back to her."

Pandora Ashley drained the remnants of her Cristal champagne, then balanced the glass gingerly on the black marble ledge, and stepped lightly from the cool, deep tub. She smiled complacently at the many reflections of her lithe, tanned form displayed in the array of mirrors which enveloped the bath enclosure. Refracted amber light played on her raven hair, casting a burnished highlight on the strands which framed her famous face, throwing into relief the small yet perfectly formed breasts displayed against her slender, tanned frame.

Not bad for thirty-four, she thought to herself. Not bad at all. She was still angry that Josh had refused to let her do that *Playboy* layout. It would have been great publicity, and a kick besides, but, no, Josh still insisted on treating her like some piece of exquisite Royal Crown Derby porcelain. Surely he knew her better than that after nearly three years of marriage.

Opium? Chloë? L'Interdit? Ivoire? She hesitated for a moment before the bewildering assortment of flacons, each promising its own enticement to seduction and romance. Opium. Decidedly, Opium. To hell with her image as the "English Rose," as a well-meaning critic had once described her when she appeared in Josh's *The Encounter*. Languidly, Pandora poured a ribbon of the honey-colored scent into the palm of her hands.

The *Moonshadows* film could be very important to her, she thought. So, for that matter, could its director, Anthony Holland. Her fingers glided deftly over her small, firm breasts, down her taut midriff, spreading the delicious scent, pausing briefly to caress the thick mass of chocolate curls before continuing down her slender thighs. Her skin was a silky brown—all over. Truly, Spain had done her a lot of good. Musk and jasmine filled the warm steamy air of the lacquered room.

An odalisque! thought Pandora Ashley. A Matisse odalisque! That is how Tony Holland must see me. And, with that, she snatched a filmy wisp of pale orange chiffon from a baroque, gilt-encrusted hook beside the marble tub. As she adjusted the Dior robe over her bosom, she noted with approval that the dark outline of her nipples was clearly visible beneath the sheer apricot fabric.

"Madame! Madame!" It was the voice of Clarisse, Pandora's personal maid, over the intercom. "It's Monsieur Holland, Madame. His car has just passed the gates."

Perhaps it was subconscious anticipation, but the name "Holland" unaccountably sent a tremor of excitement through Pandora's frame, as though she had been touched expertly in some secret place. That must not happen. Now more than ever she must be in control. Her green eyes flashed one last approving glance at her image reflected over and over from every angle of the jewel-like mirrored room.

"Merde," she whispered, not as a curse, but as a talisman, as she had whispered it to herself in the wings of so many theaters on so many opening nights for nearly seventeen years: This had to be one of her best performances.

A soft rain was falling as the silver Jaguar streaked along the M40. Anthony Holland slipped Bach's Double Concerto in D Minor on to the cassette deck and thrilled with a quiet pride as each clear note of Menhuin's recording reverberated through the luxurious automobile. His decision to buy the Jaguar—over which he had long agonized as being perhaps a premature extravagance—seemed, at this moment, vindicated beyond any shadow of a doubt. Tony

Holland faced the future with confidence and with a pride in his own achievements, which in a lesser man would have seemed smug.

There were no broken bones, no stabbed backs, no skeletal remains in closets strewing the pathway to Holland's success. He had always eschewed the cheap shot . . . the main chance . . . the fast buck . . . the easy lay. Each project to which he devoted himself had been, if not always a work of art, at least an individual creation, a work of pride to which he had given the utmost of his considerable talent, energy, and strength. Hollywood would not change him. That he would someday have to work there had been inevitable in the course of his career's progression, but he was determined that the move would be made only with the right vehicle, the right property, something he could wholly believe in and respect.

Thus when the call had come from Martin Sinclair, he reacted with exhilaration. The "Sinclair touch" was Broadway legend. Tony was familiar with several of the producer's past productions of O'Neill, Pinter, Osborne, and Bond. In each one he had pushed the stage to its limits of experimentation and creativity. Now Sinclair had chosen *him* to direct his first feature film. His moment had come, and he was ready to seize it. Holland—not readily given to displays of passion, or any emotion, for that matter—had scarcely been able to conceal his elation when the call had come through from New York.

His first feature film assignment was to be nothing less than the directorial plum of the season—*Moonshadows.* He had read the best-selling novel, and to his amazement had enjoyed it. While reading he had almost instinctively formed some visual impressions of what the rather elaborate story should look like when transferred to the screen. Tony had followed with more interest than usual the accounts in the trades of *Moonshadows*'s purchase by the famed Broadway producer for an astronomical sum of money, and the reports of directors rumored to be about to be offered the assignment (Richard Attenborough and Milos Forman were among the names most frequently mentioned). Never had Holland dared to hope that he himself, with his relative lack of experience, might be selected, nor had he even suggested to his agent, Colin Blakemore, that his name be put forward.

And then the call had come from Martin Sinclair: Now within six weeks he would be on his way to the South of France to begin shooting *Moonshadows*. He would be on his way as well to another income tax bracket. While his fee was by no means comparable to what a more experienced Hollywood director would surely have commanded, it was still roughly the equivalent of what his five ex-collaborators at the BBC—who had knowingly prophesied doom for him over their Shepherd's Bush gin and tonics when he had decided to forsake their ranks six years ago—might be expected to earn in the next ten years. It had all paid off. Yes, Anthony reflected, there were risks in life that simply had to be taken.

Others, however, seemed doomed from the outset, and Pandora Ashley as Isabel . . . was one of them. He couldn't for the life of him understand what had gotten into Sinclair, why he should be so intent on casting her. Admittedly, she had been adequate as Lady Jane Grey, but surely no one could deny that the success of the piece had been entirely owing to Josh Woodard's outstanding writing, and that any one of half a dozen actresses would have been equally good in the part.

As for *Pavlova,* what a debacle that had been. Not even her husband's brilliance could save her in that fiasco, and if even half the stories that had filtered back from location were to be believed—and Holland, for his part, was certain they were *all* true—Pavlova's exertions with the Diaghilev Ballet had been nothing compared to Pandora's bedroom acrobatics with every male on the set, from her leading man to the assistant gaffer. And all the while, of course, Josh Woodard had sat steadfastly at his typewriter, pounding out page after page of rewrites, blaming himself for what was clearly a flop film before it was even in the can, trying to write that sow's ear he'd married into a silk purse.

Holland could not fathom what spell the witch had cast over Woodard. Before he had married Pandora Ashley, Tony mused, Josh had been right up there in the front ranks of England's young literary lions, not in a league with Pinter perhaps, but still well in the running with Simon Gray, David Hare, or Peter Shaffer.

All he'd done lately, however, was to churn out glitzy vehicles for his lady love—warmed-over Terence Rattigan with a touch of Barbara Cartland thrown in. It was bloody pathetic! "Christ Almighty," Holland said aloud, "Sinclair must be mad!"

The Jag leapt forward as Holland pushed down on the accelerator. He wanted to get this farce of a meeting over as quickly as possible, so that he could tell Martin Sinclair once and for all to get another Isabel, and damned quickly at that.

Wandsworth House, the "castle" which Josh Woodard had purchased for his lady love, was situated in its own park some two miles outside the tiny village of Princes Risborough, Bucks, some fifty miles from London. The rain had stopped by the time Anthony Holland passed through the massive iron gates which opened on to a vast expanse of velvet lawn, densely shaded by great silent oaks and beeches.

The house, which rose beyond the perfect lawn, was a

long, gabled affair of great antiquity (it had, in fact, been
built under Edward VI), its weathered red brick softened by
ivy, its leaded windows shaded by creepers. It was the very
sort of house which, at any other time, would have appealed
to Anthony Holland.

This afternoon, however, the very scale of the place
seemed not grand but pretentious, and served only to in-
crease his disdain for the lady inside. His indignation was
further fueled by the assortment of vehicles lined in ostentatious display on the gravel driveway. Included were a bright
red Corniche convertible—unmistakably Pandora's, since it
sported the license "ACT 1"; a dark blue Volvo estate
wagon (it most likely belongs to Josh, thought Anthony,
since it's not flashy enough for Madame); a purple Mini
with tinted windows; and a black Porsche Targa, whose
plates read "ACT 2."

Act 3, curtain! said Anthony Holland to himself, as a
noticeable sneer played over his handsome face.

Holland was, by any standards, a remarkably attractive
man. Tall and vigorously well built, with frank, straight features and lively blue eyes, he conveyed immediately the air
of being a fortunate person. What was perhaps most striking
about his youthful good looks, though, was that they were
crowned by a thick head of hair so purely flaxen as to be
nearly white in color.

The entrance to Pandora's Box, he thought as the por-
tals to Wandsworth House were opened by a butler so solemn that Tony reflected he must have been sent around by
Central Casting. He was ceremoniously escorted to the library, where Pandora Ashley would doubtlessly—after the
appropriate pause—make her entrance upstage left.

Left alone to muse on his surroundings, however, he
could not help but be favorably impressed. The house presented no ostentatious display; there was no obvious ac-

cumulation of bric-a-brac or overpowering objets d'art, yet
it seemed to retain the imprint of centuries of placid and
commodious living. The original light oak paneling and
leaded windows had been painstakingly restored. The furniture, a harmonious juxtaposition of Georgian and modern,
was sparse, giving the impression of elegant restraint on the
part of the decorator. This understated backdrop formed the
perfect foil for the luminous beauty of a Turner watercolor
of sunset at Petworth (the only item of obvious extravagance
on display). In addition, some of David Hockney's sketches
for the Glyndebourne *Rake's Progress* dotted the walls, ac-
centuating the witty blend of antique and modern with just a
touch of the theatrical. Everything, in fact, seemed light,
airy, effortless. The very flowers were placed with such art-
ful simplicity that they seemed to have arranged themselves
of their own accord. Tony Holland could not suppress the
thought that he should be very comfortable indeed in such a
house as this. Were he left alone to enjoy it, of course.

From the moment she swept into the library in her
orange chiffon robe, Pandora Ashley sensed that she had
miscalculated. Anthony Holland, she could tell at a glance,
was not a man to be won over by tits and ass alone. No
matter. Pandora had the reflexes of a Grand Prix racer, and
she had other resources at her disposal as well. *En garde,*
she thought, my handsome Mr. Holland. You shall find me
a match for you.

Beyond the magnificence of her green eyes and her perfect body, Pandora Ashley was not, perhaps in the strictest
sense of the word, a beauty. Her features were irregular,
striking rather than chiseled, yet she undeniably created a
greater illusion of perfection than younger girls with the
faces of angels. She carried herself in such a manner that a
dime store string of pearls would around her throat be

thought incontrovertibly to have come from Harry Winston's showcase.

Illusion was in her blood. Theatricality was the very stuff of which she was made, and she played every scene to the hilt. She measured the response of her audience with the skills and instincts of a champion horsewoman approaching a six-foot jump, bending her mount to her will, measuring the pace, vaulting over the obstacle. She knew instinctively when to lower her voice to a whisper . . . when to rant . . . to tremble . . . to shed tears . . . to strike infallibly the right note in order to wring every last drop of emotion from her audience.

Utterly fearless, mercurial, willful, the intense exhilarations and depressions of her roles invariably spilled over into her everyday life. Sexually insatiable, she had, if the truth be told, only been in love once in her entire life, and that had been very long ago. Yet she went through the motions of grand passions, heartbreak, and betrayal with monotonous regularity and utter conviction, as if the outward shows of such high dramas were in themselves substitutes for some deeper feeling. Offstage, as well as on, Pandora Ashley was a brilliant performer, and she had never, never met her match.

Good Lord!, thought Holland, this is going to be even worse than I had expected. It had never occurred to him that the creature might actually attempt to seduce him, but that dress—or whatever the devil one could call the thing she was wearing—was practically transparent; plus she smelled like a walking bordello.

"Miss Ashley," he said with forced cordiality, "how good of you to find time to see me." Too bad you couldn't find time to dress.

"Not at all, Mr. Holland. It was very kind of you to drive all this way. It must have been very tiresome for you.

What can I offer you after your long journey? Scotch? Sherry?" My body?

She has a somewhat dusky, but well-modulated voice, soft, pleasant, like a high-priced whore. It certainly contrasts favorably with that garish thing she's wearing, Tony thought. "Nothing at all, thank you," he replied.

"Are you quite certain you won't join me in some sherry? I'm having some." My, my! He's quite the specimen.

"Just a small glass then, thank you." And then I'm getting the hell out of here.

He could not avoid—naturally, it had never been intended that he should—watching the rhythmic sway of Pandora's tight, small buttocks as she crossed downstairs right —he knew damn well he was witnessing a performance, and so far not a very impressive one—and poured amber liquid from a Baccarat decanter.

Now for the reverse angle, Tony mused.

Obligingly, Pandora turned: The small, round breasts strained to be free of their delicate covering; there was the faint outline of a dark triangle above the bronzed limbs.

"I wanted very particularly to meet you, Mr. Holland." A gigantic emerald flashed green fire on the tapered fingers, which held out a crystal glass. "You see, I am very much afraid that although, of course, I should be immensely thrilled to work with you, I cannot do *Moonshadows.*"

Had he been a religious man, Tony no doubt would have flung himself down on his knees at that moment and offered up prayers of thanks. Although he was not by nature demonstrative, it took every ounce of what the French would call his *sangfroid* to conjure up the proper note of regret in his voice as he asked Pandora Ashley what had made her come to that unfortunate decision. Isabel was, after all, the plum role of the season. Whoever played it, unless she was deaf, dumb, spastic, or possibly all three, was almost certain to be nominated for an Academy Award.

Pandora Ashley seated herself demurely—or as demurely as her ensemble would permit—on a quilted leather sofa opposite Tony. She smoothed her robe nervously, adjusting it to cover her legs. She placed her glass on the coffee table, then leaned forward as if to speak; she took a few short, deep breaths, as if to steady herself for what was to come; she hesitated, then snatched up the glass again. Her hand trembled slightly as she raised it to her lips. Then, abruptly, she put it down again, the sherry untasted.

"You don't think very much of me, do you, Mr. Holland?" She spoke this in a very small, weak voice, quite unlike the one with which she had greeted him. She seemed very small now too, sitting there, as if somehow all the pretense had gone out of her, as if she were tired of pretending to be a star. She was just a woman, small and vulnerable, sitting naked and afraid.

"Miss Ashley . . . I scarcely know you, I . . ."

"Please, Mr. Holland," she interrupted, holding up a small hand in a weary gesture, "there's no need for you to be chivalrous. You don't like me. I sensed it the moment I walked through that door. Human reactions are, after all, my stock-in-trade. I am an actress. Or was. You don't like me, and I'm not surprised you don't." She seemed to wish to continue, but appeared seized by violent emotion. Her tanned bosom and shoulders heaved up and down. She bit down on her full lower lip, straining to fight back tears.

Holland was bitterly ashamed of his conduct. His features were flushed with a deep and almost palpable embarrassment. He wished he could just run out of the room and leave forever behind him the spectacle of this delicate woman in torment. "Miss Ashley," he heard himself saying, "if I have given that impression, and caused any pain, believe me, I am most deeply and sincerely sorry. Even if there were any truth in what you are saying, why should my good opinion mean anything to you?"

Pandora had composed herself somewhat. Her hands swept back a strand of dark hair and rearranged it against her long neck. She turned the full force of her large emerald eyes on Anthony Holland and began again: "Have you seen my last film, *Pavlova,* Mr. Holland? No need to answer; I can see you have. And you have, perhaps, also heard certain stories, rumors about the offscreen dramas behind the scenes?"

God in heaven, why is she doing this? "I . . ." Tony began falteringly.

Pandora did not wait for his reply, but continued in her trembling voice: "No need to answer that one either; I can see that you have. To answer your earlier question, Mr. Holland, why your good opinion should be so important to me: One. I am, as I have already said, an actress. I suppose I went into this profession because there is some weakness in me that makes me need love more than most normal human beings do. Two. I have watched your work with interest for several years now. I respect and admire you. I should like that feeling to be mutual.

"It is very difficult," continued Pandora, ". . . it is very difficult—I am sure your wife will confirm this, Mr. Holland—to be married to a genius." She paused for a moment, distractedly scanning the long rows of gilded books that lined the walls of the great room. She seemed oddly lost, as if she failed to recognize the place, and couldn't fathom how she had gotten there.

"I told Josh I couldn't play Anna Pavlova, I told him I wasn't ready, that I was no dancer . . . that people would laugh when they cut away from me to the real ballerina. I begged him to get someone else. I swear it, Mr. Holland. He wouldn't listen to reason. He said I *was* Pavlova!

"It was a nightmare from the very beginning! The moment we got to the location, everybody was at each other's throats. Josh blamed the director. The director blamed me. We ran over budget in the middle, and Josh had to invest our own money just to get the picture finished. I must have had some sort of a nervous breakdown. I began doing things. I just can't explain . . . I suppose I was ready to do anything for some sort of reassurance that I . . . but there's no excuse. None. I love my husband very deeply, Mr. Holland. I am very much aware of all the sacrifices he's made for me . . . and there's nothing I wouldn't do for Josh. You must believe me."

For some moments now it had ceased to matter whether or not Tony Holland believed her. He had begun listening to her speech with detached skepticism, watching her performance with the sort of amazed incredulity one reserves for trapeze artists or high-wire acts, wondering that she had the nerve to attempt such obvious tricks on him as she glided from one effect to another. Gradually, however, and without a conscious yielding, he had ceased to be aware of the artifice. Her performance took hold. And then it struck him—sincerity had not been the point at all! It was the whole spirit with which she had created and carried the scene that mattered, that was now sweeping him away on the high tide of her passions. The idea excited him, took possession of him.

How she feels it, he thought to himself, how she sees it . . . how she creates it! All resistance melted as he allowed himself to be enveloped by the musky clouds of her perfume, allowed his eyes to focus on the soft beauty of her glowing flesh, allowed himself to be mesmerized by the rhythmic music of her shimmering voice. Desire seemed to flash like a frantic appeal from her emerald eyes. What was good theater after all but a willing suspension of disbelief, and some part of Tony Holland willed himself to believe every word she spoke.

Of course he believed her. He was even seized with a sudden impulse to cradle her small, brown, child's face in his hands, to tell her that nothing he had heard about her mattered a damn, even if it had been true. Yes, Pandora Ashley was an extraordinary woman. He could see that now. Obviously it was pointless to try to judge her by ordinary standards. Slowly he again allowed himself to distinguish the individual syllables which floated amid the sounds of her wonderfully seductive voice.

"I just seem to have no confidence left. The smallest decision paralyzes me with fear; that is why I'm wearing this ridiculous outfit at three o'clock on a Wednesday afternoon." She tore at the apricot chiffon with her long fingernails. "I had two lovely dresses laid out on the bed for me. I couldn't choose between them. I kept putting one on, then taking it off and trying the other, then taking that one off again. Finally you were here, and I still hadn't decided, so I just rushed down like this. I didn't want to keep you waiting." Her lower lip trembled. "I did so want to make a good impression."

"You have made a good impression, and . . ."—the words burst from his lips before he was quite aware what he was saying—"I want you to play Isabel for me."

"I've already told you, Tony . . ." she hesitated, ". . . it's all right to call you Tony?" Pandora asked meekly.

Of course it was.

"I can't play Isabel. I don't know when I'll ever be able to face a camera again. I couldn't live through another experience like *Pavlova*. Who knows? Perhaps someday we'll work together on another picture, but not *Moonshadows*."

Pause. "It's a pity." Pause. "I feel instinctively that you and I would get along."

Oh, yes! He knew they would! He wished there were something he could say to make her reconsider.

"Unless . . . unless . . . ," said Pandora haltingly, ". . . you could . . . arrange a screen test . . ."

Anthony Holland stared at her incredulously. It was unheard of for a major star such as Pandora Ashley to offer to test for a role.

"Don't you see?" the actress continued. "Then we would both know if I could do it, if I were right for the part. If it works out, it will be a great boost for my confidence and help me give a better performance. If not, it's saved us all a great deal of agony."

"I'll try and set something up for next week at Pinewood." Tony heard the words stumble from his mouth, the voice strained, almost childlike in its eagerness. "Of course, I shall have to clear this with Martin Sinclair, but I'm certain that will be no problem once I've explained your feeling to him. Mr. Sinclair has always felt most strongly that you're the only one for the part."

"You've taken a great load off my mind, Mr. Holl . . . Tony. You're a very kind man. Until next week, then?" The actress stood, her hand extended in a sign of friendship and dismissal.

"Next week. My secretary will call you when we've made all the arrangements. It has been an honor to meet you, Miss Ashley."

Pandora Ashley reached for the Lalique crystal box that sat atop her dressing table, an antique of Chinese ebony inlaid with mother-of-pearl. The lid of the tiny crystal box was an exquisite translucent sculpture of two turtle doves mating. Inside the box was a fine white powder, a small amount of which Pandora removed with a miniature gilt spoon and held to her finely sculpted nostrils. She inhaled deeply, then waited for the slightly acrid taste at the base of her throat to subside and for a wave of elation to sweep over her. As the drug began to work its wonders, she poured herself a glass of champagne and, kicking off her gilt sandals, pirouetted lightly around the peach bedroom, first humming a few notes from *Swan Lake,* then breaking off into a sparkling ripple of laughter: "Anthony Holland! Anthony Holland!" She hadn't believed they made them like that anymore.

She unclasped the apricot chiffon robe and draped it like a toga—à la Isadora Duncan—around her firm, brown nakedness. Still laughing, she twirled in front of the mirror. So innocent, she mused. In that way he is very like my husband. But handsome! It isn't often one sees a man that handsome. Physical beauty in a man had always been of prime importance to Pandora, and so, for his plainness, she secretly despised her husband, Josh Woodard.

She drained the champagne from her glass and flung herself on to her intricately carved Chinese wedding bed, which, like her body, was draped in silk, only peach, not apricot. She extended her languid form on the silk cushions, a smile playing on her ripe mouth as she wondered what sort of lover Anthony Holland was going to make. She pictured him before her now, thrilling inwardly as she relished the impact she knew her body would make upon him. She imagined that his clear blue eyes were fixed on her as she began to caress her rosy nipples; then, spreading her brown thighs, she plunged a tapered finger deep within herself, rubbing it back and forth in agitation and delight. The image of Holland standing before her tantalized her beyond measure. When her orgasm came, she found that it merely increased her appetite, like a forkful of meat to a starving man.

She rose abruptly from the bed and dressed hastily, not bothering with underwear or makeup. She put on a plain, tight-fitting blue skirt and jumper, and tied her hair back under a simple print scarf, then concealed her emerald eyes behind dark Porsche glasses. She would take the Mini into town and find a man—any man would do, so long as he was masculine. It would not be the first time. In fact, Pandora Ashley had lost count, so frequent were these little excursions of hers. She called them her "magical mystery tours." Taxi drivers, students from nearby Oxford, construction workers—all these had found their way into Pandora's bed as a result of her little outings. Some were, naturally, more satisfying than others, but all were, to Pandora, amusing. She made it a point never to fuck the men or boys she met in this way more than once, nor, if possible, to reveal her true identity. Not being recognized was part of the kick. If one of her random lovers began to suspect, she would suddenly cultivate a Lancashire or Cockney or Glasgow accent, and say, yes, everyone told her there was a resemblance to that actress, but she herself could never see it.

She laughed with delight in anticipation of her adventure. Patience, after all, had never been her strong point. She couldn't be expected to wait until the screen test next week and for Anthony Holland to fuck her.

The tinted windows diffused the intensity on the purple Mini of the late afternoon's light as the vehicle hurtled past Aylesbury with the velocity of a bullet. Pandora Ashley drove as she always did, flat out and with reckless abandon, narrowly missing a bicyclist who happened to get in the way of the little car as it skidded dizzily around a bend in the road. Why in hell hadn't she taken the Porsche? she asked herself. So what if it was conspicuous? If Josh didn't like her behavior, he could fucking divorce her.

The effects of the cocaine, the natural high of a triumphant performance, the thrill of knowing she was about to play Isabel, and, strangely, the image of Tony Holland's frank, handsome face, the clear, steady light of his blue eyes focused on her, had all combined to throw Pandora into a frenzy of arousal, both nervous and sexual. Something in the young director's gaze bewildered and intrigued her. True, she had won him over, but she had not beguiled him. Of that much she was certain. It did not matter. Once she got him into bed, he would be her creature.

Hadn't they all been? All but one, that is. The first one. Very long ago. The one who had so brutally stripped her, at once of shame, pride, and illusions together. The one who had taught her at age seventeen everything she ever wanted to know about men. And more . . . much more. He had been handsome too, every bit as handsome as Tony Holland. He too had had blue eyes, but in them had gleamed mockery and scorn. His name had been Robin Maxwell, and Pandora Ashley had been his wife for exactly four months, nine days, and three hours of pure, unadulterated hell.

Robin Maxwell had been an actor of sorts, but more significantly he had been a matinee idol to Pandora and the other girls in her class at the Guildhall School of speech and drama. They had giggled over his photos in glossy magazines and whispered excitedly about the bulge in his tights when he played Mercutio. She had joined nervously in their knowing laughter, fearing to betray her all too obvious lack of sophistication by a blush or a wrong word. She had wanted so badly to be accepted by the other students, and it was so rarely that they spoke to her. It was no wonder, though; she remembered her thoughts as she had disconsolately studied her reflection in a mirror. Shabby clothes—hand-me-downs from her cousin Louisa—hanging loosely on a skinny frame; thin wisps of black hair; enormous green eyes which seemed to bulge in their prominence in her pale, solemn face. How could she ever hope to be like her heroines, Vivien Leigh or Jean Simmons? She searched the mirror obsessively, trying to seek out her "best angles" . . . her "good points."

By contrast, all the other girls in her class seemed awfully beautiful, or awfully talented, or, worse, both. And yet, at bottom, her spirit never faltered. She had always known that she was meant to be an actress. Always. The fact was as inevitable as breathing. Theater, after all, was in her blood. She had been born in a squalid theatrical boardinghouse in Leicester while her father was giving a matinee performance as King John to a half-empty house.

But she had lost it all when still young. Her little world of musty railway carriages and dank dressing rooms; the ancient costumes, rank with mothballs and dried sweat; and her mother's dressing table—a pungent-smelling rainbow of grease paint; the occasional thrilling walk-on in front of the parti-colored light whenever "a child" was called for—it all came to a terrifying end when her parents were both killed in a crash of a plane taking their company of actors on tour of South Africa. Fortunately for Pandora, she had not accompanied her parents but had been left behind with her Aunt Mary in Notting Hill Gate.

Aunt Mary was a woman of straightened means and rigorous views. Her husband had been killed years earlier during the blitz, and ill health had forced her to abandon her own career on the stage and to eke out a pitiful existence giving lessons in French and elocution. Her dedication to the stage, however, remained total, in spite of her near-crippling arthritis. "I am not a woman," she would announce proudly in ringing stentorian tones, "I am not a mother, I am not a housewife . . . I am an actress!" It was not long before she began to live vicariously through Pandora, to see in the success of her brother's child the eventual triumph of her own cruelly frustrated ambition.

For a brief period in the late sixties, London had resurfaced as social mecca of the universe. The grand old city throbbed with the pulse of the new music, played by groups such as the Beatles and the Stones; it shone with a new kind of psychedelic light. Each day new discos sprang up, and new fashions and hairdos became the rage of Carnaby Street, each more outrageous than the last. The frontiers of the mind were being expanded with new drugs—hash, cannabis, LSD, mescaline, speed—and everywhere frontiers of class, of morality, of age, of convention were crashing down around the confused and disoriented of all ages.

The seventeen-year-old Pandora, however, remained oblivious to all this. Neither a grown-up nor a child, she frightened many would-be admirers by her solemn intensity. She dreamed only of the theater, of Shakespeare and Chekhov, of Ibsen and Shaw, of Juliet and Raina and Masha and Lady Macbeth and all the other roles that would be hers one day. And then, at an audition for a walk-on role with understudy duties in *The White Devil* at the Duchess Theatre, she had met Robin Maxwell—and her life had been changed.

The dress she had chosen for the audition was a bright green taffeta affair which she knew set off her pale face and bright eyes. She needed all the confidence she could muster, since she was to read with the illustrious Robin Maxwell. She had seen him before, of course, in film magazines and on the screen, but she was quite unprepared for the quiver of excitement which passed through the air like an electric current from his body to her own.

His eyes were of a cold brightness more turquoise than blue. He wore a black silk shirt, with a thin gold chain around his neck. He had just returned from Hollywood and his skin had been burnt black by the California sun. Something of a minor matinee idol in England—due almost entirely to his startling good looks and reputation as a cocksman—Maxwell had set out for America hoping to join the ranks of other English actors such as Roger Moore, Richard Burton, and Laurence Harvey who had risen to international stardom.

The market was saturated, however, and Englishmen in general were out of fashion. As a result, Maxwell's pretentions to rival Errol Flynn got no further in Hollywood than the bar of the Cock and Bull, and the beds of several second-rate starlets. Of course, there had been a couple of guest shots on *Bonanza* and the *F.B.I.,* but finally he had returned to his native shores, pushing forty, haunted by the specter of failure, and determined to show himself off to the world as a great classical actor whose disdain for Tinseltown had led him to turn his back on scores of lucrative film offers in order to return to his one true love—the THEATER!

Years later, Pandora Ashley had made up a story about Robin Maxwell, how he had first lured her back to his flat with a promise of a nonexistent party where she was to meet some of the most important people in the West End theater, then drugged and cruelly raped and sodomized her. She had told the story so often and embellished it so beautifully that over the years she had even come to believe it herself.

But in reality her seduction had been easy for Robin Maxwell. Almost boringly so. Throughout her audition for *The White Devil* he had kept his blue eyes coolly riveted on the pale, dark-haired girl, whose huge eyes matched her bright green dress. Her shy, virginal manner had fallen from her like a cloak the moment she began to read for the part, and her tiny frame had assumed the authority of a princess. He knew he had to have her, and so he did—that very night.

Of course, part of Pandora's story of that evening was

true. Maxwell had indeed spoken of a party, but something
in her eyes told him that she had understood the ruse instinctively but was drawn to him anyway. Inflamed by their
mutual deception—and by a couple of miscellaneous pills
and some marijuana—his lovemaking had been violent,
primitive, bestial. Afterward her frail body had been
convulsed with sobbing, and she had felt ashamed, confused,
defiled. Even Maxwell had experienced a twinge of conscience. After all, who could ever have expected to find a
seventeen-year-old virgin in London in the sixties, and on
stage at that. But she was back for more the next night, and
the next.

He showed her a side of London she never knew existed
—tiny after-hours clubs in the back streets of Soho and
Chelsea, where actors gathered after the curtains had gone
down and all the pubs had closed. He taught her how to
dress and how to drink. And most of all, he taught her
about sex. He was soon to find that he had never known a
woman with a hunger as intense as this frail creature possessed. As for Pandora, after her initial shock and fright, she
soon convinced herself that this, after all, must be what love
was about. It had to be. So he drank. No matter. She would
save him from himself. She even convinced herself that he
was a great actor. That she would play Vivien Leigh to his
Olivier. That they would be a great team one day.

They were married two nights after *The White Devil*
began previews at the Duchess Theatre. The play opened to
appalling notices and closed within a week. The marriage
closed shortly thereafter. Maxwell returned to old unfortunate habits of drinking and carousing and of staying away
from their flat. When he *was* there, he was violent, and became increasingly so.

Meanwhile, Pandora found other work. Her own notices in *The White Devil* had been complimentary despite the

mediocrity of the overall production and the smallness of her part, and she soon landed a coveted role in a much-publicized avant-garde production which was to open at the Royal Court. Her success, however tiny, served only to exacerbate her husband's sense of failure.

The beatings became more intense. She would regularly return home exhausted from rehearsals to find her husband sprawled drunkenly across the sheets, entwined with another woman. Worse still, even in the depths of her degradation, she still desired him. She had come to crave the hardness of his enormous cock driving roughly into her body, much as an addict craves a fix. Worst of all, she learned that she was pregnant with his child.

Terrified of her husband's reaction, she put off telling him the news until she was beginning to show, finally managing to convince herself that the baby would be just what was needed to put things right between them. In a way it did. Robin Maxwell stormed out of their Elgin Avenue flat, never to return—not before informing her, however, that their "marriage" had never been legal in the first place. It so happened that on a drunken bet one night in Las Vegas he had met and married a showgirl in one of that town's all-night drive-in wedding chapels, and had never bothered to get a divorce. He also threatened that if she "ever gave him any trouble," he would have some of his Soho friends carve up her pretty face so that she would never set foot on the stage again.

Pandora Ashley had been found later that evening by a neighbor who had become alarmed by the horrible, animal whimperings emanating from the adjacent flat. Her naked body, white as a cadaver, lay half submerged in the waters of her tub, which were tinted crimson by the blood which gushed from her slender wrists. Still breathing, she was rushed to St. Mary's Paddington where, miraculously, the doctors were able to save her own life, but not that of Robin Maxwell's unborn baby son. As a result, Pandora Ashley would never be able to have a child. Nor would any man ever use her again.

Carfax was thronged with them! Like some species of primordial fowl, they formed black clusters everywhere, their dark, winglike robes flapping in the afternoon breeze. Gaunt black forms huddled in the entrances of pastry shops along Cornmarket, while others stared bleakly at the window displays of Blackwell's. They were just what Pandora was seeking—this earthbound covey of overgrown rocks—for underneath their unruly shocks of too-long hair were to be found the ruddy complexions and fear-filled eyes of the first-year undergraduates of the colleges of Oxford, making their way to sitting their schools' examinations. For this solemn occasion, as is the centuries-old custom, donnish black caps and gowns had been thrown by the students (with varying degrees of sartorial success) over an astonishingly heterogenous assortment of eighties' haircuts and footwear.

"What a lot of silly geese they all look!" thought Pandora, as her purple Mini swung sharply into the High, and, like some larger bird of prey, slowed to a crawl as two young men in black robes detached themselves from a larger group and stood talking, framed in the archway of University College. The larger of the two was blondish and beefy and interested Pandora Ashley not at all. The other youth was quite another story. Although somewhat slighter in frame than his companion, the boy's every gesture was animated by a natural grace and his black cotton cloak was worn with the élan of a Childe Harold. Pandora's faith in Oxford was renewed once again. She inched the Mini toward the curb and lowered one of its charcoal-tinted windows.

"Excuse me!" Pandora called out to the two youths. With those two words she managed to convey not only directness, but also a mysterious suggestion of promise. The invitation implicit in her tone was apparently not having quite the desired reaction, however, as she noted that only the fairer, red-faced youth had ventured to approach the car. The other boy hung back haughtily, his dark eyes surveying her with a mixture of curiosity and disdain.

She could now see that her first impression had been correct. The boy's good looks were of the kind that could best be described as Byronic—a combination of dark brooding and scrupulous refinement which is found rarely among Englishmen, and almost never in other races. Something in the youth's haughty bearing appealed deeply to Pandora's romantic whim; indeed, her girlish dreams had once been inhabited by figures such as he now presented. His beefy companion she mentally set down as some firstborn son of Lord Haw-Haw; her hero had something rather more of the bastard about him.

"I'm in a spot of trouble, I'm afraid," Pandora began, removing her dark glasses and fixing her green eyes directly on the darker youth. "Can either of you chaps help me along to the Radcliffe Infirmary?" At this point her voice faltered, and her lower lip began a calculatedly involuntary tremble.

"Golly! I say . . . I mean, dash it . . . you're not ill, are you?" groped the boy who had come forward.

"It's my sister . . . my only sister," Pandora faltered, and through the mist which clouded her emerald eyes she perceived that the more attractive young man had advanced a step closer toward her car, and that his sardonic gaze had softened somewhat.

"You're on the wrong track, you know . . . wrong direction, entirely," sputtered the helpful one. "It's the Banbury Road you need . . ."

Pandora choked back sobs, "They say she may be . . ." Here she broke down utterly, unable to continue.

The fairer, taller boy was flushed and earnest, obviously struggling between two alternatives. "We'd take you there ourselves, gladly, you see, only it's schools," he indicated his black scholar's robes, in explanation. "Examinations . . . . We daren't miss them."

"Belt up, Charles!"

These were the first words the dark youth had uttered. In an instant, he had flung himself gracefully into the purple Mini, and impulsively taken Pandora's place at the wheel. Within seconds they were streaking at a lightning pace past the surrounding spires of the ancient city in the direction of the Radcliffe Infirmary.

Pandora Ashley and Jeremy Dain-Wilkes—the name of her young companion—sat in an electrically-charged silence as the car screeched to a skidding halt in front of the venerable red-brick hospital. Pandora took a deep breath, then slid her hand sinuously along her companion's thigh, stopping just short of its desired resting place. She fixed on him the full intensity of her emerald eyes.

"Not here!" she whispered.

"What the devil is going on here? Do you realize you've made me miss a crucial examination! I could be sent down for this. Now where in blazes is this sister of yours, anyway?" The boy's black, liquid eyes filled with indignation.

Pandora leaned back in her seat, removing the scarf she had been wearing, and arranging with her hand her luxuriant raven hair so that it fell softly about her lovely face.

"I have no sister," she announced quite languidly, "and, I'm afraid, I am very lax about visiting dying relatives in hospitals at the best of times. Fruit baskets from Fortnum's are so much less trying, don't you think?" She smiled enticingly. "Why don't we take the Bardwell Road?"

"Just who the hell do you think you are? You must be mad!"

"Not mad. Just reckless. Like you." A gleam of complicity sparked from her splendid eyes to his. "Reckless and bored."

Until now, Jeremy Dain-Wilkes had regarded her only as an anonymous woman . . . a woman considerably older than himself. It struck him now that she must be much nearer his own age than he had imagined.

"Don't tell me you're afraid," Pandora continued. "Afraid like that friend of yours . . . Charles, or whatever you called him?"

"I am afraid of nothing and no one!" the boy retorted defiantly.

"Take the Bardwell Road then, as far as the river."

"What makes you think I'd go with you? What makes you think I'd even want to touch you?"

Pandora flung her head back in laughter: "Jesus Christ! So I was right . . . you've never been with a woman before, have you?"

A dark flush overspread the youth's handsome features, a sign that she had indeed hit her mark.

"A frightened male virgin! All right then, get out of my car this instant! There is nothing I despise so much as cowardice!"

Jeremy Dain-Wilkes slammed down on the accelerator with all his might, and the car hurtled with the velocity of a purple bullet up the Bardwell Road toward the Cherwell Boathouse.

"Right, my darling!" he snarled at Pandora. "If it's fucking you want, it's fucking you shall have!"

They reached the boathouse, stopping only to pick up a bottle of Rémy Martin to take with them in the punt they hired for the afternoon.

The young man, scowling with intensity, flung his black cloak on the water-soaked bottom of the craft, then poled their punt up the far side of the Cherwell beneath the outreaching arms of the willows, which shaded their small boat from the afternoon sun.

"Want some?" Pandora took a swig from the bottle of brandy and extended it to the handsome youth.

Jeremy offered no response, but his eyes darted scorn. He peeled off the shabby sweater he had worn beneath his cloak, revealing a rake-thin but well-muscled torso. Every nerve of the youth's frame was taut with rage. Pandora's mockery had scalded his fierce pride like a red-hot poker, and he could not wait to get his revenge. His young mind filled with fantasies of cleaving her apart with his hardness until she begged for mercy, and then he would cast her, contemptuously, away!

They drifted past other punts filled with laughing young couples out to enjoy the river on this flawless afternoon. Pandora stared with a sudden pang of envy at the fresh-faced young girls in flowered skirts, many of whom had brought along picnic hampers and bottles of champagne, whose partners gazed at them with youthful adoration instead of the hurt and scorn that blazed in Jeremy's eyes. How often in the dreams of her girlhood had Pandora Ashley drifted down just such a sunlit Oxford river with just such a slim, dark youth at the helm; yet how sharply did the sordidness of the present reality contrast with the innocent romance of her imagination.

Jeremy steered their craft aside by an old drainage ditch which ran at right angles from the river and moored the punt in a shaded area where the Cherwell, shrouded by reeds and bulrushes, seemed to run black and foul. A peeling notice board which read PRIVATE! LANDING FORBIDDEN! protruded at a dizzy angle from the muddy riverbank.

"Right, my beauty," he said with strained bravado, "let's get on with this. Here! Give me a drop of that brandy!" Jeremy raised the dark green bottle to his lips and drank heartily. Then, ignoring his companion's outstretched hand, he deliberately tipped the remainder of the bottle into the Cherwell, where its golden contents blended with the brackish stream. He stripped hastily out of his denim trousers, and, without missing a beat, fell hungrily on Pandora.

Roughly lifting her skirt aside, Jeremy sought the secret entrance between her thighs and quickly penetrated her with all the pent-up force of his youth and rage. He let out an involuntary gasp of pleasure. Nothing had prepared him for the rich scent of her silken flesh, for the blinding sweetness of her warm, yielding cunt. She began kissing him hungrily now, rocking her slim hips with the motions of the shallow craft, wrapping her golden limbs around him like the coils of a serpent, awakening his senses with flickering motions of her fingers and tongue, all the while whispering soft obscenities, which throbbed in his ears like the rhythmic beating of the river against the hull of their little boat. Only after she had emitted a soft yelp of ecstasy, and he had spent himself within her in a raging torrent, only then did he stroke her gently with his young hands, and tenderly kiss her breasts.

"I am sorry," Jeremy whispered falteringly, "I didn't know . . ."

"Sorry?"

"Everything you said was true . . . about my never having been with a woman before, I mean. It made me want to hurt you. I had no idea how beautiful you were."

Pandora Ashley found to her astonishment that her emerald eyes were filled with tears. Soon she was crying uncontrollably. Jeremy gently took her face in both his hands and wiped away her tears. Then, as he stared intently at her green eyes sparkling with moisture, recognition flashed upon him.

"Good Lord! I know you. I know who you are! You're married to Josh Woodard. You've got some bloody ridiculous stage name, Anthea Pangloss or something."

At this, Pandora could not help laughing. "Pandora Ashley . . . admittedly ridiculous, but my mother's idea, not mine."

"I've seen you on stage. *Lady Jane Grey.* Three or four years ago, it must have been. I thought you were bloody marvelous. God! You *are* bloody marvelous! Look . . . I mean . . . what are we going to do?"

"Do?" The actress had by now fully recovered her composure. "About us, you mean?" Pandora stroked the youth's dark curls tenderly. There was a deep melancholy in her green eyes as she stared up at him. "Haven't I done you enough harm already?"

"Harm! Christ, you call this harm? Do you think this is such a bad trade-off for a paper on *Beowulf?*"

They both fell into helpless laughter, then held each other in a tender embrace.

Finally Pandora broke the silence. "We should be getting back," she said. "It's growing cold on the river."

"First tell me when we can meet again!" insisted Jeremy.

"We should have met when I was seventeen. You would have liked me when I was seventeen. It's too late now," she answered with simple, unaffected sadness.

"I like you now. I don't mind about your husband or your age," he protested.

"Find someone like me, then, not someone safe and tame who plants roses and does the marketing. Find someone like me before it is too late for her . . . while she is still capable of love!"

Jeremy began to protest, but Pandora put a finger to his lips and silenced him. Sensing the finality of her resolution, her proud young lover said nothing more. He dressed in silence, then grimly planted the pole into the riverbank and propelled the little punt on its homeward course along the darkening stream.

Despite the early brightness of the day, thunderclouds were gathering in the skies above Oxford as a shaken Pandora Ashley took her place again at the wheel of her purple Mini, and headed back toward Wandsworth House. Unlike previous sexual adventures, her rather bizarre encounter with the handsome youth had not appeased her hunger, but rather tormented her with forgotten yearnings and lost illusions of a bright, romantic love—dreams which she had cherished in her soul before Robin Maxwell had so brutally stripped them from her.

A tremendous sense of loss, of regret for her wasted youth, flooded over her. Could it be that she, who had spent so much of her life—both on stage and off—mimicking love, would never experience it in reality? She, who had known so many men in so many frantic couplings? The irony of it seemed suddenly unbearable. Her life had become a farce. She laughed aloud to think what a ninny she must have been as a girl, weeping buckets over the plights of lovers in books, fantasizing herself as Catherine Earnshaw or Héloïse or Anna Karenina or Juliet, reciting Elizabeth Barrett Browning out loud!

As the first drops of rain shimmered across the windscreen of the racing car, a vague thought started to take shape in her mind. Might it not still be possible to find this love? Not with a schoolboy like Jeremy, of course, a boy not much more than half her age. That would be too absurd. But perhaps with a man like Anthony Holland . . . . The clouds overhead burst with tremendous violence just as the Mini pulled into the semicircle of cars parked outside Wandsworth House. Rain streamed down Pandora's black hair as she ran toward the shelter of the vast portico. Might it not, Sweet Jesus, still be possible after all? she thought. Admittedly, Holland was not—on the surface at any rate— the Byronic type, not one to whirl about storm-tossed in a tempest of passion. Yet Pandora thought she had detected something, some deep wellspring of emotion untapped beneath his placid exterior. As she entered the library and began to warm herself by the crackling fire, her downcast spirits began to brighten. Anthony Holland. Anthony Holland. His very name excited her.

Cool water cascaded down Anthony Holland's six-foot frame. He was dimly aware of a telephone ringing in the background, and his wife, Christine, calling his name, but the sounds seemed to him to be coming from a very far-off place. Like a secret mantra or incantation, the word "Pandora" coursed through his blood, shutting out any other thoughts or images. His right hand slid down his firm belly to his erection, and his strong fingers gripped his swollen penis. She stood there before him now, laughing. She had shed the flimsy garments which had served only to underline, not conceal, the perfection of her naked flesh. Rivulets of cool water coursed over her round breasts, hardening her rosy nipples. In his mind, Anthony Holland took one of her nipples in his lips and drank as if from some enchanted fountain. His orgasm came in a shattering wave, and in the play of the splashing water, he imagined he heard her rippling laughter.

"Tony! Tony!" Christine's schoolmistress voice became more insistent. "That was Pinewood, Tony. They've arranged to set up sound stage nine for you from two o'clock onwards next Tuesday for the Ashley test, darling."

2

The bedroom of Rod Ward's house on Bellagio was hung with midnight-blue silk. Fourteenth-century bronze Indian statues of the god Siva and the goddess Devi flanked a king-size bed, whose headboard was lacquered dark blue (the decorator had authenticated it as having once belonged to Rudolph Valentino). The stunningly handsome actor lay on the satin sheets—also midnight-blue—contemplating his choice between the several spectacles which competed for his attention.

It was a sunny, nearly smogless day, and the windows afforded a breathtaking and panoramic one-hundred-eighty-degree view of the city stretching out beyond sculptured gardens, stretching toward the silver ribbon that was the Pacific Ocean. The view, however, was by now a common-place, and did not merit a glance. Receiving only slightly more of his attention was the Jacuzzi, which stood in the mirrored enclosure on the opposite side of the room, a situation somewhat surprising in view of the fact that seated in the tub were two very young girls of stunning beauty, one a Tahitian with dark hair cascading down her lovely, delicate breasts, the other a pink and white blonde with curly hair and generous tits.

Ward affected scarcely to notice that the Polynesian girl has begun to stroke her companion's breasts, her thin brown fingers teasing the blonde's large nipples. Perhaps he had noticed. Something made him smile imperceptibly, flashing for a second his perfect teeth beneath the impeccably groomed brown-gold mustache. His hazel eyes seemed to concentrate, though, on his own image (clad in a dark blue Bijan suit) projected on the screen in front of him.

Though it was about two in the afternoon, he was watching the *Tonight* show. He stroked his mustache nervously, watching the response he had made to a quip of Johnny's; then he relaxed and began laughing himself, enjoying the wave of approval he had won from last night's audience. As Carson introduced his next guest, Carl Sagan, the author and scientist, Ward switched over to another cassette. After Sagan had joined the panel, he had found little to contribute to the discussion. They should have booked him on the show with some starlet, he thought. That way he could have kidded around with her, and Carson could have come up with the racy *double entendres* he was famous for, and he could have flirted and been involved, instead of just sitting there, for chrissake.

Anger transformed the movie star's handsome features; his hazel eyes were drained of any warmth. He better get onto Lou! What was that cocksucker trying to do? Bury him? Trip him up just when he was on the brink of having everything? He snatched up the telephone as if it had been a weapon.

"Hello, Elaine, sweetheart, put me through to Lou! Lou, baby, Rod Ward . . . listen it's this *Moonshadows* deal. I'm getting kinda nervous. Yeah, yeah, I know you got us a great price from Sinclair. I know it's four times what I got on my last picture, for God's sake! It's this Anthony Holland I'm worried about. I mean, who is this asshole?

What's he ever done? How the hell do we know what he's gonna make me look like?"

Lou Sniderman took a deep breath. He had never liked Rod Ward, could never understand what that broad Leonora saw in him. Sure, he was six feet tall, had a suntan, muscles, probably a twelve-inch dick, but even that combination was a dime a dozen in this town and usually didn't get you past handing your photos and resumes to the receptionist. The guy was a smartass too, and obviously had already been around some by the time he'd entered Lou's life. Still, when Leonora Sheldrake wheeled into the office, wearing a white mink and looking like she'd just had a face-lift, and begged Lou as a personal favor to her to take him on as a client . . . well, Leonora knew she didn't have to "beg" him for anything and never would.

Punk, thought Lou Sniderman. He wondered how much longer it would be before Rod Ward would decide he didn't need Leonora Sheldrake any more. Two weeks . . . a month . . . already everyone in town was talking about Ward's escapades with the teenage girls, and the parties, and the dope. Everyone, that is, except Leonora. She was gonna take it hard.

"I hear you, Rod," said the agent. "Believe me, kid, I know what you're saying, but I swear to you on the lives of my kids, we got the best deal we could out of Sinclair. There isn't another producer in town would have given us three quarters of a million *and* that many points in the picture, so there was no way we could have gotten directorial approval too. I'm telling you, it's a sweetheart of a deal. Word is, even Tom Cruise was ready to do the picture."

Rod Ward allowed the smooth voice of his agent to relax him. Tom Cruise. No shit. He felt good. With one hand still cradling the receiver, he extended a smooth, bronzed, muscled arm toward the hot tub and beckoned the

Tahitian girl to approach the bed. As he reclined on the dark satin sheets, scarcely moving, the naked girl began making expert love to him, touching her lips to his swelling cock, her hair cascading like black silk over his muscled thighs and belly. "You're right Lou, I'm not questioning that you did your best for me . . ."

The girl lifted her delicate head, then raised her body as she deftly placed the actor's enormous member between her slim thighs. She moaned sharply as she felt herself impaled from below. Her slim brown body then rose above his hips, swaying sinuously as though in some pagan dance.

"You know how it is. Feel free to call me any time you got something on your mind. That's what I'm here for."

Rod Ward breathed in sharply as the girl brought him to a climax. "Thanks a million, Lou. I feel a lot better about the whole thing now. And just one other small thing—next time you book me on the Carson show, try and find out who the other guests are. You know, try and get some night when there's a cute piece of ass on. Take care."

"Take care, kid. And give my love to Leonora."

Rod Ward replaced the receiver. He reached out and grabbed the girl by her long jet hair and jerked back hard. "You! Bitch! Don't you ever make a noise like that when I'm on an important call again!" He twisted the silken black strands tighter and tighter until his large fist rested at the base of her skull. "Understand?"

Leonora Sheldrake stood on the redwood deck of her Malibu home and gazed out at the play of white moonlight on the dark water, at the tongues of the black waves as they licked the smooth white sand.

She was, as any observer not blinded with jealousy must have acknowledged, "a vision in white" at that moment. Her short platinum hair was impeccably coiffed. Her symmetrical features were enhanced by skillfully applied cosmetics. Her white jersey Galanos dress bared one tanned shoulder and showed her slim hips off to full advantage. She wore diamond earclips shaped like leaves (a gift from Tyrone Power) on her exquisite ears, a diamond choker from Harry Winston's (a gift from the Aly Khan) on her proud, graceful neck, and diamond bracelets from Laykin *et cie* (gifts from her fourth husband) on her beautifully molded arms.

In her twenties, Leonora Sheldrake had been thought by many the most beautiful woman in Hollywood, during an era when the cinema redefined the ideal of beauty throughout the world. Even now, as she approached her fifty-seventh or sixty-fourth (it depended upon whom you believed) birthday, her cool, blond elegance was hard to match. For the third time in ten minutes, Leonora consulted the diamond-encircled, opal-faced, white gold Piaget (also a present, but she preferred to forget the man who had given it to her) on her suntanned wrist.

"I should never have left him here on his own and gone off to Acapulco," she muttered to herself. She turned back through the glass doors and reentered her all-white room complete with white satin couches and a bright fire blazing in a white marble fireplace. Above the fireplace was a portrait of herself as Elena, from the film of the same name, the one which had earned her an Oscar nomination. In the painting she wore a wide-brimmed picture hat and a white lace gown by Irene.

As she looked about the room her eyes first settled on the portrait, then on her own reflection in a priceless Venetian mirror. She hadn't changed that much, she thought to herself. She was still a great beauty . . . no, more than a beauty . . . a legend. There were other fish in the ocean besides Rod Ward. She turned to her secretary, "Brandon

. . . try Mr. Ward's number again, will you please? See if he's left yet."

The opal dial of Leonora Sheldrake's Piaget read 7:45 as Rod Ward's midnight-blue Lamborghini Miura screeched to a halt on the driveway outside her beach house. By then, she had rehearsed the scene as she planned to play it over and over in her mind—she would remain imperious, aloof, the glacial ice queen. Ice queens had always been right up her alley. One of her finest roles had been the frigid Princess Irena von Ravenstein opposite Stewart Granger's Count Oslov, and even though the film had won only moderate praise, her own reviews had been glowing.

Accordingly, when Brandon, her secretary, admitted Ward into the vast white room, she greeted him with a line from the aforementioned epic delivered in her best Warner Bros. mid-Atlantic accent. "I hope I am not trespassing on your valuable time, sir." The words were spoken with just the right mixture of mocking seduction and sarcasm, just as they had been uttered some thirty-five years earlier.

This time, however, she was not confronted by Stewart Granger wearing an unbecoming powdered wig, who would press her delicate fingers to his lips in a gesture of meek devotion. Rod Ward—although grandly garbed in a Bijan dinner jacket and sapphire studs (presents from Leonora)— had little of the cavalier either in his appearance or demeanor. Instead, he strode across the white carpet as though he were a cowboy approaching a stubborn mare. His hazel eyes gleamed and his white teeth flashed in a broad unapologetic grin. Without a word, he grabbed Leonora by her thin shoulders and pulled her toward him, thrusting his pelvis against the white silk of her dress.

"Don't be a clown . . . and in front of my secretary!" Leonora continued to stammer remonstrances, but she did

not remove the large brown hand that pulled at the bodice
of her gown and tore hungrily at her nipple.

"We have plenty of time," the young man whispered,
rubbing his hard cock up against her. "Feel what you do to
me!"

"You don't like this dress then?" she said loudly, solely
for the benefit of Brandon who was ostentatiously shuffling
papers, trying to appear as though he had not noticed what
had passed between the two stars. "Well, come into my
room, then, and help me choose another."

Rod Ward cast a backward glance as he led the ice
queen *manqué* into her boudoir. His sparkling eye caught
that of the pale young secretary, and the young man smiled
faintly at the movie star.

Leonora Sheldrake's bed was an enormous, round affair
upholstered in white satin, with a quilted white satin conch
shell of a headboard. To reach it, Rod would have had to
propel Leonora across thirty feet of deep, white carpet
which separated it from the doorway in which they now
stood. The journey was much too long, or his passion for
Leonora too overwhelming, for the moment they were inside the room, he thrust Leonora to the floor before him.

"Tell me what you want," he said.

Leonora's eyes were moist. When she spoke her voice
was thick with desire. "You," she said, "I want you."

"That's not good enough." He thrust his hips forward,
and spoke very quietly, as if to a naughty child. "I want you
to tell me what you want."

"I want you to fuck me."

His voice grew even quieter: "What else do you want?"

"Your cock." The words came in a breathless whisper.

"I can't hear you."

"Your cock." Louder.

He placed one hand on the fly of his dark trousers but

made no motion to unzip them. Leonora bit her lips. Her diamonds flashed fire in the dark room. Rod lifted the skirt of her long white dress with the tip of his patent shoe until her sex was exposed.

"I want you to beg for it," he said.

"Please fuck me, baby," said the beautiful old woman at his feet. "Please, please fuck me!"

The flame-red taffeta of her Oscar de la Renta gown flared in the spotlight as Leonora Sheldrake stepped in front of the screen on which was projected her own image in black and white, nestled in the arms of Gregory Peck. She bowed her head in modesty as a huge wave of applause rose from the sea of people assembled in the ballroom. They were on their feet now, still applauding furiously, the polished men in dinner jackets, the women elaborately coiffed and gowned in the finest Giorgio's or Neiman-Marcus had to offer. Leonora graciously waved one diamond-braceleted hand in an effort to still the applause. All the while, her smiling eyes sought to find the red light, the sign that she was looking into the right camera, the one that would best show her beauty to the large television audience.

"Ladies and gentlemen, I cannot tell you how deeply moved I am. Truly." (More waves of applause). "But my tribute, as well as your own tonight, must be for the man who made all this, and so much more, possible for me. And for all of us . . . Mr. George Landau." With a sweeping gesture, the actress again raised her arm and pointed to a small, silver-haired gentleman in horn-rimmed glasses at the head table. He rose, bowed deeply to his peers, saluted Leonora, and resumed his seat.

"For over his more than fifty years in the cinema," continued Leonora, "George Landau has brought an artistry, a magic, that few before or after him have equaled. His name ranks among the legends of our magical town—Griffith, Hawks, Huston, Capra, Cukor . . . and (she paused for effect) George Landau!! Thank you, ladies and gentlemen. And now I must leave the podium for one of Mr. Landau's newest discoveries, a young man whose star beams bright with promise, Mr. Rod Ward!"

The young actor bounded onto the stage with feline grace and energy, affectionately placed his arm around Leonora's bare shoulder: "Let's hear it for Leonora Sheldrake, ladies and gentlemen . . . a great star and a great lady!"

The guests at George Landau's postbanquet party nibbled on champagne-poached oysters and peach croissants. Formally-attired waiters offered martinis or cantaloupe spritzers—in addition, of course, to the Moët & Chandon—in David Orgell glassware to the hundred and fifty or so of the directors most "intimate" friends whom he had chosen to share with him the conclusion of this festive evening. George had always been famous for his parties, especially in the early days. Such as the one to which a famous star was driven in an ambulance, and emerged wearing only a hospital gown with nothing underneath. Or the time Tallulah Bankhead reportedly stepped on to a buffet table laden with food, and lifted her flared skirts high above her head to reveal a complete lack of underclothing, and cried out drunkenly, "Who wants to eat me." She—also reportedly—received some very interesting offers.

Some detractors were even bitchy enough to remark, "If only his films had half the excitement or production values of his parties, George Landau would be a great director." But that was before movies became "cinema," and the work of many old hacks was exhumed and instantly shrouded in a roseate haze of nostalgia. Landau's mere survival had led him to be included in the ranks of his more talented contemporaries. At the height of his renaissance as

an *auteur,* about five years earlier, someone had actually
entrusted the old man with a thirty-million-dollar budget
film, which turned into such a high-camp debacle that it was
practically unreleasable even after the most rigorous cutting.
Landau hadn't actually directed since, and the more recent
disaster had faded in the memories of all but the investors.
And now, with rumors of his illness spreading, the old
queen had become the object of greater veneration than
ever. After all, he was part of an era that was passing . . .
one of the few living links to the days of Mayer and Gold-
wyn, and Dietrich and Garbo. Plus, of course, he gave great
parties.

Slightly in the background, but never too far from the
director's side was his "son" and protégé, Sean, a painfully
beautiful, alluring, and exotic young man—a Eurasian, the
product of a Chinese mother and a Finnish father.

George Landau had discovered his "son" on one of his
frequent trips to San Francisco. He had been summoned by
a gallery owner who claimed to have in his possession the
golden boat used to hold the image of the god Ammon when
Alexander the Great made his pilgrimage to the oracle at
Siwah.

Landau had been irritated to find that the authenticity
—if not the beauty—of this vessel was dubious at best, and
the price demanded so outrageous as to tax even the budget
of the Met. He had, however, included in his visit to San
Francisco, a pilgrimage to the Liberty Baths, one of the
city's most notorious gay bathhouses, recently driven under-
ground. It was there he had seen, through a door left
slightly ajar, a sight that literally took his breath away. For
there, lying facedown on a cot, presenting himself invitingly
to anyone who happened by, was the naked form of a young
Alexander—certainly the most beautiful boy George Landau had ever laid eyes on. Even among the carefully main-

tained beauty which filled the party room, he shone with singular splendor.

Beauty aside, the mixture of guests was, if nothing else, intriguing. At some point in the proceedings there surfaced such diverse luminaries as Joan Collins, Gore Vidal, the Countess Cohn, a black transvestite in white sequins done up as Diana Ross, a white transvestite in black sequins done up as Liza Minnelli (neither sang), Alana Stewart (minus Rod), a diminutive attorney reknowned for his Mafia connections (and his stable of nymphets) a benevolent-looking white-haired producer whose wife had died under mysterious circumstances at about the same time he came out of the closet, and a noted Beverly Hills plastic surgeon accompanied by his fiancée, a well-known actress who was a walking advertisement for his skills. (In truth, it was deceptive advertising . . . her boyfriend had done only her third and most recent nose job. A rival practitioner had already done the actress' boobs, and removed her lower ribs to give her a tiny waistline before the Beverly Hills surgeon's love for the actress blossomed.)

In one corner of the room a belly dancer gyrated frantically, naked from the waist up. No one spared her a glance. Cocaine was offered openly from a large Baccarat crystal platter tastefully flanked by orchids.

"My dearest darlings," exclaimed George Landau, sweeping up both Leonora Sheldrake and Rod Ward in his embrace, "you've helped make this the happiest day of my life!" The director looked hideous, his body as thin as a skeleton, his skin burnt black by the sun and marked by purplish patches, his thin white hair combed forward in a particularly unbecoming "Roman" manner. He wore a black velvet smoking jacket, and around his shriveled neck hung a gold seal with an Egyptian intaglio representing Osiris.

Landau was known for his remarkable collections of Egyptian antiquities, particularly funerary relics and mummies. Indeed, it was his acumen in this field—rather than his never stellar show business career—which accounted for his current great wealth.

"You both know my son, Sean," he intoned as he led Rod and Leonora to a slim youth of nineteen or thereabouts. The boy cradled in his muscular arms a cheetah cub, around whose neck gleamed a Van Cleef and Arpels diamond collar. The young man was deeply tanned, as attested by the manner in which he wore a white silk shirt unbuttoned to the waist. Around his neck was a medallion identical to Landau's, but he also wore around his wrists several golden slave bracelets. His hair was luxuriant, curly, and amber in color. There was no trace of effeminacy about him, except perhaps in the fullness of his pouting lips. The effect was stunning. Leonora Sheldrake gasped involuntarily: He was undoubtedly the handsomest man she had ever seen.

"Your son?" she asked, unable to mask the incredulity in her voice.

"Yes," replied Landau. "I've legally adopted him. Isn't it too wonderful, starting a family at my time of life!"

Sean continued to stroke the wild animal he held. He scarcely deigned to glance at the world-famous actress; Rod Ward seemed to interest him more. The eyes of the two men locked for an instant.

"His name is Osiris," said the boy, his delicate fingers stroking the animal's patterned fur.

"Osiris," repeated Ward in a whisper. Some unspoken message appeared to have passed between them, for the boy smiled.

By twelve-thirty most of the guests at George Landau's party had drifted off into the night. Contrary to the expectations of people from Kansas or Ohio, Hollywood is not a late night town. Leonora Sheldrake was one of the very few women among the group who remained, but then she and George went back a long way together. They really were friends, and had very few secrets from each other.

George Landau flicked a switch and the vast mosaic patio surrounding the terraced pool area was immediately flooded in violet light. The old man clapped his hands together, calling for attention: "Come on, children! Showtime!" He rested his withered brown hand on Sean's shoulder. "Hadn't you better get your act together? You're supposed to be the star of this little number."

From the shadowy palm trees surrounding the pool emerged black men in masks, their skin gleaming like ebony in the harsh violet light. Around their loins they wore small strips of leopard skin, which served only to emphasize the symmetry and power of their naked limbs. Some carried drums, which they beat in a primitive African rhythm; some carried odd, flutelike instruments; others, rattles made of bone.

"My God, George!" exclaimed Leonora. "What is this? A remake of *Sheena, Queen of the Jungle?*"

"Sorry, darling, it's only a little dance number. No parts for you, I'm afraid."

Sean extended his golden arms and placed the cheetah cub on Rod Ward's shoulder. The actor gave an involuntary start.

"That's all right," said the boy, gripping Rod Ward's arm and showing him how to handle the animal. "He won't hurt you. You won't, will you, Osiris?"

The African music was rising to a crescendo of unbearable urgency. The shrill notes of the flutes penetrated the hot California night as from the shadows emerged six naked black dancers, their bodies painted with abstract designs. They danced with slow, repetitive movements, edging slowly into the circle of violet light. On their heads they wore huge, egg-shaped masks. Some brandished torches vomiting trails of sparks.

"Those are Hevehe, spirit masks. They bring good magic," George whispered in Leonora Sheldrake's ear.

The dancers began to chant in a loud, uneven manner, their voices like the threatening sound of an angry sea. The dancers approached each other, lifting arms and thighs in unison, thrusting their genitals forward, their bodies convulsed by violent spasms.

Suddenly, like a golden fawn, Sean leapt into their midst. He was quite naked except for a gilt leaf. As a gold spotlight illuminated his perfect form, he seemed a pagan god incarnate. The onlookers gasped audibly, as with a proud, light tread, he joined the reeling dance.

"He's supposed to be the sun," whispered George.

The black man, still chanting, squatted down, forming a ring of panting bodies around the golden youth as he leaped into the air with effortless grace. Then, as the drumbeat increased in its insistence, Sean threw himself to the ground, gave a series of erotic jerks and lay motionless. The black men raised a devilish shriek as the gold light was extinguished, and the terrace was bathed in an eery red glow, then plunged back into darkness. There was a moment of stunned silence, then applause and shouts of "Bravo!"

Sweat streaming down his naked limbs, Sean ran smiling to the open arms of his mentor.

"He's going to be a great star!" said George Landau, gathering the boy to him in a passionate embrace, running his hand against the boy's glistening buttocks.

"Yes," agreed Leonora charmingly. "He has the grace of a Nijinsky." Sensing that George Landau and his young protégé were on the verge of being urgently in need of privacy, she murmured to Rod Ward, "Come, darling. It's getting late."

But Rod Ward stood transfixed. There was a slight twitching at the edge of his mouth, and his fists clenched as he watched George Landau slide his tongue into Sean's ripe mouth. He felt a wrenching feeling in the pit of his gut. It was only when Leonora dug her fingernails into his arm that he could be induced to move.

"That was quite an evening," said Leonora Sheldrake as the Lamborghini negotiated the curves of Coldwater Canyon at breakneck speed. "That boy seemed to have rather a peculiar effect on you."

Rod Ward removed his right hand from the steering wheel and struck her hard against the mouth.

Rod Ward tossed fitfully. In his dream he heard the droning thunder of drums, the cruel, sweet note of a flute. Sean's youthful form danced before him, his perfect face a sculpture of Eros carved from Parian marble, his young limbs moving with exquisite grace. The boy's lips parted. He seemed to smile and beckon. Rod Ward awakened, his forehead burning, his throat parched with unquenchable thirst, his body wet with clammy sweat. His brain reeled. He was seized with a blind and unspeakable lust. In the grip of this fever, he reached out in the darkness, groped for the telephone, and dialed Leonora Sheldrake's number.

The actress answered, her voice heavy with sleep. "My God, darling, it's five in the morning. If you're overcome with contrition, it could have waited till tomorrow."

Contrition? thought Rod. Christ . . . he had forgotten completely about slapping her. But maybe it would be better if he played along. "I just couldn't sleep thinking about it baby," he cooed. "I felt so bad."

"That's all right, lover. It's forgotten." Leonora's voice

was rich and caressing. "Get some sleep now, and sweet dreams." Just the sound of his voice had made her quiver with excitement. "Unless, of course, you'd like me to come over. I could make it to Bel Air in twenty minutes."

"No, baby." Ward shuddered inwardly at the thought of Leonora's imploring caresses, her clammy, leathery skin. "I'll make it through the night somehow. There is one other thing that's been really bugging me, though. The more I think about it, the more I'm convinced that Tony Holland has to go. George Landau is the man to direct *Moonshadows.*"

"George is a genius, you're right, of course. But what can we do? No one can reason with Martin Sinclair once his mind is made up."

"But you'll speak to him for me, won't you, baby? He might listen to you. You're a great star. He respects you. You personally made a fortune for him in *Of Human Bondage.*"

"I'll speak to him. I promise. Now get some sleep."

The Baccarat crystal chandelier over Leonora Sheldrake's white satin conch-shell bed shimmered like ice as it caught the first rays of morning sun glinting across the Pacific Ocean. The actress shielded her eyes as the faithful Brandon drew aside the white brocade curtains of her bedroom, revealing for yet another day the splendid panorama of the Malibu beachfront.

With consummate delicacy, the secretary placed a breakfast tray laden with a pitcher of freshly squeezed orange juice, coffee, one slice of whole wheat toast, a fluted Baccarat goblet, and a chilled bottle of Taittinger Blanc de Blancs, neatly in position above the Frette coverlet.

Brandon de Witt's duties to his film-star mistress were somewhat ill-defined in their scope by the term, "male secretary." He was a young, smallish man in his early thirties, yet with a desiccated, world-weary look about him. To his mistress, his attitude was outwardly worshipful. Indeed, he served as high priest to the cult of Leonora Sheldrake, "Goddess of the Silver Screen." He aided her with her wardrobe, advising her on what to select from among the literally hundreds of designer dresses which hung in her walk-in closet, the over four hundred pairs of shoes and matching handbags (Miss Sheldrake favored Ferragamo, Magli, or Rayne). It was he who had recommended the red flame taffeta which had caused such a sensation at the George Landau banquet (Leonora had favored a black velvet Bill Blass thing). Lovingly, he went through her legendary collection of jewelry (principally diamonds), choosing carefully the pieces that would most dramatically enhance each ensemble. This sensual passion for gems was something Brandon and his famous mistress held in common.

In reality, from a lower-middle-class Polish home (his real name was Bronislau), de Witt had set himself up as an arbiter of taste and refinement. He would readily have believed anyone who had told him Tintoretto was a kind of skin rash, or "La Gioconda" the name of a new Italian restaurant in Beverly Hills, but Brandon did, in fact, know a great deal about designer labels, and was something of an authority on Fabergé and Lalique. His taste in women's fashion was faultless. Leonora Sheldrake had not looked so well since the old studio days when she had been gowned by the likes of Irene, Jean-Louis, or Edith Head.

In addition, Brandon kept her gilt-edged press book, lovingly editing her clippings all the way back to her screen debut in 1945 as Ann Sheridan's kid sister in *Lonely Street*. He screened her calls, often in a peremptory and overbearing manner. He kept Leonora abreast of all the gossip from the outside world, always knowing the most lurid details of the latest Hollywood couplings and uncouplings. He helped her (obstensibly the reason he had been hired in the first place) with her autobiography, work on which progressed in fits and starts.

Provisionally titled *Leonora . . . The Lady . . . The Legend!*, the book was yet another chronicle of mating rituals during Hollywood's golden era. It dwelt on Leonora's romances (seemingly obligatory for any actress of her day) with, among others, Tyrone Power, Artie Shaw, Howard Hughes, Frank Sinatra, Porfirio Rubirosa, and Fernando Lamas. She denied hotly any lingering rumor that she had ever granted her favors to Darryl F. Zanuck. She also wrote of her long-standing feuds with Joan Crawford and Hedda Hopper, and of course she related the history of her seven marriages—each one shorter-lived than its predecessor. Unfortunately, however, the rate of Leonora Sheldrake's literary output was somewhat slowed by the rate of her liquid intake. Therefore, another of Brandon's responsibilities was to freshen the star's drinks regularly, a task he performed with his habitual assiduity. In a word, he had made himself indispensable.

Brandon poured a small amount of orange juice into the crystal goblet, filled it to the brim with Taittinger champagne, and handed it to his mistress. In this harsh light, he thought to himself, without makeup, she bore little resemblance to the dazzling creature in flame-red taffeta of last night's Landau gala. Although her skin had been pulled tight by a series of liftings, she was, unquestionably, an old woman.

"Brandon," she asked thoughtfully, taking a sip of her breakfast drink, "Martin Sinclair has offered me a role in *Moonshadows* . . . not the lead, Isabel . . . he's apparently made other commitments already . . . but a . . .

well, . . . I suppose you could call it a sort of 'character' part."

Brandon de Witt had no wish to disrupt the pattern of life in the Sheldrake ménage. It was not in his interest to see Leonora working again, out and about, back in the limelight, making new acquaintances, traveling abroad, where she might be exposed to other influences. Stirred from her alcoholic haze, she might even be induced to question the wisdom of signing, without hesitation, any check or document Brandon put in her way; she might start to scrutinize more closely his management of household expenses. Since these often included butcher's bills in excess of two thousand dollars a week in a household of two, such scrutiny might present problems. Decidedly, it was not in Brandon's interest to allow Leonora's dependence on him to be lessened in any way.

"A character part!" sneered the secretary with dry disdain. "Surely Martin Sinclair ought to know better than to insult a star of your magnitude with such a suggestion! What kind of 'character?' "

Leonora was rather abashed. Still she persevered, but not before directing Brandon to pour her another glass of Taittinger, unalloyed with orange juice this time. "It is a small role, you are right. And she *is* the mother of a grown girl . . ."

Brandon was appalled: "The very idea! A mother! What colossal nerve the man has!"

"That's exactly how I reacted too, at first, but Martin reminded me that Susan Sarandon played Brooke Shields's mother in *Pretty Baby,* and she is still a young and beautiful woman herself." Leonora took another sip of champagne, nibbled a crumb of toast. "After all, I've been thinking, it's an awfully long time since I made my last screen appearance, and you know I absolutely refuse, under any circumstances, to do television. We wouldn't want to disappoint my public, and Martin Sinclair's judgment was right about *Of Human Bondage*. Perhaps I should trust him. We don't want to wind up with you playing Max to my Norma Desmond."

Brandon de Witt gulped nervously. The palms of his hands were sweaty. Then, suddenly, he had an inspiration! "Madame Cassandra!" he cried. "You must consult Madame Cassandra! She will know. She will be able to advise you exactly whether the vibrations are right or not!"

"Brandon, you're a wonder! Of course . . . I should have thought of it myself. Ring her immediately, and make an appointment for this afternoon. I wanted to go into town anyway and pick out a present in Fred's for Rod. I'm afraid we had a bit of a misunderstanding again."

Madame Cassandra, "Psychic to the Stars," had her office-*cum*-residence in a fashionable town house on Burton Way. The decor was ultra modern, with gray-flannel upholstered walls and sofas, chrome and glass shelving, and Georgia O'Keeffe lithographs. Apart from the dozens of framed photos of Madame Cassandra with her heavy arms around many of her celebrated clients (including the likes of Peter Sellers and Lawrence Harvey), some odd, pyramid-shaped Lucite sculptures, and a Lucite coffee table with the signs of the zodiac embedded in bronze, one might easily have thought oneself in a dentist's waiting room. The atmosphere was calculatedly bereft of all the paraphernalia usually associated with séances in second-rate mystery thrillers. Rather, Madame Cassandra wished her clientele to feel that she proceeded along strict modern and scientific principles.

The psychic was a close personal friend of Brandon de Witt's, and through her the young man had become a firm believer in the occult. Leonora, under Brandon's auspices, had already consulted Madame Cassandra on two previous occasions with very satisfactory results.

Madame Cassandra entered. She was an imposing figure, her huge body ensheathed in a purple caftan with silver and black embroidery representing the moon and the stars. She had glossy, jet-black hair worn in a sort of pageboy, bushy eyebrows, penetrating black eyes heavily outlined with kohl, thick lips accented with a lipstick in the same shade of violet as her dress, a sallow complexion, and a pendulous double chin. Brandon stood by in attendance as, after the initial welcoming embrace, she took one of Leonora Sheldrake's bejeweled hands in her own, and, holding it aloft on the peak of a gigantic Lucite pyramid, meditatively traced the lines of the actress's palm with her forefinger. She closed her heavy-lidded eyes and seemed to go into a profound trance as she listened to Leonora's questions, all the while massaging the actress's hands with her own.

At length, Madame Cassandra began to speak in a low, plaintive voice, like the melody of an oboe heard from afar. *"Moonshadows . . . Moonshadows,"* intoned the clairvoyant. "I see a purple aura. I see a riderless horse. I see a man . . . his figure is not clear to me. Wait! I see him more clearly now. He is young . . . handsome . . . wavy, dark hair . . . a beard! No . . . not a beard . . . a mustache, perhaps . . ."

"Rod!" gasped Leonora, spellbound.

"QUIET! Now there is red. I sense a red aura. I see fire! Fire and the color of blood!" Madame Cassandra's voice trembled as she released Leonora's hand.

The star was visibly shaken. Her face went white beneath her makeup. "But, Madame Cassandra, what does it all mean?" she asked in alarm.

"It means, my child, that you must have nothing whatever to do with *Moonshadows!* I sense death all around!"

Leonora Sheldrake was still shaking as she climbed out of her white Rolls in front of Fred on Rodeo Drive to purchase a gift for her lover. She felt like one who awakens from a horrifying nightmare, comforted to find herself safe and alive in her own bed, yet unable to dispel the phantoms of her dream.

Brandon too was perplexed and troubled as he waited outside behind the wheel of the car. True, he had offered Madame Cassandra one thousand dollars over and above her usual fee to discourage Leonora Sheldrake from accepting the role in *Moonshadows*. Still, it was disturbing. He had known the psychic for years, and had never imagined she would put on a performance like that!

Rod Ward rose at the—for him—ungodly hour of nine in the morning, his brain still reeling with the phantoms of his dream. He dressed hastily in jeans and a Lapidus silk shirt, and, without breakfasting, took the black 3201 from its place in the garage beside the Lamborghini and the buttercup yellow 450 SEL convertible. He had to be inconspicuous, and the windows of the BMW were tinted black. In this sleek machine, he would retrace the drive of the night before.

He mounted Coldwater until he reached the tranquil cul-de-sac on which George Landau's rambling mansion rose behind wrought iron gates. Here, some one hundred yards from the entrance to Landau's drive, the black vehicle drew up and its driver began its vigil.

It was almost noon before Ward's patience was rewarded. The gates parted, and a white Excalibur, its top down, pulled into the road, heading for Coldwater. Sean was at the wheel. Rod Ward's pulse raced frantically as he accelerated and swung into place behind the white convertible. The sight of the boy's chiseled profile etched in the bright sunlight of the California day inflamed the actor's desires beyond imagining. The Excalibur, its curlicues of chrome flashing in the sun, swung right on Sunset and headed toward the sea. Ward scarcely knew what he did as he edged behind the young man; he knew only that he must follow.

This was a lust beyond his control or even comprehension. True, there was a part of Rod Ward's past that no one in Hollywood (with the exception of George Landau, who had discovered him) knew, or would even have suspected, a past in which homosexual encounters had played a part. But they had never been of Ward's choosing. He had always been a wild kid, especially back in Texas where he had even done time once for stealing a Chevy. And it is true that a guy that looked like him didn't last too long in prison without learning a thing or two. Then, when he first hit town looking for acting jobs, he found out quickly that it wasn't only with broads that his enormous cock could do him good. Sure, he was experienced, but he had never "wanted" sex with a man before. Even when he had butt-fucked a pudgy casting director for a shot at a *Hart to Hart* episode, he had always retained his healthy, all-American disdain for faggots. It was just one of those things that he had done because he had to do it.

They were in Malibu now. The white Excalibur raced along the edge of the blue sea outlined with ramshackle houses and bad seafood restaurants, then took a right past Trancas at the Malibu Riding and Tennis Club. The black BMW followed.

Ward remained at a discreet distance as the youth strode from the car and, exchanging a few words with a denim-clad man, mounted a magnificent white stallion which stood saddled and ready awaiting its young rider. Sean was attired in a sleeveless white T-shirt, skintight white

breeches, and gleaming leather belt. He wore no hat but
carried a riding crop.

When he rode, Rod thought he looked like a young
god, each gesture of his perfect brown limbs was in harmony
with the slightest movement of the graceful steed which
bore his weight so lightly. Enraptured, Ward donned
Porsche sunglasses and approached the riding ring stealth-
ily. Addressing himself to the man in denim who was evidently the trainer, he asked the name of the horse. "Apocalypse" was the answer. Did the boy ride here often? "Twice
a week, always at the same time. Tuesdays and Fridays.
Sometimes though, young Mr. Landau preferred to take
Apocalypse down by the ocean and ride along the beach."
Seeing that the man was eyeing him suspiciously, Ward
feigned an interest in buying the animal, but was quickly
told it was not for sale.

"Hey," said the trainer, recognition gleaming in his
shrewd eyes. "You're that film feller ain't ye? Rod Ward!
That's it. No use wasting your time though, Mr. Ward. Take
it from me, he's not for sale. If you're interested in a fine
piece of horseflesh though, there's a hunter-jumper you
oughta have a look at."

"Never mind, Mr . . . ?"

"Travis . . . Jed Travis. Pleased to make your acquaintance."

"Mr. Travis. I'm accustomed to getting what I'm after.
I'll be back Tuesday."

A flash of lightning seared the evening sky illuminating
with a blinding flash a white horse galloping across the
sands of Zuma, ridden by a youth of extraordinary grace. Its
mane flowed white as the spume of the tumultuous black
waves. Rain was falling heavily now, and the beach was
deserted except for the horseman and a solitary watcher. A

phrase he had heard once kept drumming insistently in Rod Ward's fevered brain, but he could not have said where he had heard it or what it referred to. "Behold a pale horse . . ." Dazed by the weird beauty of the spectacle, Rod Ward stood paralyzed for an instant, then broke into a headlong run toward the young horseman and his mount. Rain streamed down the high cheekbones of his handsome face as he called out to Sean.

The boy was riding bareback tonight, and the white stallion reared proudly on its hind legs at the sound of the actor's voice. The horse's hooves churned the foam, but the boy masterfully brought him under control within seconds, then turned his proud gaze upon the older man, soliciting his approval. There was something in the boy's gaze—at once bashful and enchanting—that set Ward afire with pain and longing. The rider wheeled Apocalypse round and rode toward Rod.

With a bound he leapt from the stallion, which whinnied mournfully as if lamenting the loss of so beautiful a burden. The eyes of the two men locked, and wordlessly Rod Ward traced the outline of Sean's arm with his fingers, then drew his body toward him in his powerful hands and kissed him full on the mouth.

3

"Anything else I can get for you, Mr. Woodard?"

"No thank you, Gus, this will do nicely." With one hand he reached out for the frosty glass of gin and tonic the barman had extended to him, groping with the other for his billfold on the small metal table beside his lounge chair.

"Christ Almighty!" exclaimed Josh Woodard, wincing with pain as his left wrist connected with the searingly hot metal of the poolside table which had been baking for some hours in the hundred-degree Los Angeles sun. His sudden motion upset the table and the various items he had placed upon it—Hawaiian Tropic deep-tanning oil, a rumpled Marks and Spencer cotton shirt, *The Tragic Muse* by Henry James, some drugstore plastic sunglasses, a road map (courtesy of Budget Rent-a-Car) of the Los Angeles area, Graham Greene's *Ways of Escape*, the current issue of *The Hollywood Reporter*, and the somewhat worn billfold for which Josh had been grasping. Also spilled on the poolside pavement was the cool contents of the glass Gus had just brought him.

"I'm sorry, I . . ."

"That's all right, Mr. Woodard." Gus's voice was reassuring; sympathy beamed from his dark, wise eyes. "You just leave everything to me, Mr. Woodard. We'll have this all cleaned up for you in a jiffy, and I'll bring you another one. On the house."

By this time, a large blond man of indeterminate age, dressed in white tennis shirt and shorts, had approached the scene of the accident. He glided with surprisingly small steps.

"What is it now?" Swen sighed deeply and patted his flaxen hair. "There's always something! Jason, you get right over here and fix Mr. Woodard's table for him! I swear these boys just don't do a thing. They leave it all to me." Swen leaned over and, in a mock-caressing whisper, warned, "You better watch out for that sun, Mr. Woodard. You're burning! Uh-oh, looks like Mr. Davis wants me." And it was true. A gigantic moose of a man was beckoning from a yellow-and-white striped tented enclosure across the turquoise water of the pool. "Do you know Marvin Davis, Mr. Woodard?" cooed Swen. "He owns Twentieth Century-Fox, you know. And a few other things. Suuuuch a nice man!"

Beads of perspiration trickled down Josh Woodard's bearded face as he looked down at his legs and stomach. Swen was right. Blotchy, bright pink patches were appearing on his parchment-white skin. Lord knew he had poured enough of that suntan muck on! Why had he ever set foot in this bloody place?"

"There you go, Mr. Woodard. Now you just relax!" Swen pranced off.

Gus was back. The slim barman's presence made Josh Woodard feel better instantly. Without having exchanged more than the most banal conventionalities in the four days since he'd arrived at the Beverly Hills Hotel, a tacit mutual respect had somehow sprung up between the famous writer and the barman. Josh had recognized instantly in Gus a *mensch,* a person to whom truth and honor and loyalty were more than words. As for Gus, he'd been barman at the pool of the Beverly Hills for more than twenty years. His dark eyes had seen them all come and go—starlets, agents, big-shots, hustlers, people with big dreams and bigger bank balances. And while he was invariably correct and polite to all, there were some he really liked, and he let them know. And by hotel tradition, if Gus liked you, you were all right.

Josh Woodard took a sip of his new icy gin and tonic and surveyed the poolside parade. He noted with some irritation that he appeared to be the only person who hadn't managed to acquire a deep golden tan. Even the shriveled old men who wore gold chains around their withered necks and seemed permanently attached to telephones were given a look of well-being and vigor by their dark bronze color. Josh felt doubly naked and self-conscious as his white-pink flesh began to sting. He took the checked Marks and Spencer shirt and flung it blanket-wise over his stomach. He was getting a bit of a paunch, too, he noted miserably. He glanced at his wristwatch, a Rolex Oyster (a present from Pandora, and the one item about his person that indicated his prosperity), and found that his lunch meeting with Nat Sheinberg was still more than an hour away. He picked up *The Tragic Muse*, fitfully scanned a few pages, found he couldn't concentrate, and put it down again. Who was it who had defined an American intellectual as someone who had *heard* of Henry James?

He noted with distaste his poolside neighbors' choices of literature. Except for the ubiquitous copies of *Variety*, their reading matter seemed to consist almost exclusively of *Hollywood Husbands*, or *I'll Take Manhattan* among the women, and the latest gore-drenched Stephen King among the men.

Why did he bother? They schlepped you out here because they "loved" your play; it would make a "sensational" movie of the week," they said. Then they held luncheon meetings, and breakfast meetings, and office meetings, and informal parties which turned into meetings, and stripped what you had written, idea by idea, as jackals would the carcass of a gazelle, until it bore no resemblance to your original screenplay. Except for the title, of course.

What had begun as a hard-hitting look at deteriorating race relations in Notting Hill Gate, and the gentle growth of a friendship between a plain, white working-class girl and a Jamaican reggae musician had, by infinitesimal stages, been transformed into an innocuous little sitcom that wouldn't have offended a Grand Kleagle of the Ku Klux Klan.

His scruffy little bird of a heroine was to be played by Angela Armstrong, a blonde starlet of Amazonian proportions, with silicone tits, a mass of artfully streaked blond hair, and a mouth of dental work that must have cost more money than Mildred, the character she was to portray, could ever have been expected to see in a lifetime. Apparently, though, as his agent Sid Braverman had informed him, she gave "the best blowjob in town," and this facet of the lady's not inconsiderable charm had endeared her to Nat Sheinberg, a short, round, worried man who was the show's producer.

Josh Woodard had long since ceased to care about the project. He smiled wanly when people asked him if he was writing, or "working on a concept," and spoke to him of "supportive relationships" and "euphem-izations." Just let them get on with it. He would take the money and run . . . back to Pandora.

"Paging Mark Goodson.

"Paging Elliot Kastner.

"Paging Roy Scheider.

"Paging Rex Smith."

The never-ending litany of the names of the famous and

near-famous was a constant reminder that this was no ordinary resort. True, people here might sip Piña Coladas or gaily-colored rum punches. Oiled women with breasts spilling out of minimal bikinis might totter back and forth on stiletto-heeled sandals. Children might even splash in the pool, or rush with bright plastic pails to and from the little sandbox. But this pool was like no other. Multi-million-dollar deals were enacted daily over the house phones, the careers of people whose names were household words were made or broken in the shade of the small cabanas. Scandals which would leak, sooner or later, much distorted, on to the pages of the *National Enquirer* began here. Oh sure, regulars who had been coming here for twenty or thirty years might grumble that the place had "gone down" in some way, and threaten to withdraw their custom and go over to the Heritage or Bel Air, but they never did. There was just no other place quite like The Beverly Hills Hotel anywhere on earth.

A petite blonde in a hot-pink bikini flashed Josh a bright smile as she emerged from the pool shaking the water from her long golden hair. "Water's great!" she announced in a peppy voice. She rubbed herself vigorously with a big yellow towel and sprawled out on the cot next to Josh. "My name's Cathy, what's yours?"

"Josh," he replied, in a tone that he hoped would discourage further communication. How perfect, he thought, and yet how strangely unappealing all these women are, with their small, snipped noses and exercised bodies and acres of teeth. What was that thing of Dylan Thomas's, about something being the process by which American girls turned into American women? He had forgotten.

"I'm from New York," the friendly girl declaimed. "I'm with Grey Advertising . . . we're shooting a peanut butter commercial. How about you?"

"London," mumbled Josh.

"London! Gee, that's great! I was there with my ex a couple of years ago. I really loved it. I'd love to go back there sometime. Maybe you could give me some tips . . . you know, restaurants . . . places to see . . ."

London. Pandora. How different she was from the women one met in this place. How vulgar and unfeminine these sunny women seemed compared to her. He thought back to the first time he had seen his wife in that cold, musty rattrap of a theater in Leeds. The play had been *The Tempest*. Josh had made the trip out of courtesy to Tim Logan, the director, an old chum of his from university days who had fallen on hard times. The production had been diabolically bad. Logan had attempted to give the play a surrealist Max Ernst sort of look, but had been defeated by a meager budget and a half-soused Prospero, who kept going up on his lines. The handful of people in the damp auditorium kept coughing or shifting about restlessly in their seats.

But suddenly something happened. There was a frail, dark girl playing Miranda. From the moment she made her first entrance, the audience had become hushed and attentive. By the time she spoke the line " 'Tis far off; And rather like a dream than an assurance that my remembrance warrants . . ." they were spellbound. Single-handed, this girl had transported them to Prospero's magic isle and brought Shakespeare's words to life. Josh Woodard could hardly wait for the frayed curtain to fall so that he could rush backstage and meet this exquisite, green-eyed creature, this . . . Pandora Ashley.

"What did you say your last name was, Josh?" bubbled Cathy, momentarily pulling him back to reality.

"I didn't. Woodard. Josh Woodard."

"Gosh!" said Cathy, awe and disappointment blending on her pretty face. "You're married to Pandora Ashley!"

It had frightened him for an instant when Pandora

stripped off the thick greasepaint with cream and he saw just
how young she was. He was nearing his forty-third birthday,
his hair was thinning a bit, and he had never been a matinee
idol at the best of times, with his shambling gait and hesi-
tant, professorial manner. He was mad even to have come
backstage! But she *had* heard of him, it appeared, and her
fresh young face lit up at the mention of his name. She was
his greatest admirer, it turned out. She reeled off excitedly
the names of everything he had ever written, even a one-act
radio play that had been done three years earlier on the
BBC. Oblivious to the absence of umbrellas, they had
walked through the cold, penetrating drizzle, directed by
their emotions to her tiny room in a run-down theatrical
hotel near the railway station. And there, in a tiny room
with yellowed, peeling paper, and a stained carpet that
reeked of stale beer and cheap cigars, they made incredible
love.

Two weeks later, Josh Woodard moved out of the Rich-
mond house he shared with Elspeth, his wife of eighteen
years, and their two sons. Immediately he began work on a
play about the tragic life of Lady Jane Grey. It was to make
his new love famous.

Nat Sheinberg winced as though in pain as he stabbed a
glossy forkful of lobster salad and raised it to his small, pink
mouth. Everything about the producer was meticulous and
diminutive, with the exception of the giant gold Rolex that
glinted on his freckled wrist. His thin, reddish hair was
combed forward on his pink forehead, and blue hexagonal
glasses concealed his nervous eyes as they darted back and
forth among the other tables, checking out which of his
peers had decided to put their potential deals together in the
goldfish bowl of Ma Maison at lunchtime that Thursday.

On Friday you could be sure it was all bullshit—real

estate women with jewels the size of gulls' eggs and new
listings in Holmby Hills, wives of second-rate status, cute
blondes with modified punk haircuts and too-tight Guess
jeans lunching in pairs, who had heard it was the place to be
seen. True, there was always the handful of people who
counted people like Greg Bautzer or Swifty, who never
lunched anywhere else. Yes, it was too loud on Friday for
anything but total bullshit, plus it took two hours to get
your goddam order.

"Try some of the lobster salad, Josh; it's sensational. I
promise you won't find better in Paris."

"No thank you, Nat," replied Woodard, sipping Pu-
ligny-Montrachet. "I'm fine as I am, really."

"Josh, ABC passed." Nat Sheinberg's pink face assumed an expression of great gravity. "They felt it just
wasn't their profile."

Josh Woodard stared at the producer as blankly as if he
had been told that Constantinople was founded in A.D. 324,
or that the price of soybean futures had dropped sharply in
afternoon trading.

"Now I'm not saying this isn't a terrific story we've got
here," the small pink man continued, "I think the issues
that you've raised here are very impacting . . . very impacting." He paused here, apparently feeling that some sort
of response was in order, and Josh managed a feeble "Thank
you." After all, Sheinberg had paid him a substantial sum
for the rights to his piece and was picking up the tab for his
stay at the Beverly Hills, etc., etc.

"What we need is an emotional hook . . . hit them
hard . . . titillate their expectations. For instance—I'm
just throwing this out as an idea, mind you—wouldn't it
work better if, instead of working in a second-hand book-
shop, Mildred worked in a massage parlorr . . . *that's*
where she meets the spade! See what I mean . . . *High*

Concept!" Sheinberg washed down a mouthful of lobster with golden wine.

"Look, Mr. Sheinberg," Josh was making a colossal effort to bite back his rage, and his voice took on an odd, strangled sound. "Presumably you liked something in what I wrote, or you wouldn't have paid me for it. I did not, however, write a latter-day *Fanny Hill.* Mildred is a plain, simple, *lame* shop assistant leading a drab, intolerable, *wretched* life. She is a despised, forlorn *outcast.* She is not Brigitte Bardot, Bo Derek, or Christie *Brinkley.* She is a *slattern!"* It was no use. He had a terrible temper. He had risen from the table.

"OK! OK! I told you it was just an idea, didn't I? There's no need to get your balls in a twist. It's just a question of demographics."

Josh collected himself and sat back down. He poured himself another glass of the delicious wine.

"I'm sorry. I guess I've been under a strain."

"Sure, Josh, I understand. Don't worry about it. Happens to all of us." He allowed a slight edge to creep into his soothing voice. "After all, you've got a right to be nervous. Nobody can afford too many turkeys like *Pavlova."*

For an instant, Sheinberg's eyes seemed to glint with malice behind the blue crystal lenses, but he smiled magnanimously and patted the writer's arm as he continued. "If it's Angela Armstrong that's worrying you, relax, man! The kid is determined to prove herself as a serious actress, and she just thinks the world of your writing. Get this—she even offered not to wear any makeup as Mildred and to get a haircut! I'm telling you, Josh, this is one dedicated lady!"

"She undoubtedly seems willing to make all kinds of sacrifices," agreed Josh. Happily, his sarcasm was lost on the producer, who was waving excitedly across the room, his round face now beaming with optimism.

"This is a piece of good luck for us, Josh. There's Ward Bender from Warners . . . I've had a call in to him. He can help us on this, and I'm sure he'd love to meet you . . . great . . . he's coming over!"

"Bender?" asked Josh. "Warners, you say. I thought he was at Columbia."

"That was last week." Shit, he thought, these limeys have a lot to learn.

Ward Bender, a tall, dark, polished man in a beige suit, had hardly sat down at their table and shaken hands with Josh when the entrance of a large, elderly man with a lordly demeanor caused both him and Sheinberg to leap to their feet and scurry over to pay their respects. Josh Woodard barely caught the word Nat Sheinberg had whispered in explanation as he hastened off.

"Begelman!"

"But . . . but . . . but," the author was left sputtering, but his companions were gone.

Josh Woodard sat at the crowded counter of the green and white palm-fronded coffee shop of the Beverly Hills Hotel, sipping his morning tea and nibbling a slice of whole wheat toast. Beside him perched a very small man in a dark suit and pink shirt with the largest white collar and cuffs Josh had ever seen, and a dark bush of hair combed forward on his forehead. He evidently was an agent of some kind, for he was talking loudly about the fee he had received for booking a former president of the United States on some television show. At one time, the little man said, he had represented Presidents Carter, Begin, and Sadat.

Woodard winced at the omnipresent tentacles of American show biz hype. It was truly amazing what feats they could accomplish. Josh wondered grimly at the prospect of Nancy Reagan performing opposite Jane Wyman on an episode of *Falcon Crest*. A phone rang, and he heard a shrill female voice page him. Picking up the house phone, he got Nat Sheinberg on the line. The producer sounded elated.

"Josh, baby! It's all set! HBO loved it . . . they're very high on the whole concept. All they want are a few minor changes, but no sweat; it's a definite go. I'll meet you at the Polo Lounge at one for lunch, and we'll go over the whole thing."

Josh let out a heartfelt sigh of relief. Thank God, he reasoned. They wouldn't need him to stay on in L.A. much longer. He could get back to Pandora.

Angela Armstrong was getting pissed off! She had been listening to Nat Sheinberg's b.s. for nearly six months now . . . all that crap about this Josh Woodard script doing for her what *The Burning Bed* and *Extremities* had done for Farrah Fawcett! That people would take her seriously, not only as a sex symbol, but as a sensitive actress. It was that word "sensitive" that had gotten to her, she now admitted to herself; Angela Armstrong felt her weakness was her *sensitivity*. As a matter of record, she had once confided to Tawny Schneider on *Hollywood Close-Up*, "I know I am sensitive because I am a poet. That sensitivity just flows out of me like water!" Angela Armstrong was also fond of remarking (and had already done so in "exclusive" interviews with Oprah Winfrey, *US* magazine, and the *Ladies' Home Journal*) that she was "not just another bimbo."

When she had arrived in Hollywood from her hometown of Tulsa some eight years before at the age of nineteen, she was already a graduate of Oklahoma State, having majored in Speech, and had been a third runner-up in the Miss America Pageant! Now, at twenty-seven, her career was just beginning to skyrocket. There were, of course, a couple of minor details which hadn't quite made it into the pages of the *Ladies' Home Journal* article, "Angela Armstrong—an Intimate Glimpse of Hollywood's Newest Sex Symbol."

Angela had indeed arrived in town, as the article duly informed its readers, in the spring of 1979, equipped with a shiny red Camaro (part of her winnings from the beauty pageant) and a husband named Ken, a former college football hero who worshipped the ground his new bride walked on. Ken's chances at a pro career in football had been torpedoed abruptly by a knee injury in a final game with Brigham Young, but after his initial despair wore off, it was decided that he would accompany Angela to Hollywood and there seek a career in sports broadcasting, while his young wife pursued her acting ambitions. There was no reason to suppose he didn't stand a good chance of success, either. With his rugged all-American good looks, and his deep, bass voice, everyone in Tulsa agreed he looked just like a young Charlton Heston . . . only with Rob Lowe's nose.

As for Angela, her imminent stardom seemed almost a foregone conclusion. She had been entering—and usually winning—local and state beauty and talent pageants since she was a baby. She had brought with her the red leather portfolio, lovingly started for her by her mom, in which photos of all these triumphs were carefully documented. True, her bright blue eyes were slightly crossed, and her cute uptilted nose a trifle bulbous at the tip, but the smile was a forty-carat dazzler, and her long, slim legs and golden hair had wowed them every time.

Ken and Angela began their Hollywood lives in a cute one-bedroom apartment in West Hollywood on a street where it was said Kim Novak had once lived. The beautiful, loving couple then blissfully ushered forth in pursuit of the inevitable Fame and Fortune which somehow seemed their inalienable right.

At first, everything proceeded right on track, for Angela anyway. Her showing in the Miss America Pageant proved successful in landing her an agent her second week in town—not with one of the giant firms, I.C.M. or William Morris, where she had never been able to get past reception, but with a feisty ex-New Yorker named Fran Taubman who ran her own three-member agency.

Taubman had a reputation around town for integrity and shrewd judgment, and the time, energy, and persistence to fight for her clients. Producers and casting directors respected her instincts, having found by experience that most of the people on her client list tended to show up on time sober, hit their marks, say their lines, and, generally speaking, get the job done, a feat by no means as unexceptional as might be supposed in this town.

"Wholesome," was the thought that entered Fran Taubman's mind when Angela Armstrong found herself unexpectedly touched by the girl's naivete, her unswerving belief in the Lana-Turner-in-a-sweater-at-Schwab's myth of the route to stardom. The older woman warmed to the way the girl exalted the attributes of her young bridegroom, and her glowing faith in his shining prospects. Fran Taubman found it refreshing that the girl was totally oblivious to the fact that ex-beauty queens and handsome hulk ball players were a dime (if you could get that much) a dozen in this town and decided, impulsively, to take them under her wing. Whenever she sent the girl out on a casting call, Fran made a practice of telephoning the producer and sounding a *haymische* note of caution: ". . . and no funny business. This is a sweet girl. Married."

Angela got work. Commercials at first. Nytol. Special K. Alberto VO5. Camay. Camay was the one that did it for her. People actually started asking for "a girl like that one in the Camay ad." She got a *Rockford Files* and a *Little House on the Prairie* in rapid succession, and then came what looked to be her big break—the second lead in a sitcom pilot about two sisters trying to make it in the Big Apple. The producers of the show had had a string of hits, and the girl signed to play her older sister was an actress named Amelia Sterling, who had gained some popularity in a series two seasons back.

Angela, Ken, and Fran Taubman celebrated with dinner at Chasen's (which Ken, in a fashion becoming typical of late, ruined by drinking too much and being sick afterwards), and the purchase of a cocker spaniel named Taffy—after the character Angela was to play in the new show, *Two Sisters.* The pilot sold, and taping began immediately on the first eight episodes. Stardom was just around the corner! The happiness which was supposed to accompany it, however, seemed more elusive. A subtle change had gradually crept into the cozy West Hollywood apartment. After a few initial rebuffs—owing, naturally enough, to his total lack of broadcasting experience—Ken Harding had decided to quit the sports game and act as his wife's manager. It had seemed like a good idea at first: Angela was thrilled that she would shortly be famous enough to need a manager at all, and why shouldn't it be Ken? Soon, however, it began to seem to Angela that his duties as manager consisted of sitting around the house all day, swilling beer, spending *her* money, and watching ball games on television.

In truth, Angela Armstrong had quickly picked up the Hollywood fear, which approached paranoia, of even the most casual contact with a "loser." And that was what Ken appeared to have become. Suddenly, he seemed provincial and oafish in her eyes, so unlike the sophisticated types she was meeting on the set. The other girl in the series, Amelia Sterling, was openly incredulous when Angela confided that she had still been a virgin when she and Ken got married, and would never so much as dream of making it with another guy. But Angela was lying through her pearly teeth even as she said it. She did dream of it. She dreamed of it all the time now.

Angela had to spend a lot of time on the road promoting *Two Sisters,* appearing on local talk shows, and at photo sessions, suburban malls, and supermarket openings all across the country. She also spent lonely nights in Holiday Inns, making tearful long-distance calls to Ken, quarreling . . . making up . . . then quarreling again. "Why hadn't she let him accompany her?" he pleaded. After all, he was supposed to be her goddam manager, wasn't he? She explained to him, again and again, that the network was paying for her travel expenses only. There was no way they could afford to pay his way out of their own pockets.

Secretly, though, she was glad he wasn't around. He was just getting to be a colossal pain in the butt with his endless whining and self-pity. Ken accused her of infidelity. It was not true. What was true was that she had encouraged one or two flirtations with local TV personalities on whose shows she had appeared, but had, each time, at the last minute, withheld the final act of intimacy. Ken's mistrust, therefore, made her feel like a martyr. These conversations would invariably end with the same words of apology from her downcast husband: "I'm sorry, honey . . . it's just that I can't stand being away from you. I miss you so bad!"

"I know. I miss you too, hon. Now put little Taffy on the phone for a minute, will you, darling . . . I just want to say hello to her too."

Ken would then hold the little puppy near the receiver so that Angela could hear its canine "woof, woof, woof." The sound of her little pet's barking always made Angela homesick and invariably brought tears to her bright blue eyes.

Despite the loneliness, however, Angela at first loved her new-found life in the limelight. She even took the time to send presents to Fran Taubman, a scarf from every town she visited. The agent's scarf collection had grown to about forty or so when they suddenly stopped coming, and were replaced by a barrage of telephone calls. At first Angela pleaded, then she nagged, and finally she became downright abusive, demanding that Ms. Taubman get her out of this or that appearance. Amelia Sterling, her costar on the *Two Sisters* show had just done the *Tonight* show. Why couldn't Ms. Taubman get the network to put *her* on Carson, instead of parading her around one-horse towns like some kind of goddam circus freak? Amelia Sterling was on the cover of *TV Guide,* while *her* name had only been mentioned in the accompanying article.

Then, finally, *Two Sisters* hit the air! It went on opposite *Dallas* and got slaughtered. The network shifted the show to Saturday nights. Nothing. They moved it to Monday nights, opposite a long-running detective show they hoped was starting to run out of steam. It got creamed. They aired a fourth episode, but the smell of death was already in everyone's nostrils. *Two Sisters* was among the first and least lamented casualties of the 1987 season.

Fran Taubman dropped Angela Armstrong from her client list. Angela filed for divorce from Ken. Their little dog, Taffy, had been run over by a neighbor's car, an accident for which Angela blamed Ken, saying that he had been too drunk to look after their pet. Then Angela's mom died during an unsuccessful kidney operation. The bad years had begun.

Angela Armstrong learned, with brutal alacrity, what it means in Hollywood to be July's flavor of the month in September. She found herself, overnight, on the lowest rung of the ladder—even below the newest arrivals in town, whose photos and resumes were daily flung, unheeded, into trashbins. They, at any rate, were unknown commodities whose lucky break might come one day. At least they had no black marks against their names, no shadow of failure to dog their steps as they made their rounds of the casting offices. Angela Armstrong had had her shot, and she had blown it! Even worse, word spread like cancer of her "ingratitude" to Fran Taubman; she was marked as "difficult." In addition, the flaws in her appearance suddenly seemed to take on great importance. Blond? OK, so who wasn't? Her tits were too small. She was cross-eyed. Her legs were too gangly. There seemed to be every reason not to hire her.

Soon, what little money she had saved ran out. There had never been any real money to begin with, and just about every penny she had earned had gone to buy clothes, or into the furnishings of the West Hollywood apartment. The red Camaro had been consigned to Ken's use; Angela herself had bought a shiny buttercup-yellow Mercedes 450 SEL with the proceeds of the Camay ad, and a floor-length white mink on the signing of the series deal. Ken got the red Camaro and a couple of thousand dollars as part of the divorce settlement. The Mercedes went next. Then the mink.

She experienced her first affaire with Gino, the photographer who had done a layout which was sold to *Gallery* magazine. At first she had thought him sleazy. He was, for openers, a good six inches shorter than she. And she disliked the mustache he wore; the flashing rings on each finger; the too-flared trousers; the shirts of too-thin silk that tapered narrowly at the waist, which was encircled by a too-shiny alligator belt decorated with an enormous "G" buckle. But finally his flattery won her over.

Starved for praise, she believed him all too eagerly when he told her she was the best-looking broad he had ever photographed. He made her feel relaxed too, much less guilty about posing in the nude. He knew the names of all the stars who had taken their clothes off for the camera, and soon Angela convinced herself that it was just another step on her stairway to stardom.

On her first night in bed with Gino, he tried desperately to bring her to orgasm. After his failure to do so, he told her she was "frigid as a brick," and thereafter sought only to please himself. She never questioned the truth of this statement. She had never known an orgasm with Ken, but had never felt any deficiency in their lovemaking, having relished the pleasure of his strong arms caressing her, his handsome face breathing softly next to her own. She had honestly thought that was all there was to it—for the woman, anyway. At least sex with Ken had never seemed bad or ugly. Not like this. Gino now appropriated her, body and soul. He paid the two months back rent she owed in West Hollywood, and she moved into his Tarzana pad. Gino always knew where there was a party, knew people she could "do herself a favor" by being nice to.

Rather rapidly, Angela found herself being sucked deeper and deeper into a vortex from which there seemed to be no escape. Each "step" her new protector urged her to take in her "career" only made her slide further backwards into the abyss of degradation. The low point came with a porn flick filmed in a warehouse which surfaced at an embarrassing moment in her later rise to stardom. Vicious tongues around town referred to it as Angela Armstrong's "Oreo sandwich," since, in the film in question, Angela's naked form was entwined in a somewhat acrobatic sex act between two blacks—one male, the other, female.

Angela's sudden rescue from this way of life came from an unlikely quarter. A chance encounter with her *Two Sisters* costar Amelia Sterling at Gelson's supermarket in Century City was followed by lunch at La Scala Boutique. It emerged from the luncheon conversation that Amelia's current good fortune—as attested to by her Rodeo Drive attire —owed nothing whatever to show business, nor even to a wealthy husband or lover. Her career, like her costar's, had gone flat as a pancake after the cancellation of their series.

"But I don't understand," gasped Angela. "Your dress! Your jewelry! Everything! It's just fabulous!"

Amelia Sterling laughed heartily. "But sweetheart, it's all lying out there in gobs, just waiting to be scooped up! All you need is a real estate license!"

Halfway through the second glass of wine, Angela had begun unburdening herself. She talked about the bad time she had gone through, about the divorce, about Gino, about the movie (the latter only after the third glass), and about her despair.

Amelia Sterling was a good-natured, sympathetic person. If she had ever borne a grudge against her former costar, for any past bitchiness or backbiting on the set of their ill-fated series, it was rapidly discarded at finding the woman in such an awful plight.

"The first thing we've got to do, is get you away from that bum, Gino!" She paused for a moment in thought. "Consider it done. You've just moved out on him!"

"But where to?" Angela's eyes brimmed with tears. She shook with involuntary sobs, inwardly ashamed of the harm she had once wished on this pretty girl who was now spontaneously extending her hand in such a display of friendship and generosity.

"My place, of course," responded Amelia.

"I'm rattling around in a four-bedroom home I'm doing over up on Benedict Canyon, with no one for company."

Angela shook her head forlornly. "I could never accept such generosity."

"I'm not being generous," Amelia continued. "You'll pay me back, all right, and I'll see to it that you are able to. I'll introduce you to my boss first thing tomorrow morning." (Here Amelia mentioned the owner of the most prestigious real estate firm in Beverly Hills, whose sign on a property was tantamount to notice that, if you weren't interested in the one-million-dollar-plus price range, you needn't bother making further inquiries.) "As soon, that is, as we get you into some decent clothes, and do something about your hair and makeup."

Angela hesitated momentarily, dabbing with a Kleenex at the mascara which was now streaming down her cheeks. "How can I ever thank you for this?" she stammered. "You must forgive me, but I've been so long with Gino that my mind must be getting warped . . . I mean, there are no strings attached or anything . . . you don't like girls, I mean, or anything like that?"

Amelia Sterling drew back for a moment, stung by the affront, but her companion looked so genuinely abject that she decided to shrug it off.

"No . . . no, Angela, nothing like that. Don't worry! You'll be able to repay me sooner than you think, just as I've said. And I always liked you, even in the old days. I thought it was rotten of Fran Taubman, bad-mouthing you that way; and your no-good husband walking out on you! You've always been a sweet kid. You just need a few breaks, that's all. Now you come along home with me!" And that was precisely what Angela Armstrong did.

Amelia Sterling's prophesies of Angela's golden future in the world of Beverly Hills real estate were not long in being realized. Irving Samuels, Amelia's boss, had taken a personal interest in his crack saleslady's protégé from the moment he first set eyes on her, attired in a navy-blue and white Ralph Lauren ensemble she had borrowed from her friend, which was at once businesslike and feminine, and which set off her long-legged, all-American good looks perfectly.

"My Golden Girl!" Samuels christened her instantly, and, with her speedily acquired broker's license and cream Cadillac Seville (in which to chauffeur potential buyers to the poshest sections of Bel Air or Holmby Hills), the name seemed appropriate. As a salesperson, Angela turned out to have the Midas touch. In addition, she had entered the field just in time to catch the tail end of the boom which had inflated property in the Beverly Hills area by as much as five hundred percent over a six-year period.

By the end of 1984, despite a general tapering off in the real estate market, Angela Armstrong's personal fortunes were riding high. She had long since repaid Amelia Sterling for the latter's kindness with a present of a Blackgama mink jacket she had particularly admired in Révillon.

Angela's bank balance had by now risen to an impressive sum. She acquired, however, a reputation among her colleagues for spending as little as possible on anyone other than herself. Her desire for money—not only the outward trappings of wealth, but money in and of itself—mounted almost to a physical craving. It became her practice to entertain many of her wealthy foreign clients by wining and dining them in L'Orangerie or Jimmy's, then accompanying them on the following day to the expensive boutiques along Rodeo Drive, where, along with their other purchases, they might feel disposed to reward her with some expensive trinket. In addition to the real estate company's Seville, which she drove for business purposes, Angela had bought herself another yellow Mercedes convertible. More significantly, she had purchased for herself a condominium in the most luxurious of the opulent new high-rise structures which had sprung up to form a steel and glass forest along the Wilshire

Westwood corridor. The price tag had been a mere million, and this figure, Angela reasoned, would be likely to double in the next few years.

Thus Angela approached the start of 1985, and her own twenty-fifth birthday (which happened, coincidentally, to fall on New Year's Day) as a success story—rich . . . beautiful . . . dynamic . . . at the top of her profession. Yet, if the truth be told, Angela Armstrong was still not happy. Her real dream, her dream of "stardom," had not come true! It was something she would have to rectify.

She began her campaign to reenter the show business scene by making tentative inquiries among the many successful industry people she had encountered in the course of her real estate work. The response was uniformly friendly, but discouraging.

"Forget it, Angie baby!" was the gist of their reaction. "What does a bright kid like you need all that shit for? Actresses are a dime a dozen! You are more than just another bimbo!"

But Angela was not deterred. This time her mind was made up. She'd just have to find some other way. She managed a one-night stand with a world-famous movie star superstud who picked her up one morning around two as she was coming out of Kathy Gallagher's, but the superstud was sloshed to the gills and fell asleep on her . . . so nothing came of that. She bought a knockout zebra-stripe Norma Kamali suit and tried jogging back and forth for days along the Malibu strip of beach in front of Johnny Carson's house, but she never succeeded in attracting his attention. Angela did go out once or twice with Robert Evans, whose mansion was listed with Irving Samuels Realty, but the producer was still trying to get over his recent break up with one of his wives or girlfriends or someone, and was very moody on both occasions. He didn't call again after the

second date. She heard some rumor about a "fuck party" at
a top director's house, but wasn't sure whether to believe it,
or whether going might not do her more harm than good,
even if it were true.

Then, one morning, just as Angela was beginning to
feel discouraged, a new client marched into the luxurious
Irving Samuels office on Canon Drive. Her name, she said,
was Marci Sheinberg. She and her husband were interested
in putting their large Encino home on the market. They
wished to purchase a home in Beverly Hills—not post office,
not school district! The Sheinbergs had two children, so they
would require at least four bedrooms plus a maid's room
and pool, and would prefer something in the flats. Their
maximum was 1.9 million.

Marci Sheinberg was a dark, petite, well-preserved
woman. Although she had lived in California for many
years, everything about her appearance bespoke the New
Yorker. There was a big city, pulled-together look that most
Beverly Hills women just never managed to achieve, no matter how feverishly they spent their husbands' money in Giorgio's. At the moment she was dressed in a dramatic, yet
casual Claude Montana outfit. Angela Armstrong knew for
a fact that the sweater alone had cost nine hundred and fifty
dollars. She had admired it herself in Theodore's, but rejected it as exorbitantly overpriced. She regretted her decision now; it looked so smart on Mrs. Sheinberg. But then,
all Marci Sheinberg's outfits did. She devoted a great deal of
her time to shopping, traveled often to Europe on buying
sprees, kept pace with the latest trends in fashion, and
adapted them to what was right for her. She had charge
accounts in every major store from Neiman-Marcus on the
West Coast to Bloomingdale's on the East, and if she found
an item she liked—say, a Saint Laurent silk shirt at four
hundred seventy-five dollars, or some Maud Frizon shoes at

three hundred fifty dollars a pair—she would usually take a
dozen in her size in every available color. Marci Sheinberg
had elevated shopping to an art form.

Sheinberg . . . Sheinberg . . . the name rang a bell
somewhere in Angela Armstrong's mind. Suddenly it came
to her. One of the judges of the Miss America Pageant the
year she had been chosen as third runner-up had been
named Sheinberg! Nat Sheinberg, a Hollywood producer!
She could picture him quite clearly now. His eyes had been
glued to her during the swimsuit competition. Angela remembered thinking at the time that the little pink-faced one
was bound to give her the highest marks! She could barely
conceal a tremor of excitement as she flashed her most dazzling smile at Marci.

"Why, certainly, Mrs. Sheinberg. I am sure we will be
able to find the perfect house for you. By the way, your
husband doesn't happen to be named Nat, does he?"

"That's right. Nat Sheinberg, the producer." Marci's
dark, shrewd eyes narrowed with suspicion. "How do you
happen to know my husband?"

"Oh, I don't!" Angela's smile radiated sweet simplicity
and warmth. "I've just heard of him . . . that's all."

Nat Sheinberg had thought more than once about di-
vorcing his wife. On one occasion, he had moved into the
Beverly Wilshire for a week and consulted an attorney. Talk
about JAP, he had married a JAEMP—a Jewish-American
Empress. "Princess" wasn't good enough for Marci! Nothing was ever good enough for her. Not a goddam thing!
Everything Nat did was wrong. To Marci he was a "coarse
vulgarian." Far too many times he had heard her moan that
it would have been so much better if she had married Ben
Josephson, who was so crazy about her and became a sur-

geon. It was useless to remind her that if she had married Ben Josephson, she would still be back in Scarsdale.

Furthermore Nat reminded her, his money wasn't too "coarse and vulgar" for her to spend, was it? And now this latest business about buying a new house! The place they had in Encino all of a sudden wasn't grand enough for Her Highness! The house was a fucking palace, for chrissake! Eight bedrooms, ten bathrooms, six fireplaces, a fucking tennis court, even . . . the list went on and on! Two acres in the most beautiful residential neighborhood of Encino, and he had paid only half a million for it five years ago! There was no telling what they would ask for a place like that in Beverly Hills these days. God alone knew! Ten . . . fifteen million, maybe. They were comfortable. Not rich. Comfortable. They just didn't have that kind of money. No way. But it was no use arguing. Marci had made up her mind. She was not going to live in Encino a day longer! She pronounced the word "Encino" as if it were "Auschwitz."

Marci was very active socially on several charitable committees: cancer, opera, and the rest. She was sick and tired of the contemptuous glances she received from the other impeccably groomed matrons when, in response to their smiling inquiries as to where she and her husband lived, she was forced to mention the name of the accursed place. Besides, Mitchell would be ready to start high school in the fall, and Stacy two years after that. Her children, she vowed, were going to attend Beverly Hills High!

There was nothing for Nat Sheinberg to say. Marci had worn him down with that high school business. Besides, divorce in the State of California was just too expensive a proposition. He shuddered to contemplate how much the attorney had told him Marci could take him for. Nat still managed to get around, see other women, have a good time. So let her have the house! But it couldn't cost more than 1.9

million! "One point nine million!" he yelled at her at the top of his lungs. "Not a broken penny more! Do you understand me?"

   "Now, look here, Miss Armstrong," snapped Marci Sheinberg from the backseat of the cream Cadillac Seville, "I don't know what kind of fool you take me for! Do you seriously expect to drag me around like this, from one broken-down shanty to another, so that when you finally do show me something halfway decent I'll go into ecstasy over it? I know all about those tricks! I intend to speak to Irving Samuels, personally, about this!"

   "I'm trying to show you everything that is available in your price range," piped Angela Armstrong sweetly, flashing her sunniest smile. In truth, she had been dragging the search out deliberately, reasoning that sooner or later Mr. Sheinberg would join in the house-hunting expedition.

   "Dear, your charm is wasted on me. You know perfectly well which are the two or three best houses in this area. So I expect you to show them to me right now, without any further nonsense about the owners being away and your not having the keys, or any of that other bullshit you've been giving me for the last ten days. Now I think we understand each other. Do you want to make a sale, or don't you?"

   Daunted, Angela ventured to inquire, "But what about your husband? Isn't he interested in what kind of house you are buying?"

   "He trusts my judgment completely," Marci stated flatly. "Once I've found the right place, he'll come and look it over, naturally. But my husband is a very busy man."

   Shortly after this hostile exchange, Marci Sheinberg found her dream house. It was on Crescent Drive just south of the Beverly Hills Hotel, and was built in the style of a miniature French château, complete with turrets and ornamental fountains. Château Sheinberg, Angela nicknamed it mentally. The owners were asking 2.5 million, but Angela said she thought there might be some flexibility. She suggested that they put in an offer at two million and see what happened.

Marci meditated grimly on the tone in which her husband, Nat, had thundered "One point nine million . . . not a penny more!" She had been married to Nat for nearly nineteen years, and she knew that tone—it was the only one that worried her. Maybe if he saw the house. It really was an exceptional buy; he would realize that. If nothing else, he was a shrewd businessman, and once he saw it, he would feel the same way about it as she did.

Nat Sheinberg was, accordingly, shown over the Crescent Drive property by his wife and Angela Armstrong. Nat actually liked the place, and agreed to sign an offer at the two-million-dollar figure. This offer was duly accepted by the sellers, and an escrow entered into by the Sheinbergs. The sale, however, never went through. During the time it would normally have taken for the escrow to close, Nat Sheinberg walked out once more (this time for good) on his wife, Marci. So what if divorce in California cost a fortune? He'd make it back. Financial considerations were forgotten. Something incredible had happened. Angela Armstrong— twenty-seven years old, beautiful, successful in her own right, a girl who had nearly been Miss America, for chrissake—had fallen in love with him! And he *knew* he was in love with her. So the hell with everything. He was fifty-one years old, and he wasn't going to throw the rest of his life away on a woman who didn't understand him.

It didn't take long for Angela Armstrong to let her new lover know of her show business aspirations. Happily, the producer was not in the least averse to the idea of his lovely girlfriend getting back in the business. On the contrary, the idea of guys all over the world eating their hearts out over the broad he was making it with gratified his ego enormously. He liked the idea that he, Nat Sheinberg, had the power to create a new star, and he relished the thought that any success or fame for Angela would be bound to irritate his ex-wife Marci still further. Plus, Angela actually had what it took to make it. There was one thing, however. Her tits were too small. She'd have to get them done. That's why he had given her an "eight" in the swimsuit competition!

"You're a big girl," Sheinberg said. "What are you? Five nine? Five ten? You need big boobs!"

At first Angela was hurt, and she burst into tears, for she always had been a sensitive girl, but ultimately decided it was a small price to pay for stardom. Her new silicone implants were soon seen to maximum advantage in a sequin-spangled confection over flesh-colored net, which Sheinberg hired Bob Mackie to design especially for Angela.

For the talent portion of the Miss America Pageant, Angela had sung a medley of "When the Saints Go Marching In" and "America the Beautiful," and it was Sheinberg's idea that if they could put together a nightclub act, it might prove a great showcase for her talents. He had connections in Vegas that owed him, and he called in the favor. In addition, he hired the finest arranger, vocal coach, and choreographer money could buy to work with his lady love.

When the moment for Angela Armstrong's Las Vegas debut arrived (as the opening act for Rich Little), Sheinberg took out full-page ads in the trades, hired a giant billboard on Sunset—right above the Cock and Bull—to display Angela in her nearly transparent Vegas costume. None of his publicity efforts were enough to cause a sensation, however. Especially in view of the fact that the lady, in spite of the best efforts of the vocal coach and choreographer to drill her, could neither sing nor dance. Her act met with a luke-warm response.

Undaunted, Nat hired Harry Langdon, one of Holly-wood's leading photographers, to take some stills of Angela. A stunning poster resulted from this photo session: Angela Armstrong, clad only in the bottom half of a gold lamé bikini, was pictured emerging from the Malibu surf, her massive breasts burnt golden brown by the sun, her gold hair streaming wildly against a gold-red sunset. She looked the living image of the California dream, and the poster began to sell.

A top publicist named Norman Winter was hired to keep Angela's name constantly in view. The publicist had a bright idea: He also happened to represent a strikingly handsome young actor who, on screen, was macho personi-fied. Offscreen was another story. Disquieting rumors were beginning to penetrate beyond the innermost core of silence into the civilian world. Moreover, the macho actor's career had recently begun to slide as a result of two poorly received films in a row. The stigma of homosexuality, especially now, could be the coup de grace to his faltering popularity. What could be better, reasoned Starke, than to organize a highly visible romance between this young man and his new client, the budding star, Angela Armstrong? No one (outside the business, that is) knew yet about her relationship with Nat Sheinberg. Talk about killing two birds with one stone!

Soon there they were, Winter's two clients—Love's Young Dream—he of the piercing green eyes and rippling biceps; she of the golden hair and magnificent breasts. The year's most perfect couple stared out everywhere from the pages of *Us, People,* the *New York Post,* the *National En-quirer,* et al. There they were, cuddled up before a crackling fireplace at his Santa Barbara ranch; emerging from Spago; discoing at a private party at Nell's in N.Y.C., following the premiere of his latest film (another turkey, which finished his career entirely).

Still, half the publicist's strategy had worked. Without her having done a thing, Angela Armstrong's name was suddenly on everyone's lips. Without having appeared on television in nearly four years, her TV Quotient skyrocketed. A starring role in a mad slasher horror film was next. It made a fortune. She made several "guest" appearances on a highly-rated nighttime soap, and was offered a continuing role in the series. Sheinberg, however, advised her to turn it down. He was going to buy the rights to a stage play, *Lost Souls* by the famous British playwright, Josh Woodard, and he would develop it as a made-for-television movie to star Angela.

Miss Armstrong was unimpressed. She had never heard of Josh Woodard. "For chrissake!" Nat exclaimed. "The guy is married to Pandora Ashley . . . you can't get much bigger than that!" (Suddenly Angela was interested. Very interested.) The play had a great part in it for Angela, Sheinberg enthused. It would do for her what *Sybil* had done for Sally Field; what *Burning Bed* had done for Farrah Fawcett! It would prove to the world that she was a *sensitive* actress.

Sheinberg's arguments had all made sense at the time. But that had been over six months ago, and now Angela Armstrong was starting to get pissed off!

It was all very well and good for Sheinberg! The little producer, known for cheapie, exploitative productions, had wanted to upgrade his image in the community. What better way than by producing something indisputedly high-toned and cultured by an author of Josh Woodard's standing? *Lost Souls,* he figured, was a sure bet to put him in the running for some very respectable Emmys.

Meanwhile, the series role Angela had turned down at Nat's urging had catapulted the actress who'd accepted it to overnight celebrity status! And while Sheinberg was jerking off with his "culture" (and Angela was being forgotten), Victoria Principal had already written two best-selling beauty books! So had Morgan Fairchild, Raquel Welch, Sophia Loren, Linda Evans, and everybody's Aunt Harriet! Yet here she was, Angela Armstrong, one of the greatest beauties in modern Hollywood (to quote the *Ladies' Home Journal)*, and Sheinberg wouldn't even listen to her book idea, *Angela Armstrong's Guide to Inner and Outer Beauty.*

"The market's saturated," he said.

What does he know anyway, Angela fumed. Sheinberg was turning out to be a colossal pain in the ass! What kind of a big shot was he if it was taking him over six months to set up a crummy television movie? On top of everything, she'd never met such a horny little bastard. He was after her morning, noon, and night, especially since she'd had her boobs done! The image of the pink, sweaty Sheinberg sliding his prick in between her now ample bosoms nauseated her. How had she ever let herself get mixed up with a loser like this creep in the first place? She had to get away.

It was when she was dressing to attend the George Landau testimonial banquet that Angela Armstrong decided to pay more attention to this Josh Woodard character. Tall, a bit stooped, professorial in his manner, but not bad . . . not bad at all, Angela thought. After all, Pandora Ashley must have known what she was doing. She was an international star; why, she had even been on the cover of *Vogue!*

Josh Woodard struggled with the bow tie, remembering the advice of Jeeves that "one should always strive for the butterfly effect." How to achieve this eluded him entirely, however, so he poured himself another Scotch from the bottle of Chivas he had bought in the hotel gift shop, and picked up the bedside phone in his hotel suite. At least the

sound of Pandora's voice would cheer him up. Unfortunately, when the Beverly Hills Hotel switchboard put him
through to Wandsworth House some ten minutes later, all
he got was Clarisse, the maid, explaining snottily that Madame was out. Josh tried to calculate mentally the time difference between California and England, and was on the
point of working himself up into a state of alarm about his
wife's well-being, when the desk rang and informed him that
Mr. Sheinberg's car was waiting for him out front.

Christ all-bloody mighty! thought Josh. All I bloody
need right now is a bleeding banquet. "Tell him I'm on my
way downstairs."

Angela Armstrong half-heartedly patted one hand
against the other, making her feeble contribution to the tor-
rential wave of applause which greeted the entrance onstage
of Leonora Sheldrake at the George Landau A.F.I. tribute.
On either side of Angela, Nat Sheinberg and Josh Woodard
were both on their feet, yelling "Bravo!"

"You've got to hand it to the broad," enthused Nat
Sheinberg, "over sixty, and still a great piece of ass!"

Angela's blue eyes narrowed to slits as she appraised
the diamond bracelet and rings on the graceful arm Leonora
raised to still the audience. Leonora's jewelry made what she
was wearing look like paste from Woolworth's. But that was
not all that bothered her, and she could not help admitting
to herself that as far as true stardom was concerned, she
herself was still in a galaxy very remote from that inhabited
by Leonora Sheldrake. The older woman was not some in-
vention of media hype or clever p.r. management, a "star"
which could be extinguished by the cancellation of a TV
series. No, she was the genuine article, dutifully worshipped
by generations of fans the world over.

Angela's feeling of inferiority was reinforced later in

the evening when she and Sheinberg had put in a brief appearance at George Landau's private postbanquet party at his fabulous mansion above Sunset. Josh Woodard had excused himself, pleading that he was too exhausted to attend, and was waiting for a long-distance call from his wife. It was painfully clear to Angela that many of the show business legends present, including Landau, Jimmy Stewart, and Leonora Sheldrake herself, had little idea of who *she* was. As for Nat Sheinberg, Angela was beginning to find it positively embarrassing to be seen with him. She pleaded a migraine and dragged Sheinberg home early, her mind racing with sudden revelations. She had never realized so clearly what a long climb she still had to get to the top. It was high time, she decided, to scale the next rung of the ladder!

In the early morning hours following the George Landau testimonial party, Josh Woodard was awakened from a profound and dreamless sleep by a loud and persistent hammering at the door of his room. He turned on a bedside light, illuminating a copy of *Swann's Way* and a digital clock which read 2:57. Alarmed, he groped for his bathrobe (a faded, well-worn paisley affair) and stumbled hurriedly toward the door.

"It could be a telegram," he reasoned, worriedly. "Something must have happened to Pandora!"

He opened the door, not to a telegram, but to none other than Nat Sheinberg's leading lady. Angela Armstrong's smile was on high beam, and she was still wearing the skimpy, blue, silver-spangled Fabrice creation she had worn to the Landau banquet. Her thick mane of golden hair cascaded abundantly over her shoulders, mingling with the rich, light fur of her arctic lynx coat. With one well-manicured hand, she held forth a bottle of chilled Dom Perignon, with the other, a large and unwieldy shopping bag from (of all places) Brentano's. Nat Sheinberg was not to be seen.

"May I come in?" Angela asked sweetly, not waiting for the answer, but striding on her long, suntanned legs past the dumbfounded playwright into the tiny hotel room.

Oh, well, thought Josh, this is Hollywood. Apparently it is a place where one must expect the unexpected.

"I can't believe this!" gasped Angela Armstrong, wheeling about, hands on hips, her blue eyes flashing with indignation. "I can't believe they'd give you a little cubbyhole like this! My God! This is an outrage to an author of your standing! A guest from a foreign country! Oh, this is just awful! You must believe me, Mr. Woodard, I have no idea about this . . ."

Josh reeled with bewilderment and exhaustion. "Look, Miss Armstrong, it's very sweet of you, uh, very kind of you, to take an interest . . . but I assure you, I'm perfectly all right here. The room suits me perfectly. I'm quite comfortable. Now . . ."

"Comfortable! Hah! This place looks like a Salvation Army shelter! How much are they soaking you for this dump, anyway?"

"I don't have any idea, I'm afraid. Mr. Sheinberg is taking care of it," mumbled Josh forlornly, feeling rather as though he'd passed through the looking glass.

"Well, that explains it, of course. We'll see about that! They have some magnificent rooms here. Some of the bungalows are great. You might like one of them better. You know. The quiet? For your writing?" Angela lowered her voice to an intimate whisper: "I write a little myself, you know."

Josh felt obliged to evince a polite interest. The girl seemed well intentioned, if foolish. "Oh, really? What sort of thing do you write?"

"Poetry," Angela confided. "I don't know. It just seems to pour out of me. I've always been very sensitive."

A bleary-eyed Josh mumbled words to the effect that that would account for it, he supposed. Whatever did she come here for? he wondered.

"Well, I guess we're stuck with this room for tonight, anyhow," said Angela stoically, tossing her arctic lynx on the unmade bed. "I'll call Nick Papas first thing tomorrow, myself!"

"Much obliged," smiled Josh wanly.

"Shall we open this?" asked Angela, indicating the Dom Perignon.

"By all means!" agreed the writer, wishing he had something stronger on hand at this juncture. But champagne would have to do—anything to help him through this ordeal. His head rang with the unreality of the situation. Tinseltown Kafka!

"I'll fetch some glasses from the bathroom," Josh volunteered.

When he had left the room, Angela sprawled out in a floral armchair, extending her long golden legs in their silver Andrea Pfister evening sandals. Almost involuntarily, her snub nose wrinkled in distaste. She had to keep reminding herself that Pandora Ashley *must* know what she was doing with this man, although the evidence up to this point was exceedingly thin.

The bathroom glasses were duly brought, the champagne cork gaily popped, and the couple clicked their glasses in a toast.

"To *Lost Souls!*" said Angela, flashing her brightest smile.

"*Lost Souls!*" repeated Josh Woodard, smiling also.

After the second glass of Dom Perignon, the atmosphere in the room lightened considerably, and it was in an almost affectionate tone that Josh Woodard finally asked his glamorous visitor why she had chosen this unorthodox hour to pay her social call.

"I just felt we should get to know each other better. You know, I want to do a really good job playing Mildred. I don't know whether Nat told you about this, but I've even offered to go without makeup!" Angela paused to let the immensity of her dedication sink in.

Josh nodded politely.

"I want," Angela continued intently, "to learn my craft. To grow as an actress!" Here she leaned forward so that her massive golden bosom nearly touched the playwright's beard. "You'd like to help me do that, wouldn't you?"

Woodard agreed feebly that he would, but he backed off, noting that as the champagne bottle was nearly empty, he'd ring room service and order another.

So that's what the little minx has been up to all along! he mused. But why the Brentano's bag? And why pick on me, for pity's sake? What on earth does she imagine I can do for her, even if I wanted to?

Josh was under no illusion that the lady had arrived in the grip of uncontrollable physical passion for him. He thought bleakly of the tired joke about the Polish actress who was so dumb she came to Hollywood and fucked the writer. This woman already had the producer—Sheinberg! What did she want with him? The devil of it was, Josh realized, he was becoming aroused in spite of himself.

"Hello, room service? This is Mr. Woodard in . . . Woo . . . dard . . . yes, that's right . . . in 303. 3 . . . 0 . . . 3. Yes. I need a bottle of Dom Perignon, and," Angela was pointing, "some glasses. Yes. And you might as well send a bottle of Scotch also. Yes, J.B. will do nicely. No. No ice."

A silver Andrea Pfister sandal flew heavenward. "Come here, Josh, baby!" cooed Angela Armstrong.

When the room service waiter had been tipped, and the second bottle of Dom Perignon uncorked, the full nature of Angela's errand spilled out, together with the contents of the Brentano's bag.

"Joshie, you think I'm a beautiful woman, don't you?" asked the actress, thrusting her breasts provocatively forward once more, fixing the playwright with what she intended to be a "soulful glance."

Josh Woodard fidgeted nervously. He must have been mad to let this farce get this far! What had he been thinking of? "Look, Miss Armstrong . . ."

"Angela . . ."

"Angela. Angela, it doesn't matter what I think. I'm a happily married man. Anyway, I'm only the writer . . ."

"Right!" smiled Angela triumphantly. "That's exactly what I wanted to talk to you about." Rising, she shimmied out of her chair and spread the contents of the Brentano's bag on the floor. There lay every beauty and fitness manual in print. Everyone from Jane Fonda to Christie Brinkley to Jane Seymour stared up at Josh, in every imaginable shade of leotards and leg warmers, lifting weights and toning tummies.

"But . . . but . . . but . . ." he sputtered incoherently.

Angela, however, was no longer listening. She had approached the bed, and, with the undulations of a golden serpent, was slithering out of her clothes.

"Don't you think," she demanded, her tanned frame revealed in all its naked splendor, "that I have a better body than any of them?"

She stretched out cat-like on the bed, posing suggestively, running her long brown hands over the splendid curves of her bosom, down into the golden reaches between her thighs.

"Don't you see, Josh? Together we could write the best beauty book of all! We'd call it the *Angela Armstrong Inner-and Outer-Awareness Beauty Concept Book!* You will do the inner part, and I will do the outer part!"

Josh Woodard poured himself a stiff Scotch and gulped it down in panic. He might have known something like this would happen. How had he ever let things reach this stage! What an idiot he was! Worst of all, he could not tear his eyes away from the golden Amazon on the bed. He was hard as a rock. He despised himself for it, but at that moment he wanted her desperately. Still, he made no move toward the bed. Angela, seeing his hesitation, reasoned that there was only one possible explanation. She rose from the bed, approached Woodard, reached for his belt buckle, and was about to unzip his fly in a matter-of-fact, professional manner when Josh let out a yelp and backed away.

"No! It's no use. It won't do. Look, my dear, I don't wish to offend you in any way. . . . The whole thing is my fault. I should have asked you to leave ages ago. But I simply must insist you put your dress on now and go home!" Josh reached for the spangled Fabrice and gently held it out to her.

Angela, though, had a one-track mind: "Don't feel bad, sugar! If you can't get it up, I know how to fix that . . ."

Woodard's feeling of self-disgust now mingled with contempt for this girl . . . so hard and ultimately unsensual, for all her voluptuous attributes. Using her sex on poor, pathetic little Sheinberg who loved her. Now trying to use him. Worse, trying to turn him into someone who would use her. Just another partner in a game of sordid trade-offs! And it had very nearly worked. He picked up Angela's arctic lynx and draped it over her bare shoulders.

"I'm sorry. I'm genuinely sorry if I've hurt your feelings . . ."

"You motherfucking louse!" Angela was screaming like a fury, her face scarlet with rage, the reality of rejection finally sinking in. "You stinking faggot! You're off the picture . . . you're off *Lost Souls,* do you understand me? You listen to me, Mr. Motherfucking Shakespeare: When I get through with you, you'll curse the day you ever set foot in California!"

He already did, thought Josh Woodard grimly, as his glamorous visitor finally slammed the door behind her, leaving in her wake a pile of beauty books. He already did.

4

It was hot as an oven inside the trailer. The Elvis Presley record had wound down, but Tim, Lucinda's baby brother, was still howling his guts out. The stifling room looked like a garbage can, with empty beer bottles littering the floor, and scraps of paper lying on the furniture. The upholstery on the furniture had faded from what had originally been bright, clashing colors of orange, lime green, brown, and purple. The garishness was muted somewhat by age—and a layer of dust. The crowded room also held a makeshift play-pen for Tim; inside were dusty plush animals missing ears or eyes. Claiming even more space was a brown leatherette Barcalounger Frank had bought on payments when he was still working up at the mill.

The TV was on and Dan Rather was saying something about the marines in Honduras and whether Central America could ever become another Vietnam. Cindy changed channels and gave Tim a bottle of Coke. His little red face was blotchy from the heat, and his eyes were swollen from crying.

Marines. She looked at the framed photo of her dad in his uniform on top of the TV set. He stood in front of a flag and was smiling. He wore a white cap and had eyes like

Clint Eastwood. Lucinda stared at the picture. It was the photograph of a man she had never known.

She had been only seven when her pa had started in on her. That was about the time he stopped working regular hours and Tillie had started waitressing nights. He would sit in his bathrobe in the tiny living room, watching TV, drinking beer, and he would make the little girl sit in his lap. She would sit as still as she could, almost holding her breath, praying each time that this night would be different, that the moment would not come when he would open his robe and ask her to "play with daddy." But it had only gotten worse. One night, when she was nine or so, he had come home and caught her trying on a bright red lipstick in front of the mirror. He called her "a dirty little tramp, just like your mother," and picked her up and started to shake her by the throat. "You've been begging for this!" he screamed, pulling down his jeans. "Tramp," he muttered over and over as he plunged into her child's body.

That had been eight years ago. Over the years he gradually came to bother her less, mostly due to the drinking. But Lucinda had also learned when to avoid him, and she managed to find excuses to keep her away from home. She knew she had to get away—for good. And she would. Soon. She just had to.

The red blouse had arrived that morning. It was actually more cherry than red, and had a V-neck cut way down to there with just two small ruffles on either side. And even though it was only polyester, one would have sworn it was silk, the way it clung to her body. Best of all, however, was the label—Saks Fifth Avenue! You could bet your ass that nobody, but nobody, in Northern High—except maybe that cunt Maureen and she was so flat-chested no one would look twice at her no matter what she wore—had ever had anything from Saks Fifth Avenue before.

"$39.95!" her mother had screeched. "And just how the fuck did you happen to get your hands on $39.95, you little whore?" By that time, Lucinda was out the door. Nothing was going to spoil her joy in owning that blouse. Not even Tillie's mouth. Not this time. Besides, she had come by the money honestly, or almost.

She ran through the bleached-out dust and hot pastel metal of the trailer park, her red bundle clutched to her breast. Only when she reached the gigantic white wagon wheel that marked the entrance to the "Shady Lane Mobile Home Park" did she pause for breath.

"The old bitch!" she thought. Defiantly, she peeled off the sweat-streaked, pale blue T-shirt she had been wearing and threw it in the dust at her feet. For a moment she stood half-naked in the trailer park entrance, her cinnamon-colored hair blowing wildly in the hot wind, her pearly skin gleaming like alabaster in the relentless sun. Then, slowly, she unfastened the buttons of the red blouse and slid the silken fabric over her glistening breasts. Lucinda Bayes could hardly wait to see herself in a mirror, she felt so beautiful.

The blouse meant so much to her. Ever since she had seen Madonna wearing one just like it in one of her videos, Lucinda knew she had to have it. She also knew it would help her at the "Madonna Wanna-Be" contest in Portland. She was determined to win, despite the fact she wasn't blond, and was several inches taller than the singer. It could be her ticket to get out of this hellhole, and she was determined that nothing would stand in her way.

Lucinda had only a few minutes to spare before catching the bus to Portland—just enough time to stop by Helen's Grocery to pick up something she urgently needed.

Helen kept a kind of hair color you could just spray on and turn your hair any shade at all you wanted, and today Lucinda wanted to be blond.

"Beachcomber Blond," or "Spun Sand?" Lucinda decided the rock singer's hair was closer to "Beachcomber Blond" on the color chart. Heart racing wildly, she reached out and slipped the pink-silver can of tint into her oversized purse.

No voice called out. No hand reached out to grab her. In fact, as usual, no one paid her any mind at all. It wasn't surprising actually, since Lucinda Bayes was as much a fixture at Helen's as the peeling posters advertising Coca-Cola and Coppertone, the corkscrew strips of aging flypaper laden with their prey, or the mangy, underfed dogs that whined day and night outside the rusted screen door begging for scraps. Cindy was at the store nearly every day, reading over and over Helen's meager assortment of paperback romances and movie magazines.

It wasn't until she was on the Portland bus that Cindy started to feel bad about stealing from Helen. The fat lady had always been good to her, even treating her and her baby brother to ice-cream bars a couple of times when it was really hot and they had no money to pay. No mind. She would pay her back with the prize money. Just as soon as she won.

Once in the Portland bus terminal, Cindy headed straight for the ladies' room and began spraying her hair with the contents of the stolen aerosol can. The golden-yellow shade looked even better than she'd dared hope; it lit up her young face, and set off her bright eyes like jewels.

On her way to the Roxy Theatre, Lucinda stopped off at the cosmetics department of Montgomery Ward. Ignoring the dirty looks from the salesgirls, she lingered there for over an hour, painstakingly applying testers of pale blue and

pearly-white eyeshadow, dark brown mascara, peach
blusher, and honey lip gloss. With each stroke of the
makeup brush, Lucinda Bayes's heart leapt within her. Part
of her had always dared to hope she was pretty. But now she
realized that she was more. She was beautiful!

The line outside the Roxy stretched for what seemed to
be blocks and blocks. It giggled and squealed and squirmed,
composed as it was of hundreds of teenage girls, all dressed
in one of the various styles of their idol. Most had opted for
the funky look of layered castoffs which had become
Madonna's trademark. Lucinda, however, had chosen instead to mimic the singer's sexier, more grown-up look.
First prize in the contest was fifty bucks in cash, plus
Madonna's record albums and two tickets to her Portland
concert next month. And as if that wasn't enough, the local
girl selected would then become eligible—together with win-
ners of similar contests being staged all across the country—
for the grand prize—an all-expense-paid trip to Hollywood
and the chance to audition for a part in Madonna's next
movie.

Lucinda's heart sank as she took her place in the snak-
ing line of girls. So many of them were beautiful, and most
of them had class too. What was she even doing here? She
was nobody. Nothing. As far back as she could remember,
people had been calling her a "no-good tramp . . . Cindy
Super-tits from Trashtown." In a way it was true, she reasoned. Sex had never been a mystery to Lucinda Bayes. She
wasn't the kind of girl boys had to invite out to the pictures
or take to the prom. She'd never learned to tease them or to
lead them on . . . to put any value on her own embraces.

She had no right even to be here. It was stupid. All
she'd ever get for her pains would be a beating from her pa if
he found out. Hadn't he told her a million times that beauty

contests were for whores! Frightened by the image of her father, she decided to give her name as Lucinda O'Rourke, using her mother's maiden name. That way, she wouldn't get into any trouble even if, by some miracle, she did win, and it was announced on the radio. Even if it got into the papers, she reasoned, no one would know her with her new blond hair.

The line was moving forward rapidly now. Lucinda's hands were clammy with sweat. She had never stood up on stage before in front of a lot of people. It had been madness to come.

She was inside the stage door now. A cold blast of musty air assaulted her, as though she were entering a tomb. As the girls filed in, a young man with a clipboard patiently wrote down each contestant's name, and handed her a placard with a number on it to wear around her neck. The girls were instructed to step out onto the stage and mime and lip-sync to one of Madonna's recordings. Lucinda could make out the panel of judges sitting in the front row of the orchestra pit: a minor Paramount executive; the head of Portland's most successful charm school, Melanie Childs; and Stan "The Man" Luboff, deejay from radio station KNOW, whose brainchild the contest had been. Before this panel, the contestants were to act out selected numbers in groups of six. Lucinda's luck was running high. The song chosen for her to mime was, "Borderline," the very song she'd been practicing ever since she'd first heard about the contest. Even better, she was easily the best-looking of her group of six. She was bound to stand out.

When a rough voice called out "Next," and her group shuffled awkwardly on to the stage, Lucinda drew on some hitherto-undreamed-of wellspring of passion within herself and took possession of center stage as if it had been hers by inalienable birthright. The music took possession of her body as she moved gracefully along with the recording. She was good. She knew it. An almost palpable hush descended over the orchestra pit. Even so, it had come as an undeniable shock when Stan Luboff called out the winner's name— "Lucinda Lee O'Rourke!" Her knees had turned to Jell-O, and brown mascara coursed relentlessly down her cheeks as Stan "The Man" hugged her and presented her with her winnings—the albums, the tickets, and five crisp ten-dollar bills!

Lucinda was still shaking as she washed the yellow dye out of her hair, using green liquid soap from the dispenser at the bus terminal washroom. It was incredible! Lucinda Bayes—for once, a winner! It felt great, and furthermore she was going to keep it that way.

On her way home to the trailer park, Cindy stopped off at Helen's just as the fat lady was ready to shut up shop for the night. She let one of the crisp ten dollar bills drop to the floor in a place where Helen would be bound to find it.

The rest of her prize money would go toward finding her escape from this place. Yes, Lucinda Bayes's life was going to be different from now on. A whole lot different . . . and there was nothing anyone could do to stop it! Not Tillie! Not Frank! Not anyone!

When Frank Bayes had gotten back from 'Nam, Tillie O'Rourke had been practically the only girl in Bend, Oregon, who wasn't afraid to go out with him. It wasn't that he was ugly; in fact, Frank was a good-looking guy, tall and well built, with thick sandy hair that he wore down to his shoulders as if to show he wasn't in the Marines anymore and he'd just like to see somebody try to make him get a haircut.

Maybe it was something in his cold, green eyes that scared people. They were old eyes, with all the youth drained out of them, eyes that never seemed to look straight at you, yet could at the same time pierce you through. And if that wasn't weird enough, he wore one gold earring, a badge of fierceness and defiance that seemed to say, "I've lived through things you motherfuckers couldn't even begin to imagine. I live by my own rules from here on out."

But none of the weirdness bothered Tillie. After all, she'd been best friends with Janey, Frank's kid sister, since she was eight, and had had a crush on Frank Bayes as far back as she could remember.

When Frank first came back from Vietnam, he would sit all day in his tiny bedroom, smoking dope and listening to Bob Dylan records. Sometimes he'd point a hunting rifle out the window, tracking passersby on Grant Street as if they were V.C.

Then one day his sister Janey had knocked on his door and told him to clean himself up for dinner that night. She was bringing home a real nice girl for him to talk to, and she wanted everybody to see that he could still "behave like a gentleman." If anyone else had used those words to him, he would have torn his head off. Janey, however, could get away with anything. Their momma had died when Frank was only five years old, and even though his sister was nearly two years his junior, Janey had, in many ways, become the closest thing to a parent Frank ever had.

It was Janey who always interceded in the fights between Frank and his father, stopping them before they erupted into real violence. Shit, when he'd come back from the war, it was all Frank could do to keep himself from strangling the motherfucking old bastard. All those stinking letters he'd written him about *duty*, for chrissake! What did the old fart think this was—some fucking John Wayne movie on the fucking Late Show? The war hadn't been black and white, man. It had been live, and in living color. One time, Frank had been the only survivor when his platoon had got caught in a Cong ambush in the Ia Drang valley. For what seemed an eternity, Frank had been forced to hide, lying motionless under the still-warm bodies of his buddies, while the V.C. kept poking at the pile of corpses with their knives. Whenever he thought of that time, the stench of fear and death would come into his nostrils, and he would gag. And now, all of a sudden, this old cocksucker, who never had a good word to say to him till he joined the marines at eighteen, wanted to start that flag-waving crap with him.

But Janey was all right. Janey was worth coming home to. That's why he didn't even mind it too much when the "real nice girl" she brought to dinner turned out to be Tillie O'Rourke.

The meal had gone about as well as Janey Bayes could have hoped, all things considered. Old man Bayes had mostly kept quiet, and Frank had seemed content to listen to Janey and Tillie gossip. He had showered and shaved and had put on the short-sleeved, pale pink Arrow shirt that his sister had bought him as a coming-home present. Janey noted with approval that he had answered politely when Tillie asked if he didn't think we'd win the war pretty soon now, instead of launching into one of the sarcastic tirades that similar questions usually provoked. Janey also noted the way her brother kept his eyes locked on Tillie's boobs. Tillie didn't seem to mind his attentions, however; in fact, she seemed to be lapping it up like a kitten would a bowl of cream. Janey couldn't really blame her, she guessed. Tillie had always had a thing about Frank. Still, there was something in the whole scene that made her uncomfortable. Maybe she had done wrong in bringing them together.

Following that dinner, Frank Bayes started seeing Tillie O'Rourke. He didn't exactly invite her out on dates, or anything, but he didn't seem to mind her hanging around all the time—and she seemed to want nothing more. He would drive around in his clapped-out '62 Chevy Impala for hours, going nowhere; Tillie sat by his side, her pale eyes timid as a rabbit. The music of Jimi Hendrix blared on the radio, his electric guitar sending shock waves up Tillie's spine.

Frank would take a swig of bourbon, and shout, "Shit! Did you hear that riff? Man, that Hendrix is unbelievable! Did you know he used to be in the 101st Airborne? We had a black guy in our unit, Tommy Mitchell . . . used to play this music all the time . . . one time when we were pinned down for about three hours behind a wall with the gooks shelling us real heavy from the trees . . . he was a real badass nigger, Tommy . . . best guy in the world to have beside you in a fight. Shit, he used to have this big old chocolate chip cookie, you know, that his old lady had baked for him and sent him in a package. He never did eat the damn thing . . . just kept it all wrapped up in some kind of tinfoil and carried it around with him everywhere . . . said it was his good luck charm."

"What happened to him?" asked Tillie.

"Got his legs shot off."

Sometimes he'd tell her jokes he'd heard in 'Nam, and Tillie would try to laugh or smile, despite the fact that to her his stories weren't funny. Some of his stories just plain scared her, like the one about the American soldier who was "building his own gook" out of bits of dismembered corpses, or the officer who had a plan to drop piranha into the paddies of the North to "shorten the war." It was hard to remember sometimes this was the man she had worshipped years ago. Some things about him had changed so much. But he still had the same half-ashamed grin he'd had as a boy, and he was surprisingly gentle with her when they made love in the back of the old green Chevy. It was as though he really respected her.

Then one night they went to see a soft porn movie at the drive-in on the edge of town, and when Frank saw those actors up on the screen getting in bed together, he got horny and made Tillie do it right away, even though she didn't like the idea that somebody might look into the car and see them at it. Not long after that, she knew she was pregnant. At first she was scared, but Frank seemed not to mind. He even said he would marry her.

By the time Lucinda Bayes got back to the trailer park, it was nearly six-thirty. Tillie was standing in the doorway of their mobile home, dressed for work in the hot-pink shorts and low-cut top with white fringe that the waitresses at the Bar None Ranch wore. She was drinking Coors from a can. Though it was almost evening, it hadn't cooled down much, and her face looked shiny and pink under the heavy makeup. Time had not been kind to Tillie Bayes.

An Elvis Presley ballad was playing loud on the stereo inside. Her ma sure had a thing about Elvis, thought Lucinda, as the plaintive notes wailed into the Oregon night. She never played any other kind of music. She even kept a scrapbook with pictures of Elvis she'd cut out from all kinds of fan magazines and old newspapers, and she talked about how one day she was going to save up enough money to take a trip—she called it a "pilgrimage"—to Graceland, and see Elvis's mansion and put flowers on his grave. She'd go on her own, she said, without Frank or the kids.

Except for Frank Bayes, Elvis Presley had been the only man Tillie ever loved, so it just seemed natural, when things with Frank turned out so bad, that she gave her heart more and more to Elvis. She cried for three days when he died, till Frank slapped her around and told her to stop her bawling or he'd smash her "fucking Elvis records" over her head: Tillie shut up, but she knew deep inside her that she was the only woman in the world who would have understood Elvis Presley and saved him with her love.

Inside the trailer the song ended, and Lucinda's kid brother started yowling in his rickety playpen. "Well," sneered Tillie, "if it isn't Brooke Shields! You get your ass in here this minute and look after your brother. Are you trying to make me lose my job?"

Some job, thought Lucinda to herself, being pawed by half the beer-soused rednecks from here to Seattle, but she didn't answer back. She swept past her mother. In her Saks blouse, she felt she belonged to a different, better world already, full of standing onstage and hearing applause.

The TV was already on, so Lucinda turned up the volume and willed herself to be transported to a different world. She was just in time to see the telecast of the A.F.I. tribute to veteran screen director George Landau.

Lucinda had never heard of the A.F.I., and she had no idea who Landau was, but her young heart thrilled as the camera panned across the sea of glittering celebrities assembled in the Hollywood ballroom. The girl tried to imagine what it would be like, just once, to sit like Linda Evans or Angela Armstrong dressed in a sequined ballgown, sipping champagne while Tom Selleck or Rob Lowe sat smiling at her side. And who knew? Maybe she would be there some day.

Lucinda had to pinch the silken sleeve of her new red blouse to remind herself that she had really won, that she, Lucinda Bayes, was now an actual semifinalist in a national beauty contest. Well, maybe it wasn't really a "beauty" contest, but it was close. It was just too good to be true!

She slithered her denim-clad body as close as she could get to the screen as she heard Leonora Sheldrake announce. "One of Mr. Landau's newest discoveries, a young man whose star beams bright with promise and . . . a very dear friend of mine . . . Mr. Rod Ward!"

Good God, Rod Ward was handsome, thought Lucinda as she stretched out on the rust carpet. Now that was somebody she really would like to go to bed with! She remembered a nude picture of him she'd seen in *Playgirl,* and the thought of it made her horny. She watched as the handsome actor put his arm around Leonora Sheldrake. Lucinda wondered if what she had read in the *National Enquirer* about the two stars being engaged could possibly be right? How could somebody as perfect as Rod Ward possibly be in love with an old broad like that? Hell . . . she must be almost a hundred. She stared with envy at the set as Leonora swept off majestically in her taffeta creation. Lucinda shut her eyes for a second, imagining what that dress would look like on her, and how the bright diamonds would set off her long chestnut hair and white bosom. Then a dog barked and a door slammed and Frank Bayes was home.

He was drunk. That went without saying. "Shit," he snarled, "this place is like an oven, and it stinks in here! Cin . . . what's that stink?"

"I dunno. Dinner, I guess. It's been heating up for nearly an hour. I didn't know when you'd get in."

Frank's green eyes lit on a glossy black box stuffed with fluffy tissue paper and bordered in a fancy red scroll-like lettering which lay open and looked oddly out of place on the dingy lime couch. "What's this?" He strode over to the couch and, with the deliberate, purposeful movements of a drunkard trying to behave sober, lifted up and began to examine the package. As he did so, a pink slip of paper dropped to the floor.

"Saks Fifth Avenue!" he exclaimed with as much shock as if the parcel had been postmarked from the Soviet Union. "Saks Fifth Avenue! Just what the fuck is going on in this goddam house, anyway?" He picked up the pink slip of paper and tried to decipher its meaning. One lady's blouse. Red. $39.95 plus tax! They gotta be joking! Who the hell here is spending that kind of money?" His eyes flew to his daughter's lithe body sprawled on the rug, her firm buttocks squeezed into skintight jeans, her upper back encased in shiny red fabric.

"You bitch!" he shouted. "You bitchin' little whore! Where do you get off spending that kind of money?" He grabbed her by her hair and pulled her to her feet. "What did you do to earn that kind of money, as if I don't know, you little cunt!"

"I didn't!" she started to scream. "I didn't do anything bad for it! I swear to God . . . I borrowed the money . . . so I could win the contest . . . and I did . . . 'cause I was the prettiest!"

"Lying little cunt! I'll teach you to lie to your father!" Lucinda's face stung as Frank slapped her hard with the open palm of his huge hand. Then she saw him get that look in his eye . . . that special, weird look that he always got before he started in on her, and she knew what was coming. "Show me," he said. And his voice was not rough anymore. It was low and caressing. He pulled her to him and put his tongue in her mouth. His spit tasted of bourbon. The room was hot, and Lucinda gasped for breath as Frank put his hands on her crotch and started rubbing back and forth on the tight denim. For a split second, her head spun with the heat and fire that was shooting up from her crotch; for a moment, she actually wanted him.

Frank sensed his daughter's submission, and gave a weird, lopsided grin. He clutched at the red fabric like a wild beast tearing at its prey. Lucinda gave a shriek of agony as the pretty shirt was ripped mercilessly from her body. She flailed out wildly, scratching Frank's face with her long fingernails as his rough hands began mauling her breasts. A thin red line appeared on Frank's cheekbone as he pushed her to the floor.

"You're no child of mine, you little cunt! You're a whore just like your ma!"

Cindy's hand groped wildly along the top of the television set until it came to rest on the object it sought. Without pausing a second, she lifted it up and brought it down with all her might on the skull of her attacker. There was a hollow, piercing crack, then Frank Bayes pitched forward on to her. She thought for a moment that she hadn't stopped him and began to sob hysterically with fear. Then she saw that he remained motionless.

When she rose to her feet, sticky blood from her father's forehead trickled down her breasts. She was still clutching the heavy silver object with which she had hit him —the framed photo of Marine Corporal Franklin R. Bayes. The glass had shattered, and splinters of it were imbedded in her arm. Still sobbing, she picked up the shreds of red fabric from the floor beside her, then went into the tiny bedroom where she knew her mother kept money hidden in a coffee can on a top shelf of the closet. She found twenty-four dollars, mostly in ones. That, along with the forty she had left from the contest would be enough to get away from here.

She took a yellow shirt and her mother's best pink dress. When she was dressed, she tiptoed past her father's body lying on the floor, her mind filled with fear that he might spring up at her, might rape her again. Easing the door shut, she ran out into the hot Oregon night.

Countless pairs of headlights illuminated the forlorn and bedraggled figure of Lucinda Bayes as she marched desperately along the side of the freeway, one arm outstretched. It was nearly eleven o'clock. Tillie wouldn't get back from waitressing at the Bar None for at least another three or four hours. It wasn't likely anyone would find Frank till then.

What the hell difference does it make? Cindy sobbed to herself. Her life was over now for sure, just when it had begun to look as if things were going to turn around for her.

Then she lucked out. A Dannon truck heading south pulled over to the side and offered her a ride. The old guy driving the rig turned out to be real polite too, not asking too many questions and telling Cindy she reminded him of his youngest daughter, Cynthia. He said she was working as a secretary in Houston now; it was obvious he was proud of her. He fished out some pictures of Cynthia and his other kids. There were five in all, three boys and two girls. The snapshots showed them standing around a Christmas tree; Cynthia, who was dark and had buckteeth, was holding an Alsatian puppy. Lucinda looked at the photo with longing, wishing that she could have had such a happy home. At that moment she would have given anything on earth to trade places with Cynthia, buckteeth and all.

The truck driver dropped Lucinda off at Eureka, saying he was real sorry, but this was the end of the line for him. It was nearly five hours before she got her next ride. By then, her thin cotton dress was soaked through and sticking to her skin, and her legs were ready to give out. There was also a giant lump in the pit of her stomach and her right arm ached from holding it out imploringly to the passing parade of vehicles.

Each time she saw a highway patrol car she would freeze with terror, figuring for sure that they must have found Frank by now, and would be out searching for her. But so far they just drove on by, like everybody else, paying her no attention.

She had already planned that as soon as she got to San

Francisco she would find some small hairdressing parlor and
have her hair bleached out, so she'd be harder to recognize.
That, she knew, would use up a lot of the money she had, so
she couldn't afford to waste any on food.

Just when Lucinda had all but given up hope of ever
getting another ride, a bright red Corvette going at least
ninety miles an hour streaked past her, and then, seconds
later, with a squeal of brakes, pulled over on the shoulder. A
tow-haired boy stuck his head out through the passenger
side of the sunroof, yelling, "Hey, baby, move your butt if
ya wanna ride!"

The red convertible pulled into the rain-soaked parking
lot of a Red Lion Motor Inn. The red glitter of the neon
"vacancy" sign spilled like blood on the black pavement.
Davie Bowie blared on the car stereo. Lucinda Bayes sat
rigid on the lap of the tow-headed boy, as he began kneading
her breasts insistently in time to the driving beat of the rock
music.

The boy whose name was Dan, shifted his position
slightly so that Lucinda could feel the pressure of his hard
cock against her thigh. "I'm gonna get us a room," said
Alan, the dark-haired boy. "You guys stay here!"

In only a short time, Lucinda Bayes lay back in a tub of
bubbles. The scented steamy tub, the bright fluorescent light
over the big mirror, the gleaming beige tiles, the fluffy towels, the wallpaper streaked with silver bamboo shoots—all
these things represented to Cindy a new world of luxury.
From the bedroom outside came Jagger's sensual wailing of
a Mick Jagger song.

The connecting door opened abruptly, and Dan stood
before her—naked, pink-fleshed, and grinning. Stoned out of
his mind, he tried singing along with the music as he approached the tub. "She was hot . . . hot . . . hot," he

sang inanely, as he leaned over, thrusting his erection in
Lucinda Bayes's face. "C'mon, babe, gimme some . . .
gimme, gimme, gimme some . . ." he moaned as her soft
lips parted for him. "Holy shit!", he yelled, "Hey, Alan
. . . c'mere! We got ourselves a winner!"

Almost immediately, the dark boy was in the room,
watching greedily as Dan pumped in and out with his pink
buttocks, grinding his hard-on deeper and deeper down
Lucinda's throat.

"That's right, baby . . . suck me. Suck me good. Hey,
Al, she likes to suck cock, ain't that right, baby?"

The dark boy helped Dan to carry her from the bathtub
to the bed. They had some good grass, and Cindy took a
couple of hits. After that, she felt a lot of things as from a
haze. The two boys spread her legs, taking turns penetrating
every part of her. Alan was the cool one, making her go
down on him while Dan was fucking her. His dick was
longer, slimmer. Cindy cried out with pleasure when he
opened her with his expert fingers, then, finally, slid it into
her. Dan looked on, grinning, as she writhed on the bed in
her first blinding orgasm.

In the morning, the boys and the red Corvette were
gone. Cindy began to sob in disappointment and fear. What
had she done wrong? Hadn't she done everything to make
them like her? Dan had even told her how beautiful she was!
Why, oh why hadn't they taken her with them? She had
been sure they liked her.

A wave of panic gripped her like icy fingers clutching
her throat. What if they hadn't paid for the room? Her
meager bankroll wouldn't be nearly enough, she was sure.
They were bound to call the police, and then what would
become of her? Then she glimpsed the crumped green
twenty dollar bill on the pillowcase beside her, and her sobs
gradually subsided. To her great relief, she found Dan and

Alan had paid for the room, after all. She felt a lot better after she had treated herself to hotcakes and sausages and coffee at the Denny's across from the motel parking lot. It was the first food she had tasted in nearly forty-eight hours. Lucinda Bayes smiled. Finally . . . she was on her way!

5

As Emilio presented the bottle of '78 Lynch-Bages for Martin Sinclair's scrutiny, he tried to keep up the usual waiter's mixture of banter and subtle flattery with which he had always entertained the producer. For more than thirty years, Sinclair had been dining at Sardi's, always attended to by Emilio, although more recently he had taken to having the restaurant cater his meals in the privacy of his office a little farther west on 44th Street.

As a special courtesy to a valued customer, the restaurant kept to tradition by assigning Emilio the task of seeing to it that Mr. Sinclair's consommé *madrilène,* cornish hen stuffed with wild rice, and *marons glacé* (the menu selections never varied, except for the wine, and the producer's taste ran generally to the finest Bordeaux) arrived at his office intact and properly heated, no matter what the weather outside.

For his own part, Emilio was more than willing to carry out this unusual task. Not that Martin Sinclair was a big tipper, or even that he spoke much, responding with only the most occasional nod or grunt to Emilio's good-natured ramblings. And he certainly never smiled—that was a given. Yet nobody had ever been able to convince the

waiter that Sinclair was in any way the ogre the press and
some of the theater crowd made him out to be. That's why it
made him sad today to see the producer looking so haggard
and white. Then suddenly it came to him: Martin Sinclair
was an old man, just like him. An old man with the best of
his life behind him.

As he busied himself setting out the meal, Emilio
thought back to 1954 when he had been just starting out at
Sardi's, and was still so dazzled by the place he nearly
dropped his tray and smashed a dozen glasses every time
some big star—not like these jerks they had these days, but
real stars like Mary Martin or Rex Harrison—would walk
in. Those people. They were larger than life. You couldn't
put your finger on it, but when they walked into a room
something happened. A charge. Like a good shot of booze
on a snowy night.

The first Mrs. Sinclair had had it. Heads would turn
when she and Martin were led to their booth, even though
she wasn't an actress, and in those days he was still virtually
unknown. They were just such a handsome couple. She,
with her pearly skin and flaxen hair, always laughing at this
or that, gesturing animatedly with her small, pale hands.
He, dark and erect with his hooded eyes and prominent
nose, never smiling exactly, but radiant with affection, gazing with unmistakable pride at his lovely wife, a reflection of
her happiness. What was her name? Margaret? . . . Melanie? . . . Madelaine! That was it. Sure. Madelaine Sinclair. She had class. Not like that last one, that German
broad.

Madelaine Sinclair . . . he wondered what had become of her. Didn't they have a kid together, or something?
Oh, yes. Now he remembered. That was a terrible tragedy!
Terrible. As he prepared to return to Sardi's, the waiter
paused to look at the producer and was struck with a strong

sense of pity. I wouldn't trade places with him for all the money in the world, he thought, no, sir, not for all the money in the world.

Martin Sinclair had been born in 1920 as Mendele Sniderman, the son of an immigrant father from a wretched little village in Poland, and a mother who was an aspiring actress in the Yiddish theater. His father had begun life in America selling herring out of a barrel on the corner of Hester Street, and, like so many of his brethren, made the slow climb to prosperity by backbreaking stages . . . selling odds and ends from a pushcart, becoming a traveling salesman in neckwear, opening a small shop on Rivington Street, eventually becoming a prosperous manufacturer of ladies' lingerie. His father was a grasping, ruthless man, who cherished both his money and his low opinion of the rest of humanity.

Mendele's mother—Martin's mother—poor creature, had been a very different sort of person, at least in the beginning. She was full of ardor and independence, defying convention which looked down on young girls who went on the stage. There was always a wildness in her, and when she was happy, her gaiety was without parallel. Martin remembered her sprightly walk and sparkling brown eyes as she had walked with her tiny son down Canal Street, where the store windows were stacked with Hebrew books, mezuzahs, hats, prayer shawls, and hourglasses, or haggled with the pushcart vendors on Orchard Street for the ingredients of that evening meal. She was special! Yet even in those simple, relatively happy days, there were signs of trouble. There was always another side to her, and at times she would withdraw into herself. Breaking off abruptly in the middle of a story or a song, she would sit frighteningly still, staring vacantly ahead for hours on end, oblivious to the cries of her little boy tugging anxiously at her skirts. Then just as suddenly she would come to herself, laugh brightly, and clasp her child so tightly in her arms that he couldn't breathe.

As the boy grew older, she would take him to the Grand Theatre, which seemed to young Mendele to rival in splendor all the cathedrals and palaces of the world depicted in his school books.

Paradoxically, as the family's fortunes mounted, mama's condition deteriorated. Sniderman would always complain of her "extravagance," accusing her of "throwing out good food." He was forever shutting off lights, bellowing that the boy was being spoiled, reproaching her for this or that.

Rumors reached Martin's mother that he was seeing other women, *shiksas* who worked for him at the plant. Mama said nothing, but would fall into spells of silent weeping culminating in shrieks of hysterical laughter. At such times her eyes would dart wildly, and she seemed not to recognize her son. By the time Martin, always an honor student, was ready to enter college, she had had several violent outbursts in public and was under a doctor's care.

Two weeks after Martin learned that he had been accepted at Princeton, and announced his plans to leave home, his mother lost complete control of her faculties, groveling on the floor, tearing at her clothes like a wounded animal, attempting to end her own life by slashing her wrists.

Sniderman had her committed to an institution without a moment's hesitation. Months later, she managed to hang herself there, knotting together strips of bedclothes to form a noose. The boy could never forgive her. Instead of sharing in the moment of his greatest triumph, his acceptance by one of America's foremost universities, his beloved, his mother, had deserted him. What is more, he was secretly convinced that the madness was there in him too, a fettered beast just waiting to burst its chains. From that moment on,

the vigil began, and he peered inwardly into the dark re-
cesses of his soul . . . waiting. When he arrived at Princeton he shed his father's name and assumed that of Sinclair,
after his favorite author, Sinclair Lewis. With his new name
and his new start, he was leaving the ghetto behind. Only its
demons remained with him.

Despite his new anglicized name, Martin Sinclair soon
found that, even though his academic brilliance had earned
him entrance to Princeton, *entrée* was quite another matter.
The year was 1938, and, while German troops marched into
the Sudetenland and Europe stood poised at the brink of
catastrophe, much in the venerable college town of Princeton remained as rigid as the stones of its graduate school
tower, which stood immobile, gray against a gray autumn
sky.

As a freshman, Martin's own pathological shyness,
masked by a pose of aloofness and dignity, would, in combination with his undesirable background, have set him apart
from his fellow students, in any case. In addition, there remained more than a tinge of anti-Semitism at Princeton.
Even some of the recently emigrated European Jews who
had been added to the faculty were looked upon with well-
bred and unconcealed hostility by staff and students alike.
So for his first several weeks at Princeton, Martin Sinclair
felt very much like an outsider.

All of this changed, however, as abruptly as may be
imagined, when on an autumn day of incredible clarity a
white Auburn Supercharger convertible drew up along the
curb below the window of Sinclair's college room. The car
was an enormous ivory-colored affair, with coils of brightly
polished nickel and deep-red leather upholstery. The canvas
top was down, and Sinclair from his window, could see the
Louis Vuitton cases piled high in the rear seat. His eyes,

however, were drawn to the driver of this fantastic vehicle, a woman whose bobbed hair was almost as light as the shade of the car, and who wore a cream-colored suit with the skins of some fantastic animal slung elegantly over one shoulder.

She was locked, at the moment, in what was evidently a farewell embrace with the youth seated beside her in the Auburn. When they finally drew apart, the effect was rather like that of Narcissus withdrawing reluctantly from the adoration of his own image in a crystalline pond . . . so strong was the resemblance between the two. Fair, with light grayish eyes, high-arching brows, and full, sensuous lips that wore, perpetually, the suggestion of a pout, both the boy and the girl radiated the self-assurance that comes from the knowledge that one's place is, by birthright, at the very center of the universe.

"Lucky man!" gasped Martin Sinclair aloud to his roommate, Doug, a solid football-playing type with whom he was on normal, albeit minimal, terms of sociability.

"You bet your ass," agreed Doug. "That's Parker Whitworth, heir to the powdered food fortune! I should think he'll be good for at least sixty million when old dad Whitworth kicks off!"

"That's not what I meant," said Martin, "I meant the girl! Who is she?"

"Oh! The girl. You're wrong there . . . she's only his sister. His half sister that is . . . they have different mothers . . . Cornelia Whitworth. My God, Sinclair, where have you been hiding yourself? You can't open a society page from Park Avenue to Nob Hill without having her mug pop out at you! 'Deb of the Year' . . . 'America's Number One Heiress,' they call her . . ."

"Mug!" exclaimed Sinclair. "Why, she's the loveliest creature I ever saw!"

"Oh, she's all right, I suppose. If you go in for the

fragile type. I prefer 'em with a little more meat on their
bones, if you get my meaning. Besides, I think there was
something about her being engaged to Skip Potter."

What Martin could not know then was the extent to
which these two glorious creatures would ultimately change
his life. Of course, given their diversity in backgrounds and
social graces, added to the fact that Parker was already in
his junior year and Martin was still a freshman, the two
might never have met had Sinclair not chanced to walk out
in disgust in the middle of what he regarded to be a very
amateurish theatrical presentation by the Princeton Triangle
Club. Closing the auditorium doors behind him, he bumped
squarely into a drunken Parker Whitworth, whose views of
the production seemed to coincide exactly with his own.

Martin stood abruptly still, paralyzed by the mere
proximity of the brother of his dream girl. But then, with
equal abruptness Parker Whitworth clapped Martin on the
shoulder with a fluid gesture of camaraderie, as if he were an
old school chum, and announced with easy grace, "Terrible
rubbish, eh, old sport? Worst of it is . . . I've got to scrib-
ble something nice about it for this week's *Princetonian*.
Promised the director I would . . . we were at Groton together, and all that. Come on! Let's get out of this mausoleum and find something to drink!"

As he sat in Parker Whitworth's Auburn roadster,
Martin Sinclair now had his first chance to examine his sudden new friend. He was an arrestingly handsome youth, although his blond hair was slightly darker than his sister's,
and his gray eyes, more prominent than hers, were somewhat lusterless, no doubt dulled by the effects of too much
alcohol.

For his part, Parker seemed to take an instant fancy to
his new companion. Martin Sinclair, he found, spoke little,

but his pointed, caustic views on Princeton life accorded very well with Parker's own opinion of the venerable university. Just as Martin's race and background had proclaimed him an outsider, so too had Parker Whitworth's wealth—inordinate even by the standards of his classmates—his arrogant and eccentric behavior, and his contempt for such typical Princeton pastimes as football and fraternities, set him apart from his fellow students.

The Whitworth millions, moreover, were not untainted by scandal. Parker's mother, Julia, had been Stanford Whitworth's second wife, and their marriage had been performed with haste, following as it did so closely on the heels of the tragic and mysterious death of Whitworth's first wife, Constance, Cornelia's mother, while Cornelia was still in her cradle. Although the cause of her death was officially reported as "heart failure," Constance Whitworth had in fact taken her own life in a fit of despondency over her husband's infidelities, hanging herself by looping her braided bathrobe belt over a shower curtain rod in a bathroom of their Palm Beach estate.

Stanford Whitworth's second marriage, to Parker's mother, Julia, also ended in tragedy. While on a shopping trip to Paris, the second Mrs. Whitworth, age twenty-one, had been discovered lying dead on the floor of her suite at the George V. Malicious tongues whispered that a hypodermic syringe had been found beside the body, and that young Julia Whitworth had for some time been addicted to morphine. Whatever the facts of her death, Julia left behind her two young children by Stanford Whitworth—Parker and his younger sister, Pamela. Since their father had never remarried, they, along with their half sister, Cornelia, stood to inherit one of the largest fortunes in the country.

Another interest which soon bound Parker Whitworth and his new companion closer together was their shared passion for the theater. Martin soon aided his friend in writing the squibs of drama criticism of college productions which Parker periodically contributed to the *Princetonian,* and the two youths began making frequent forays into Boston, New Haven, even New York, to attend the latest hits or would-be hits headed for Broadway. Often these excursions would evolve into marathon drinking bouts, culminating in a visit to some "house of ill repute" in the area, all of which Parker Whitworth was intimately acquainted with. Indeed, Parker seemed to have little or no interest in women other than the inhabitants of these dingy brothels, choosing their company in preference to the fresh-faced girls from Smith or Bryn Mawr so eagerly pursued by his classmates. As in all things, here too Martin Sinclair followed Parker Whitworth's lead, and the two became virtually inseparable companions.

On one of their excursions, Parker and Martin shared an odd experience which was to bind the two friends closer together. One late October evening the two boys found themselves in, of all places, Newark, New Jersey, en route to a whorehouse Parker knew about where the girls were "absolute peaches!" As they drove through the city, they were confronted by incredible traffic snarl-ups and scenes of mass hysteria. On one block, they saw people emerging from their houses with wet towels thrown over their faces, scurrying about in panic. Others were hurriedly cramming articles of furniture into vans. The sound of women wailing and children crying was heard everywhere around them. Martin's first thought was of Hitler and an invasion, and his instinct was to panic as well. But Parker, leaning out the driver's seat of the Auburn, stopped to make inquiries of a policeman who seemed little less panic-stricken than the rest of the populace. Upon hearing the officer's breathless declaration, Parker Whitworth threw back his handsome head and laughed uncontrollably.

"What on earth is going on?" asked Martin.

When he had recovered his composure sufficiently to speak, Parker replied, "Nothing on *Earth* at all! It appears the Martians have landed, at least according to our friend, Mr. Orson Welles! At this very moment, they are thrusting their foul, leathery heads out of a meteorite right here in New Jersey!!!" Again, he collapsed in laughter. "You would have supposed an extra-terrestrial intelligence would have more sense than to visit New Jersey!"

By this point, Martin was also convulsed with hilarity. It was decided that, since it was the end of the world, they had damn well better enjoy it! That night, in a seedy Newark brothel, the two friends shared a magnum of Mumm and a dark-haired whore with the unlikely name of Prue, and swore, drunkenly, undying friendship.

At Christmas, Parker Whitworth was to motor to New York, where he would rejoin his sister, Pamela, and half sister, Cornelia, and proceed with them, by private railway car, to the Whitworth compound in Palm Beach, Florida, where the family would spend the holidays. It was only natural therefore that Parker should invite Martin to join him as his guest during the Christmas holidays at the Whitworth compound in Palm Beach.

The trip south was made in the Whitworth private railway car. It was a glorious thing, boasting three bedrooms, two baths, a dining room with paintings by Cézanne, Rouault, and Manet, and a glass-domed observation platform. Its grandeur was diminished, however, by the unexpected absence of Cornelia Whitworth. The heiress—presumably in order to attend to the arrangements for her forthcoming wedding to Skip Potter—had decided at the last moment to remain in New York for several days longer. She would join the family in Palm Beach the following week, after Christmas, but before the New Year.

His half sister's absence threw a noticeable pall over young Parker's spirits on the journey south. He drank too much, not—as was his usual habit—boisterously, but in a sullen, despairing way, locking himself in his sleeping compartment and refusing almost all food. Martin, himself disappointed in the postponement of his long-awaited introduction to the girl of his dreams, was thus thrown into the company of Parker's seventeen-year-old sister, Pamela. The scales between judging the young girl plain or pretty were fairly evenly balanced, although it was obvious that she had made little effort in her own behalf to tip them in favor of beauty. She shared the family trait of clear gray eyes, but her face was somewhat too rounded, and her stature rather too short. Her mousy blond hair was brushed back from her forehead and held severely in place by two ordinary tortoise-shell combs. She dressed simply and, in fact, seemed to make a virtue out of shunning any of the fashion-consciousness of her older, lovelier sister, Cornelia. And where Cornelia was famous for her wit and charm, Pamela prided herself instead on her bluntness and outspokenness.

"So you're the Jewish boy Parker has taken up with!" was her opening remark to Martin Sinclair, who, taken aback, could only mutter that he "supposed he must be."

"You are not at all what I expected," continued Pamela, staring at him in an analytical way. "You are much more exotic-looking than I thought you would be. Prouder."

"Were you looking for something more along the lines of Fagin?" Sinclair inquired testily.

"Oh, no! You mustn't be angry . . . I didn't mean anything like that at all!" Pamela flashed a good-natured smile which instantly put the young man at his ease. "You're just so different from the people Parker usually turns up with. I'm so glad he's found a nice friend at last. God knows he needs one."

"He seems very upset at your sister's not being here."

"Cornelia is NOT my sister!" The words were spoken quietly, but with such a profound undercurrent of hatred that the speaker's features were instantly transformed. Regaining control of herself, Pamela continued, "Yes. It's the idea of her marriage that's upsetting him."

"But why?" asked Sinclair, scenting a glimmer of hope for himself. "Doesn't Parker like the young man? Is there something wrong with Potter?"

"Oh, no . . . Skip's all right. I mean it's papa's idea of a suitable match. Paynes marrying Whitneys . . . Vanderbilts marrying Astors . . . Whitworths marrying Potters, that sort of thing. It's all very suitable."

"But then, why?" queried Martin Sinclair. His question remained unanswered as the train rumbled along in silence for some moments past the flat, gray countryside, blanketed with snow the color of old newspapers.

Pamela Whitworth felt herself powerfully drawn to the dark, brooding man opposite her. Some magnetic force seemed to emanate from his hooded, intense gaze. He seemed, with his slim, dark looks, and his withdrawn manner, so different from the spoiled, empty-headed young men who clustered around her half sister.

"My brother, Parker," she ventured with a smile, attempting to draw Martin out, "tells me you share his interest in the theater. Parker dreams of becoming a stage director, but naturally father won't hear of it."

"I don't see what right your father has to interfere. Parker is very talented . . . I mean . . . why can't he decide for himself what his future should be?"

Pamela laughed out loud at her companion's naïveté. "You don't understand, Martin. Cornelia's money, the great bulk of it, that is, comes to her directly from her mother. It was her grandfather who built the foundation of the Whitworth estate. She will be free to do with it as she pleases on her twenty-first birthday a few months from now. Parker and I, on the other hand, are completely dependent on our father. He could cut us off without a cent at any time. Parker would never defy him openly. He's just not strong enough." She paused thoughtfully for a moment, then added, "I should like very much though to hear about some of the productions you two would like to do together. Parker tells me you have startling, original ideas."

Pamela's comment seemed to unleash a wave of energy in Martin, and he began to speak with mesmerizing intensity of his love of the stage. He spoke of the need not only to foster new young playwrights but to bring a revolutionary, relevant approach to the classics, of the need for experimental workshops for actors, and the need to blur the distinction between actor and audience.

Pamela Whitworth scarcely understood or cared about half of what he said. What enchanted her was the rich whisper of Martin's deep voice, the passionate glow in his dark eyes, the intensity of his movements as he leaned forward, gesticulating, to make some deeply-felt point. Suddenly she ached to feel his intense gaze fixed on her with passion of another sort. It was a futile wish, however—at least for now. Pamela realized that, for now, he was scarcely aware of her presence as a person, let alone as a woman. That could be changed, but it would take time.

Young Martin Sinclair gaped in undisguised awe as the huge twin bulks of the Breakers and Royal Poincania rose from the bright, gleaming expanse of sand, and Palm Beach sparkled before him in the winter sun, bounded by the sapphire of Lake Worth and the turquoise of the Atlantic Ocean.

"Truly," he thought, "this is an enchanted kingdom." A wave of panic swept over him. What place, after all, had he here among these people? His every move, word, gesture was bound to proclaim him an outsider to Cornelia Whitworth and her circle. Still, he and Parker had exchanged vows practically amounting to "blood brotherhood," and even the brattish Pamela had treated him as an equal during the train journey south. Might not Cornelia do the same?

These and similar thoughts flitted through the young man's consciousness as the family Silver Phantom threaded its way through the palm-lined avenues toward the Whitworth estate. Despite all he had heard by now of the Whitworth fortune, Sinclair was totally unprepared for the splendor of the domain he now entered. Second only in its magnificence to Mar-a-Lago, the Marjorie Post Hutton palace, the Whitworth mansion sprawled elegantly over sixteen acres. Conveniently located near the posh Everglades Club, the estate was bounded by Lake Worth on one side and the ocean on the other. The house itself boasted some eighty-six rooms, and was, according to Pamela, one of the ten largest residences in the country. Martin's brain whirled as he crossed the threshold of this palatial building. To think that he—to whom a few short years ago wealth had meant no more than a full belly and a warm coat—should be standing, a welcome guest, amid such grandeur!

The first days of the visit passed in relative calm, although an undercurrent of hostility obviously existed between Parker Whitworth and his father, Stanford. The latter was a heavy-set, hard-drinking, irascible man of florid complexion, and with a well-deserved reputation for unmatched ruthlessness, both in his personal and professional dealings.

Stanford Whitworth had little affection and less time for his offspring, except perhaps for Pamela, in whom he recognized something of a kindred spirit.

"Let's face it," the elder Whitworth was fond of remarking, "ninety-nine percent of the people in this world are born out of a bottle of whiskey on a Saturday night!" Whereupon he would fix his only son with a look of undisguised loathing, for in his eyes, the boy was a weakling—a class of persons for whom Stanford Whitworth had no use at all. Take this latest prank of his son's . . . filling the house with Jews! Lord only knew what would be next! With Parker, he was aggressive and sarcastic. With Martin, he was barely civil.

Christmas at the Whitworth estate was thus passed under a cloud of tension, a cloud which would, no doubt, be dispelled only by the arrival of Cornelia, now slated for the twenty-seventh. Pending her arrival, Parker's behavior was alternately high-strung and irritable, or listless and morose. He locked himself in his room for hours on end, in bouts of solitary drinking, immune to the entreaties of Pamela or Martin to come out for a sail or a game of tennis.

As soon as Cornelia appeared, however, wearing a ravishing dove-gray linen Chanel traveling costume, and a three-hundred-fifty-thousand-dollar pearl necklace (Skip Potter's engagement present), her brother's somber mood brightened. At her announcement that the engagement to Potter had been broken off, Parker's mood soared. (as did that of Martin Sinclair). Cornelia seemed to Martin a complete, infinitely delicate, quite perfect thing of beauty. In fact, taken separately, the beauty of the Whitworths . . . brother and sister . . . Parker and Cornelia . . . was arresting. Together, the pair quite literally made one gasp.

Now, at last, Martin found himself plunged headlong into the mainstream of Palm Beach social life. Cornelia had

responded to her brother's introduction of Martin with the
unruffled charm of a woman who has worn beaux like rings
on her pretty fingers since the age of twelve. The soft, low
voice, the lowered eyelashes, the apparently heartfelt sincerity of her simple greeting—"So glad you were able to join us
down here"—thrilled him to the very depths of his soul. Did
his ice princess live atop a dizzying glass mountain too steep
or slippery to climb? No matter. He, Martin Sinclair, would
find some way to scale that precipice!

The *Palm Beach Daily News,* or "Shiny Sheet," was
soon full of snapshots of the glamorous Whitworth siblings
. . . playing in an Everglades tennis tournament, dancing
cheek to cheek at the Bath and Tennis Club, watching the
polo matches at Delray.

The winter season in Palm Beach that year was even
more brilliant than usual, owing to the influx of the international set, fleeing in the threat of war in Europe. Prince
Serge Obolensky, the Countess Dorothy di Frasso (together
with her lover, mobster Bugsy Siegel), Elsa Maxwell, the
Cole Porters, Barbara Hutton, the Laddie Sanfords, Alfred
Gwynne Vanderbilt, and Doris Duke were among the trend-
setters who frequented the round of parties, tennis tourna-
ments, polo matches, and gala luncheons at which Cornelia
and her brother shone so conspicuously. The climax to these
festivities, though, was to be the Whitworth's own New
Year's Eve Ball, invitations to which were among the most
sought-after and talked about in all Palm Beach society. The
theme of the party, proclaimed in the coveted invitations,
was to be: "1939! LA VIE EN ROSE!"

In preparation for this gala, hundreds of yards of pink
satin were draped over the walls and ceilings of the Whitworth mansion's ballroom; the pool area had been flooded
with pink spotlights, and hundreds of café tables with pink
satin cloths had been set outside, centered by thousands of

pink roses in crystal vases. The two hundred waiters wore pink and red color-coordinated uniforms. Three orchestras had been engaged to play until dawn. Two thousand 6:00 A.M. breakfasts had been laid out. A veritable jungle of pink and scarlet poinsettias had transformed the Whitworth gardens into a winter fairyland, complete with a frosting of artificial snow. Each of the privileged guests had been requested to wear something pink, and most of the ladies had gracefully complied with this request—every shade from the palest pink to deepest fuchsia was on display in the costliest fabrics imaginable. Among the gentlemen, most contented themselves with the simple addition of a pink boutonniere or bow tie to complete their evening costume. Alone, of all the women present, Pamela Whitworth had elected to wear a simple, black evening frock.

As for Cornelia, certainly to Martin she was the living embodiment of a perfect rose. Her petallike pink organza Balmain imparted a peach glow to her alabaster skin, and a collar of matchless rubies and diamonds lent fire to her cool, poised beauty. She glided effortlessly through the swirls and eddies of people about her, detaching herself from the groups of admirers who clustered about her like a bird flitting from one branch to another. Martin watched her constantly, yet it was always to Parker she returned.

Her brother had procured for himself a pink swallowtail coat and trousers. These he wore with such easy nonchalance that the effect was neither effeminate nor ridiculous, but consummately chic.

A groundswell of whispers arose from the guests as Cornelia and Parker swirled in a pink haze across the dance floor to the strains of "Night and Day."

"Why ever did she break off her engagement to Skip Potter? It was a brilliant match."

"They say it wasn't *she* who broke it off!"

Martin Sinclair felt angry blood surge to his temples at the sound of such disrespectful gossip about his beloved. Yet he was only too aware that he had no claim on her. Since their initial introduction, Cornelia had spoken barely two words to him. His body was so rigid with confusion and so intense with anger that he barely felt the pressure of an arm on him. With a start he looked up into the face of Pamela Whitworth. Her hair was, as usual, swept back from her forehead, although diamanté combs had been substituted for the usual tortoiseshell variety. These combs, a touch of lipstick, her simple yet elegant black dress, and a single strand of pearls were Pamela's only concessions to the festivities. In attire, that is. In her hand she clutched a glass of champagne, and by her manner it was clear that it was by no means the first she had drunk that evening. The orchestra struck up, "I Can't Get Started."

"Dance?" asked Pamela.

Why not? thought Sinclair. It would, at least, bring him on to the dance floor, and put him in closer proximity to Cornelia. He might even summon up enough courage to suggest a change of partners. As they danced, however, Pamela realized that Martin was propelling them toward the spot where her brother and Cornelia swayed in perfect unison. Stiffening, she detached herself abruptly from her partner's grip.

"*Et tu, Brute!*" she hissed sharply, and was on the point of flouncing off and stranding Martin in the middle of the dance floor when Parker and Cornelia swirled toward them. Parker, abruptly suggesting a change of partners, swept Pamela off to the strains of "Moonglow." Suddenly, magically, Cornelia was dancing with Martin! One of his arms was actually around her! When he had sufficiently recovered his senses to appreciate anything at all, he noticed that she was trembling slightly. Her face, he noted, seemed unnaturally pale beneath her flawlessly applied makeup. They danced on, Martin floating in a trancelike state, exchanging fragments of conversation. Despite the exhilaration of holding his dream girl at last, Martin was uneasy. He sensed that beneath her icy calm exterior, Cornelia Whitworth was profoundly agitated by something. He felt the dizziness of one poised at the edge of a precipice. Events seemed to be moving along independent of his will or actions.

Cornelia's gaze was once again riveted to her brother, who, having changed partners, was now dancing with a striking brunette. The tempo of the music accelerated. The brass section of the orchestra was on its feet, horns swaying in unison. The insistent rhythm rolled over the dancers like the crashing of the surf beyond the moonlit garden. Slim and elegant in his pink outfit, Parker numbly executed a number of dazzling dance steps, dipping almost to his knees in a series of semi-splits, then bounding to his feet again. His new partner, her suntanned face glowing with excitement, swirled and spun delightedly around him. The music and the noise seemed to be building to a crescendo. Midnight was fast approaching. A flock of pink balloons was released, and they floated upwards in the starry Palm Beach sky. Martin Sinclair felt Cornelia stiffen, and her eyes, as she stared at Parker and the brunette, were as cold and gray as the winter sea. Suddenly she gripped Martin by the arm, almost convulsively, whispering urgently, "Come with me! I want to get out of here!"

It was midnight as they ran toward the beach. Behind them, a roar like the clash of a thousand cymbals erupted. Above them, pink balloons floated drunkenly. Despite the clamor from within, an almost palpable feeling of emptiness seemed to emanate from the great house behind them. Ahead, the beach sprawled black and forbidding, illumi-

nated by a cold sliver of a moon. Cornelia raced ahead of
Martin on to the sand, flinging off her delicate pink evening
slippers, and lifting the pink organza petals of her skirt so
that her slender legs gleamed like marble in the moonlight.
Sinclair hung back on the stairway.

"What's the matter with you?" Cornelia called out to
him, mockery dancing in her cool gray eyes.

"But your beautiful dress . . . you'll ruin it!" gasped
Sinclair.

Cornelia burst into high-pitched laughter, "You are a
fool! You don't suppose I mean to wear this twice! Come
along!"

With a few quick strides he was beside her. In a trance
he folded her in his arms and drew her soft body against his
own, silencing her laughter with a burning kiss. He was
convinced that at any moment she would contemptuously
thrust him from her, but he was unable to stop himself,
impelled by a desire such as he had never known. To his
mind, her rose petal lips responded to his with ravenous
fervor. Abandoning her cool body to him, she drew his hun-
gry mouth to the marble smoothness of her breasts, arching
her neck backward like a swan. Then, just as abruptly as her
outburst of passion had begun, she froze and stood motionless, gazing in triumph at the approaching figure of a man in
pink.

Martin Sinclair too stood rooted to the spot, his heart
pounding more wildly within him than the waves which
crashed at his feet. He scarcely knew what to make of the
bizarre scene in which he had played, so briefly, a leading
role. Only one thing was certain. He must possess Cornelia
Whitworth! She had used him, played with him, but it didn't
matter. He must possess her—utterly. A last balloon danced
mockingly toward the pale crescendo of the moon. It was
1939. A new year had begun.

* * *

On New Year's Day—the last of Martin Sinclair's visit to Palm Beach—it was as though the events of the previous evening had been not merely dreamlike, but, in fact, a dream. In Cornelia, there was no trace of the passionate siren of the night before; in Parker, no trace of the furious youth who had stumbled upon their embrace. Perhaps there was a slight hint of intimate mockery in the way Cornelia stared at Martin, and perhaps Parker's manner toward him was a bit more forced than natural in its geniality. But nothing was overt, and he could have been mistaken. It was only Pamela who glared at Martin with open hostility and contempt.

When they returned to Princeton, both Martin and Parker threw themselves feverishly into an off-campus student production of Brecht's *Arturo Ui,* an attempt, in its scathing portrayal of tyranny, to arouse the consciousness of their fellow students to the specter that was darkening all of Europe. The bond between the two youths at this time was renewed, even strengthened. Their theater-going visits to New York, where the Whitworths maintained a vast residence on Fifth Avenue near Eighty-sixth Street, increased in frequency. On these visits, Martin Sinclair was able to upgrade his status to become one of the dozen or so admirers who always hovered about Cornelia Whitworth. He was not fortunate enough, however, to number occasionally among the half-dozen men with whom the heiress might have a half-dozen dates on any given day. Their moment of intimacy was never repeated.

One day in late April, however, Parker approached his friend with a miraculous request. It seemed that the young man who was originally to have escorted Cornelia to her upcoming twenty-first birthday celebration (the boy was the heir to one of the largest steel fortunes in the country) had

been forced to cancel, owing to urgent family business
which required his presence in Europe. Would Martin, as a
favor, take his place on such short notice? The ball was to
take place at the Plaza in less than two weeks. Martin's
heart leaped within him as he answered in the affirmative.
So he had been more than the whim of a moment . . . he
had meant something to her, after all! Her passion had been
no more than the spiteful caprice of a spoiled child!

The ball in honor of Cornelia Whitworth's twenty-first
birthday was reportedly to be the most extravagant such
affair since the debut of the Woolworth heiress, Barbara
Hutton, nearly a decade earlier. Yet, as preparations for the
ball progressed, and florists and decorators labored to trans-
form the hotel ballroom into a silver and white fantasy land,
the mood in the Whitworth household was somber. After
the reported expenditure of the then incredible sum of one
hundred thousand dollars, the party seemed to be regarded
by everyone, essentially, as some sort of ordeal that must be
gone through.

Were it not for the presence of Cornelia, Martin would
have found the atmosphere in the Whitworth home unbearable, and even she wore an expression of acute anxiety.
Parker, too, seemed worried and preoccupied, and—as was
his usual fashion in this mood—drowned his sorrows with
drink. The usually overbearing Stanford was even more hostile than ever in his sarcasm. Only Pamela seemed to look
forward to the festivities, and even appeared to be in an
uncharacteristically playful mood.

Matters came to a head one evening as the family gathered gloomily around the immense mahogany dinner table.
Stanford Whitworth, his face flushed with drink, presided at
the head. "It would be fatal to let that damned fellow Roo-
sevelt use any of his fool tricks to draw America into a war

that is none of her business," he declared without preface. "Such a war would be only in the interests of the Jews, and it is they who are promoting it." Sinclair felt the blood rise to his cheeks as the older man expatiated on the "unquestionable soundness of many of Hitler's views." Feeling that both his position as an invited guest, and the respect due the elder Whitworth as the father of the girl he loved prevented Martin from speaking out. Struggling to restrain his anger, he begged to be excused from the dinner table and retreated to the library.

Still shaking with suppressed rage, he was surprised a moment later to hear the library door open softly behind him. He had hoped it might be Cornelia, but it was Pamela Whitworth who stood in the doorway. She was dressed in what was, for her, an unusually feminine creation of dark blue silk, cut low over her full, round breasts. She had allowed her dark blond hair to cascade in loose waves, imparting a new softness to her roundish face. Her gray eyes had been given new depth and luster by the careful application of a grayish shade of eyeshadow and their long lashes accentuated with mascara. She looked, thought Martin Sinclair, almost lovely.

"You mustn't mind father . . ." she said softly, then adding, "or any of us, for that matter. We are all mad, I suppose . . . the whole family. Some more than others." Pamela crossed to the bar, and poured drinks for both of them. Her gray eyes looked searchingly into his.

"I've wanted to apologize to you for a long time," she said. "I was beastly to you on the train, and in Palm Beach. It's just that . . . well . . . I liked you, and I hated to see the way they were making a fool of you! There. I've said it!" She let out a sigh of relief.

"I don't understand. Making a fool of me? Who are *they*? What exactly do you mean?"

"Parker and Cornelia, of course!" Startled at his lack of comprehension, she gasped, "You can't mean you haven't suspected . . . you haven't guessed . . . ? Why do you think Skip Potter broke off his engagement to Cornelia?" Pamela lashed out, now giving full vent to her hatred for her half sister. "Don't you see? She has destroyed my brother, Parker, and she will destroy you! It is she who has turned him into an alcoholic weakling. She is evil! Please, please believe me . . . I'm telling you this for your own good. I'm telling you this . . . because I love you."

Pleadingly, Pamela reached out her arms toward Martin, but he stepped back from her, appalled and disgusted by what she had said, and by the obvious malice she intended. "You must be sick to think that I would believe you! How you must envy her . . . to invent such a tale about your own brother and sister!"

Pamela's face hardened in an expression of hatred and determination as she spoke. "My sister, as you call Cornelia, is about to have my brother's baby! Why do you think your services as an escort were enlisted at the last minute? The boy who was supposed to take her got wind of the scandal— oh, not the whole sordid story by any means, but enough to warn him off. That's why *you* were selected; they didn't want to ask anyone who might conceivably refuse. The ball will go off as planned. Then Cornelia will take a short trip abroad—Bali has been mentioned—and return home, after a convenient abortion, to resume her rightful place at the head of society."

Martin could contain himself no longer. He grabbed Pamela roughly by the shoulders, and shook her until she cried out in pain. "You monster," he screamed. "You vicious little monster!"

"Very well," said Pamela as she pulled free of his grasp. "You still don't believe me. Then I will show you!

It was she felt, her blue eyes radiating sincerity, only fair.

Martin Sinclair spent the night preceding Cornelia Whitworth's twenty-first birthday extravaganza in sleepless torment. Mocking images crowded in upon his fevered imagination. He remembered Parker and Cornelia as he had first seen them, locked in an embrace in the Auburn coupé. Had not his first impression been that they were lovers? He pictured their golden bodies tangled on the Palm Beach sand as they emerged from the surf. He saw again the expression on Cornelia's face when her brother had confronted them on New Year's Eve, the unmistakable expression of a triumphant woman who had succeeded in stinging her lover into a jealous rage! He recalled a conversation he had held with Parker only a few days earlier, motoring up from Princeton.

"We are twins . . . Cornelia and I . . ." his friend had told him. "Both Gemini . . . the Twins, you see . . . born a year apart, and to different mothers, but twins all the same. We think, feel, breathe as one!"

But this was insane. He couldn't allow Pamela's venomous words to poison his mind against the girl he worshipped, and against his closest friend. Pamela had admitted her own love for him, Martin, so surely it was his indifference to her that had prompted her to fabricate this horrible slander purely to torture him.

Still, so many questions remained unanswered. Why did Parker stay away from the nice, eligible girls of the Seven Sisters colleges, seeking instead the company of whores? No one could ignore the abrupt changes that occurred in his friend's mood when Cornelia was absent. Why had the spectacle of her brother dancing with the brunette at the "Vie en Rose" party so enraged Cornelia? Why had Skip

Potter broken off their engagement? Pamela had threatened to "show him." Very well, then, let her try! He would believe it when he saw it!

And yet, even as he thought these words, Martin Sinclair knew in his soul that he believed Pamela. He knew that he should leave the Whitworth house that instant and return to Princeton. Yet in his heart he recognized his desire—his need—to be shown, to see it for what it was . . . something morbid and twisted and unclean. He acknowledged a nameless desire for vengeance. He yielded to a desire to humiliate and punish.

Cornelia Whitworth stood, poised and assured, at the top of the ballroom staircase. She thought of her own appearance, sensing the impact of her silver and white Schiaparelli creation, listening to the gasps of admiration at her matchless diamond necklace and earrings, once owned by Pauline Bonaparte. With Martin Sinclair on her arm, Cornelia floated down the staircase into the throng of guests and admirers. Martin, in his new dress coat felt, for the first time, rich and assured, as if this were his natural milieu. He was aware that he and Cornelia made a strikingly handsome couple; his dark good looks contrasting pleasingly with her silver and white fragility. Behind the pair followed Pamela Whitworth on the arm of her elder brother, Parker.

Whirling about moments later on the ballroom floor, Cornelia sensed that something was disturbing Martin, that he was preoccupied and not with thoughts of her. It was almost as though he didn't even want to be there. She was well aware of Pamela's infatuation with Martin, and, indeed, spite for her detested half sister had been one of her motives for leading Sinclair on. Perhaps Pamela has been filling his head with malicious stories about me, she mused.

Leaning her head against Martin's shoulder in a kitten-ish way, she said teasingly, "You know I believe my little sister, Pamela, is very fond of you."

"Oh? She confides in you, then?" Sinclair inquired sarcastically.

"No," responded Cornelia with her most beguiling smile. "We have almost nothing in common. Except of course, our love for Parker, and . . . our affection for you."

"I am indeed flattered. It is quite a compliment . . . to appeal to such diverse tastes as yours and your sister's." There was an edge of harshness in Martin's voice which startled her, yet she responded with a silvery laugh. Martin Sinclair was beginning to intrigue her.

"Pamela tells me . . ." he continued, his black eyes glowing like live coals, ". . . that you are thinking of taking a trip almost immediately. She mentioned something about Bali?"

Cornelia Whitworth flushed noticeably. Then the color drained from her cheeks until her face was almost as white as her chiffon gown. "The horrid little bitch!" she gasped. Even she had not suspected that Pamela would go so far in betraying family secrets! "I should like to rest for a moment," she said, pulling away from Martin and turning toward the bar where Parker stood. Martin watched from the dance floor as Cornelia spoke animatedly, even distractedly, to her brother, fluttering her arms like a white bird. Parker put a reassuring arm around his sister's waist, then led her from the ballroom.

Martin strode to the bar and began downing one Scotch after another. Gradually the evening blurred into a swirl of sound and color and smells. At some point Parker and Cornelia reappeared on the dance floor, gliding with unconcerned grace. And then they vanished again just as abruptly.

The sight of Cornelia's inviolate, silvery beauty galled

Martin into an even deeper sense of loss and betrayal. It was with a shock that he realized the evening was drawing to a close. The acrid fumes of stale tobacco and spilled champagne permeated the ballroom. Violins scraped feebly as the last dancers swayed uncertainly on the dance floor. Of Cornelia and Parker, there was no trace. Pamela Whitworth was making her way toward him across the nearly deserted floor. She was dressed in a voluminous, but unflattering dark blue satin dress which only served to underline the dumpiness of her round figure, her too-square shoulders, her too-short legs. For a moment, Martin thought she wanted him to dance with her, but she gripped him firmly by the arm and led him toward the grand staircase.

Her small eyes lit by mischievous triumph, she said to him, "Come on! There was something I promised to show you."

Martin followed her blindly, drunkenly, down the seemingly endless corridors of the Plaza Hotel. He wanted to break her grip on him, to run away, but her small fingers might as well have been made of iron. He was impelled forward by an almost morbid obsession. Finally they halted in front of a door which bore a notice reading, "Do Not Disturb!" Pamela produced a key from her bodice, and quietly opened the door.

There was a fireplace in the living room of the suite, and, though it was May, a fire had been lit in the grate, casting an eerie red glow which was the room's only source of illumination. This red light reflected off the naked forms of two perfect bodies which lay enmeshed before the hearth. It danced in the sparks which flashed from the diamonds encircling Cornelia's throat, so that she too seemed to be on fire.

Parker Whitworth lay back, his graceful form extended before the flames, as his sister raised her elegant white body above his and rode upon him, as though he were a magnificent stallion under her, spurring him on with her finely molded ivory legs. Tongues of flame reached out as if to lick at her cool body, darting over her small, pointed breasts, down her long, graceful back. At last, in the final paroxysm of pleasure, she arched her white neck backward with the grace of a swan. At the same moment, Parker quivered violently, dissolving within her in a powerful spasm of love.

Afterwards, they lay for an instant quite still, enfolded in each other's arms; then, sensing the presence of an intruder, betrayed, perhaps by the shaft of light penetrating from the corridor, Cornelia turned her head and stared at the doorway. The lurid red glow from the fireplace imparted a horrible sensuality to her chiseled features. Her mouth seemed distorted by a fierce, animal lust. Her bright eyes smoldered with defiant disdain as she stared fixedly at the narrow ribbon of light from the doorway, behind which, she must have known, Martin Sinclair and her sister stood transfixed. Then Cornelia Whitworth laughed—a rippling, arrogant, icy laugh that lacerated Martin's very soul.

Her laughter reverberated in his fevered brain as he thrust Pamela from him and raced blindly down the corridor, lurching drunkenly into the elevator. Lust gripped him like a vise. He was unbearably hot. Suffocating! His throat was parched. He felt as though his body were on fire.

The creamy light blue of dawn already glimmered in the spring sky as Sinclair spun through the revolving glass doors of the Plaza, into the chill morning air of Fifth Avenue. It must have rained during the night, for the steps were slippery as Martin descended uncertainly toward the pavement. He heard an angry shout behind him and turned to see Parker, clad only in shirt and trousers, rapidly descending the slippery steps behind him.

At the first blow, they both slipped and fell heavily to

the sidewalk. The hotel doorman ceased his attempt to flag down a passing taxi and rushed toward the pair, trying vainly to separate them as they thrashed about wildly on the pavement. For ten, fifteen, twenty minutes, they fought senselessly in the growing dawn light. Martin's new evening coat hung from his shoulders in tattered shreds. Both young men were torn and bleeding . . . so exhausted that they could remain erect only when, for an instant, by their position they mutually supported each other, swaying together like dancers. Then a crunching blow from Parker's left collided with Martin's jaw. The dark young man sank to the pavement, blood pouring from his cut lip. Parker stood over him, soaking wet and dripping with perspiration. There was no longer any hatred in the blond youth's stare, only hurt and exhaustion.

"I'll be damned if I'm going on with this any longer," said Parker Whitworth brokenly. "Damn you to hell, Sinclair! I was your only friend!"

Martin Sinclair's remaining years at Princeton were solitary. The one remaining link with the days of his past friendship to Parker was in the frequency with which he continued to patronize the local whorehouses. The fiery vision of Cornelia Whitworth in her frenzy of incestuous lust had dispelled any bright illusions of womanhood he had cherished. Why delude oneself with fancies; all women are whores! he reminded himself.

While, beyond the cloistered walls of Princeton, the world erupted in war, Martin Sinclair nursed his sense of injury in melancholy brooding and self-absorption. He read bitterly, in the fall of 1941, of Cornelia Whitworth's marriage to Count Roger Faucigny de l'Estroy, a French nobleman of impeccable bloodlines but sorely diminished wealth. (It was to be the first of the heiress's seven marriages.)

Immediately following Pearl Harbor, Parker Whitworth enlisted for active service in the U.S. Navy. Resisting all efforts by his father to have him transferred to a safe command, he was killed in action in the South Pacific at the age of twenty-two. Pamela Whitworth, grief-stricken, and in an attempt to bind up old wounds, tried desperately to contact Martin Sinclair after her brother's death, but she could not locate him. By then, Martin Sinclair too was at war.

On April 11, 1945, Lieutenant Colonel Martin Sinclair was one of the American officers present at the liberation of Buchenwald. The nameless horrors of that torture chamber, of the suffering which had been inflicted on his own people, lived with him ever afterwards. The revelation of man's inherent bestiality seared his brain, leaving an indelible scar. The world seemed a blasted, withered wasteland . . . humanity sunk beyond all hope of redemption. The stench of the crematoria lingered in his nostrils, infecting the very air he breathed for decades to come. The eyes of the starving wretches who had survived stared out at him in dreams for the rest of his life. He gazed at them as though into a mirror, feeling a kinship deeper even than that of race, for he too, the "liberator," was surely one of the "damned." With the end of the war, Martin returned to New York, embittered far beyond his years. The dead tissue in his soul could never grow back.

Martin's father, Itzhak Sniderman, had died peacefully in his sleep while his son was away at war, leaving the boy a legacy of some twenty thousand dollars. Upon his return to the States, Martin immediately made use of his inheritance to secure the stage rights to a controversial novel, *Cry of the Native,* a stirring description of race relations in the South written by a black author, Thomas Langforth.

The project was an ambitious one, since the play based

on the novel traced the plight of a black family over three generations, and involved many scene changes and an enormous cast, both black and white. The black novelist, Langforth, had no experience as a playwright, and a young, white dramatist, Philip Norwood, was brought in by Sinclair to adapt the unwieldy six-hundred-page book for the stage. For the first, and—as it turned out—last time, in his theatrical career, Martin Sinclair elected to direct as well as produce. Almost from its inception, the production was beset with problems.

Norwood's adaptation, when it was finally ready, in Sinclair's opinion, did much to distort and dilute the impact of the original novel. The production was slated to open at the Colonial Theatre in Boston in mid-January. Sinclair drove himself and his company relentlessly, working almost literally around the clock, transposing scenes from the original novel into the virtually unusable script by Norwood, endlessly shifting the order of scenes and sequence of speeches. Sinclair's determination was fanatical, almost to the point of monomania. He brooked no opposition, regarding any difference of approach by the actors in the light of a personal attack. The atmosphere was unbearable. Days and nights went by, and no one left the theater.

A complex arrangement of three different revolving sets had been constructed on a thirty-foot platform in order to accommodate the action of the play. It was a multi-generational story, spanning almost a hundred years, beginning with the slave grandfather and ending with a modern-day rebel falsely accused of rape.

With the beginning of technical rehearsals at the Colonial in Boston, it was apparent that *Cry of the Native* was in deep trouble. Costs were skyrocketing. Sinclair had already sunk every penny of his inheritance into the play, plus an additional seven thousand he had been able to scrounge from the few "angels" strong enough to back such a controversial piece mounted by a novice producer-director.

The first run-through with the revolving stage was a disaster, nor did it improve greatly on subsequent nights. Postponement of the opening was unthinkable, however, since it was simply out of the question to consider refunding any money that had been taken in at the box office. So *Cry of the Native* did open on schedule, but the play was so long that it ran until one in the morning with two intermissions. Half the audience left during the first of these. The remainder trickled out grimly during the remaining two and a half hours. During one scene involving the burning of fiery crosses by the Ku Klux Klan, the revolving stage accelerated accidentally, hurtling bits of flaming wood into the terrified orchestra.

Crew bills for "golden time" and all-night rehearsal hours came flooding in, amounting to nearly fifteen thousand dollars over the original budget. Despite all the problems, Sinclair remained adamant that the show must, somehow, reach Broadway. It was scheduled to play a second try-out stint at the Chestnut Street Theatre in Philadelphia. By dint of all-night writing sessions with Thomas Langforth, Martin managed to prune the script to a workable length. He went personally into debt for ten thousand dollars, and was able to tap the remaining five thousand needed to pay off the crew from his original investors, but the prospect for a Broadway opening remained bleak.

The end seemed inevitable when, on surveying the stage of the Chestnut Street Theatre, Sinclair found, to his horror, that it was raked in such a fashion that it would have to be leveled and restructured to accommodate the temperamental turntable. Four days before the scheduled Philadelphia opening, Martin sat with his head in his hands as a crew of carpenters and masons toiled on stage with lumber, asbestos, and sandbags. A woman's voice at his side roused him from his gloomy reverie.

"If you are not fully financed," the voice asked, "would you consider the possibility of my becoming an investor?" The voice belonged to Pamela Whitworth.

"That is one characteristic I share with my so-called sister," Pamela was fond of repeating, "I always get my way with a man . . . sooner or later!" The heiress was to recoup every penny of her investment in *Cry of the Native,* and even to turn a tidy profit, for Martin Sinclair's first theatrical production did eventually open on Broadway, where it met with lively critical acclaim and ran for eighteen months to enthusiastic and packed houses. Nor was Pamela's boast an idle one, for, on the night of the first preview in Philadelphia, Martin Sinclair became Pamela's lover, and remained so for several years. The relationship, however, was by no means idyllic.

In her heart, Pamela could never forgive Martin for preferring Cornelia. Martin likewise could never forgive Pamela for not being Cornelia, and for destroying his dream by revealing her sister's guilty secret. Still, Sinclair had by now become sufficiently hardened to be willing to compromise himself, especially in order to lay his hands on the Whitworth millions. Married to Pamela, he would at least be able to avenge Cornelia's scorn of him so many years ago. The Whitworth millions would make him king of Broadway, able to mount any production he wanted.

Pamela, for her part, sought to bend her lover to her will. Her plan was to allow Sinclair sufficient independence to make him a suitable consort for a Whitworth, but never enough to enable him to be independent of her and her money. For this reason, marriage was out of the question; she was under no illusions about the nature of the ties which bound her lover to her. Still, in her own way, she loved him. She owned him now, on whatever terms, and she was not about to relinquish him.

Matters had reached this bitter stalemate between the pair when Martin Sinclair was approached with a business proposition by one Arthur Eckstein, a dress manufacturer from New Jersey with a passion for the theater. He informed Martin that he had been "bowled over" by his production of *Cry of the Native* and wished to join him in a long-term producing partnership. Since much of his time would still be taken up, of necessity, by the family dress business, Sinclair would have almost total artistic control. His contribution would be purely financial. Martin Sinclair lost no time in entering into this advantageous partnership. He lost even less time in abandoning his mistress, Pamela Whitworth, to whom he never spoke another word, despite her attempt to commit suicide by a barbiturate overdose after he left her.

It was in the second year of his partnership with Arthur Eckstein that Martin Sinclair left, alone, on a trip for Europe, with a view to securing the rights to *Outcasts,* the smash hit of the London season. It was on this journey that he was to meet his first wife, Madelaine.

6

Anyone watching the manner in which Merle Greene paced up and down the length of her cramped Sixty-third Street apartment, all the while clenching and unclenching the fingers of her large white hands, could not have failed to draw a comparison between her behavior here and that of a tense jungle cat hurling itself in fury against the bars of its cage. While her body moved constantly, jerking in angry anticipation, her gray eyes never wandered from the gilt and ivory telephone beside the damask love seat. She seemed to be willing it to ring with her gaze, but the ornate instrument remained obstinately silent.

"How dare the old fossil not take my call!" she repeated to herself over and over again, willfully nurturing the hurt till it inflamed her to a kind of frenzy.

The painful smallness of the apartment was made more acute by the massiveness of its furniture and the abundance of bric-a-brac. Admittedly, it did contain some fine pieces: A baroque Spanish console vied for attention (and space) with a vast Jacobean armoire. Cloisonné tables from India found themselves in incongruous juxtaposition with Dresden shepherdesses and ormolu clocks, all the while jostling for position with Louis XIV chairs upholstered in boldly patterned

Clarence House fabrics. The effect was rather as if the contents of several spacious rooms in a gracious manor house had been piled willy-nilly on top of one another for storage in a warehouse, and this, indeed, was not far from being the true history of Merle Greene's present surroundings.

Merle Greene was a tall, fair woman of a certain age . . . fifty, perhaps. Her figure was rounded and voluptuous, yet without heaviness, and she moved with the suppleness of a young girl. Her straight fair hair was a becoming shade of ash blond, and her clear, translucent complexion still required very little aid from makeup. There was something about her tiny nose, though, which suggested that it had perhaps not been quite so *retroussé* since birth, but had needed skillful hands to make it so. Another distinguishing feature was her smile, which tended to draw itself upward to the left in an odd, affected manner.

Merle gave this smile now, as a pleasing thought crossed her mind. "We shall see, Martin Sinclair, we shall see," she said aloud to the cluttered room.

In truth, Merle Greene's life had had its share of successes and disappointments. She had been born in Philadelphia, in one of those rambling gray stone mansions with imposing fireplaces and acres of parquet floor, the kind built by wealthy manufacturers in imitation of the English gentry homes, all to please their Bronx-born wives. Merle never really knew how her father had made his millions—they were simply there by the time of her birth.

Merle was an only child, born to her parents late in their lives. As a result, her every whim was catered to, especially since her sweet face and precocious disposition added charm to even her most outrageous requests. By the time she was fifteen, she owned her own thoroughbred, Rhinemaiden, and everything she wore, down to her hand-embroidered silk underwear, was imported from Paris.

Even at this state, though, when she was still the belle of the Center Point Country Club dances, Merle showed a headstrong inclination to get "mixed up" with the wrong kind of men. A romance with an Italian boy—a construction worker's son—had had to be broken up, and it was rumored that the Greenes had paid him a thousand dollars to leave town. Shortly thereafter, when she was only seventeen, her parents discovered to their horror that she was having an affaire with one of her teachers—a man some twenty years her senior, married, and with three children. It was not necessary for them to do anything about this romance, however, as it fizzled of its own accord when Merle left for Sarah Lawrence.

Her college days were numbered, however. In her freshman year she met and fell in love with the brother of one of her classmates, a handsome young man named David Sachs, just returned from Korea. They spent a passionate week in Atlantic City, where they married quietly, later presenting the Greenes with a *fait accompli*. Such secretiveness was essential since David had no tangible assets besides his dark good looks and splendid physique.

The Greenes, although heartbroken that their only daughter should have eloped with someone so unsatisfactory, decided to make the best of a bad bargain. At least he was a nice Jewish boy. Deciding to ignore the first ceremony as if it had never taken place, they formally announced their daughter's engagement, and organized a lavish wedding on a grand scale, at which Merle wore white from Lanvin, and Mrs. Greene wept copiously. David was installed as vice-president at Mr. Greene's factory, and a second mock-Tudor mansion with parquet floors, not two miles from her parents' home, was purchased as a wedding gift.

Despite these advantages, however, Merle's marriage proved not to be a happy one. Much to her consternation, her husband showed no inclination to wait on her hand and foot. In fact, Sachs proved to have very much a mind of his own. He expressed boredom and contempt for both Merle's father and for his own job at the factory. He was also quite a ladykiller, and it was not long before he was blatantly flaunting his affaires under his wife's nose. Moreover, noone, not even Merle, could run through money as quickly as he. Even when the factory had several slow seasons, David saw no reason to curb his extravagance, clearly regarding his marriage as a blank check. Merle too had embarked on several extramarital affaires, and the couple became masters at taunting each other, and at inflicting pain.

It was at this stage that Mr. Greene had his first stroke, one which left him virtually paralyzed on one side of his body. Under David's management, the factory began to operate at a loss, a situation which did nothing to deter his own reckless expenditures on gambling and women. By the time Merle's father died, some seven years later, it was found that the firm had been bled dry, and he left his wife and child nothing but massive debts.

Mrs. Greene did not survive long. Her husband's death, her daughter's divorce, and the auctioning off of her beloved treasures all in rapid succession proved too many blows for the old lady to endure. Merle Greene found herself alone, an attractive but spoiled woman in her mid-twenties, bereft of all she had loved. And if she was not quite penniless, she was, at best, in circumstances which—for one accustomed to her degree of luxury—seemed almost the same thing. At first she clung to the hope that one of her lovers—a prosperous business man from her social sphere with whom she had been carrying on an affaire for several years—would leave his wife for her. When he didn't, Merle resolved to leave Philadelphia for New York, and to seek the advice of one of her father's dearest friends, one Arthur Eckstein, a theatrical producer who was sometimes partners with the notorious Martin Sinclair.

As though auditioning for his next production, Merle burst unannounced into Eckstein's office one afternoon, and collapsed in sobs. Her histrionics had an effect, although they did not quite produce the results Merle had anticipated. Eckstein was a shrewd, hardened old man, and certainly not one to regard the voluptuous blonde before him in a paternalistic spirit. It was as a mistress that he decided to provide for her. His generosity, however, extended only to paying the rental on a modest apartment on Sixty-third Street, as well as the costs for moving the bulk of her Philadelphia possessions with which Merle refused to part. As a "sugar daddy," Eckstein left much to be desired.

And so it was that Merle's destiny became bound up with that of Eckstein and, eventually, Sinclair. For many years since then, she had subsisted on the fringes of their glamorous lives, making herself as indispensible as possible. She was, she knew, now too old to begin again elsewhere, and so if she was to recoup her fortunes, it must be through either Eckstein or Sinclair. Once that had been accomplished, then on that day she would avenge herself for all the humiliations they, and all men, had made her suffer. That vengeance she had sworn.

Merle's arrival at Eckstein's office coincided with Martin Sinclair's return from Europe with his new bride, the cooly refined, exquisitely blond, hauntingly beautiful Madelaine. Following a honeymoon in Jamaica, they settled in New York—a king of the theater and his stunning queen. Merle set out immediately and with absolute determination to become the new bride's best friend, and to insinuate herself in Madelaine's life with Sinclair.

Merle had quickly assessed that her relationship with Arthur Eckstein was going nowhere. Not only would he probably never leave his wife, Miriam, but the old fart was too stingy even to keep her in style! Still Merle clung to him like grim death, reluctant to forego even so tenuous a foothold in the glamorous haut monde of Broadway. As discreetly as possible, however, she began to shift her attentions to Sinclair. Although the presence of his blushing bride made it unlikely that he would succumb to her charms anytime soon, still she thought it best to prepare for the future. Surely she had more to offer Sinclair than the insipid blond girl!

In the first years of their marriage, all seemed to go well. Triumph followed triumph; Sinclair appeared to have the Midas touch—every play he brought to Broadway was not only well received critically, but made money for its investors. To Madelaine, the joy of living in the charmed circle of the theatrical world was inexhaustible. Even the black moods of melancholy which unaccountably assailed her now-famous husband from time to time did not dim her love for him, although they did arouse concern. During these episodes, he would withdraw into his study for days at a time, speaking to no one, taking neither food nor drink. However, each time, just as Madelaine was beginning to become seriously alarmed, he would emerge her same dear Martin. No, in those days, there was truly no shadow on the horizon—except one: Madelaine Sinclair could not have a child.

For years she visited a succession of gynecologists, hoping to remedy her infertility. Then, at last, shortly before the opening night of *Charades,* her husband's most ambitious musical to date, she learned that the miracle had happened —she was pregnant!

Pregnant with Alison . . . Alison!

* * *

The brisk voice of Martin Sinclair's secretary, Liz, snapped the producer back from his revery of times past . . . chances missed.

"I have Merle Greene on line one again, Mr. Sinclair. She is most insistent that I put her through."

There was a long moment while he tried to focus . . . to pull his thoughts together . . . to return to today. "Insistent is she?" The thought seemed to amuse the old man. His mood brightened perceptibly. "Well, we shall see about that. Tell her to hold. First get Tony Holland in London for me." During the silence which followed, Sinclair willed himself back to the present, and to the immediate concerns at hand.

The connection to England had been made: "Tony, my boy, how did things work out with Pandora Ashley?"

"I must admit, Martin, better than expected. I was much impressed by the lady . . . much impressed. She seems to have an elusive quality. One that has never been captured on film. If we could just get that up on the screen, I feel we would have a magnificent Isabel. For that reason, I'm going to take the liberty of shooting a test of Miss Ashley over at Pinewood tomorrow. To be frank, Martin, she appeared to have some misgivings about tackling this role. Her nerves seem to be in a very delicate state. She's not yet fully recovered from the ordeal of *Pavlova* . . ."

"Fine, Tony, just go ahead and do whatever you think necessary. Call me as soon as you've shot the test on Ashley. Good-bye, my boy." Without a break, he shifted to the intercom: "Liz, try the Beverly Hills Hotel once more. Try paging Woodard out by the pool."

"Right away, Mr. Sinclair . . . and I still have Merle Greene on the line for you. Shall I put her through now?"

"No! Devil take the woman! I'm not in the mood for her cat and mouse games! Tell her I'll get back to her."

"If you don't mind my saying so, Mr. Sinclair, Miss Greene really does sound quite overwrought. She says it's an emergency. Perhaps you should talk to her; she seems in a very bad state."

"All right. All right. Put her through."

When Merle's voice came on the line it was low and honeyed and seemed to throb with concern.

"Martin! Oh, Martin, thank God I was able to find you in!"

"Of course, I'm in," he mumbled gruffly. "Where the devil should I be? Well, what is it?"

"It's . . . it's Alison, Martin!"

Perhaps it was a trick of the light in his office, as dusk began to fall, but a dark shadow had seemed to cross the producer's face at the mention of the name "Alison."

"Martin, they're refusing to keep her at Clover Hill any longer . . . there's been some trouble about some animals, apparently."

"Well, have a word with Bradshaw, dammit! You know I have to be out on the coast in less than three weeks, and there's that blasted business with Ingrid and the lawyers coming up. Deal with it yourself!"

"I did speak to Bradshaw, Martin. I tried everything. I swear it. He just won't listen to reason . . . said his decision was final. I told him we'd be over there as soon as possible."

"You told them WHAT?" Sinclair's voice pulsated with rage. Merle dripped sympathy. "I told him we'd come there to talk. There was no other way. I know how difficult things are for you at this moment, how much pressure the picture and that horrible woman are subjecting you to. I know you

just couldn't face having to look for another place for Alison
right now."

Martin Sinclair cursed Merle Greene from the bottom
of his soul. Her and Alison. But she was right. In a barely
audible whisper, he told her he'd pick her up first thing the
next morning and they'd drive out to Clover Hill and see
what was to be done about Alison.

Alison, my "love child," Sinclair mused with irony. My
beloved daughter, born of Madelaine.

Several thousand miles away, it was well past midnight
and the sullen waiter in the grimy café on the Rue de Sèvres
had lost his patience with the old woman in the shabby coat
who stared vacantly before her at a nearly empty glass of
cognac. Raising her glazed eyes, she demanded *"un autre,"*
her voice raw and throaty. The only others remaining at this
hour were a frowsy-looking *putain,* whose painted features
looked gross and bloated in the neon light, and a haggard
Arab-looking man with drawn features and a deep scar on
his left cheekbone—perhaps her pimp. Even they appeared
to be on the point of leaving, and Jean-Claude, the waiter,
had no intention of staying up all night merely to pour an
endless stream of cognac into the old hag before him.

"On ferme, Madame."

Something of an authoritative, even of an aristocratic
manner came into the voice of the withered old lady as she
stared the waiter directly in the eye and again demanded,
"un autre, s'il vous plaît."

Jean-Claude yielded. There was something in the woman's face he had not noticed before. True, her skin was
weathered, and the blond hair which she had pulled back in
a disheveled bun was stringy and matted. Also, she wore no
makeup, not even a trace of lipstick, and he had at first
guessed her to be almost sixty. He now saw that she must be

closer to forty. She still had lovely eyes, blue-green and al-
mond-shaped, fringed with dark lashes which needed no
trace of mascara to make them outstanding. As he placed
the glass of cheap cognac in front of her—her fifth for the
evening—Jean-Claude concluded that she was certainly a
woman with such a past as cheap novels are written about.
There was no question: This ragged creature who drained
her glass with frightening avidity had once been a great
beauty.

"*Salut!*" called the Arab to the waiter, as he and the
prostitute swayed out the glass doors.

"*Salut. Bonne nuit!*" Then more softly he said, "*Je
regrette, Madame, on ferme.*"

The woman fumbled in the pockets of her dark coat
and threw several coins on the table. "*C'est assez?*" she demanded.

Jean-Claude realized for the first time she was not a
French woman. Not German either, he thought to himself.
English? Or perhaps American? No, Americans always had
money. The coins she had thrown on the table amounted to
no more than twenty-five francs and the bill had been for
forty-two, but Jean-Claude knew that her pockets were all
but empty, and he was not disposed to cause her more trouble. "*Elle en a assez,*" he reasoned. "*Ah, oui, Madame, ca y
est.*" He assisted her with her chair and escorted her to the
door of the dingy café with as much ceremony as if he had
been the maître d'hôtel at Maxim's and she the Duchess of
Bedford. "*Bonsoir, Madame, bonne nuit.*"

"*Bonne nuit.*"

La pauvre, thought the tired waiter as he shed his soiled
apron and turned out the lights. He was in the process of
locking the glass door when the darkness was pierced by the
loud squeal of brakes and a woman's heart-rending scream.
He knew instantly what had happened, and he ran like a

man distracted down the black rain-slicked Paris pavement. No more than two blocks away, Madelaine Sinclair lay in a dark bundle in the center of the street. The driver of the Peugeot which had struck her was on his knees before her limp body. He was a young man and kept rocking back and forth in obvious panic and remorse.

"Ce n'etait pas de ma faute," he cried as Jean-Claude arrived on the scene, *"Elle courait juste devant la voiture. Elle s'est complètement soûlée."*

Martin Sinclair and Merle Greene sat stiffly, scarcely exchanging a word in the backseat of Sinclair's maroon Bentley as it sailed past the lush verdure of the Connecticut landscape, glistening in the early morning sunlight. Merle was wearing a dresden-blue Adolfo suit, with a matching blue silk shirt, firmly believing that its ruffled neckline and the soft large bow at the throat gave it an added femininity and set off her creamy skin and gray eyes. She had added a long strand of cultured pearls and liberal lashings of a Bal à Versailles. If, however, the ensemble was having the desired effect upon Martin Sinclair, he had, as yet, not given the slightest indication. Merle's feline glance surveyed her companion as he in turn gazed, lost in thought, out the car window. It was becoming hard, even for her, to believe that the hunched, silent man who sat beside her with hooded eyes had been her lover.

Not that the torridness of their romance had ever threatened to set the world on fire. Even Merle couldn't claim that. It had begun in a matter-of-fact, perfunctory fashion. Merle had quarreled bitterly with Arthur Eckstein, at the time joined with Sinclair in the production of a musical which had been having trouble during its tryouts in New Haven, but which the partners were still determined to bring to Broadway. Eckstein had, with varying degrees of sincerity, been promising to divorce his wife and marry Merle for years now, but this time, the fight over it had become particularly acrimonious, and words and threats were exchanged on both sides which would long be remembered. A tearful Merle had fled to Sinclair for sympathy, cried on his manly shoulder, and, well . . . one thing had led to another, and he had demonstrated it in a physical manner. Fondling her large breasts and lifting her skirt with the brusque movements of a man who knows what a woman wants and isn't about to waste words giving it to her.

Merle Greene smiled slightly now as she stared at the somber man in the dark suit beside her. She thought of him now, undressed. The sparse graying hairs on the white flesh of his chest. The small, infantile gasps of pleasure that he had emitted sucking at her tits. The pleading look in his dark eyes as her nimble fingers brought his cock to life.

Merle Greene knew the truth about Martin Sinclair. And the truth was that, despite his embitterment at the sex, his misogyny, almost, Martin Sinclair was a man over whom a woman could obtain power . . . real power. Of that there was no question. The only problem was how to become that woman, how to attain that ascendancy.

It had been obvious to Merle at the time their affaire began that Sinclair was still brooding about Madelaine. Although she had pretended to be her Madelaine's dear, dear friend, Merle hated that woman with a passion. She was dying now, they said, her health gone, her beauty ravaged by alcoholism. They said she lived like an animal . . . that her squalid flat in Montparnasse stank of urine and cheap cognac . . . but none of this could quell Merle Greene's hatred or soften her envy of the image of Madelaine Sinclair clad in Nina Ricci silver lamé, her flaxen hair swept back from her shell-like ears, her blue eyes dancing with love of her husband. That had been the opening night of *Charades,* a collaboration between Sinclair and Eckstein, and one of the producers' greatest triumphs. Arthur had escorted his wife, a dark-haired woman with a beak of a nose and a fortune of her own. And Merle, in off-the-shoulder black velvet, had been forced to attend on the arm of the choreographer, a high-strung gay, who was relentlessly bitchy to her all evening.

It was that night, or rather in the early hours of morning, when the papers came out and their feelings of exhilaration were confirmed by ecstatic reviews, that, amid the popping of champagne corks, Madelaine had chosen to crown the triumph of the evening with her own joyful news. She was pregnant! Martin Sinclair had clasped her small white hands in his, and some who were close enough to him to get a good look later claimed to have seen him cry tears of joy. But it was likely that they were just embellishing the story in the light of what happened afterwards. The couple decided that night too to name their child after the hero or heroine of *Charades* in honor of that auspicious opening night. Thus, if the infant were a boy, it would be called Christopher . . . if a girl, Alison.

Herbert Bradshaw leaned out the mock-Tudor window of his spacious book-lined office and looked thoughtfully at a group of children playing on a perfectly manicured lawn. To be sure, the concern at hand was an affair of the utmost delicacy, and Martin Sinclair was not a man whose wrath, once kindled, could be easily assuaged. In the past, Bradshaw had gone to extremes to accomodate the famous producer, and this solicitous attitude had in turn had a beneficial impact on Clover Hill. But this latest business, well, that was a different matter . . . His train of thought was interrupted by loud peals of laughter from one of the group of children on the lawn. It rose in pitch and intensity, gradually translating itself into a harsh, braying sound.

At the sound of this wild laugh, Martin Sinclair jumped to his feet and wrung his hands in agitation. Drops of sweat broke out on his pale forehead. His dark eyes seemed somehow to reflect the primitive fear evidenced in the child's shrill wail from outside.

Merle Greene slowly crossed her legs; soundlessly she lit a mentholated cigarette. The unseen child's weird outburst ended as abruptly as it had begun. The sudden silence which filled the oak-paneled room was like that of a funeral parlor where the mourners abruptly find that they have exhausted all polite forms of condolence and are confronted with the naked face of death.

Sinclair's husky voice penetrated the stillness: "Look here, Bradshaw, I'm a busy man, and over the years I've contributed a great deal of money—a great deal—to this institution. I am aware that my . . . that Alison is a difficult child. But surely that is what you are equipped to deal with. If you were not, she would have no need for you . . ."

Bradshaw was hushed, his posture deferential. Still, he felt he must strike a note of firmness: "That is, of course, so, Mr. Sinclair. But we have many children in our care, and it is our fear that your daughter's violent behavior poses a threat to their well-being. Furthermore, it is, as you know, our policy at Clover Hill to avoid physical restraint whenever possible, and to rely on other means of therapy. Regretably, Alison does not seem to respond favorably to this regimen."

"Still, she's only a child," Merle interposed, again in honeyed terms. "I thought that she had made remarkable progress on her last visit with me."

Bradshaw crossed to his massive desk and appeared to consult some files before responding. "Since your visit two weeks ago, Mrs. Greene, Alison assaulted an eight-year-old patient in the dormitory, attempting to violate her sexually with an empty bottle. She deliberately broke an aquarium in one of the schoolrooms, killing more than thirty rare and beautiful specimens of tropical fish. *And* she managed somehow to seize my own son's spaniel puppy and hang it. But that was not the end of the poor dog's agony. Shall I describe to you in what condition my little boy found his cherished pet?"

By now the principal's voice throbbed with emotion as he told how Alison had stubbed out lighted cigarettes on the dying puppy, relishing every second of its death throes. He seemed no longer to care about the exalted position of his visitors. Sinclair was silent, apparently plunged into a wave of the deepest melancholy by the details of Alison's atrocities. His eyes darted about wildly, and he seemed to wish only to be able to rush from the room.

Of the threesome, only Merle had retained her composure. Her liquid voice was more soothing than ever as she raised her large white hand and pointed out the window at the sprawling grounds. "Look, Martin, wouldn't that just be a lovely spot for a riding stable? Imagine the fun the children would have with their very own ponies. Oh, how sweet it would be!" She seemed very elated by the prospect and clapped her hands like a little girl. Her gray eyes were bright with wonder and excitement as she asked Herbert Bradshaw for his opinion of her plan.

It was determined, by the close of their meeting, that (a) Alison Sinclair should remain at Clover Hill on a "provisional basis," and (b) construction of the Martin Sinclair Equestrian Center for Children would begin that April.

7

Arthur Gershon leaned across his lustrous Jean-Michel Frank desk, and offered his client a light. This client, like most of his clients, was a lady, and an extremely beautiful one at that. By the way she drew deeply on her cigarette, it appeared she was also an extremely agitated one. Agitated in spite of the fact that everything about the offices of Gershon, Fine, and Silver was calculated to soothe the eyes and nerves with quiet luxury.

Gershon himself was quite an authority on Art Deco and had filled his office with handcrafted twenties-era furniture of superb quality. The rich beige walls formed a decorous background for an enviable collection of paintings by O'Keeffe, Malevitch, and Stuart Davis. Everything about the room was subdued, well proportioned, and refined. Gershon, too, spoke in a slow, well-modulated voice, each syllable calculated to reassure the listener. He used this technique as he addressed his lovely client, the second Mrs. Martin Sinclair: "I can assure you, Mrs. Sinclair, that we will do our very best to bring this matter to a conclusion you will find satisfactory."

"Satisfactory!" Her German accent gave the word a hissing sound. "I was told you were the best divorce lawyer in New York, and you call this pittance he is offering me satisfactory! Thirty thousand dollars a year! It is ludicrous. I spend more than that in Bergdorf's alone! I would be left with nothing to spend on my poor child."

Gershon was soothing, unruffled. "Be calm, Mrs. Sinclair. Remember, I'm on your side. Of course, there is no question of our accepting so derisory an amount, but there are certain factors in this case which make it to our advantage to settle out of court. . . ."

"Factors!" Ingrid Sinclair spat out the word. "What factors?"

"Mrs. Sinclair, this is not a simple case. Your husband, it appears, is inclined to be most, shall we say, vindictive in this matter. Only this morning I received a communication through his attorney, George Radcliffe, to the effect that, should you decline this offer, your husband is prepared to furnish proof in court that you were—and I use his words—'never his legal spouse,' and that Melissa is 'not his daughter.' Naturally, I informed Mr. Radcliffe that Sinclair's offer is totally unacceptable."

Ingrid Sinclair made no response, but the color seemed to drain from her scuptured face, and she compressed her rather thin lips together tightly. Finally she whispered in an almost inaudible voice, "He's bluffing. He wouldn't do it. The child means everything in life to him."

"Nonetheless, Mrs. Sinclair, it is imperative that, as your attorney, I be in possession of any facts, no matter how unpleasant, which may be brought out against you. Have they any means whatsoever of substantiating such accusations?"

"None! None whatsoever! I swear it! Melissa is Martin's child. Unless . . ."

"Unless?"

"It's impossible. She would never do such a thing."

"I don't quite follow you. Who would never do such a thing?"

"Merle Greene."

It was a bright, sunny afternoon on Madison Avenue, where Merle Greene had managed to get one of the prized outside tables at Le Relais. She glanced in irritation at the imitation Cartier tank watch on her wrist (bought from a black hustler outside Bloomie's for fifty dollars, but no one seemed to be able to tell the difference). Her dear friend, Rosemary Smythe-Hutchison, the celebrated author of romance fiction, was late—a good twenty minutes late. The old cat does it on purpose, thought Merle as she sipped her kir. She loves rubbing it in that I have a nine-to-five job, and don't get all day off for lunch. She felt a prickling sensation on her skin, as if these small humiliations were physically so many needles stinging her white flesh.

"Merle, darling!" exclaimed a large red-haired woman in a red suit, advancing toward her. "I'm so sorry I'm late. I simply had to meet with my publisher, and it went on and on!"

Merle rose, bubbling with girlish enthusiasm at the sight of her oldest friend. She had worn her Adolfo again, although it was a bit warm in today's heat, and she allowed herself a smile of self-satisfaction that she still looked better-dressed than Rosemary, who had at least ten times her money to spend. Gypsyish, she mused, evaluating the red number. It would look all right on a much young, thinner, woman . . . and those earrings look positively vulgar. "Darling," she burbled, "you look fabulous! Wherever did you get that outfit? It's so becoming; you should always wear red."

"Thanks, darling. What are you drinking? Kir? I think I'll have one too . . . no, I'll make it a kir royale—that is, if they make it with decent champagne. Walter, what champagne do you use by the glass?"

"Mumm, Madame!"

"Oui. Ça va. Un kir royale, s'il vous plaît."

What bullshit, thought Merle to herself, speaking French in New New York City. And her accent is lousy.

"I suppose we better order," said Rosemary Smythe-Hutchison, her voice dripping with pity. "I know you have to get back to work. Their chicken salad here is simply marvelous—the best in town. I think I'll have that. Don't look now, but I think that very distinguished-looking man at the bar is staring at us . . . he looks Italian, don't you think?" She flashed a bright red lipsticked smile in his direction, but it appeared to have no noticeable effect. The two ladies giggled conspiratorially, their demeanor—despite the fact that their combined age would have been more than a hundred years—resembled nothing so much as a pair of naughty schoolgirls repeating their first risqué jokes.

"Now!" said the author, after the waiter had taken their order for two chicken salads and two glasses of white wine. "Tell me everything about Martin!"

"Well . . . he's taking me to California with him!" exulted Merle. "And he has managed to get Ingrid to give him custody of Melissa over the summer . . ."

"Managed!" snorted Rosemary. "That bum of a boyfriend of hers can't stand the sight of the brat. She'll be delighted to get her out of the house . . ."

"True . . . and naturally, there's no way he can look after the child himself. . . ."

"So. You're going along as a glorified nanny. Is that the idea?"

"Certainly not. We'll have an au pair girl, and we'll have adjoining rooms in the Beverly Hills Hotel. I would hardly call that the position of a nanny!"

"Darling, may I be frank? You know you're my dearest friend in the whole world. May I ask you a blunt question? You won't hold it against me?"

Merle replied somewhat sourly that she might, she could, and she wouldn't. Of course.

"How long has it been since you last went to bed with Martin Sinclair?"

"Not that long ago. Once. Six months ago. Just after Ingrid first left him."

Rosemary gave her unpleasant all-purpose "I told you so" snort again. "And the other day, when you went out to Connecticut with him and Alison?"

Merle Greene had to concede that Martin Sinclair's expressions of affection on that occasion had been minimal, to say the least.

"Let's be realistic about this, Merle," Rosemary continued smoothly. "You and I both know he will never marry you."

The glint of naked steel flashed in Merle's gray eyes as she responded. "Neither you nor I know any such thing. He's not even divorced yet."

Rosemary nodded condescendingly at her friend's outburst. "Darling, I'm not trying to hurt you. On the contrary, I want you to get something out of the old fart. But it's basic masculine psychology and mathematics. A man of sixty-eight is left by his beautiful thirty-five-year-old wife for a twenty-eight-year-old stud. What must he do to prove his beleaguered masculinity? Simple. Marry an *even younger* woman who is going to persuade him that sexually he is a sort of cross between Errol Flynn and Mick Jagger. You could be Jackie Onassis. You could be Princess Grace of Monaco risen from the grave. He will not marry anyone older than thirty. Maximum." It was hateful to hear her friend say these things, but inwardly Merle Green knew the bitch had a point.

"And to be blunt . . . my dearest, if you hadn't realized you hadn't a prayer of marrying him yourself, you would never have steered him on to Ingrid."

Merle argued, but her heart wasn't in it. "But he'll be more practical now. Surely he's smart enough to know that another child-bride will only do the same thing to him all over again—only worse. He nearly went out of his mind last time with his wounded pride. He wouldn't dare risk it."

"But you must make him risk it?"

"I! What the hell are you talking about?"

"You must make him. Provided, of course, *you* select the child-bride. It's the only way to get power over him."

Merle began to listen more attentively to her girlfriend. She adored the sound of the word "power." They ordered a second round of drinks to pursue their conversation. Merle decided not to worry about the job. She would soon be leaving it behind for good.

Heads swiveled and momentary lulls occurred in babbled conversations as they entered the room. The long-legged blonde in the beige Versace was led to her table at the Plaza Hotel's Palm Court by an obsequious maître d'. At her side was a flaxen-haired little girl of five or so, dressed also in beige, whose beauty at once enhanced and rivaled that of her lovely mother. Violins in the background scraped a deeply saccharine rendition of "Memories."

As Ingrid Sinclair and her daughter Melissa were seated at their table, the brusque manner in which the beautiful lady demanded a Stolichnaya straight up somewhat dispelled the aura of Madonna and Child which had surrounded the pair. In fact, so far as Ingrid resembled a Madonna at all, she was much more along the lines of a

Dürer than a Raphael. Her beauty was of the Northern
School, sharply etched yet clouded with melancholy. There
was none of the warmth of Italianate rapture in the gaze of
her blue eyes as she drained the colorless liquid before her
and stared piercingly at her little daughter. She searched the
child's sunny face—beaming as it was with this rare treat of
accompanying her mother to a wonderful place—for any
resemblance to the features of the dour old man she had
married. She could find none.

Melissa's round blue eyes filled with wonder as the
waiter brought a basket of piping hot scones, then a large
bowl of fluffy whipped cream, accompanied by delicate porcelain dishes filled with bright red gooey raspberry jam.

"OOOHHH!" exclaimed the delighted child. "Raspberry, my favorite. Is it your favorite too, Mummy?"

"Yes, darling. Now have you ever had scones before?"
she asked, for, in truth, the beautiful young woman was not
terribly familiar with her child's eating habits.

"Scones?" asked the bewildered little girl, shaking her
flaxen curls, opening her blue eyes still wider.

"Those," Ingrid pointed at the basket, "are called
'scones.' They come from England. Now this is what we
do." Deftly she slit one bun with a knife, cut it carefully into
bite-size pieces, laced it with foamy cream, placed a generous dollop of red goo on top, and put the whole confection
in her daughter's tiny mouth. She laughed for the first time
that afternoon as the little girl struggled eagerly with this
new delicacy. Melissa had never been so happy. The sweet,
rich taste in her mouth, this sparkling, laughing, unknown
woman who was her mother, the sentimental music swelling
in the background—the child felt herself to be in paradise.
Through this veil of happiness she did not notice the anxious look which came into Ingrid's eyes as her nervous
laughter died away.

Melissa was Martin's child, all right; the dearest wish
of his heart; a beautiful, perfectly-formed, normal child. Of
this, Ingrid was certain. She was not like that other child,
that monster. Yes, Melissa was Martin's child. And he
would pay for her. And pay. And pay. Ingrid had risen this
far, and not even the claws of that treacherous bitch, Merle,
would pull her from her pedestal. It had taken her too long
to reach it. She surrendered to the richness of the room,
with the discreet scurrying of the waiters hurrying to perform her slightest command, the flash of jewelry on perfumed women, the rich aroma of the men's cigars. Her mind
erased all concern, her surroundings enveloped her in a feeling of security and belonging.

Above the hushed conversation, the violins were scraping a mawkishly embellished version of "Send in the
Clowns." Ironic, she thought, it was the very tune the
would-be actress had sung on the day she first met Martin
Sinclair.

Ingrid's bittersweet reminiscences were interrupted by
the arrival of a tall, dark young man in jeans and a leather
jacket, who strode through the Palm Court of the Plaza
Hotel around the end of the tea hour and seated himself
between Ingrid Sinclair and her child. He was perhaps a few
years younger than his lady friend, not being much more
than twenty-five or -six, and his burning black eyes and olive
complexion hinted at his Italian ancestry. But something in
the scornful expression of those eyes, or the slight twist of
his mouth, counteracted the pleasing impression given by
the regularity of his features.

"So," said Lou D'Antonio, glancing disdainfully
around him, "I see it's Mary Poppins time."

The violins were still scraping away, the theme from
Love Story this time. "Jesus. How can you stand that fuck-

ing racket? So, come on. Give. What did Gershon have to say? How much does he think the old buzzard is good for?"

Ingrid looked pointedly at Melissa, whose smile had faded immediately upon D'Antonio's appearance, as if to say "not in front of the child," but Lou was not to be restrained.

"Look, don't pull that motherhood shit with me. This is Lou, baby, remember? Now, give."

Ingrid's German accent gave her reply a slight hissing sound. "He thinks it may not be as . . . as 'straightforward' was the word he used . . . as straightforward as we had hoped. It seems Merle Greene is ready to support any wild accusations that Martin tries to make against me. If I accept his offer, which of course I cannot do, he will make no effort to dispute the legality of our marriage or (she lowered her voice to a whisper) the legitimacy of *Liebchen*. She will remain his sole heir, and, furthermore, if he should still be alive at the time of her twenty-first birthday . . ."

Lou interrupted with a sneer, "A mathematical impossibility . . ."

". . . She will receive the sum of five million dollars, which is being held in a trust fund. If, however, we fight, he claims to be able to prove in court that we were never married, that *Liebchen* was Arnold Stockman's child, and he says he will disinherit her utterly."

Lou's fist smashed the linen-draped tea table sending a Meissen cup and saucer crashing to the floor. "The old bastard is bluffing! He's gotta be. Besides, you swore to me the brat really is his. Well, is she or isn't she?"

"Yes! Yes! Yes! A thousand times yes! It is only that Merle Greene has in her possession certain letters which could be very embarrassing . . . which might give a bad impression in court. We could compromise. After all, it is

my own child's future we are talking about . . . Can I de-
prive her of five, perhaps fifty million dollars?"

"That's beautiful. I mean, that is really beautiful, Ingrid. Maybe we could get those violinists over here to play
"Mother Machree." But where do you think I'm gonna be
when Melissa has her twenty-first birthday party? And how
about you? You'll be fifty-two fucking years old by then,
remember!" Lou reached out and stroked her lovely face.
"Don't you see, honey, it's only you I care about. You and
me. That old bastard put you through hell. He deserves to
pay for it."

"You are right," said Ingrid Sinclair *née* Von Albenstein. "He will pay."

Merle's session with Rosemary Smythe-Hutchison had
not left her in the best frame of mind. She felt by no means
disposed to sweeten Ingrid Sinclair's afternoon. She poured
herself a stiff Scotch, seated herself on her ivory damask love
seat and, picking up the receiver of her gilt rococo telephone, dialed Ingrid Sinclair's well-remembered number.
For all that, her voice was liquid honey when Ingrid answered with a Germanic, *"Ja."*

"Ingrid, darling, I'm just sick that this awful business
has prevented us from getting together! How *are* you, sweetheart?"

"I have nothing to discuss with you," hissed Ingrid
Sinclair. "You had better be in touch with my lawyers."

"But, sweetheart. You mustn't feel that way . . . and
we've been so *close* to each other, *remember!* Besides, there
is little Melissa to think of. How is the little angel?"

Ingrid had been ready to slam down the phone, but
something in the older woman's words made her hesitate.
"What do you want from me?" she asked in a whisper.

"Sweetheart!" Merle seemed shocked and wounded.

"Want from YOU! Why, haven't I always been your very dearest friend, ever since we met at Dr. Stockman's? Didn't I introduce you to Martin? Didn't I even introduce you to Lou D'Antonio? Just think, Ingrid, you were in terrible trouble when I first met you."

Ingrid lit a cigarette with an onyx Cartier lighter and inhaled deeply. Her brain seemed clouded. Her temples throbbed with pain. Her mind wandered as she thought back over the past few years. It was obvious that Merle wanted to do the talking, so Ingrid relaxed somewhat, listening, thinking. She surveyed her own reflection in the mirrored paneling of the Sinclair's Beekman Place apartment. She looked, she thought, worn-out and exhausted, with every tiny line around her eyes magnified tenfold after her ordeal with the lawyers. Did she need a face-lift yet, she wondered. Some of Arnold Stockman's patients she knew had been younger than herself when they started "lifting." No, she decided, she didn't need a face-lift. All she needed was a rest. Two weeks at La Samanna. No Melissa. No Martin. No lawyers. Just sun and sand and Lou D'Antonio's caresses.

Lou . . . he could be such a bastard when he wanted to. Her true age was thirty-eight, yet Lou was the first man Ingrid Sinclair had ever genuinely loved. Except, of course, for her father, but the memories she held of him were blurred and fading like the sepia photographs of him in his Wehrmacht uniform.

In truth, she was in love with the legends her mother had spun about General Friedrich von Albenstein, who had died only a few months after her birth. The stories of her father had provided the sole glory in her bleak childhood. Ingrid had been born in the charred rubble and blackened steel of postwar Berlin. Her father had been among nine generals taken prisoner by Allied troops in the final mop-

ping-up operation. In November 1946, Friedrich von Albenstein, general of the Third Reich, was executed by a Soviet
firing squad, leaving behind a widow and infant daughter to
forage for survival in the wasteland of Berlin.

It was, to Ingrid, a bitter irony of fate that her father
should have been shot as a "Nazi" war criminal. Von Albenstein and his class had always despised Hitler and everything he stood for. His family had belonged to a military
élite that could number among its ancestors not only
"Junkers" who had fought under Frederick the Great of
Prussia, but warriors who followed the banners of the cross
to Jerusalem under Frederick II, Holy Roman Emperor in
the Fifth Crusade. Such was the noble ancestry related to
her in the evenings by her mother who had spent the day
rummaging in garbage cans behind restaurants on what remained of Unter den Linden for the scraps of potato peels
that kept them alive. One grew up fast in postwar Berlin.
That is, if one grew up at all.

When Ingrid's mother died shortly after the girl's
twelfth birthday, the already-embittered child was sent to
America to live with a cousin who had married an American before the war and who now lived in Yonkers. There, in
the dingy suburban home with its Macy's colonial furniture,
where Ingrid was treated more like a charity case than a
family member, the young girl dreamed of the glittering life
of aristocratic Europe, of gala evenings at the opera, of
weekends at the Schloss, hunting, of waltzes danced in white
satin.

By the age of fifteen, her high young breasts, long legs,
and scuptured cheekbones gave her a sophistication far beyond her years. At Christmastime she lied about her age and
was able to secure a job behind the cosmetics counter at
Lord and Taylor. There she met a sportswear manufacturer
from Seventh Avenue, a round man named Fischman. He

complimented Ingrid on her appearance and asked if she had ever done any modeling. He then presented her with a card that said Élite Fashions, and told her to step up to his office any time if she felt like working for him. Modeling! Ingrid had clutched at the thing—haughty, swan-necked women in Dior gowns on the pages of *Vogue* or *Harper's Bazaar*. She was altogether unprepared for the grueling reality of work in a Seventh Avenue showroom, displaying the ill-fitting wares of Élite to a leering assortment of buyers from third-rate department stores.

At times, if there was an especially important buyer from out of town, one who could be relied upon for a heavy order, Ingrid was expected to "entertain" him. For her added efforts there would be a bonus, an extra fifty dollars or so at the end of the week in her pay envelope. It happened also that Nate Fischman's marriage was not a happy one, and he was known to seek solace in the arms of his prettier employees. By February, Nate Fischman was paying the rent on a small apartment on East Thirty-third Street; Ingrid von Albenstein was the tenant.

She stayed with Élite and Fischman for nearly two years. At the end of that time Ingrid discovered she was pregnant. Fischman offered her five thousand dollars and a ticket to Los Angeles "not to make trouble." Ingrid accepted. The abortion was routine without complications, emotional or otherwise. She cashed in the airline ticket to the Coast, however; she had no intention of leaving New York just when things were beginning to go well for her.

After she had left Élite Fashions, Ingrid von Albenstein spent five hundred of her five thousand dollars on a portfolio of photographs of herself by a well-known photographer. These she took to the Ford Agency, and then, when she was rejected there, to Wilhelmina and several other prestigious modeling agencies. It was no good, they said; she didn't have the look of the moment. Or she had the "look," but too strongly resembled several girls they had on their books already. Or she was too inexperienced, and had no formal training. Things were slow, and they just weren't taking on any new talent. Try again in a few months perhaps. Ingrid was becoming desperate. She had already paid out a two months' deposit in advance on an apartment on East Fifty-third Street, and had bought an expensive outfit at Bonwit's to wear for interviews. At last, when she was down to eight hundred dollars, she went into Saks and managed to get a job as a floor model in the Park Avenue Room, showing off elegant Chloës and Halstons to the store's clientele.

Some weeks afterwards, Ingrid was modeling a dark blue sequined Bill Blass, priced at two thousand seven hundred fifty dollars, when Dr. Arnold Stockman came in looking for a birthday present for Denise, his current love, with whom he was flying to Puerto Vallarta the following week. Arnold Stockman liked the blue dress and asked to examine it more closely. Ingrid von Albenstein approached gracefully, pirhouetting around him. Stockman decided he especially liked the way the dress looked on Ingrid. In fact, he decided it looked better on her than it would have on Denise, so although he bought the dress, Denise received only a bouquet of red roses for her birthday gift; thereafter, she was never able to get through to Stockman on the phone. Ingrid von Albenstein quit her job at Saks and flew with the doctor on his holiday.

Although she was by no means an innocent, young Ingrid found herself totally unprepared for Stockman's swinging life-style. The young doctor owned a luxurious villa in Puerto Vallarta, not far from the Garza Blanca Beach Club. He was very friendly with several other fun-loving men who had been vacationing there for several years, among them an entertainment attorney from Beverly Hills, a young producer of soft porn films, and a broker from Merrill Lynch. Each, of course, brought with him his lady of the moment. These men seemed ready to try anything, usually at least twice, and Stockman was the ringleader of the group.

Evenings began at Oceano's, where they would meet around eight for margaritas or neat tequila. They proceeded to the City Dump or Capriccio's, where they would take over the dance floor, couples forming and re-forming to the pulsating beat. Ingrid soon found herself taken from Arnold's arms by David, who held her close in his hairy brown arms, thrusting his pelvis against her crotch. She turned toward Stockman, her eyes appealing for help, but the young doctor laughed, obviously enjoying her discomfort. Her next dance partner was the attorney, Ken, who thrust his tongue into her ear and muttered obscenities. His date, Karen, was on the dance floor with Samantha, the broker's friend. Samantha, a redhead with gigantic tits, cupped the other girl's buttocks in her hands, and rested her head on her partner's bosom, as her hands traced the curve of the other girl's hips.

Patterns of sensuality emerged as the urgency of lust permeated the hot air of the small discothèque. Sweat ran down Arnold Stockman's forehead as he grabbed Ingrid's arm, and calling out, "C'mon, you guys, we're going to my place." There, on the moonlit Mexican beach, clothes were discarded, and the orgy—to which the activities of the tiny dance floor had been merely foreplay—began in earnest. The couples lay in a tangle of brown bodies on the white sand, all but Ingrid, who stood to one side, still wearing her thin, pink silk dress, her blond hair blowing wildly, her thin shoulders shivering in the hot night. But Arnold held out his hands to her, speaking softly and reassuringly: "What's the matter, baby? It's all right. We're all friends. You don't need to do anything you feel uncomfortable with."

He undressed her slowly, gently, like a child undressing a favorite doll, covering her breasts with kisses, sucking at her nipples until their nubs were hard between his teeth. He drew her down with him on to the warm sand, caressing her, comforting her. Soon he was thrusting deep inside her, murmuring words of endearment as if they had been the only two on the beach. Just as Ingrid was on the brink of coming, however, Stockman withdrew, leaving her to writhe in a frenzy of sexual arousal. He turned his back on her, walking over to where Samantha and Karen lay rolling on the sand, penetrating each other's bodies with searching tongues and fingers. Ingrid bit her lips in frustration, watching helplessly while Stockman entered Samantha from behind: Samantha, in turn, moaned with pleasure as she buried her tongue inside Karen's cunt. When David approached Ingrid, his erect penis thrust toward her like a weapon, she made no protest, opening her legs for him.

By the time the two-week vacation was over, Ingrid had experienced every permutation of the sexual act the various combinations of the four young couples could offer. Samantha, a thin, high-strung New Yorker with black hair, had awakened her to the pleasures one woman could kindle in another. Stockman seemed to particularly enjoy watching the two women together, his brown eyes bright with lust as Samantha brought his young blond German *Prinzessin* to a paroxysm of desire.

When they returned to his brownstone on Seventy-eighth Street, the parties continued, and Ingrid found she looked forward to them more and more. She craved the sensation of being kissed, licked, and fucked by one person after another. As her voluptuous pleasure became more and more apparent, however, the young Doctor Stockman began to lose interest in her. It had been her coolness, her haughty ice princess quality which had attracted him. Now he ignored her advances when they were alone, and was quick to pass her on to his male friends when they were not. Her days at Seventy-eighth Street were numbered, and she knew it. Beyond the expensive clothes Stockman had bought, she had nothing—no money, no job, no friends. It was at this point in her life that she met Merle Greene.

In Manhattan, the guests at Dr. Stockman's special evenings often included some of his wealthy clients—women and, occasionally, men, who wished the benefits of their reconstructive surgery to provide a passport to a reinvigorated, exciting way of life. Some were older women who had been abandoned by their husbands for younger girls, and who were now eager to reaffirm their sexual attractiveness, so recently restored by the surgeon's knife. Others were young girls whose flat chests or prominent noses had hitherto relegated them to the category of ugly ducklings, but who were now transformed into beauties, eager for their share of male attention and sexual fulfillment.

In a very real sense, Stockman was a dream merchant who catered to a select group of his patients' fantasies long after they had left the operating table. And so, Merle Greene, her relationship with Arthur Eckstein crumbling, her affaire with Martin Sinclair going nowhere, had come to Arnold Stockman to have her face "done," and later had begun to visit the good doctor socially for his particular brand of recuperative therapy.

Merle never actually participated in Stockman's orgies, but instead sat off to one side, fully dressed, curled up like a large white cat, smiling her peculiar smile, her gray eyes glued always to Ingrid's naked body. She seemed to drink in every nuance of Stockman's behavior toward the girl, and once, when he had behaved toward her with particular arrogance, Ingrid looked up to find Merle Greene's large white hand resting comfortingly on her shoulder, her eyes promising sympathy.

They began their affair in the afternoons when Stockman was at his office. During one session, when they were in bed together in Merle's tiny apartment, Merle Greene turned to Ingrid and whispered, "Leave him."

"How can I?" replied the girl. "He's all I have. I have nowhere to go."

"That is exactly why. Leave him before he throws you out. I've been watching him. Leave while you're still capable of wounding his pride."

"Where can I go?" asked Ingrid von Albenstein, opening her wide blue eyes wider.

"Here, to begin with. But there's someone I want you to meet." Kissing the German girl full on the lips, she added quietly, "I have a plan."

"Who is it? Who is it that you want me to meet?"

"You may have heard of him. His name is Martin Sinclair."

The following morning, when Stockman had left for his office Merle Greene came by the doctor's house and helped Ingrid pack her belongings. They were careful not to touch anything of Stockman's, for the move might not be permanent. Merle even dictated the note Ingrid left on Arnold's pillow. It read: Darling, I still love you, but I cannot bear this way of life any longer. I must go away and try to find myself among my own kind of people. The life that you are leading disturbs me deeply. Please do not try to find me. *Gräfin* Ingrid von Albenstein.

Merle thought the title on the signature was a neat touch, since Ingrid had always boasted to Stockman of her aristocratic Aryan lineage.

And so it came about that Dr. Arnold Stockman, who

only a few days earlier had been trying to think up the easiest and cheapest means of getting Ingrid out of his Seventy-eighth Street brownstone, went berserk when he found that she had walked out on him.

Merle Greene made several subtle changes in Ingrid von Albenstein's appearance before presenting her new-found young friend to Martin Sinclair. First, she took Ingrid to Eric at Louis Guy D, a positive "wizard" at color who lightened her hair one tone and removed any brassy yellowing tinges. Her coiffure was also altered so that instead of the long flowing mane she had affected, Ingrid's hair was pulled back in a sleek chignon. All her large pieces of "fun" costume jewelry were discarded along with half her eye makeup. From the extensive wardrobe purchased for her by Dr. Arnold Stockman, Merle selected a palette consisting mostly of beige and ivory, relieved only by simple black. "From now on, baby," said Merle, "you're strictly a pearls-and-oysters girl!"

One startling by-product soon emerged from Ingrid's "new look"—the German girl now bore a striking resemblance to the young Madelaine Sinclair.

"Isn't it riiiiiiich? . . . Aaarre we a paaaiir?" A thin girl with a hooked nose and prominent collarbones stood alone (except for her accompanist) on the bare stage. As she peered out into the darkness, her face reflected an odd blend of defiance and fear, resulting in an expression much like that of St. Joan facing her tormenters.

Martin Sinclair wearily lifted his head and turned to Val de Lisle, his director, who sat in the red plush seat beside him. He asked wearily, "Must they *all* sing "Send in the Clowns"?! By God, I'll get up on stage myself and strangle the next one who does!"

"Next!" cried Val. In an attempt to appease the producer, he added, "This one'll be better. I've worked with
her."

"That's hardly a guarantee," mumbled Sinclair irrita-
bly.

The next girl *was* prettier, if somewhat arch and confident in her manner. She obviously thought her choice of
material clever and original, for she announced that she was
going to sing a Noel Coward song in a manner that indicated quite clearly she was going to knock 'em dead. In a
surprisingly raucous voice she began to belt: "I'll see you
again, whenever spring breaks through again . . ."

Val de Lisle looked up at Sinclair, beaming encourag-
ingly, but the expression on the producer's face withered his
enthusiasm. "Next!" the director called feebly.

The confident girl continued for a minute, uncomprehending. Then she turned red in the face. She did not
leave the stage, however, but clenched her fists and began
blubbering, looking out accusingly into the audience at Val.

"You've obviously 'worked with her' all right," Sinclair
muttered under his breath to de Lisle. "Get that hysterical
bitch off my stage, and in future confine your casting to the
theater, or you can get out with her!"

"Oh, Martin!" said a silvery voice behind the producer.
"Don't be so hard on the poor girl. I thought her little song
was very sweet." Merle Greene took off her Blackglama
mink and draped it over a row of seats in the darkened
theater. "Martin darling, I'd like you to meet a dear friend
of mine from Germany . . . the Countess Ingrid von Albenstein." Throughout her vivid memory of that fateful day
which had, ironically, served as her own audition for the
role of Mrs. Martin Sinclair, Ingrid had been vaguely aware
of Merle Greene's sugared voice droning on at the other end
of the line. Now, a change in Merle's manner made Ingrid

suddenly aware of the fact that a threatening edge had crept into her voice.

"All right! You introduced me to Martin Sinclair. A thousand thanks! *Danke schön!* Now what the devil do you want from me?"

"Honestly, Ingrid," cooed Merle Greene, suddenly subdued. "I just can't understand your attitude. You know, you're your own worst enemy. Why don't you just concede custody of Melissa to Martin? That's all he really wants. I'm sure that in those circumstances, any embarrassing matters would never come to light, and I could persuade him to be much more *generous.*"

"Give my child up . . . into your hands! Never!"

"Be reasonable, darling. You know how *important* Lou D'Antonio is to you . . . and how restless he gets, especially with children."

"Lou has nothing to do with my decision. I will never give up Melissa. Don't forget, Merle, I am not the only one who can be embarrassed."

"Yes, precious, I know. Unfortunately though, you are the only one who put it down in writing." This was Merle Greene's parting shot. "Just be sure Melissa is all packed and ready to go with us to California by the weekend. It will do the child so much good to get used to being with her father."

Merle paused a moment after hanging up the phone. She had actually accomplished a lot that day. So what if Ingrid were no longer her friend and bed partner. Surely another blonde will turn up soon, Merle thought to herself, and smiled.

8

A small set intended to represent a modest hotel bedroom in France had been hastily put together on Stage 9 at Pinewood to accommodate Pandora Ashley's test for the role of Isabel, Lady Dunsmere, in *Moonshadows*. Anthony Holland had chosen the scene in which Isabel, the bored, pampered wife of a cabinet minister, with whom she is vacationing at the elegant Hôtel du Cap in Antibes, is persuaded by her young lover, César—the role for which Rod Ward had already been signed—to aid him and his friends in a terrorist kidnapping conspiracy.

During the course of the scene, Pandora would need to display the cool poise of the aristocrat, as well as the fierce sensuality of a woman ready to risk money, power, position, even her own life, for a chance to escape the banality of her gilded existence. Rod Ward's lines would be fed to her by one Pete Bolton, a solid enough actor, and one of Anthony Holland's drinking buddies from the Shepherd's Bush days . . . a thoroughly workmanlike professional, who nonetheless lacked the needed spark or sex appeal, or whatever the magic formula was, that would ever enable him to scrape more than the bare bones of a living from his chosen profession.

Pandora Ashley sat tensely on the bed, dressed in an ivory satin nightdress that dipped revealingly and displayed her rounded breasts to full advantage. A hairdresser stood before her, fluffing out her raven hair, giving it an artfully disheveled look; above her, an assistant played with a baby spot so that her best features, her enormous green eyes and splendid cheekbones, would be emphasized.

The coiffure was complete. "Right, luv!" called the lighting man. The red light went up, indicating quiet on the set; no one was to leave or enter while it flashed its message: "shooting in progress."

"Moonshadows test. Take one."

"Turn over," called Anthony Holland.

It took only five takes to get the scene right. Bolton had flubbed his lines on the first one, and Pandora had seemed a bit stiff, her movement puppetlike, but on take three she seemed to catch fire, and a current of electricity passed through the skeleton crew. Holland knew he had it on three, but ordered a retake just for good measure. On four, she was somewhat mechanical, but on the fifth one, the spark was back.

"Cut. Print. That's a wrap, fellas! Miss Ashley, I think none of us need have a sleepless night over this. As far as I'm concerned, the part is yours."

"Tony, I'm deeply grateful to you. I could never have done it without you. You gave me the courage," Pandora said in her most professional voice.

"May I invite you for a drink?" Tony asked his new leading lady.

"Of course. If you'll wait for me to get dressed." She added in an undertone, "I don't believe you've ever seen me with my clothes on."

"I'm not altogether certain that I don't prefer it that way." Laughing, he escorted her to the door of the portable

dressing room that had been set up for her on the sound-
stage.

Moments later, seeing that the last of the film crew had
drifted off, he went inside. Pandora sat in front of a large
mirror surrounded by lights. She was naked, and her full
lower lip trembled as she saw Anthony's handsome face
appear in the glass behind her own. She closed her eyes as
he drew her body to his. The caress of his hands on her
warm skin seemed the continuation of a dream. In a moment he drew her down and stretched her on the floor, all
the while his hands sought out the secret parts of her body
that were throbbing with desire. Her body was in a frenzy of
longing. This dark woman, with her mouth open to receive
his kisses, her slim legs parted for him, aroused in Tony
Holland a devouring passion he had never known. He became like an animal, pinning her beneath him, stabbing her
with his sex over and over until she moaned in ecstasy.
Their desire did not exhaust itself, but grew, feeding on itself.

Briefly they uncoupled, while Pandora climbed over
him like some agile jungle cat, her green eyes beckoning, the
wetness between the legs enticing him, rubbing her firm
body against his penis. A current of electricity seemed to
pass between them, recharging their frenzy.

"My God!" said Anthony Holland. "I never knew it
could be like this."

Following Angela Armstrong's unceremonious departure from his hotel room, Josh Woodard poured himself a
large tumbler full of room service Scotch in a vain attempt
to quiet his frayed nerves. He then placed a call to Wandsworth House with the usual results: Madame was out.

Angela Armstrong's vile torrent of abuse had shaken
Josh profoundly. He had thought the girl shallow and vapid,

but would never have believed her capable of such vicious spite. Beauty books, indeed! His recent visitor—although unquestionably a walking advertisement for the latest advances in plastic surgery, cosmetic dentistry, and hairdressing—could not, at least to his Englishman's mind, have been more lacking in all the qualities of charm, feminine grace, true sensuality, warmth, and intelligence which combined to make a woman beautiful. How different from Pandora. Yet his lovely wife was unfathomable to him at times. She had even proposed once, in all apparent seriousness, that they sell Wandsworth House, leave England, and come and live in this diabolical place (she had mentioned Bel Air, no less)!

The mere idea of this strange non-city with its grandiose mansions serving as monuments to ill taste and worse breeding depressed him unutterably. F. Scott Fitzgerald had been a fool, Josh thought. The rich were not different. Money could no more halt the onslaught of pain than a facelift could deny the passage of time. Before his marriage to Pandora, Josh Woodard had spent months in a Jeep, traveling with the Bedouin in the remotest stretches of the Sahara. He had joined Red Cross volunteers in war-torn Ethiopia, bringing nourishment and medicine to babies whose shriveled limbs could scarcely support their grotesquely distended stomachs. He had spent weeks in the hospital wards of Hiroshima, among wretches whose inherited fate might well foreshadow that of all mankind if the mad nuclear arms race were not halted.

Josh Woodard had built his considerable reputation as a writer on his ability to transmute, by his wit, compassion, and eloquence, this "heavy," often controversial subject matter into riveting entertaining theater that appealed to a wide audience, yet pulled no punches in its uncompromising view of reality. His words had force, and, to Josh, words were sacred, the last remaining weapons in a crusade for justice and understanding.

And so, not the least of the reasons for which he loved his wife was the beauty and conviction with which she spoke his words. He took the same joy in his wife's performances that a boy might feel when he sees the bird, whose broken wing he has patiently and lovingly reset, soar at last into the heavens. If only Pandora would let him enter more deeply into her innermost thoughts . . .

But Josh knew there remained a door in his wife's heart irrevocably locked against him . . . against all men. No matter, he would keep trying. And maybe someday she *would* open it. To him. To him only. Until then, how could he resist showering her with all the material joys for which she had yearned so long, even if it did mean working occasionally for the Nat Sheinbergs of the world, or temporarily neglecting the stage for the more lucrative world of films. Had she not told him that after Robin Maxwell she had never thought to love again, and did she not, miracle of miracles, love him now, in spite of his paunch and his thinning hair and his chronic shyness?

Extravagance, he knew, was one of his wife's weaknesses. It rankled her deeply, for instance, that she had to buy her clothes "off the rack"—as she termed shopping in Browns, or Saint Laurent Rive Gauche—and couldn't afford to go to Paris and make her selections from the couture collections. He attributed this to her childlike vulnerability and her insecurity after years of struggle. In fact, it was only one of the many facets of her vulnerability, and it made his protection all the more vital to her.

For the same reason, he had, after the initial shock, forgiven her numerous infidelities. True, when he had first learned of her affaires with other men on the set of *Pavlova,* he thought his brain would burst through his skull. Of all the people on the production, Woodard had been the one most oblivious to Pandora's liaisons. He had not learned of her infidelities until the wrap party—actually less a party than a wake, for the air was heavy with the feeling of failure —when the intoxicated wife of the leading actor had screwed up her courage and marched up to Pandora Ashley as she stood chatting with Josh, and, with controlled deliberation, poured the contents of her glass of red wine down the front of Pandora's peach chiffon frock.

The assistant director had had to restrain Josh from going after the woman, and it was then that the terrible truth came out in a tearful confession by Pandora, delivered in front of everyone. The woman was not to blame. She had reason to be upset. She, Pandora, had had a brief, meaningless affair with her husband. It had meant nothing to either of them, of course, and it was over now. Josh was the only man she had ever truly loved. She begged him to believe that. She had been under unbearable pressure. The role was so demanding. She knew she was doing badly and had been groping desperately for reassurance of any kind. Josh hadn't been there for her—he was so busy with rewrites, and with the financial worries of the film. It had just, well . . . happened. And it would never happen again!

Josh believed her, despite the fact that he would later hear of other "meaningless affairs." He believed in her love for him, and, in truth, Pandora at heart had a deep and abiding fondness for Josh, a real gratitude for the wondrous change he had effected in her life. Despite his unprepossessing appearance, she had even found him to be a surprisingly skillful and pleasing lover, had even tried, valiantly, for a matter of nearly five months following their marriage, to remain faithful to him. But it was just no good! Not only were her sexual appetites gnawing at her constantly, her husband's very high-mindedness, paradoxically, seemed to exacerbate Pandora's desire for mischief! The more Josh treated her like a porcelain shepherdess, the more she felt compelled to prove herself a creature of flesh and blood. At the end of her five months of fidelity, she had been bored to distraction and had sought release with a particularly handsome A.S.M. on *Lady Jane Grey*. After all, Pandora reasoned, she had only taken marriage vows, not holy orders!

The phone rang in Josh's hotel suite.

"Pandora darling! You're up early. I would have rung, but I was afraid of waking you."

"I know, darling, but I have such good news, I couldn't wait to tell you. I did that test for *Moonshadows* yesterday. Anthony Holland loved it. I've definitely got the part!"

"That's wonderful news, but hardly surprising—you'll make a splendid Isabel. Pandora, darling, I've got to get out of here. I don't know how much more of this damn town I can take. . . ."

Pandora's voice was rich, voluptuous with promise, yet decidedly abrupt. "Well dear, I'm sure it will all be fine."

"Good-bye, dearest . . . and remember, don't let the bastards get you down. You know how much I love you."

"I'll try. I miss you so, my darling," said Josh.

"I miss you, too. I'll ring again tomorrow evening." With that, Pandora Ashley put the phone down and rejoined Anthony Holland in the departures lounge. There, she thought, now he won't try to reach me at home.

Anthony Holland, surrounded by Louis Vuitton cases, and looking incredibly handsome in a gray suede Armani jacket, rose to greet her. He held up a parcel from the duty free shop.

"Dom Perignon," he said. "I thought it might come in handy."

Air France announced the departure of Flight 801 to Paris, Charles de Gaulle. "All passengers are requested to present themselves at Gate 32 for boarding. *Air France announce le départ . . .*"

Pandora Ashley slipped her tongue between Anthony Holland's teeth. "That's us!" she said.

The forty-eight hours he spent with Pandora Ashley in Paris were among the happiest of Anthony Holland's life. Paris, the enchantress, opened her arms in welcome, like a celebrated courtesan displaying her charms to a favored client. Parisians have always shown a special fondness for lovers, and when a couple has the grace of Anthony Holland and Pandora Ashley . . . well, nothing could be too good for them. The concierge, the flower vendors, the book sellers in their stalls along the Seine, the Africans with their fierce masks and ivory trinkets, the snobbish salespeople on the Faubourg St. Honoré, the surly cab drivers—all of them had an indulgent smile and a lively word. *L'amour,* they all said to themselves with a sigh as the handsome Englishman with the flaxen hair and the dark woman with *les beaux yeux* marched off, laughing, arm in arm.

Anthony relied on Pandora. Her French was so much better than his, almost fluent, in fact—but spoken with just enough of an English accent to give it an added touch of charm. He loved to watch her order seemingly complicated items from the menu, discussing nuances of nouvelle cuisine with the chef of Jacques Cagna, tingling with surprise as each beautifully prepared dish was presented for his delectation.

Pandora seemed a sorceress. In each shop, a few softly spoken words and the most exquisite creations appeared, fantasies of net and sequin at Saint Laurent, delicate bouquets of floral chiffon at Dior, dramatic black taffeta at Valentino. In each creation she looked more ravishing than before—he wanted to buy them all for her. (He had never bought a dress for a woman before. Of course, he paid Christine's accounts at Harrods and Harvey Nichols, but would never before have so much as entered a woman's clothing boutique except on the last shopping day before Christmas.) Pandora wouldn't hear of it. After much argument, however, she let him pay for one, a sequin and net Saint Laurent—as a souvenir.

Beauty was everywhere around them and they were as one with it. They rode horseback in the Bois de Boulogne, bought hot dogs on crusty bread and munched them in the elevator to the top of the Eiffel Tower, listened to a would-be Piaf sing in the Place du Testre in Montmartre, climbed to the top of Sacré-Coeur, lined up at the counter of Fauchon to nibble on an incredible assortment of pastries, ran up and down the métro, going nowhere in particular, just getting on because they liked the look of the Art Nouveau métro signs.

They spent hours sipping espresso and gazing into one another's eyes at the Café des Deux Magots. There they met for the first time a young musician whom Pandora was to dub their "shadow." It is true that Tony rewarded him quite lavishly for his off-key serenade, but he somehow managed to appear—singing quite out of tune, and accompanying himself ineptly on an old guitar—at every restaurant the couple visited, whether on the Île St. Louis, or at La Coupole, or at the funny place in what remained of Les Halles, where they still found *gratinée* at four-thirty in the morning.

They sat on the steps of the Opéra, and visited Victor Hugo's house, and kissed in the shadow of Nôtre-Dame and cruised down the Seine. These things they did in a mere day and a half, a feat possible only to those who are in love.

They could not keep their hands off each other for a moment. They danced at Privilège and saw *La Double Inconstance* at the Comédie Française and, alone, listened to a solitary organist play Haydn in the dark, incense-filled church of St. Julien-le-Pauvre.

That Sunday night, their last, on the road to Versailles, a pale opal moon rose in the sky for them. They parked their rented Mercedes in a lot in full view of the magnificent château, gleaming in the night, illuminated by amber spotlights. Pandora's hands traced the line of Anthony Holland's thighs. Tony fell into a delicious trance of pleasure as she ran her hot tongue up the length of his straining penis. He closed his eyes in rapture, intoxicated by the perfume of her dark hair, the expert motions of her velvet lips as she moved rhythmically back and forth, enveloping him within her ravenous mouth. All at once, starbursts of pink, blue, and amber shot up in the black sky above the palace.

"Look!" cried Tony Holland, stroking her raven hair gently, "I don't believe it . . . it's pure Hitchcock!"

"Feux d'artifice!" exclaimed his beautiful lover. "They must have known we were coming. No pun intended." She laughed a silky laugh, then her lips sought his in a passionate kiss. *"Je t'adore,"* said Pandora Ashley.

"Je t'aime," said Anthony Holland.

At dawn, they returned to their suite at the Plaza-Athénée for hours of long-drawn-out lovemaking. It left them exhausted, but still tingling, wanting more.

When Anthony Holland woke from his blissful sleep, late morning sunlight was streaming through the windows of the suite. Outside there was the bright splashing of the fountain, and the carmine awnings reflected brightly in the sun. Far away, a church bell tolled.

Pandora had risen early and ordered their breakfast, and now she smiled at her lover as she gestured to a little table covered by a crisp white cloth on which golden croissants and little crystal pots of gaily-colored confitures, blue and white china, and a gleaming silver coffeepot were arrayed with exquisite symmetry. Tony Holland's blue eyes radiated happiness, and a broad grin spread over his handsome features. "Good morning, my love," said Pandora.

"Come here," said Tony, as he peeled the light peach-hued silk Dior wrapper from her shoulders as she knelt by his side.

That morning there seemed to be even more magic in Pandora and Tony's lovemaking. Each seemed to sense intuitively the very pulse of the other's most secret desires. Their caresses had a strange quality: at times soft and melting in their tenderness; at others, fierce and demanding in their animal urgency. They could not look at each other without being drawn to touch each other's flesh with their hands, their mouths, their whole bodies. Her heart raced wildly as he lay the full length of his powerful body on hers. She felt the honey flow from her as he parted her with his warm fingers, and then, in a moment of blinding sweetness, she cried out in ecstasy as he entered her. They moved together as one being, undulating in waves of immeasurable bliss.

At much the same time, thousands of miles distant from the straining lovers, a depressed Josh Woodard opened wide the windows and leaned forward to peer out at the quiet Hollywood night. As he gazed at the starlit heavens beyond the pink cupolas of the hotel, bathed in their garish, blue floodlight, the old MGM boast of "more stars than there are in heaven!" could not help entering the writer's mind. What glamour the word "Hollywood" had once held for him! He thought with sudden nostalgia of his endless hours spent as a boy in shabby Nottingham cinemas, weaving dreams from the black and white images on the screen, while war waged in the world about him. What creatures for dreaming the stars of those films had been—Rita Hayworth,

Barbara Stanwyck, Gene Tierney, Ingrid Bergman, Leonora Sheldrake—the list was endless. How those beautiful women had stirred his adolescent longings, kindled his first boyish desires! What enchanted world could have produced those exquisite creatures?

In a strange frame of mind, at once aroused and dejected, and still more than a little drunk from the evening's excesses, Josh Woodard wondered if, perhaps, somewhere in the Hollywood night, some trace of that vanished beauty might not linger, and, if so, shouldn't he try to find it? He flung on a shirt and trousers, and set out on foot, past the astonished hotel doorman, down the slope toward Sunset Boulevard.

Josh Woodard walked for hours, walking into daybreak past the grandiose mansions which sprawl along the famous boulevard as far as the border of Beverly Hills. Past the seedy rock clubs, trendy boutiques, agents' offices, hairdressers, and restaurants which dot the strip as far as Laurel Canyon. Here, where the urban landscape gives rise to burger joints, gas stations and cheap motels, the hookers were already at their posts, scanning passing motorists. None seemed to pay Josh any attention; dressed as he was, he scarcely seemed worthwhile propositioning. One girl, dressed in a purple mini and hot pink boots, brushed past him by inches as if he did not exist, her face intent on attracting the attention of the occupants of a passing Mercedes sedan which had slowed its pace. Josh Woodard was horrified to detect that, beneath the garish makeup, the girl was only a child . . . no more than thirteen or fourteen.

Christ Almighty! thought Woodard, Is everyone in this blasted town a whore, himself included? Hadn't he too in effect been whoring by working with Sheinberg, attempting to retailor his play, *Lost Souls,* to fit the little man's particular needs?

Sick at heart, he wearily pointed his steps back in the direction of the Beverly Hills Hotel. It was around seven A.M. when he was stopped by a passing patrol car at the corner of Foothill and Sunset. Guns at the ready, the officers spread-eagled him at the side of their vehicle and conducted a body search. Unable to produce any identification—in the haste of dressing, Woodard had inadvertently left his wallet in his room—Josh was equally at a loss to explain his conduct, except to state that he was a guest from England, staying at the Beverly Hills Hotel, and had decided to go for a walk.

One of the officers was inclined to put on the cuffs immediately and take him in for vagrancy, but the other policeman did note what he believed to be a genuine British accent. He figured they might as well at least drive him by the hotel, as he was by now loudly demanding that they check out his story with the front desk.

So Josh Woodard ended his bizarre night by being led into the lobby of the Beverly Hills Hotel with one police officer on either side. Naturally, the front desk duly identified him as a guest, and he was released by his captors with an apology—after all, these foreigners can't be expected to know these things—and a warning. It is against the law to walk in Beverly Hills.

Pandora leaned across and unfastened the metal buckle of Anthony Holland's seatbelt. As she rose from her own seat, she slightly brushed his lap with her buttocks, then took a few steps down the aisle of the first class cabin in the direction of the lavatories. Halfway she turned toward her traveling companion and parted her lips in a beguiling smile. Having carefully noted the door she entered, Tony paused a moment, then rose to follow her. The sign on the door still read "Vacant."

Within seconds, Tony was inside. He found Pandora leaning against the mirrored cabinet, her skirt already lifted above her brown thighs in anticipation.

"I just can't get enough of your cock," she said.

Within seconds he had entered her, moving tentatively at first, then thrusting deeper and deeper in a desperate frenzy. Her hands moved imploringly down his back, drawing his firm buttocks toward her.

"All of it," she gasped, trying hard not to call out, struggling to prolong the ecstasy as the powerful rhythm of his cock plunged deeper into the innermost reaches of her body.

As her paroxysm came, it seemed to her that she had melted into some evanescent substance of heat and light . . . that she was no longer flesh and blood. Lovingly, she caressed his flaxen hair.

"Come. I want you to spunk inside me. Come for me, baby," she whispered.

A momentary spasm as if of suffering furrowed her lover's handsome brow, and then Pandora felt the hot liquid burst between her thighs. They clung to each other fiercely, then broke into uncontrollable peals of laughter as the "Return to Seat" light began flashing on and off.

"London. Looks like we'll have to return to earth," said Anthony Holland.

9

For once, in her vow to have Josh Woodard removed as writer on *Lost Souls*, Angela Armstrong proved to be as good as her word. Turning a deaf ear to Nat Sheinberg's moaning and groaning about "contractual obligations," and "pay-or-play deals," Angela Armstrong had made it clear to her producer and lover in no uncertain terms that either Woodard went or she did!

She had not mentioned it at the time, not wanting to spoil the mood of a festive evening, but Angela now confessed to Sheinberg that the Englishman had approached her drunkenly at the George Landau banquet, stared down her dress, and had made the most lewd and obscene remarks to her! She had never been so insulted in her life, and had held her tongue only out of consideration for Nat; but it was unthinkable that she could ever work with that horrible man!

And so Sheinberg had expected an unpleasant scene when he met with Woodard the next day over lunch at the Polo Lounge. In fact, the luncheon meeting went splendidly, at least from Josh's point of view, though the diminutive producer was at a loss to explain the playwright's reaction to what he had to tell him. The producer had begun cautiously, secretly fearing that Woodard would, as he was fully entitled, threaten to sue him when he announced that he was bringing in another writer for what he delicately termed "polishing" on his play.

However, instead of expressing any hostility when Sheinberg began his spiel about "the American marketplace," and "getting a fresh perspective," Josh's face registered not only approval, but delight.

"Sheinberg, old man, say no more! This calls for a celebration! Waiter! Dom Perignon, and make sure you give *me* the check! You know, Sheinberg, I had never realized till now what a splendid chap you are. Quite splendid." And with that the author gave the small man a hearty slap on the back, nearly knocking the astonished producer out of his chair. Woodard then raised his glass, and in a loud voice proposed a toast. "Let us drink to . . . demographics, Mr. Sheinberg! Demographics!"

When Pandora Ashley bade good-bye to Anthony Holland at Heathrow, she still felt little inclination to return to the country and the solitude of Wandsworth House. She was on an adrenaline high—as though she had just stepped off stage after receiving a dozen curtain calls. The lady's spirits were soaring, and the glitter of London was much more in keeping with her mood of elation. *Moonshadows* would be *her* picture now that she had the director eating out of the palm of her hand.

She headed for the little *pièd á terre* furnished like a miniature jewel box that she maintained in Pont Street, and rang an old flame of hers, a titled fashion photographer with whom she'd had a brief fling during the run of *Lady Jane Grey* at the Haymarket. He proclaimed delight at hearing from his "favorite film star," as he called her, and suggested they dine at Le Suquet or Tramp. As much as she thirsted for a night out on the town, Pandora, however, decided that discretion was called for, and opted for a quiet dinner at her tiny flat. After all, she didn't want word of her assignation drifting back to Anthony Holland at this point, to say nothing of her husband.

It was with a light heart that Josh Woodard turned the key in the door of room 303 of the Beverly Hills Hotel. The floor was littered with a sheaf of telephone message slips, and a red light flashed on the phone beside the bed. He opened the messages eagerly, certain that they would be from his wife, but all six of them were identical, delivered every half hour. Each read, "Call Martin Sinclair's office regarding *Moonshadows* script" followed by a New York telephone number. When he got the operator at the switchboard, the message was the same.

He chose to ignore the command to call Sinclair, however, and instead placed a call to Wandsworth House. Clarisse said that Madame was in, but had been feeling unwell and had taken a sleeping tablet and was not to be disturbed. Obviously there was nothing to do but to ring Sinclair's office and see what the old boy was up to.

Woodard had already turned down the opportunity to do the screenplay adaptation of *Moonshadows*. In fact, he had been the first writer to whom Martin Sinclair had offered the assignment. The fee was astronomical, and Woodard had read the novel, actually finding that it was not without some interesting elements. He had been very tempted to undertake the job, but Pandora was dead set against it from the start. The moment she heard the book was to be made into a film, she had been absolutely determined that she would play the lead role of Isabel, and she did *not* want to work in another film written by her husband. It made people think she was merely a marionette, she argued. No one

would believe she could do anything on her own. No matter
how brilliant her performances had been in the past, Josh
received all the credit. When a production failed, however,
as in the case of *Pavlova*, it was all her fault. It was she who
was inadequate and had failed to live up to her husband's
conception.

Regretfully, Woodard had bowed to her wish and accepted the Nat Sheinberg deal instead. But now it would
appear that *Moonshadows* was back in his life again. The
role of Isabel was already Pandora's. That had happened
quite on its own, without any participation from him, so
that his wife could fairly regard that as very much her own
accomplishment. The deal with Sheinberg was mercifully
over, and now Sinclair was evidently more eager than ever
to work with him. Everything he had heard about Anthony
Holland pointed to his being a bright, inventive young man,
precisely the sort of director he would most like to work
with. The film was to be shot largely in Europe, primarily
the South of France, and the thought of leisurely weeks on
the Côte d'Azur with his ravishing wife made him giddy and
filled him with longing. It was all rubbish, anyhow, Pandora's insecurity! He would be insane to turn down this assignment. He'd call Sinclair straight away and do the deal himself—agents be damned. And if Pandora were still angry,
the money Sinclair was offering was good enough to enable
him to step into Cartier and buy a bauble with which to
appease her. Cartier always had a soothing effect on his
wife.

Pandora Ashley stared with uncharacteristic discomfi-
ture at the dark head of the titled photographer, still blissfully asleep beside her on her Porthault sheets. It was a very
curious thing, but she regretted the night they had spent
together and wished momentarily she hadn't thought of

calling him. She poured herself a glass of Krug champagne
from the ice bucket beside the bed and wondered moodily if
she might not be falling in love with Anthony Holland.
Something had unquestionably happened in Paris.

After Robin Maxwell, Pandora had quickly learned to
gratify her sexual appetites with the same singleminded intent as a man, reversing with each of her lovers the role she
had played with her first husband, using each only for the
momentary pleasure he could bring her, then contemptuously discarding him when his services bored her. And Pandora had a very low threshold of boredom indeed.

Inexplicably, however, she felt no desire to wound
Tony Holland, not even to laugh at him. There was something in his blithe, trusting spirit, his frank good nature, his
sense of wonder and discovery at everything they shared,
that made her look at the world through his eyes. And what
she saw seemed fresh and new, as though washed by a
cleansing rain.

There was nothing sordid in their passion, in the pleasure they gave one another in bed. She had soon learned
better than to mistake Tony's gentleness for weakness. Once
he had determined on something, all her cajoling and caresses, her tears or entreaties, were in vain. Yes, Anthony
Holland was good. She felt almost guilty and definitely foolish for having betrayed him so soon.

"Mmmmm . . ." her dark companion stretched his
athletic limbs, yawning languidly, "good morning, milady
. . . breakfasting without me?"

"Of course not," murmured Pandora, pouring him
champagne.

The young lord took a hearty swig of the golden liquid;
then, suitably refreshed, he placed his companion's hand
between his legs. She removed it as abruptly as if his penis
had been the proverbial red-hot poker. Leaping from the

bed, she flung on the print silk Ungaro she had purchased in Paris and fled from the room, leaving her titled companion to wonder what he had done to offend her. No matter; she would be back. Pandora's unpredictability was part of her charm.

Cold rain streaked Pandora Ashley's tear-stained face as she emerged into the London dawn, shivering in her thin silk Ungaro frock. Her full lower lip trembled involuntarily as she scanned the passing traffic for a taxi.

"Sweet Jesus!" she exclaimed out loud, remorse, fear, and elation vying for top position in the actress's heart. Last night's folly had only proved one thing—her life of one-night stands and anonymous fucks was over. She was in love with Tony Holland! Pandora craved the warmth of his flesh only . . . the liquid velvet of his soft voice whispering his innermost desires in her ear.

Pandora Ashley was at last in love again, and she would follow her passion wherever it might lead her. "After all," she reminded herself: *"Il faut toujours aller jusqu'au bout!"*

With the departure of Josh Woodard from the *Lost Souls* project, a writer was brought in by Nat Sheinberg whose credits included two *Fantasy Island*s, one *Love Boat,* and several episodes of the old *Mary Tyler Moore Show.* The writer's first decision, arrived at at a luncheon meeting with Nat and Angela at The Ivy, was to scrap the title. *Lost Souls* sounded like a "downer"! Angela Armstrong, beaming triumphantly, agreed. Nat Sheinberg, disregarding the advice of his new psychiatrist to show more assertiveness with women, acquiesced. The show was henceforth to be titled *Mildred . . . Portrait of a Massage Parlor Hostess.* "High concept," said the new writer.

Angela's makeup was back, but she retained the limp (Mildred was, after all, supposed to be lame) for "audience identification." The romance with the black musician became substantially less subliminal than it had been in Woodard's play. When it was finally aired, the show received a twenty-eight share and won its time period, beating out *Dynasty*! Angela Armstrong was, indisputably, at last a "star!" She made the covers of *People* and *Los Angeles Magazine*. Her performance as Mildred won her an Emmy nomination as Best Actress. *Playboy* begged her to pose for a layout. She agreed, provided that it be "tastefully done." She made an appearance on the Carson show (although on a night when some obnoxious comedian was guest-hosting), to promote the publication of her new beauty book, which would, she told the host, stress the overwhelming importance of inner, as well as outer, beauty.

Pandora Ashley's emerald eyes sparkled as brightly as the green gems in the Cartier necklace which her husband fastened lovingly around her swanlike throat. Josh flushed with happy embarrassment as his lovely wife kissed him impulsively on the lips. "There's another surprise, too," he began tentatively when the embrace was over. Pandora's ripe mouth narrowed instantly into a thin tight line. She knew instinctively what was next. So the neckpiece had been merely a sop. She would see about that!

Josh continued stumblingly, "I've decided, that is, Martin Sinclair has been on to me . . . and he's convinced me that it would be best for me, that is, for you, for both of us . . . if I were to become involved with *Moonshadows*, after all." He paused at this point, hoping for some response, but Pandora was as cold as the shimmering diamonds around her pretty neck.

"Darling, to be honest, I've never understood what's bothered you so much about the idea of my writing it. This way you can count on the role of Isabel being played up for all it's worth. You should have seen the treatment McAlastair wrote. The whole focus was shifted onto the terrorists. He'd left out half of Isabel's scenes from the book. I swear to God, you were turning into little more than decoration." Pandora, although still silent, seemed to soften somewhat. The pleasing curves returned to her full lips.

"Besides, Sinclair is paying nearly three times what I was getting from Sheinberg, and I've talked him into paying for us to fly down to the Côte d'Azur immediately. I've convinced him that that's the only place where I can get into the proper mood to write the piece."

At this, Pandora melted completely. She flung her arms wide open and waltzed her bewildered but ecstatic mate around the room. "How could I ever have doubted you. Oh, what an idiot I am! What a perfect ninny! I don't know how you ever put up with me!" She lifted Josh's rough hand to her lips and kissed it tenderly. "First, I was terrified I wouldn't get the part . . . and then I was frightened that if I did, people would say it was only because of you. But it's only my idiotic insecurity again; I can see that now. I don't know why you put up with me."

"Because, you silly bitch," said the playwright, cupping his wife's buttocks firmly in his hand and drawing her toward him, "you're a great lay."

Anthony Holland ordered a second gin and tonic from the barman at the White Elephant. Although he was normally not a drinker—certainly not at this time of day—his approaching meeting with Josh Woodard, filled him with an uncomfortable blend of guilt and hostility, not unmingled with apprehension. How could he go through the farce of a polite luncheon meeting with a man who knew every delicious curve and entrance of Pandora's body as well as he did himself. The idea of sharing her with another man had suddenly become a torment to him. He had never thought of it in Paris. That had seemed a schoolboy holiday, with him playing truant, exploring vistas of the world, of his own body, that he had never dreamed existed.

Their bed had become—during those few precious days —the center of the universe. There had seemed no limits to what they could ask of one another, no limits to the ecstasy their bodies could yield. And, incredibly, there had been a rightness to it all . . . an inevitability . . . as if they had both known all their lives that the moment must come when they should find themselves entwined in this sweet combat. Until now, Tony Holland's life had followed a straight, steady, upward path, veering neither to the left nor the right. Now, suddenly, doors to new realms of sensuality were opening all around him. It was as if a painter, whose palette had hitherto been restricted to pastel watercolors, were suddenly presented with all the brilliant hues of the Fauves and given the wide world for his canvas. Everything suddenly became a possibility.

Pandora had told him all about Josh Woodard. How he had saved her from the privations and poverty she had endured after her first husband had deserted her. How gentle Josh had been at first after their marriage, nurturing her talent, giving her the courage to tackle the role of Lady Jane Grey, which he had written specially for her.

But all that had changed recently, Pandora explained. Josh had turned into some sort of a mad Svengali, allowing her no thoughts or independence whatever. He was stifling her! Suffocating her! Driving her constantly, relentlessly, past her breaking point, pushing her to play roles—Pavlova, for instance—she was not ready for, simply to aggrandize his own self-image as a writer, refusing to let her appear in anyone else's projects. In the beginning she had idolized

him, but now she was terrified of his drunken rages, his
insane outbursts of jealousy. Furthermore, she had remained
unswervingly faithful to him for the longest time, but lately
his drinking had led to frequent bouts of impotence. And
after all . . . she was a young woman still. She had a right
to lead a normal life.

All the same, she would never hurt Josh. She would
never hurt him in spite of everything he had done to her.
She would always be grateful to him. She would never leave
him—just as she would never ask Tony to leave his wife and
children for her. In fact, she would even forbid him to speak
of such a thing. Still, theirs was undeniably a great love.
More than that, it was a great adventure. They would hurt
noone. Their love was a beautiful gift to each other, not
something they were stealing from anyone else. There could
be no question of guilt.

Tony Holland felt the gentle pressure of a hand on his
shoulder; he looked up to see a bearded man with a genial,
intelligent countenance smiling down at him.

"Mr. Holland, I believe. How do you do? I'm Josh
Woodard."

A slight flush suffused Tony's handsome features. "A
great honor, Mr. Woodard. Let's get our table, shall we, or
can I get you something to drink here?"

"No. Let's sit down straightaway. I'm famished for
some decent food after all that California muck—all gua-
camole and cold pasta and arugola with melted goat cheese.
Meant to be frightfully chic, I expect, but not my cup of
tea."

Holland could not help reciprocating the older man's
good-natured grin. "So," he said, "old man Sinclair's finally
roped you in as well, has he? As captain of the *Titanic,* let
me be the first to welcome you on board."

By the conclusion of their luncheon—grilled Dover

sole washed down with a vintage Chassagne-Montrachet—
Tony Holland and Josh Woodard found that they shared the
same hopes and aspirations for the film version of *Moonshadows*. Together they would create something really fine—
not just another cheap thriller, but a film which would examine the cynicism of power politics as practised by both
superpowers, and the frightening implications that the intri-
cate web of international terrorism could have on innocent
lives.

Josh spoke with enthusiasm of Tony's selection of Pandora to play Isabel and of the great passion she could bring
to the role. Tony began to feel distinctly uneasy. Pandora
was right, of course: There could be no question of guilt.
Still, he sensed uncomfortably that there had been something not quite right in Pandora's portrait of her husband.
Josh drank sparingly and spoke of his young wife with particular tenderness and caution, as though fearing that every
word and gesture might compromise the angelic purity of
his beloved. Tony Holland wished to God that he were not
in love with Josh Woodard's wife. But he was. God help
him! He was.

10

Martin Sinclair's face was contorted with rage. His dark eyes seemed ready to start out of their sockets. His color was ashen. His gravelly voice rose to a crescendo, like a giant wave crashing down on the sand.

"Why am I surrounded by incompetents?" he thundered. "I don't want a guesstimate! I don't want a 'ballpark figure'! I want a goddam budget, for chrissake. One that I can take to the studio. I'm the one that's going to be held accountable for any overruns."

The small man sitting in the red leather wing chair on the other side of Sinclair's desk squirmed uncomfortably. Sure, he'd been warned about Martin Sinclair's tantrums. He'd heard stories—the Broadway musical star who'd been driven to nervous collapse by Sinclair and lost his voice for nearly a year through hysterical paralysis; Sinclair throwing a martini in a critic's face at Sardi's after a particularly vitriolic review of one of his productions. Willie Howard had worked with some *monstres célèbres* in the course of his fourteen years as a production manager, including such notoriously temperamental directors as Otto Preminger, but he couldn't remember ever having been subjected to such a display as this.

As Sinclair ranted, purplish veins stood out on his fore-head. He slammed his fist down on the mahogany desk for emphasis. Howard was badly shaken, but he attempted to appear calm as he remonstrated that it was simply impossible to come up with a budget in only eight days for a film as complex as *Moonshadows,* particularly when there was still no film shooting script, and they were still basically working from the novel. What was the point of doing elaborate cost-ing-out on a scene that might later be cut from the film completely, or changed in its background or characters?

"I didn't hire you to be a screenwriter!" thundered Sin-clair. "God knows I'm paying enough jerks for that already. From you I don't need imagination. I need figures. Sched-ules. Breakdowns. *By Monday.*"

Willie Howard rummaged in his trouser pockets, found his Valium tablets, and gulped two down hastily. He said a silent prayer, for just then the phone rang, interrupting Martin's tirade. It was Paris, France, on the line, appar-ently. The American Hospital.

"Vous allez mieux, Madame?" The kindly face of the white-haired nun beamed with sympathy as she adjusted the cushions beneath Madelaine Sinclair's head. Madelaine tried to smile, to respond to the woman's kindness. It had been so long since anyone had shown her such compassion.

The sister patted her withered hand tenderly: *"Oui, oui. Je comprends. Il ne faut pas parler. On a essayé de contacter votre mari, Monsieur Sinclair. Vous verrez, il viendra sûre-ment vous voir. Tout finira pour le mieux, grace à Dieu. Re-posez-vous ma petite."*

Madelaine Sinclair began to toss her head frantically back and forth on the pillow at the mention of Martin's name. Her dry lips formed words, but no sound came. *"Ma*

fille . . . ma fille . . ." she mouthed over and over, but
the good sister did not understand.

"*Reposez-vous. Tout va bien passer. Vous allez voir.*"

"*Madame. Madame . . . vous avez un visiteur!*"

For an instant, Madelaine's blue eyes flashed with the
hope that somehow, miraculously, Martin had flown to her
bedside. But it was only an unkempt man in a worn
trenchcoat holding out a small bunch of violets.

"*C'est moi, Madame, vous vous en rappelez . . .* from
the café . . . I was the waiter who served you. *Je, m'ap-
pelle Jean-Claude.*"

Merle Greene had no sooner replaced the ivory receiver
on its gilt cradle than it began to ring shrilly. When she
lifted it up, Martin Sinclair was on the line, speaking in a
gruff, strangled voice.

"Jesus! I've been trying to get through to you for ages!"

"What is it, darling?" Merle was soothing. Her voice
rippled like fluid silk. "You sound very upset."

"Upset! Hah! Only you would use a pussy word like
'upset.' It seems Madelaine has got herself run over by a
truck in Paris. They say she's not expected to live. She's
asking to see the child. Well, I won't have it! I won't have
her seeing Alison! I've given them your number. I want you
to deal with it."

"You poor angel! How simply awful for you! Now just
don't give it another thought. You know I'm always glad to
help you. How dare that woman think she can just come
back into your life making demands . . . even if she is ill?"

"Look, Merle. You and I understand each other pretty
well, I think, so you can save the 'sympathy,' and any other
thoughts you might have on Ma . . . my ex-wife. Just keep
the whole thing away from me. I have enough on my mind
already with this damn *Moonshadows.*"

Merle Greene assented and put the phone down. She rubbed her large white hands together and smiled her special smile. To think—both Mrs. Sinclairs were now in her power, and their brats with them.

". . . but, Madame, I am afraid you do not comprehend the gravity of the situation. There is a very little time to be lost."

Merle Greene tapped the gilt receiver impatiently with her long scarlet fingernails. "I assure you, doctor, Mr. Sinclair understands perfectly. He has given this matter most careful consideration, and has decided that it would assuredly be against his child's best interest to travel to Paris at this time to see her mother."

Dr. Le Maire was a small man with an aquiline nose and a thinning head of sandy hair. He bit nervously at the handle of his eyeglasses as he tried to give form to his thoughts in his far-from-perfect English. Clearly these Americans were mad . . . it was simply not possible to refuse the wish of a dying woman to see her only child. "Yes, Madame. I understand you, but perhaps you do not appreciate that she may never have another chance. I have no wish to alarm you, but Madame Sinclair is not expected to live more than a few days."

"Yes, yes, but Mrs. Sinclair gave up all rights to the child when she abandoned her some years ago. Besides, it is Mr. Sinclair's feelings that Mrs. Sinclair would be a bad influence on Alison. After all, it was Mrs. Sinclair's alcoholism which led to the child being born—let us say—less than perfect. There would be no point in placing them in contact now."

"Madame Greene, I am at a loss . . . I do not even know who you are or what your interest in this case is. I must be allowed to speak to the husband. *En fait, j'insiste.* I insist to speak to Martin Sinclair."

"I am sorry, Dr. Le Maire, that is simply not possible. Besides, I assure you there is no possibility that even your entreaties will change his mind. I am not without compassion, Doctor, but you must see our point of view. Madelaine's life is over. Alison's is just beginning. We must think of her. There is nothing further to be said, Doctor, good day." And with that, she hung up.

The good doctor's hand trembled with rage as he replaced the receiver. *"Incroyable, ces gens-là. Quelles brutes!"* He turned to a slight man in an old trenchcoat who had been sitting patiently, waiting for the outcome of the conversation.

"Qu'estce qu'ils disent?" asked Jean-Claude. *"Ils vont envoyer la petite?"*

"Non," replied the good doctor. *"Ils refusent absolutment."*

"Salauds!"

Martin Sinclair stood before the windows of his Carlysle suite, staring bleakly in the direction of Central Park South, where Alison's "Sweet Sixteen" party was in progress. It had always struck him as appropriate that the birth date of his eldest child should have coincided with Tishah be-Av, one of the days of darkest mourning in the Hebrew calendar.

For sixteen years he had kept the day as a sort of somber personal ritual, taking no calls, receiving no visitors, transacting no business. As he gazed forlornly at the Manhattan skyline, Martin Sinclair saw, with crystal-clear memory the vision of a child's nursery bathed in morning sunshine. In honor of the forthcoming birth, the sunny, buttercup-yellow walls had been painted by Cecil Beaton himself in a festive mural with a carnival motif.

Never, outside the realm of fairy tales, had the preparations for an infant's arrival exceeded those made by Martin Sinclair and his beautiful young wife, Madelaine. Their joyful anticipation was heightened by the fact that their marriage had, for many years, been barren despite many attempts by Madelaine to have a baby. An antique rocking horse (valued at twelve thousand dollars) stood proudly in the center of the yellow nursery, almost prancing, it seemed, in its eagerness to welcome its new rider. A handsome music box in the shape of a miniature carousel nearly four feet high—complete to the most minuscule details, with bright flashing lights and an array of high-stepping horses—whirled gaily, playing as its welcoming theme one of the hit songs from the latest Sinclair Broadway smash, *Charades.* A veritable Noah's Ark full of giant Stieff stuffed animals stood sentry at their posts, waiting. For weeks every possible variety of infants' wear had been arriving from Baby Dior in Paris. A cradle, the most beautiful imaginable, had been festooned with yards and yards of handmade Belgian lace. The finest pram available had been specially flown in from Harrods, London. A pastel carpet with the central design of a huge hot-air balloon had been hand-knotted to the Sinclairs' custom order in India. All was in readiness.

Madelaine's labor pains began at round eight-thirty in the morning. Despite her excruciating pain, her face, nestled on her husband's shoulder, was serene and suffused with happiness, as their chauffeured Bentley headed at breakneck speed for Columbia Presbyterian. This baby, she was sure, would wash away the bitterness of the last few years of married life with Sinclair, would allay his terrible outbursts of unfounded jealousy, mitigate his black, impenetrable moods. They would be a real family now, find again the happiness they had once known in Jamaica so many years ago.

Some thirteen hours later, an ashen-faced Martin Sinclair was still to be found in the waiting room of the maternity ward, pacing like a caged beast, accompanied in his ordeal by his partner, Arthur Eckstein, and the latter's wife, Miriam. The sterile room was shared, much to the producer's irritation, by a shabbily-attired, ill-shaven man with coarse features, a construction worker, as he proudly announced himself to be, who could not be restrained in his eager attempts to make conversation with the Sinclair party. This, he told the producer and his friends, was to be his fifth *bambino*. *"Nummere* five! *Nummere* five!" he kept repeating, beaming proudly at this fine testimonial to his manhood.

It was around twenty minutes past eleven that night— more than fifteen hours since Madelaine's labor had begun —when an unsmiling Dr. Brunstein gravely approached Martin with the words: "Mr. Sinclair, your wife has just given birth to a baby daughter."

Sinclair was too relieved to catch the note of gravity in the physician's voice, and with a shout of joy he clapped Arthur Eckstein ecstatically on the back. Eckstein, however, having instantly sensed some calamity, solemnly placed a restraining hand on Martin's shoulder and bade him listen calmly to what the obstetrician had to say.

Suddenly Sinclair responded. "It's not Madelaine . . ." Martin's voice faltered. "Oh, God, not that . . . please tell me she's all right . . ."

"No, Mr. Sinclair. Your wife is quite all right. So, for that matter, is the baby. However, the child is . . . well, to put it bluntly, Mr. Sinclair, we fear there may be some brain damage."

Dr. Brunstein's somber pronouncement was interrupted by a loud outburst of joy from *"nummere* five," whose wife, Carla, had just given birth to a strapping, eight-pound boy, which was now being exhibited through the glass partition by a smiling nurse. Excitedly he rushed over, attempting to thrust on Martin and Arthur Eckstein some of the fifty-cent cigars with which his pockets were bulging.

The howl which Martin Sinclair emitted when, at length, he was shown his infant daughter was indescribable —that of a soul in torment. Alison's tiny limbs were grotesquely proportioned. Her little, purplish face was twisted in an expression of unmistakable malignity. The sight instantly recalled to Sinclair the face of his mother as she had been taken away to be institutionalized, her once lovely features unrecognizably distorted by madness.

"The child must be put down!" he thundered at Brunstein without hesitation.

"I am sorry, Mr. Sinclair, I can appreciate that you are very agitated at the moment, but that is, of course, completely out of the question! There is no reason whatever that, with the proper care and attention, your daughter should not grow up to lead a relatively normal and happy life. I have not yet, however, explained the situation to your wife, feeling that you might wish to speak to her yourself first."

Sinclair physically thrust the good doctor away from him and dashed wildly from the room, racing through the corridors of the hospital, not pausing even when he reached the street. Without looking for his waiting Bentley, he continued to run as if pursued by the Furies—through the New York streets, not pausing until he reached his Beekman Place apartment. Once inside, he headed straight for the bright yellow nursery. Within moments, the twirling carousel lay in splinters at his feet; the yards of Brussels lace were strewn in tatters on the floor. Helpless, the dumb toy beasts looked on as the producer, his fury spent, sank exhausted to his knees on the balloon carpet, and wept like an infant.

Madelaine Sinclair, her ill-formed daughter cradled lovingly in her arms, returned home to Beekman Place escorted only by Jones, the family chauffeur. Her arrival was greeted only by Travers, the family butler. Her beloved husband had not so much as set foot in her room at Columbia Presbyterian following the delivery. The weakened young woman, already traumatized by the agony of a difficult birth and the news that her little baby was "not quite perfect," was nearly numb with the shock of Martin's cruel treatment of her. Still, Madelaine tried desperately to understand what her husband must be suffering, remembering the fear and horror with which he had spoken long ago of his mother's tragic illness and death, his almost preternatural fear of inherited madness.

She was prepared to forgive him. Surely once he came to know little Alison better, as their baby improved with tender care and patient training—after all, as Dr. Brunstein had reminded her, they could afford the finest treatment and advances were being made daily—Martin would come to love their daughter as she did. Besides, they could have another child. The doctors had assured her there was nothing congenitally wrong with her; there was no reason why a second baby could not be perfectly healthy. All this, she told herself, Martin Sinclair would learn to accept in time. She knew him better than anyone in the world. Beneath his gruff exterior, he was the kindest, the gentlest of men.

Every Sunday Jean-Claude was released from his responsibilities as waiter in the small Parisian restaurant, and he spent the day with his sister Jeanette, her husband, and their five children. The meal Jeanette offered this Sunday

was simple but excellent, a *salade d'haricots verts,* hearty
cassoulet with warm crusty bread, and a good bottle of red
wine to wash it down, but she noticed that her brother did
not eat with his usual gusto. He seemed distracted and far
away in his thoughts. She also thought strange the manner
in which he was staring fixedly at Claudine, his sixteen-year-
old niece, as if a plan were forming in his mind. It was true,
of course, since the night of the accident involving *l'Améri-
caine,* that her brother had been depressed and preoccupied.

Jean-Claude reached over and ruffled his pretty niece's
dark hair. Sixteen, he thought, sixteen . . . just the age of
the girl for whom the dying woman called out in the night
. . . the age of the daughter she had not seen in thirteen
years. Suddenly he smiled broadly, and lifted his glass in a
toast: *"À la famille! Aux enfants!"* Yes, he thought, it would
work. He would ask Dr. Le Maire's permission in the morning.

The idea was an unconventional one, to say the least,
but it could do no harm. So, after some little deliberation,
Dr. Le Maire gave his consent to Jean-Claude's scheme.
After all, Madelaine Sinclair was fading fast. She was not
expected to live out the week, and if perhaps she could be
given one moment of happiness before the end, even by such
unorthodox means, he was not going to be the one to deny it
to her. After all, it was the duty of a physician to relieve
suffering.

Therefore, the next day Madelaine Sinclair was told
that her ex-husband had consented, and that her daughter,
Alison, would arrive in Paris the following day to visit her.
Jean-Claude brought little presents for her—some lipstick
and mascara—and the nuns helped her to arrange her flaxen
hair. Rouge was unnecessary, for the prospect of seeing her

daughter for the first time in thirteen years was enough to bring a glow to her pale cheeks.

"*Ravissante!*" gasped the waiter as he witnessed the transformation.

"*C'est un ange!*" agreed the good sister who had helped brush Madelaine's silken hair. "*Un ange de Botticelli!*"

Merle Greene stood at the top of the stairway leading down from the side entrance of the Plaza Hotel to Trader Vic's. Beside her stood Alison Sinclair, attired for her birthday outing in ballooning black velvet trousers which were meant to minimize but instead drew attention to her bulk. They were waiting for one more celebrant, Rosemary Smythe-Hutchison, who was late as usual.

Some moments later the celebrated author swept in, her red hair worn loose and frizzy, her body obscured by a red silk caftanlike affair (Halston, Merle noted). Enormous gold bracelets clanked on her wrists. "So sorry I'm late, darlings, but you know how Donald is. So amorous! I could hardly make him let me tear myself away. So this is the birthday girl!" she burbled shooting a meaningful look at her friend. "My, my, my . . . we have grown haven't we?"

"Sweet sixteen!" chirped Merle Greene, her own voice as sweet as honey. "Shall we go down? Our table must have been ready ages ago." She put her white hand on Alison's shoulder. "Come, darling." The child refused to budge, however, and she swayed clumsily, shuffling back and forth on her heavy feet, trying to free herself from Merle's grasp.

"She certainly has a will of her own," mumbled Rosemary, clearly enjoying the spectacle.

Merle tried another tack. "Sweetheart, you like this place. This is your favorite, remember?" Alison threw back her large head. Her brown eyes darted wildly about her. Then she emitted a harsh, snorting laugh, still swaying to and fro. "That's right, you like it here . . . now, come along with Auntie Merle like a good girl."

Moments later, sipping rum concoctions from coconuts fringed with orchids, the two girlfriends began to get into a party mood.

"She's so like her father, don't you think?" smiled Merle at her best friend, winking broadly.

"Very like. Such a pity he couldn't be here tonight, isn't it?"

"I'm sure he was dying to come." For some reason, this innocuous remark threw the two ladies into paroxysms of delirious laughter. Alison began to mimic them and joined in with her odd, snorting laugh.

"Speaking of coming," giggled Rosemary, "have you ever had a 'screaming orgasm'?"

"Please, darling, not in front of the child!" This provoked more gales of laughter.

"Not that kind, honey, though it's almost as good—it's a drink!"

"What's in it?"

"God knows. Vodka, I think. Crème de cacao, brandy . . . anyhow, I'm sure they'll know how to fix them here." Raising her jeweled hand at a waiter, Rosemary called out in her most forceful voice: "Waiter . . . two screaming orgasms! No! Make that three!" glancing at Alison who was by now grinning with total incomprehension. "After all, she's a young woman now, and it's only right for her to know about such things."

"You'd be amazed at what she knows," said Merle, lifting an elbow. "She's a hot-blooded little thing. She's gotten into the pants of several boys *and* girls at Clover Hill. You'd be astonished."

"Mmmm . . . she really does take after her father then."

Alison let out a harsh braying sound, "Faaa . . . thee . . . rrr." Heads turned in the restaurant as her voice rose and fell.

"That," said Merle Greene, "is precisely what he is most afraid of."

On a fine, mild Paris Sunday, when the great city was tranquil and at peace in the soft sunshine, Jean-Claude sat quietly by the hospital bed. He knew that Madelaine's time was nearly come: She looked so worn and emaciated.

"Madame . . ." he whispered gently. Her eyes opened, and a gentle smile appeared on her pale face. *"Madame . . . votre fille . . .* your daughter, *Madame . . . Mademoiselle Alison . . .* she is here, *Madame.* You are ready to see her, *Madame?"*

The dying woman stretched out a pale hand, squeezing his arm with all her feeble strength in a sign of gratitude. *"Merci, monsieur, merci,"* she whispered in a trembling voice.

For nearly thirteen years now, Madelaine Sinclair had had but one recurring image in her mind. It was an image flickering, distorted, then frozen—like that of a cinema when the reel freezes on one burning frame. She saw her husband, Martin Sinclair, flanked by two male nurses and Merle Greene, dragging her little girl from her arms. "Unfit . . . alcoholic!" Sinclair had raged at her as she stood paralyzed, wailing, wringing her hands, calling out for her baby. "You have only yourself to blame," Merle Greene had added contemptuously. Her only comfort came from one of the orderlies, who placed his hand on her shoulder and spoke gently as if she were a child herself: "Your little girl is not well, Mrs. Sinclair. This way we'll see to it she gets the

proper care. We'll have her back home with you soon."
Soon, thought Madelaine, soon.

By the time of Alison's birth, Martin's swings of mood
had become wild and incomprehensible—one moment, an
affectionate, loving husband; the next moment, sullen,
brooding, enveloped in the blackest melancholy and prone
to mad outbursts of unprovoked jealousy. The only time he
seemed to believe he really possessed Madelaine was when
he lay in her arms, inside her. At all other times, her movements were questioned. Martin in a rage was a terrifying
figure—his dark eyes would narrow with a controlled and
focused malice, the heavy lids would lower and become
more hooded, like those of an enormous bird of prey. His
lips would tighten in a joyless smile. His vocabulary of
scathing abuse seemed limitless. Madelaine cringed pitiably
before him, protesting her innocence, her love for him. But
it was to no avail.

These outbursts would later be followed by equally
spectacular acts of remorse and contrition on her husband's
part: gifts of a floor-length Barghuzin sable coat from Ben
Kahn, a priceless Fabergé egg studded with sapphires, a
roomful (literally) of yellow roses. These outbursts were
only one of the many reasons Madelaine had wanted so
desperately to become pregnant. She felt the added security
of a child would reknit the bonds between them, reassure
Martin of her complete devotion. That is why, during the
rehearsal period for *Charades* she was ecstatic to learn of
her pregnancy. It was also during the rehearsals for *Charades,* during the long, often eighteen-hour days that her
husband spent at the theater, that Madelaine Sinclair began
—discreetly at first—to drink.

Martin Sinclair's door remained locked against Madelaine from the day of Alison's birth. Only once—about two
weeks following her return from the hospital with her baby

—did her husband see fit to speak to her, and that was in the form of an impassioned, semi-hysterical plea that they give the "cursed changeling," as he called Alison, up for adoption. When Madelaine adamantly refused even to hear of this, all further communications from the producer to his wife were relayed via the household servants.

Increasingly (and in this he was egged on by Merle Greene, whose personal knowledge of parallel cases among persons of her acquaintance could fill a textbook), Sinclair began to shift the blame for the misshapen infant squarely on to his wife's drinking during pregnancy. In truth, Madelaine had, with her husband's frequent absences at work, his tyrannical outbursts and uncontrollable fits of jealousy if she so much as spoke civilly to another man at a cocktail party, begun to drink more than was, strictly speaking, merely "social."

She had never, at the best of times, been the possessor of what is referred to as a "good head for liquor." One or two glasses of wine or champagne had always been enough to make her tipsy. But as for being an alcoholic, someone who secreted bottles in nooks and crannies throughout the house, who drank neat vodka at nine A.M., who shook like a leaf if deprived of booze, and devoted every minute to thinking about procuring more—it simply was not in her. All that had happened later, months after Madelaine Sinclair returned home from Columbia Presbyterian with her baby daughter in her arms, to find the yellow nursery smashed to pieces as if by a tornado, and her husband's heart closed pitilessly against her.

Jean-Claude exited the hospital room and returned with a shy, dark-haired girl in a navy-blue dress with dark, solemn eyes and a kind demeanor. She hesitantly approached the bed and held out a small bouquet of flowers to the dying woman.

"Alison! Oh, Alison, my child! Do not be afraid. I am not afraid to die. Truly, I am not any more. I am quite content . . . now that I see you again. Now that I see how lovely you are." Madelaine stretched out her fragile arms to the young girl who, touched by the pathos of the moment, responded with all her heart to the woman's embrace . . . as much, perhaps, as if she had really been Madelaine and Martin Sinclair's child.

"You must be kind to your father; he is not a cruel man. How could he be? He has sent you back to me. But he suffers so much; he is so very unhappy. I tried to help him, but I failed. You will succeed. I know he must love you dearly, as I do. Do not cry . . . we shall meet again . . . I am very happy now. Tell Martin . . . I am very happy. . . ." With that, Madelaine closed her beautiful eyes and fell into her last slumber. Jean-Claude called frantically for Doctor Le Maire, but when the physician bent over his patient, he knew instantly that it was over. He put his arms around Jean-Claude's niece and gently led her from the silent room. *"Vous avez bien fait, ma petite. Vous pouvez être très fière de vous-même. Très fière. Vous avez montré beaucoup de courage."*

It was past midnight on that Sunday evening when the three birthday revelers reeled tipsily out of Trader Vic's and the Plaza on to Central Park South and into the sticky summer night. Merle Greene was about to tell the Plaza doorman to hail a taxi so she could head home, but Rosemary Smythe-Hutchison—whose face was by now as red as her hair from the effects of the cocktails—placed a restraining hand on her shoulder.

"What's the matter? Where are you going? It's early!" The author's voice was thick . . . her speech slurred. "We haven't given Alison her birthday present yet!"

"Present?" Merle was baffled. "We haven't bought her any present."

"Gotta get her a present! She's sweet sixteen!" insisted Rosemary, bending her head conspiratorially toward Merle and whispering drunkenly in her friend's ear. Merle Greene emitted a shrill scream of laughter at Rosemary's suggestion. The two were soon giggling helplessly, rocking back and forth in each other's arms. Soon, uncomprehendingly, their young charge chimed in, mingling her harsh braying laugh with their own, attracting the stares of many passersby.

"We wouldn't dare!" said Merle, finally managing to restrain her mirth, but there was a gleeful, malicious twinkle in her feline eyes.

"Why not?" asked Rosemary. "Her father doesn't care. Come on, I know just the place. Taxi! . . . Driver, the Lone Ranger . . . it's a nightclub over in Soho . . . West Broadway, I think."

The Lone Ranger was one of the smaller and seedier of that breed of nightclubs spawned by the women's liberation movement in which male rather than female striptease artists performed. The ladies' cab drew up in front of a shabby brick building in a rundown part of Soho, distinguished from the adjoining deserted warehouses only by a huge cowboy hat outlined in neon with the establishment's name in a sort of electric lasso. The only other exceptional feature was the presence of a three-hundred-and-fifty-pound black bouncer at the entrance.

"Maybe we should tell the driver to wait," suggested Merle, put off by the building's unappealing exterior.

"That's a good idea," agreed Rosemary, slipping the cabbie a fifty-dollar bill and instructing him that they'd be back in about twenty minutes. It was decided that Alison, for the time being, should wait in the car.

Once inside, the two girlfriends descended a narrow, ill-lit staircase to a sort of subterranean brick cavern, eerily illuminated by pulsating strobe lights. On a primitive stage at the front of the room, over which hung an impenetrable haze of marijuana and the reek of cheap perfume, a tall dark man was sinuously divesting himself of a black rhinestone-studded cowboy outfit. Surrounding him was a squealing, seething mass of females who mimicked the dancer's gyrations to the beat of some hard-driving country rock music.

Near-naked men, their muscles gleaming with sweat in the oppressively hot cellar, carried their trays of drinks over the heads of the slithering women. These waiters wore the male equivalent of a Playboy Bunny costume—black leather jock straps with gold chain suspenders. In keeping with the Lone Ranger motif, they also wore partial black face masks. These waiters, as well as being noted for their trim, muscular bodies, also were reputed to be willing to make their services available privately to the guests of the establishment. Apparently the management—far from frowning on this moonlighting by its employees—actively encouraged it, taking for itself a part of the action. So notorious was the club, in fact, that the police department had been trying for some time to shut it down.

"Well, what do you think?" Rosemary Smythe-Hutchison asked her friend.

"It's hard to tell, with those masks . . . but that one over there is pretty good-looking!" Merle indicated a well-built bronzed youth with reddish-blond curly hair and a mustache.

Rosemary nodded her approval, and began frantically signaling to get the waiter's attention.

At length, the young man shouldered his way toward the pair. Merle was pleased to note that, on closer inspection, they had chosen well. He flashed them a bright smile.

The boy had even, white teeth, a good complexion, and couldn't have been much older than twenty.

"Hi! My name is Steve. I'm your waiter for this evening. Now what can I get for you ladies?"

"Do you have screaming orgasms?" asked Rosemary sweetly.

"We've been having those all evening," Merle added coyly.

"Is that a drink?" asked the boy, becoming nervous.

"Not necessarily," replied the author of romantic fiction.

Steve paused for a moment to check out the two women. They were no spring chickens, that was for sure, but they weren't that bad-looking . . . especially the blonde. The redhead looked like she was the one with the money, though; he had spotted her heavy gold Ilias Lalaounis jewelry straight off.

"What time do you get off work?" cooed Merle.

"Oh . . . I could get off pretty soon, I guess. Get one of the other guys to take over my shift. We're kinda slow tonight. It kinda depends . . ." He flashed his most seductive smile at Merle. This, he thought, is going to be a pleasure!

"Five hundred dollars!" announced Rosemary brusquely, annoyed to find that the boy evidently preferred her friend.

"I'll be ready in ten minutes . . . just gotta clear things with my boss," nodded Steve.

"Our cab is outside," smirked Merle Green. "We'll be waiting."

On entering the taxi some moments later, the young waiter, his mask removed, wedged himself cozily in the backseat between Merle and Rosemary. Without his Lone Ranger mask, the boy was less handsome; he had small, ferretlike eyes and a venal expression. Unceremoniously, he placed a hand on each of his female companion's knees, and began to nibble on Merle Greene's left earlobe.

Merle, much to his astonishment, checked his embrace, cooing softly, "I'm afraid you misunderstood. Your 'services' are not for us, but for our young friend here!" She indicated Alison, who had been sitting all the while in the front seat, unseen by the boy, rocking back and forth and muttering to herself.

"My friend and I just want to watch!"

"As a matter of fact," added Rosemary Smythe-Hutchison, "you are her birthday present."

Once again, the two dear friends collapsed in girlish laughter.

11

"Go over it again, from the beginning. I want to hear everything," said Lou D'Antonio, stretching out his long legs on the fawn suede sofa in Martin Sinclair's den.

"Do we have to . . . now? Can't it wait till morning? I'm exhausted." Ingrid felt drained, haggard. This court case was becoming an obsession with him. She was painfully aware that she must look every year of her age, for Lou's dark eyes regarded her so scornfully at this moment. There was no trace of the ardent desire she had inspired in him not so long ago.

"Now! I wanna hear it now. Christ, Ingrid, you're only gonna get one shot at this motherfucker! Now it's important that we go over every bit of the past, figure out what kind of ammunition they're gonna hit us with. That's the only way we'll be able to fight back." He drew her toward him and kissed her gently on the back of the neck. "Come on, baby. It'll all be over soon. Then it'll be just you and me."

"And Melissa . . ."

"Sure. Sure. And Melissa. So you walk out on Stockman, and Merle Greene takes you to some theater and you meet Sinclair. Then what?"

Ingrid poured herself a glass of Rémy Martin from a

Baccarat decanter, sighed deeply and began: "They were in the middle of casting. The theater was empty except for Martin and Val de Lisle, the director, and a production secretary. It was very creepy. I had never been in an empty theater before. It was cold, I remember, and the look he gave when he first saw me . . . that I will never forget as long as I live. Never." Ingrid shuddered, took a quick gulp at her brandy, then continued.

"It was as if I were a ghost. Merle explained later that it was because I so strongly resembled Madelaine, his first wife—particularly perhaps in the darkness of that auditorium—but at the time it chilled me to the bone. There was some small talk then. Merle had made a point of introducing me as a countess from Germany, and I spun some story about my family and where in Germany we came from, trying to give the impression that I had only recently left and that I had been leading some sort of jet-set life-style.

"Sinclair became much more charming. I don't remember too much of what he said. He spoke a lot about Brecht and Berlin as a cultural influence on world theater and some production of *Galileo* he had always wanted to do starring Albert Finney. He seemed very knowledgeable. No longer so intimidating. Believe it or not, at that moment I was really impressed with him." She emitted a dry, bitter laugh. "He began explaining about the production they were working on . . . a musical version of *Of Human Bondage*. He asked whether I had ever read the book by W. Somerset Maugham and appeared to be pleased when I said I had. Then he asked if I didn't agree that it would make an excellent subject for a musical. That sort of thing. We spoke in this way for ten minutes or so before I realized that Merle had slipped out of the theater, leaving me alone with him."

"Were you aware at that point that Merle herself had had an affair with Sinclair?" interjected Lou.

"No. Not at that point. I knew that she had been seeing Arthur Eckstein, Sinclair's partner, but that he was married and was refusing to leave his wife for her."

"Go on. What then?"

"He asked me to accompany him to dinner. We went to Nanni's Il Valleto, and our entrance made quite a stir. I had never known before the special thrill one gets arriving on the arm of someone famous and powerful. The special hush. The envy in the other women's eyes. It was a feeling I liked. But there was also—I cannot express it—a 'rightness.' *Das hat mir gut gefallen.* I began to see him. I was careful not to disturb his image of me as an aristocrat. Merle helped me. We both agreed that we must be very, very careful."

"You were still staying with Merle?"

"Yes."

"Did you tell him anything about Stockman at this point?"

"Only that I had had a relationship with a well-established plastic surgeon, but that it was over."

"Why did you tell him anything in the first place."

"Merle said that Sinclair was very suspicious, very inquisitive. He would hear anyway, and it would be better if he heard it from me."

"Go on. What next."

"After two or three dates I began having sex with him. I would come here, spend two or three hours, but he would always send me home with his chauffeur. He would never allow me to spend the night. I could see that he was reluctant to commit himself, that it wasn't going to be easy. I also knew there were all sorts of difficulties with the play as well. Things were going very badly. He wanted to replace the unknown girl they had gotten for the lead with a famous actress, Leonora Sheldrake. The director protested that it was ludicrous; he said she was thirty years too old for the part, and he threatened to walk. This was the situation ten days before the play was to open to Boston."

"Never mind the *Variety* chitchat. What about you?"

"I wanted, of course, to accompany him to Boston. He objected. Merle was going. She had managed to patch things up with Arthur Eckstein for the umpteenth time. I was frantic. I knew that if I let him go to Boston alone, it was over. Then Merle had an inspiration. She managed to run into Stockman accidentally on purpose and let him think I wanted to get back with him. He began calling incessantly. At first I refused to see him, but then, when we did go out, I made sure that we were seen in all the right places so that Martin would hear about it."

"You were fucking Stockman again?"

"Yes."

"And Sinclair? When you saw him, you were fucking him too, right?"

"What is this? An inquisition? Yes. Yes. I was fucking him too. I was fucking Merle also, if you must know. Now are you satisfied?"

"Calm down, will you! I'm not blaming you. I'm just trying to find out the way it all came down so we can prove Melissa is Sinclair's kid. I'm on your side, remember?"

"All right, then. It worked. At least to the extent that Martin became extremely jealous and begged me to come to Boston with him. I agreed, naturally, but it was no good. The atmosphere on the production was by now unbearable. Everyone was at each other's throats. Leonora Sheldrake was brought in over Val de Lisle's objections. The show had to be completely rewritten around her, naturally. Martin and Leonora wanted Val off the show completely, but Martin didn't want to pay the vast sum of money he'd be owed if he were fired. Cabals were formed. The whole company took sides: pro Val, pro Martin. Martin had his spies everywhere. It was like the court of Nero; it was unbelievable! Off with their heads! Off with their heads! Scheming . . . everyone was scheming for their moment in the spotlight. And I, God help me, was scheming with the best of them to marry this tyrant, whom I had by now learned to fear and despise. Boston was a disaster, but Martin was determined to bring the show into town. The next stop was Toronto. We were booked in a vast barn called the O'Keefe Centre, where the sets looked like they had been built from a child's Erector set, and Leonora Sheldrake's voice couldn't carry beyond the twelfth row, even with a mike.

"By then I was pregnant with Martin Sinclair's child, and he still would not marry me. I was desperate. Merle, as usual, had a solution. I vanished. For two weeks. In fact, I was in Montreal, but Sinclair thought I was with Stockman, and Stockman thought I was with Sinclair. We composed a masterpiece of a letter—a sort of cross between Elizabeth Barrett Browning and Barbara Cartland—saying good-bye forever, our romance had been wonderful while it lasted, but I now knew I loved ANOTHER. This letter we typed in duplicate, changing only the names of the addressee, and we mailed two identical copies, one to each of my lovers.

"It only remained to wait and hope that one would take the bait. Sinclair bit first. He had the greatest ego. The thought that I could actually prefer someone else to him—especially a man twenty years younger—was intolerable to him. All of a sudden he was on the phone to Merle, my dearest friend, demanding to know my whereabouts. She, of course, refused to tell him at first. It was only when she saw that he was determined to make an honest woman of me that she told him of my whereabouts. Then we flew to Acapulco for a long weekend, and it was there that we were married. And so began my life with Martin Sinclair. The rest you know."

"And she has those letters! Both of them? The one to Stockman too?"

"Both of them."

The maroon Bentley halted momentarily outside Beekman Place, merely pausing in its stately progress toward John F. Kennedy. In the backseat sat Martin Sinclair, wearing dark Brooks Brothers' pinstripe suit, a Turnbull and Asher shirt, a maroon tie, and incongruously clutching a Cabbage Patch Kid under one arm.

Andrew, the chauffeur, strode briskly into the opulent lobby and informed the concierge that he was there to pick up Mr. Sinclair's daughter. Inside the car, Martin wiped his brow with a linen handkerchief and went over in his mind for the twentieth time that day how he would greet the six-year-old. He looked up to see the little girl approaching, clad in a pale yellow organdy frock, her flaxen curls dancing, her blue eyes solemn and afraid. But she was on the arm of, not his chauffeur, but her mother.

Martin bit his lip in rage at the sight of Ingrid. She approached like a Wagnerian fury, her blond hair streaming wildly behind her. She was clad in some sort of a loose-fitting, tiered, white linen garment (it was, in fact, a nine-hundred-dollar Yohji Yamamoto from Charivari, but to Martin it looked like Ophelia's mad scene). Thrusting her head inside the window of the Bentley, she shrieked at the producer: "You must speak to me! Don't think you can dismiss me that easily . . . I'm not one of your chorus bitches. I am still your wife. I won't let you and that witch, Merle, destroy my child. Our child! I demand you speak to me." Sinclair changed color, but he bit his lip and remained silent, instructing Andrew with a gesture to remove Melissa from her mother's grip and place her alongside him in the car.

"I was a good wife to you. Do you seriously think you will find a better one, old man? Old, old, old man! Look at yourself! Don't think I am through. Don't think I will keep silent. I will let the world know exactly what goes on behind the scenes of a 'prestigious' Martin Sinclair Production. I will tell . . . sell . . . the story of backstage life on *Human Garbage* to every cheap scandal sheet from the *Enquirer* on down! You will be the laughingstock of the profession. No top director will want to work with you again when they hear what you really did to Val de Lisle. Equity will bring you up on charges when they know the truth about how you fired Gloria Wolff!"

Martin's face was purplish but he ignored her, speaking to Andrew. "Pull away!" The chauffeur hesitated. The young woman's head was still inside the open window of the Bentley.

Andrew protested feebly, "But, Mr. Sinclair . . ."

Sinclair pushed a button on the door panel, and Ingrid drew back abruptly as the glass panel began to climb rapidly toward her throat.

"Pull away, I tell you!" screamed Martin at the top of his lungs. The little child sat beside him on the soft leather seat. She emitted no sound, but her tiny frame was racked by sobs.

Arthur Gershon clasped his hands together at the back of his neck, leaned back in his Jean-Michel Frank leather chair, and emitted a long, low whistle. Ingrid Sinclair demurely crossed her svelte legs encased in Carina Nucci snakeskin boots. Lou D'Antonio, seated beside her, gnawed anxiously at his fingernails, as he waited to hear the lawyer's reaction. Gershon began cautiously in his deliberate, methodical way, weighing each syllable for its possible repercussions.

"You realize, Mrs. Sinclair, that if what you are telling me is the truth . . ."

"It's the truth, OK" interjected D'Antonio impatiently.

". . . then we are dealing here with a very serious matter, very serious indeed. There are two separate crimes here —statutory rape of a minor, and attempted blackmail. Why did you not bring these matters to light earlier?"

"I had no wish, naturally, to damage my husband's reputation, or Mr. de Lisle's either, for that matter."

Gershon paused thoughtfully for a moment, licked his lips, flicked a switch on his telephone, and told his secretary to get Harry Schatzberg on the line, or Schatzberg, Schatzberg, Cohen, and Gelfand, the firm representing Martin Sinclair in the divorce.

"I'm gonna try something here," he whispered to his client. "Harry! How are you, *bubi*? How's your squash game coming? Nah! You're getting too good for me! Listen . . . I've got Ingrid Sinclair in here, and I think I can see a way we keep everybody smelling like a rose . . . no headlines . . . everybody happy. Your client's already happy? I love it. But, Harry, between you and me, you tell your client we're gonna subpoena a Mr. Val de Lisle, and a Miss . . . what's the kid's name, Mrs. Sinclair? . . . that's it . . . Carol Bancroft, and see how long he stays ecstatic. Oh, by the way—I tell you this strictly as a friend—this could be something I have to go to the D.A. on. Procuring a minor for immoral purposes, illegal wiretapping, blackmail . . . this could be very deep shit. Harry, I'm leveling with you. In fact, if it were anyone else but you, I would have spoken to the D.A. first."

"What's with this D.A. horseshit, Artie? Procuring minors! You know as well as I do, Sinclair's a pillar of the establishment. Sounds to me like your *fraülein* there, who, by the way is not *Mrs.* Sinclair—she's not *Mrs.* anybody—

has a hyperactive imagination. Tell her to do herself a big favor and take the thirty grand—it's all she's gonna get. And that I tell you strictly as a friend."

Gershon put his feet on his Art Deco desk and began rocking back and forth complacently. "OK, *bubi*, OK. Just humor me. Ask your client about Val de Lisle, Carol Bancroft, and the adjoining rooms in the Royal York. We want five hundred thousand a year, sole ownership of the Beekman Place apartment, and we'll give him very generous visitation rights. Strictly as a friend." With that, Gershon put down the phone, and turned to his beautiful client who was smiling triumphantly. "Well, we gave it a shot. We ran it up the flagpole. Now we have to wait and see if Sinclair salutes."

The connecting door of Martin Sinclair's adjoining suite at the Beverly Hills Hotel at which Merle Greene had been poised all night, like a cat waiting to spring, did not open on to rooms similar to her own—full of floral curtains and overstuffed chairs and Impressionist prints—but rather on to a private sanctum of burgundy lacquered walls, indirect lighting, antique Chinese rugs, and Martin Sinclair's extensive art collection.

Sinclair had not found the décor of the ordinary hotel rooms to his liking, so once he had decided that his new interest in the motion picture industry would entail spending three or four months out of the year on the Coast, he rented a suite by the year for his own exclusive use. He had it completely gutted and redone to his own specifications by his own designer. Unique among the great luxury hotels of the world, the Beverly Hills acceded to his wishes gladly.

The walls of the producer's suite were hung with a priceless collection consisting primarily of the hallucinatory images of the Surrealists, such as De Chirico, and Dali. The

deep-shadowed arches of De Chirico's silent arcades seemed
to have the power to draw the old man into a dark reverie of
an irrecoverable past. Sinclair seemed to have a profound
affinity for these strange melancholy paintings with their
theatrical intensity of clear and mordant light. The sinister
version of Dali's morbid imagery of sex, blood, decay, and
deliquescent flesh, seemed to conform to and reinforce his
own pessimistic view of humanity.

A patch of brilliant dust-filled light streamed sharply
through the window, bathing the dark red room and its
priceless objects in a lucid, yellowish light. On a marquetry
table beside Sinclair's bed, a telephone began to ring insistently. It was a call from New York, from his divorce attorney, Harry Schatzberg. It looked as if there was going to be
trouble.

Beads of perspiration stood out on Martin Sinclair's
pasty forehead. His fingers had turned a purplish white from
the force with which he clenched the telephone receiver in
his hand as though it were a blunt instrument in search of a
victim. "Sinclair . . . Sinclair?" came Harry Schatzberg's
voice over the line, "Are you still there?"

"Yes . . . yes, I'm here . . ." came the reply, so low
as to be almost inaudible.

"Looks like you better tell me the whole story about de
Lisle and the Bancroft girl. This could be ugly."

"You better fly out here. When's the first plane? I'll
have Liz arrange everything. Just have your secretary call
my office." Sinclair was in control again, forceful, authoritative. Schatzberg was soothing, but noncommittal. "You
know I can't just do that, Martin. I have a practice here.
Other clients, other cases."

"To quote Paul Newman, 'There are no other cases.
This is the case!' Don't argue with me, goddam it; I'll make
it worth your while. You have assistants, haven't you? Now

get your Mucius' bull out of Sticus' china shop, and get your ass on a plane!"

"OK, OK. I'll be out there by tonight. We'll go over the whole thing."

Sinclair crossed to the connecting door leading to Merle Greene's apartment, and hammered on it with all his might, crying: "Madame Greene, get the hell in here! Your darling protégée, my wife, is at it again!"

Merle Greene reached out to touch Martin Sinclair's hand in an attempt to comfort him, but was quickly rebuffed.

"Let us make one thing clear, Merle. I *employ* you in a position of trust *not* because I have any illusions about you, but, in fact, precisely for the opposite reason. I know by your conduct in dealing with your so-called best friend, Ingrid, the full extent to which you are capable of betrayal. I find comfort in this. Others may be taken in by your kitten-with-a-bowl-of-cream act. Even I find it occasionally amusing. This, however, is not one of those occasions."

Merle appeared to be genuinely devastated. She dabbed at her blue eyes with a powder-blue linen handkerchief. Her soft voice throbbed with emotion as she answered the producer. "Oh, Martin, how can you be so cynical? It's true that I did 'betray' Ingrid, if you can call it that, after the way she treated you, but it was only after much soul-searching and many sleepless nights. I only did it for you. How cruel it is of you to taunt me with my loyalty to you and Melissa! You know I'd do anything for you."

"That, my dear, happens to be a true statement. Unfortunately, I also know why. You know my wife better than anyone. Is she bluffing about this Val de Lisle thing, or will she use it?"

"On her own, no. She wouldn't dare. Besides, she

doesn't hate you enough, and she cannot believe you hate her. *She'd* keep trying for an amicable arrangement . . . but with Lou D'Antonio pushing her . . ."

"Ah, yes! the charming young Mr. D'Antonio. You introduced him to Ingrid, I believe?" sneered the producer.

"How was I to know what would happen?"

"How, indeed?"

Merle thought it an expedient moment to return the conversation to the matter at hand, namely the threat by Ingrid Sinclair to expose certain occurrences more happily left uncovered. There was no denying, however, that while Sinclair's girlfriend prior to her marriage, she was privy to a somewhat underhanded scheme by the producer to remove Val de Lisle from his post as director of *Of Human Bondage,* without paying him the fee he was entitled to if fired. It had been well-known in the profession that de Lisle had a penchant for "jailbait," and that on more than one occasion his escapades with under-age young ladies had even cost him large sums of money to appease irate parents and generally smooth troubled waters. De Lisle, moreover, was a happily married man with a beautiful wife, three children, and a gabled house in Connecticut.

Among Martin Sinclair's *bêtes noires* were stage mothers. In certain productions, they could not, of course, be avoided—children were required, and the inevitable viragos descended at casting time, making Martin's life a veritable hell with their multi-talented progeny until the least objectionable of the little monsters had been selected.

Of these formidable creatures whose persistence knew no bounds, the most strident and insistent was a certain Mrs. Betty Bancroft of the Bronx, whose infant phenomenon, Carol, had been thrust—at regular intervals for the last ten years—upon Sinclair for consideration for dozens of roles, all of which she was equally incapable of playing. The girl had a pretty face and lovely dark curling hair, but despite the fortune Mrs. Bancroft had obviously expended on singing and dancing lessons, she was lamentably and spectacularly untalented. The mother and daughter pair had, in fact, become something of a standing joke in the Sinclair offices.

Through her tenacity, however, Mrs. Bancroft had somehow managed to wheedle Carol into the casting sessions for *Of Human Bondage,* even though there was no part imaginable for her in the play. The girl was certainly growing up fast, Sinclair remembered thinking at the time; she looked at least nineteen or twenty. Her shapely legs had none of the coltish awkwardness of girlhood, and her large breasts, free of any bra, bounced enticingly as she went through the paces of her amateurish dance number.

Her charms were not lost upon Val de Lisle, who had been in favor of giving her a bit part and of letting her understudy the ingenue. At the time, Martin Sinclair had rejected the idea out of hand. Months later, however, on the road when Leonora Sheldrake had been brought in to play Mildred, against De Lisle's hysterical protests, and the atmosphere backstage was like a snake pit, Sinclair began to think that the presence of Betty and Carol Bancroft might just be an asset to the production after all. Accordingly, Mamma Rose and Baby Carol, as they were known around the Sinclair production office, were summoned at Sinclair's expense, to Toronto, where *Of Human Bondage* was being restaged, relit, rewritten, and rechoreographed almost daily.

At this point, however, each change seemed to make the show worse instead of better. The company was completely demoralized, and most blamed the entrance of Leonora Sheldrake, superstar, for the debacle. Any number in which she was not featured, and which seemed to have a life of its own, or which threatened to be a showstopper, was almost certain to be cut by Sinclair over the frenzied objections of de Lisle. It was obvious that they wanted him to walk, and equally clear he would be damned if he was going to give the old bugger that satisfaction.

The gypsies took to calling Sinclair "Robespierre" behind his back, and it was true that one never knew whose head was likely to roll next. The lighting designer was close to a nervous breakdown; all his beautiful effects had to be thrown out so that Madame Sheldrake could be constantly bathed in more and more white light in an effort to hide her age. The actress playing Nora, the woman who comforts the young doctor with her love after he has been cruelly jilted by Mildred, was replaced. The cast mumbled that it was not because she had been inadequate, but rather because her sweet soprano voice pointed up too sharply the deficiencies of Leonora's singing.

The bickering went on and on, and such was the atmosphere into which Carol Bancroft and her mother were now introduced. Sinclair ensconced them in a suite at the Royal York Hotel, where the company was staying, and let Betty Bancroft know, in no subtle terms, exactly what was required if her daughter's career was, at last, to be launched.

Although Carol Bancroft, at fifteen, was no virgin, the negotiations were long and hard. Mrs. Bancroft would settle for nothing less than a speaking part in *Of Human Bondage,* five thousand dollars in cash, and the ingénue lead of Kim MacAfee in a revival of *Bye Bye Birdie,* which Sinclair was planning for the near future. No one, after all, could say Betty Bancroft wasn't a good mother. This matter settled, the rest of the scheme was easily effected. It was—quite literally, in this case—child's play for Carol Bancroft to linger late one night in the darkened theater after the rest of the exhausted cast had drifted off after rehearsal, and to ask reverently for Val de Lisle's advice about a piece of business.

The remainder of the director's advice was given in room 614 of the Royal York Hotel. Room 616 was conveniently occupied by Martin Sinclair, and it had been supplied with several extra features for the producer's comfort and enjoyment, to wit, a hidden camera and video recorder.

In the morning, Val de Lisle found himself summoned to Sinclair's office where he was confronted with a pictorial souvenir of the preceding evening's exertions, the birth certificate of his paramour, and a letter of resignation from the production awaiting his signature. It specified he was withdrawing on grounds of ill health, by the terms of which de Lisle waived any and all rights to future compensation.

"Statutory rape," said Sinclair, and Ingrid, who had been present, later told Merle Greene that it was one of the few times she had seen her husband smile.

Merle Greene curled her lips slightly and snuggled cat-like on the burgundy velvet sofa in Martin's Beverly Hills suite.

"What the devil are you smiling at?" asked Sinclair gruffly. "This could be a very ugly business; 'blackmail' they're calling it."

Merle merely extended her long white legs on the dark red couch and purred, "It's nonsense. Who will press charges? Val de Lisle? He can't accuse you without destroying himself. Carol? Thanks to you, she's well on the way to being a star now. She's not about to drag her own name through the mud. I can't even understand why you're upset, frankly."

"It's not a legal question. When I picked up Melissa to go to the airport, Ingrid ran shrieking after the car like a harpy, threatening to sell her memoirs to the gutter press. This sort of thing in the papers for every farmer's wife in Nebraska to cackle over—to say nothing of my colleagues in the business. I'll be made into a laughingstock! They could also use it to show me as an unfit parent in a custody fight."

Merle regarded her red-lacquered nails contemptuously. "How much are they asking?"

"Five hundred thousand a year. Beekman Place, and sole custody."

"Hah! The last thing D'Antonio wants is sole custody. Agree to that instantly."

"You're insane! The only thing that matters to me in this whole mess is the child!"

"I know that, but it will throw them off-balance. You've said you don't think Melissa is yours, so make them believe you're convinced of that, and they've lost half their bargaining chips."

"Go on. I'm listening."

"As I think I've mentioned, the key to this situation is Lou. Now I happen to know Lou D'Antonio rather well . . ."

"Yes. One of your few unmarried boyfriends, I believe."

"Lou is a very impatient man, and a very greedy one. We must arrive at the minimum figure it will take to make him feel that it is worth his while to stick with Ingrid . . . no more . . . no less. If Lou leaves her, Ingrid will have nothing but the child to live for, and she will fight you for custody like a tigress, regardless of financial considerations. Ingrid can be a very silly girl at times. She lets herself get carried away by her emotions. Very silly."

Merle's line of reasoning had calmed Sinclair considerably. "What sort of 'minimum figure' are you thinking of?"

"Well, as long as we maintain that the Mexican marriage was never valid, and your decree from Madelaine was never finalized in London, whatever you give is pure charity. But it must be a lump sum, say a quarter of a million?

You'd keep Beekman Place, of course. Lou would be very hard put to keep his hands off a quarter of a million."

"And Melissa?"

"They'll throw her right back at you. Lou won't stand for that child around the house."

"I'll speak to Schatzberg. That's the line we'll take. If it works, my dear, needless to say you'll be well taken care of."

Merle made no reply, but as she extended herself languidly on the couch in her powder-blue chiffon, she looked the picture of relaxation and contentment. In fact, she looked very like a kitten with a bowl of cream.

12

For an instant, some magical time machine seemed to be in operation as Leonora Sheldrake made her entrance down the stairway to the pool of the Beverly Hills Hotel, followed, at an obsequious distance, by her secretary, Brandon. She crossed gracefully to cabana number 5, where a luncheon had been set for Martin Sinclair and his companion, Merle Greene. Leonora wore a white jersey costume, with a bare midriff and shorts cut high on her shapely brown legs. Her platinum hair was pulled back and concealed under a matching white jersey turban. Her choice of jewelry had been unusually discreet, for she wore only some platinum and diamond loop earrings, and a single diamond solitaire pendant around her proud neck.

To the gasping onlookers, it was as though she had stepped off the screen in *By Desire Obsessed*—a film she had made in the early fifties with Joel McCrea and Farley Granger—in which she had worn an almost identical ensemble. In fact, the most striking and noticeable change from the image one had of her in that film was that the memory was in black-and-white and the reality in color. In the lady herself, there appeared to have been little alteration, although some thirty years had undeniably come and gone.

She was perhaps a little thinner now, that was all, but then it was no longer the fashion to be frankly voluptuous.

Merle, in an oversized straw hat to protect her delicate complexion and an ankle-length black skirt over her black maillot, which served to protect (and conceal) the rippling white flesh of her thighs, smiled gaily. Inside, however, she nearly choked with envy: She knew for a fact the woman was at least ten years older than she was!

Sinclair, who had hitherto seemed miserable and out of place in the hot August sun, dressed as he was in a checked wool sport jacket with a silk ascot around his throat despite the broiling heat, brightened noticeably at the sight of the movie star. Casting her as Mildred in *Of Human Bondage* some seven years ago had been one of the brightest coups of his career.

Naturally he had been ridiculed for casting a woman in her—to be charitable—late forties as the young cockney waitress who seduces a medical student and leads him to his doom. Furthermore, even Leonora's greatest admirers had never accused her of being much of an actress, and in her long career she had never before set foot on a stage—except perhaps at an Oscar presentation ceremony. Val de Lisle had quit the show, obstensibly with a bleeding ulcer, and so Sinclair had his way.

Sheldrake's movie career might be over—"they just weren't making her kind of film anymore"—but her name was known in virtually every household in America, so the publicity attending her stage debut would be immense. There were legions of people, complacent suburbanites now, who years ago had thrilled to her in darkened cinemas in small towns all over the country. Now some of her films had achieved a kind of cult status. It didn't matter how awful she might be as Mildred—they would pay to see her in the flesh.

Pay they did, and—if the truth be told—in the end, Leonora Sheldrake was not that bad. Of course, she was not Maugham's Mildred. She was neither a young girl nor a cockney. She could not sing, and, although she moved incomparably, she was not really a dancer. But, somehow, when she stood on that stage, people felt they were getting their money's worth, and when the curtain fell every night for eighteen months, her loving public rewarded her with at least half a dozen curtain calls. Eventually her professionalism had even earned her the respect of her co-workers.

"Darling!" exclaimed Merle. "You look ravishing, as always. Where's Rod?" Merle's features assumed an expression of grave concern. "I do hope there's nothing wrong between you."

"Not at all. Never happier. How's Arthur Eckstein," smiled the star, adjusting her chair so that the harsh sunlight would not catch her at a bad angle. "Rod is just itching to begin work on this *Moonshadows* of yours, Martin! I wish I were five years younger. I would have simply adored to play Isabel."

"Five! Hah!" murmured Merle inaudibly under her breath.

"I thought Ward was coming along with you," said Martin. "There are things in the part I want to discuss with him."

"He said he might be along later. Apparently he's taken it into his head to buy a horse, or something, and he's chasing around looking at the creatures."

A waiter made a discreet entrance into the cabana, bearing a huge platter of iced crab legs and a bucket containing chilled Pouilly-Fuissé.

Sinclair is looking in a bad way, reflected Leonora, who had not seen him in some years. His skin color was pasty and ashen; his eyelids puffy; his dark eyes lackluster, the circles beneath them purplish and cavernous. His dark hair looked obviously tinted in the unrelenting glare of the sun, and his wintry attire made him appear, to her eyes, oddly naked and vulnerable. In the pool, a child's voice could be heard calling out to him: "Daddy . . . look! Look at me! I'm diving!" *That German bitch has certainly been putting him through it*, thought Leonora. *Still, what did he expect? A man his age. So what if Ingrid had decided to get a little action on the side? One could hardly blame her.*

"A horse, by God! So your Mr. Ward considers a horse more important than *Moonshadows*, does he? Well, you can tell Roy Rogers that it may interest him to learn that I've fired McAlastair and brought Josh Woodard in on the screenplay. In fact, he's in the hotel here now, and will be joining us later."

"Woodard!" gasped Leonora. "But he's Pandora Ashley's husband. He'll write the thing so that she's the whole center of interest."

"Nonsense. Woodard's a first-class author. He had a tremendous reputation even before he knew his wife. He has a great grip on the book. I'm convinced he'll do a splendid job."

"Yes. Yes, of course, but frankly, you know, Martin, people are surprised that . . . well, a film of this importance, that you haven't entrusted it to a director of . . . well . . . more stature. After all, your own expertise is primarily in the theater and this, this Tony Hill, is it?"

"Anthony Holland."

"Yes . . . well, that's just it. I mean . . . no one's ever heard of him. What's he ever done? Whereas you take, for instance, George Landau . . ."

Sinclair silenced her by raising her delicate hand to his mouth and brushing it with his lips. "Now, now, Madame Sheldrake, do not confuse me with the seven or eight husbands you have twirled so elegantly around your pretty fingers. *I* control *Moonshadows,* as I have controlled every one of my productions . . . not Josh Woodard . . . not Pandora Ashley . . . not Anthony Holland . . . not George Landau . . . and certainly not that hyperactive stud of yours! We both know, I think, where Mr. Ward's talents lie. I should advise you to tell your young man not to get above himself. Do I make myself clear, Leonora?"

Leonora flashed a dazzling smile and squeezed the producer's hand affectionately. "Perfectly, darling. Only you mustn't blame poor Rod. I'm afraid it's only silly me. You know how fond I am of George, and how anxious I am for Rod to prove himself. I, of all people, know how wonderful your judgment is. You will forgive me!"

Martin did so readily. He knew better than to do battle with Leonora Sheldrake with anything less than full armor. The woman was lethal, but, by God, as a fellow killer, he admired her style. "Besides," continued the producer, with something of a sneer, "don't be too hard on Tony Holland. You might just find him to your liking, after all. The ladies consider him quite a dish, I believe."

It was a coup! There was simply no question about it. True, a lot of ground rules had been laid, and a lot of preconditions met, but the bottom line was a half-hour exclusive interview by Barbara Walters with the legendary and reclusive Martin Sinclair for *20/20,* taped in the intimate surroundings of his personal suite at the Beverly Hills Hotel. A small coup, perhaps, for a lady who had gazed penetratingly into the eyes of the Shah of Iran and Prince Charles—to say nothing of Burt Reynolds and Sally Fields—but even the anchorwoman herself was pleasantly surprised by Sinclair's urbane acquiescence to her request for an interview on the eve of his first venture into film production. Moreover, Ms. Walters knew for a fact that he had repeatedly turned down *60 Minutes*.

The Broadway producer's relations with the press over the years had been only marginally less hostile than Frank Sinatra's, and his feuds with newspaper people in general, and critics in particular, had been spectacularly acrimonious. In fact, Sinclair's own personal relations with Barbara Walters had lately been somewhat frosty after he learned that she had lunched socially at Grenouille in the company of the latest ex-Mrs. Sinclair, Ingrid, and an ex-Mrs. Mark Goodson. This little incident had apparently been forgiven, however, for now ABC technicians were threading cables along the Aubusson, and rigging lamps so that the priceless Surrealist collection in the producer's suite would be shown to full advantage on camera. In preparation for his descent upon the film capital in the character of movie mogul, Sinclair had hired a top consultant from the p.r. firm of Rogers and Cowan, at whose instigation the on-camera tete-à-tete with Ms. Walters was about to take place.

Rivers of sweat coursed down Martin Sinclair's face and on to his Turnbull and Asser cravat, as a makeup artist fretted with the cavernous bags under the producer's eyes. Already he cursed himself mentally for agreeing to this circus. Schatzberg, his attorney, had advised him it might be wise to drum up some public sympathy in advance of his pending child custody fight with Ingrid. Rogers and Cowan had advised him that it would give him "credibility" in the Hollywood community. Ultimately, however, he was forced to admit to himself that the desire for media exposure had been his own, despite his lifelong hatred of the press. On Broadway, his name was legend, looming as large as the productions he had mounted. He would not permit his stature to be dwarfed in this new Hollywood realm of studios run by the corporate executive officers of multi-national conglomerates.

Ms. Walters has been a good choice, he calculated thoughtfully. Too prestigious to be thought of as a mere Hollywood gossipmonger, and less likely to go for the jugular than Mike Wallace or Morley Safer. Sinclair and Barbara had actually known each other for some time. He remembered her from the days when she had been starting out on the *Today* program.

She had aged well, he mused, almost too well. There was certainly more of the beauty about her now than there had been at thirty. Success had blurred the outlines of aggression, softened the edges, "feminized" her. She was wearing a peach wool Bill Blass suit that was just a little too youthful for her, he thought. American women never get these things right, never attain the ultimate polish which comes with dressing appropriately for their age.

She was advancing toward him now, extending a reassuring hand, smiling her ingratiating smile, and, on the whole, he was beginning to feel that the idea for the interview had been a good one, after all.

Barbara Walters adjusted the triple strand of freshwater pearls at her throat, leaned raptly forward on one graceful hand in such a manner that her Buccellati cabochon ruby ring was in frame, pursed her lips in an earnest manner, and lowered her eyelashes to intimate that the holy of holies was about to be penetrated.

"Martin Sinclair! You are known to all of us as a man of the theater. For years we have been hearing the doomsayers tell us that 'Broadway is dead.' Does your move out here show that you agree with them?"

Sinclair reproduced what was calculated to emerge as an affable chuckle, but more resembled a harsh clearing of the throat. He bared his teeth in awkward intimation of a smile. "No, Barbara! I would be the last man in the world to say that the theater is dead . . . or even to attempt to say what *is* theater, for that matter!

"You know, in the seventeenth century, the upper classes used to visit the madhouses . . . Bedlam . . . and watch the ravings and torments of the inmates. It was considered a polite form of entertainment. Now, of course, they've closed down the asylums and let the patients out into the streets, so that form of entertainment is no longer available to us." (Here, he once again attempted his chuckle as a token of jocular amiability.)

". . . Seriously, I think that to be valid, theater, like all art, must essentially be plastic, must move in harmony with . . . no . . . in advance of the times. You see that painting over there, for example . . ."

The B camera moved in for a tight shot of an early Dali canvas of a wasted landscape where rock fragments sprouted female genitalia, and limpid clocks poured frozen time over a bleak eternity.

"Dali, isn't it?" Barbara Walters gushed. "A masterpiece! You really are very close to those paintings, aren't you?"

"Once that painting was not merely, as it is now, a priceless decorative object. It possessed the power to shock! To make man look at himself in a new way. Now no matron in Minneapolis would so much as raise an eyebrow at it . . . it has become what it set out to mock—a venerable institution. In the same way, theater has lost much of its power to move us, to stir us to action, to effect change. Without that electric charge, young people turn away from us. Broadway becomes just another dinosaur—a tourist attraction, like the Spruce Goose or the Queen Mary, and just as obsolete as either."

"And that is why you've decided to abandon the stage for films?"

"No, by no means. You've not seen the last Sinclair smash on Broadway, Barbara! But there are exciting new technologies out there, new tools of showmanship in the film world, and I mean to try my hand at them before I get too old. Theater is where you create it, in the creation of spectacle. I think I know how to do that, and I'm sure that with *Moonshadows* I'm going to do that."

"All the world's a stage!" smiled Ms. Walters.

"On the contrary! As Ken Tynan once observed: 'If all the world's a stage . . . we might as well burn down all the theaters!' I just wish the critics and even the general public would take into account the staggering amount of hard work, really backbreaking work, money, logistical planning, and downright heartache that go into mounting even the smallest production on Broadway nowadays, and the equally staggering amount of talent that can sometimes participate in some of the worst turkeys ever to close on opening night. Even the greatest can make unbelievable mistakes. Hal Prince, for instance, once begged David Merrick to drop the title number from *Hello, Dolly!,* said it would ruin the show!"

Barbara Walters radiated warmth, from the soft honey shade of her flawlessly groomed hair, to the soft peach tones illuminating her flesh in the light from the baby spot, and the deep red glow emanating from the ruby on her delicately arched finger. She was evidently doing a good job of what she was so highly esteemed for—establishing an easy camaraderie with her guest, making him forgetful of the technical apparatus surrounding them, which scrutinized minutely their every gesture, magnified the significance of their every phrase.

Barbara's sibilants became more pronounced as she

lowered her voice to a whisper suggestive of intimacy. The cabochon gleamed brilliantly, as she leaned her chin against her hand for support. "We've spoken till now of your public world, the world of theater! But what of that other world . . . the private world of Martin Sinclair? We've all heard the stories . . . the divorces . . . the litigation. Is Martin Sinclair a happy man, even with . . ." there she made a sweeping gesture to indicate their opulent surroundings . . . "all this?"

Sinclair winced perceptibly. Walters was treading on territory that had been privately agreed to be off-limits. He managed a smile, however, of feigned good humor, replying: "As you know, Barbara, Sophocles believed you could judge no man happy or unhappy until his death. I will not attempt to out-guess Sophocles." His dark eyes narrowed perceptibly beneath their hooded lids, flashing an unmistakable warning.

The interviewer recognized his signal to change direction, but she chose to disregard it, pursuing her line of inquiry. "Still, you have a little daughter, Melissa. How old is she?"

"She will be seven in November."

"Surely, she must give you a great deal of happiness . . ."

Martin's response came in a lethal whisper: "A great deal."

Emboldened, Walters continued, "And you have, I understand, another daughter by a previous marriage . . ."

The question was well beyond Sinclair's limit of permissibility. "I have no other children! You are misinformed," snarled the producer, abandoning any pretext of amiability.

Grave concern and compassion transfused Ms. Walters's carefully made-up features. "But didn't you have a

daughter, Alison, by your first marriage, some fifteen or sixteen years ago?"

"The child was stillborn. I do have a ward by the name
of Alison, a relative of a former wife, whom I look after as a
charitable gesture."

At this point in the 20/20 broadcast, the interview was
to be interrupted by ads for Toyota, Tylenol, the ABC Movie
of the Week, Budweiser, Weight Watchers lasagna, Lavoris
mouthwash, next week's segment of Dynasty, in which
Krystle loses her temper with Alexis, Roman Meal bread,
and Apple computers, following which the remaining fifteen
minutes of Barbara Walters's in-depth, but heart-warming
chat with Martin Sinclair was to be aired.

In its final form, however, the show was aired in the fall
and devoted only a twelve-minute spot to the much-her-
alded interview with the legendary producer, deleting all
reference to the personal life, changes made only after repeated threats of litigation. The balance of the show was
devoted to an exposé of the counterfeiting of Gucci bags and
Cartier wristwatches.

Laura Broadhurst, Sinclair's p.r. rep at Rogers and
Cowan, lunched with Barbara Walters at Le Dôme. Henry
Rogers dined with Roone Aldridge at Chasens. The 20/20
show, as broadcast, won its time segment for ABC, and,
ultimately, although a few feathers were ruffled, the incident
passed with no residue of bitterness on either side.

Leonora Sheldrake, sleek in Zoran white cashmere,
nursed her fourth vodka of the evening in front of the crackling fire which blazed in the white marble hearth, oblivious
to the pounding of the surf which crashed against the pilings
of her Malibu home, the sound partly obscured by the quiet
hum of the central air-conditioning which kept the room a
cool, wintry temperature. On the stereo, a record of an old

lover repeated itself over and over: "Darling, down and down I go/Round and round, I go/In a spin and loving that spin I'm in/Under that old black magic called love."

Many were the phantoms whose faces peered out at Leonora from the flames, lovers in whom she had once kindled insatiable passions and torments of jealousy—tycoons, film producers, racing drivers, crooners, matadors, stars of a bygone era. Forgotten scandals from yellowing fan magazines. All dead now. Ashes.

Leonora laughed bitterly to herself and poured another drink. Some people had even thought she was dead, until her romance with Rod Ward catapulted her once again into the limelight of supermarket check-out notoriety. References to these tabloid headlines had often been the unthinking preface to a request for an autograph when she did go out—which she did less and less now.

She relied increasingly on Brandon, her secretary, to get through the mundane chores of life for her. When she did emerge, it was imperative that she look perfect. Never would she let herself be seen like so many of these so-called "stars" nowadays, wearing a smelly jogging suit and sneakers. She was from the old school. No one would ever catch her looking less than every inch a star.

Now there was the question of this role Martin Sinclair was offering her—a "cameo" in *Moonshadows*. Sinclair had left things open, given her time to think it over. She would, of course, follow Rod Ward to the South of France in any case—a separation of months during filming would be out of the question. The role—no matter how small—might give her the opportunity to be present on the set as a costar in her own right, not merely as a hanger-on. Sinclair's judgment had been good for her in the past. It was he who had convinced her to overcome her lifelong fear of the live theater and led to one of her greatest triumphs in *Of Human Bondage*.

Weeks had passed since Leonora Sheldrake's disturbing session with her personal tarot card diviner in which the great Madame Cassandra had warned her to stay away from the film, and from France, and—the most impossible warning of all—from Rod Ward. With each passing day, the star's inclination to dismiss the psychic's warnings as "nonsensical mumbo jumbo" had increased. Her proximity—because of her relationship with Rod Ward—to the pre-production excitement of an eighteen-million-dollar-film about to go before the cameras had instilled an overpowering urge to the actress to be back on screen again herself. The more she thought about it, the more Sinclair's offer tempted her.

She had taken to calling her agent, Lou Sniderman, two or three times a day to see if there were any offers other than *Moonshadows*. Lou always took her calls immediately. The agent had worshipped Leonora Sheldrake when he was still a kid in the mail room, and she was one lady he always had time for, even when she rang him at home after office hours. Still, now he could only tell her, once again, as he had for years—with the exception of some television guest shots that Leonora had rejected out of hand—that "things are dead." Lou Sniderman urged her in the strongest terms to accept the cameo in *Moonshadows*.

It was a prestigious, big-budget film, just the sort of vehicle in which Leonora could return to the screen with undimmed luster. They were offering good billing—"And with a Special Appearance by . . ." Josh Woodard, the screenwriter, was one of England's leading playwrights. He didn't have to tell her about Martin Sinclair's track record on Broadway! Tony Holland was young, but he had a growing reputation and was becoming "hot as a pistol" in the business.

"Go on . . . Leonora! Take it!" advised Lou Snider-man, almost pleading with her for her own sake. "The part is small, but at least it's glamorous; you know how rare that kind of part is nowadays. She's supposed to be one of the wealthiest women in the world, right? That means clothes, furs, jewelry—the whole *schmeer*. You'll be seen at your best."

"But she's the mother of a girl of twenty!" Leonora responded. "My public won't accept me in that persona."

Being a friend, Lou Sniderman did not remonstrate with Leonora that she was, in reality, the mother of a twenty-two-year-old (by her third marriage to a Brazilian tin magnate with whom she had not been on speaking terms for seven years). Instead, he replied patiently, "So the wom-an's a mother, so what? Who doesn't like mothers? Next thing you'll be telling me there's something wrong with America, baseball, and apple pie! Sweetheart, listen to Lou. Just get back up there on that screen, and their tongues will be hanging out to see more of you!"

"Lou! You are right!" Leonora was already glowing with excitement; her heart was beating fast. All thought of Madame Cassandra vanished from her head. "Call Martin and tell him I'll do it, as a personal favor to him, of course. Just make sure I have complete approval of my wardrobe and all the rest!"

Lou Sniderman let out a sigh of relief. "Don't worry about a thing, Leonora . . . just leave it all to me. You've made the right decision."

Leonora tingled with excitement as she put down the receiver. She *had* made the right decision! She *knew* she had!

At that instant, the glass door to the sundeck rattled horribly, and Leonora let out a startled scream before she recognized the figure of the man who stood pressed against the pane, water streaming down his muscular frame, sand covering his clothing. A gust of wind struck her face, as she slid the panel open to admit her lover, Rod Ward. "My God! Where on earth have you been? What have you been doing? Sinclair was furious that you didn't turn up at lunch today."

"I've been looking at horses. I told you," said the actor as he casually peeled off his wet jeans and shirt and threw them carelessly in a dripping pile on the white carpet. Leonora shuddered involuntarily at the sight of his erection. She was hypnotized by the power of his young body, the golden bronze of his smooth skin, the curling auburn hair above the smooth, firm penis. She approached him, falling eagerly on her knees before the erect sex.

As it was almost within reach of her mouth, Ward pushed her away, saying, "Not now. I'm frozen and starving. Get me a drink, will you?"

When he was curled up in a robe beside her on the white sofa, with a large brandy and a roast beef sandwich on crusty bread, Ward became more affectionate.

"Leonora, darling, I've had an idea. The more I think about this Holland guy directing, the less I like it. This is a complicated part . . . not just the pretty-boy stud shit I've played till now. If I do it right, it will mean people will take me seriously as an actor, at last."

"They will, darling. You're wonderfully talented. All you need is a chance to show it."

"But if I screw up on this, they'll crucify me. I don't know if I can make it on my own, without a director I can rely on, and this English prick is gonna be worse than useless. Do you think if you and I invited George Landau to come along on the picture, you know, as my personal drama coach, you know, as a favor, all-expenses-paid, he might go for it?"

Leonora looked into the eyes of her handsome lover, startled at how brilliantly they reflected the reddish glow of the firelight. He seemed to be like a little boy, lost and frightened.

She ran her diamond-encircled fingers through his thick, wavy hair. "Don't worry," she whispered. "I'll see to it that George comes along. After all, who'd be so stupid as to turn down an all-expenses-paid trip to the Cap d'Antibes? Besides, I'll point out that things have been known to go wrong on many films—directors sometimes have to be replaced—and in the remote event that something terrible like that were to happen on *Moonshadows* . . . God forbid . . ."

"God forbid . . ." repeated Rod with an appreciative smile.

"Well, it certainly couldn't hurt George to be on the scene, as it were."

Only then did Rod Ward fold Leonora Sheldrake in his strong arms and satisfy the stirring hunger inside her body.

George Landau, his mottled, emaciated frame naked save for a tropical shirt of orchids and begonias, which hung loosely over his brief swimming trunks, watched transfixed from behind metallic mirrored sunglasses as his "son," Sean, emerged from the turquoise waters of his mosaic-tiled pool, his body like a straight sharp knife, a Hockney fantasy of masculine perfection come to life.

"What's that you're drinking?" the boy asked, lightly rubbing his golden frame with a Hermès towel with a nautical motif.

"Compari and bitter lemon. Shall I have Chen get you one?"

"Hell, no! It looks like another one of those fucking medicines you're always taking. Let him bring out some Dom Perignon for chrissake!"

The old man summoned a delicate-looking Oriental

houseboy, and the refreshing liquid arrived momentarily in an ornate vermeil ice bucket.

"You got home very late last night," Landau said with feigned nonchalance.

"What do you expect? I'm sick of this bloody tomb of Tutankhamen. I can't spend my whole life cooped up in this mausoleum . . ." Seeing the muscles of Landau's face twitch with irritation, the boy modulated his petulant tone to one of tempting entreaty. "Can't we go away together on a trip someplace? After all, you promised to show me the world . . . I've never even been outside the States."

"An odd coincidence, this sudden wanderlust . . ." mused Landau, taking a sip of the poppy-red liquid and arranging a pyramid of white powder on the glass table at his elbow into narrow lines. "Only an hour ago I had a call from Leonora Sheldrake begging me to fly to the South of France and coach Rod Ward on *Moonshadows.*" He raised a quizzical eyebrow, but Sean betrayed no visible reaction at the mention of his new lover's name.

Landau held a silver straw over the white powder and inhaled deeply. "The Riviera! It's changed of course. They've killed Juan-les-Pins with tawdry discos; Cannes is like a souk; St. Tropez is overrun by gawkers; and that silly Irish bitch turned Monte Carlo into a concrete junkpile condo. Still, if you've never been, it might be a giggle. If it will please you, my boy, we shall go."

It was nearly three o'clock on a smoggy August afternoon when Lawrence J. Rifkind, production chief at the studio, returned to his cavernous office for his meeting with Martin Sinclair. Rifkind had played two sets of tennis during lunch, and as he flopped into an overstuffed leather chair and buzzed his secretary to admit the Broadway producer, he was still tieless and a trickle of shower water ran down the side of his face. The air-conditioning in the dark-paneled suite was turned up so high as to make the room almost polar.

Except for several art department sketches of upcoming studio productions hanging on walls, there was little hint of show business in Rifkind's office. There were no signed photos of the stars who had made the studio great, framed *Variety* headlines, or Oscars adorning the handsome room. Its luxurious anonymity would have been equally well suited to the corporate offices of a manufacturer of baby food or steel-belted radial tires.

Lawrence Rifkind was a comparatively young man who had risen through the ranks of the Morris office, remaining there until the studio had offered him a lucrative position as Vice President of Creative Affairs some three years ago. He had advanced steadily, so that when Sol Hirsch—an older man whose record as production chief had failed to live up to the box-office expectations of the officers of the parent multi-national firm which controlled the studio —Rifkind was the unanimous choice as his successor.

Rifkind had gone for the *Moonshadows* package on the strength of Sinclair's legendary Broadway reputation and the notoriety of the bestseller. The studio was in for about half of what had been budgeted originally as an eighteen-million-dollar picture. Now shooting was scheduled to begin in less than a month in the South of France, and there was still no script. More troubling was the fact that the estimated cost had risen to around twenty-five million dollars. Of course, that amount was no longer a record, certainly, and the book alone had a built-in audience factor.

Still, Rifkind was beginning to get edgy, wondering if he had been wrong in deferring to Sinclair's judgment in going with Pandora Ashley. Sure, she was a star, particularly in Europe, but would she draw at the U.S. box office,

where it really counted? Actresses in general, except maybe
for Jane Fonda or Streisand or some such, didn't mean shit
as a draw. And they could have saved a fortune by building
the "Eden Roc" and shooting the whole thing in Mexico,
but Sinclair had insisted on the "authentic ambience" of the
Riviera.

"Jesus Christ Almighty," Rifkind had wailed, "a
rock's a rock, a tree's a tree . . . shoot it in Griffith Park!"
But the decades-old Hollywood maxim had failed to move
the adamant producer. *Moonshadows* was his. It was a hot
property. He would simply take it to another studio.

Well, at least they should have gone for Fonda or Streep
or somebody big. Rifkind chewed nervously at a manicured
fingernail and poured himself a diet soda as Sinclair, a tow-
ering figure, muffled in enough dark woolen clothing for a
New England winter, entered the room.

Fuck it, thought Rifkind. The old asshole's a legend; he
knows what he's doing.

"When will we have a script from Woodard?" began
Rifkind, after a perfunctory handshake, avoiding any unnecessary preliminaries.

Martin Sinclair held his hands out, palms upwards.
"Two . . . three weeks, maximum. He's already on his
way down to the South of France to write it."

"The South of France, for chrissake! Why can't he
write it here! You got a problem. We can't start with half a
script! You might add locations, drop locations; add speaking parts, drop speaking parts."

"We can't alter the start date." Sinclair was firm and
unruffled. His implacable confidence transmitted itself to
Rifkind. "It was an enormous coup to get the Hôtel du Cap
to allow us to film there for three weeks, and to block off the
pool area for our use only. It is imperative that this be done

in the off-season, but while the summer weather still holds. We go on the twentieth of September, script or no script."

Rifkind appeared satisfied. "There's just one other point, Martin. Now these terrorists—in the book they're P.L.O., right? And the Rod Ward character's an Arab. Now there's no way we're gonna show our heroine fucking Yassar Arafat here. We'll lose the whole New York audience, to say nothing of the Israeli market, so in the movie they'll be just your average A & P terrorists, right? Woodard understands that, I hope?"

Sinclair nodded gravely.

"What we're making here is not, in my eyes, a political film. It's a great romantic adventure with a glamorous international backdrop." Rifkind spoke in a questioning tone.

Sinclair again nodded, then narrowed his bright black eyes so that their hooded gaze was that of a cobra about to strike: "Larry, I've waited for over thirty years to make a picture, for the right property . . . the right moment. *Moonshadows* is that property, and nobody but nobody is going to cut the fucking balls off it! Relax, kid! I know what I'm doing."

Rifkind relaxed and took another sip of Diet Coke. It would be all right. Sinclair knew what he was doing.

13

It had been a hot, smog-filled day at the beginning of July when Lucinda Bayes reached Hollywood. The air on Hollywood Boulevard was heavy and foul. The sun, burning through a slate-colored haze, beat relentlessly on the filthy pavements—the last refuge of the homeless, the degenerate, and the mad. On the steps of Mann's Chinese Theatre, where *Star Trek IV* was playing, a beggar woman squatted, mumbling an unbroken string of obscenities at any and all passersby.

Lucinda, her hair bleached out to a strawberry blond, her mama's pink dress clinging provocatively to her youthful curves, walked stiffly in an effort not to show how afraid she was. Afraid of the strange men who lurked in corners and whispered suggestively as she passed; of the black men in leather jackets with metal studs; of the strange youths with hennaed Mohawks and painted eyes.

She walked, as though with a purpose, past Fredericks of Hollywood and the Pussycat Theater, past at least a dozen bookshops with porn for sale. She looked down at the sidewalk, at the stars with names like Marilyn Monroe and Jean Harlow and Mabel Normand—names she knew and names she only thought she knew. She walked till her feet bled, and all hope died within her.

As night fell, she stood beneath the red neon heart that pulsated over Love's Barbecue and cringed as the white-hot beam of a police helicopter's search light seemed to seize on her in the darkness. Hysterical, she began to run aimlessly. Her flight took her down toward Sunset, and, there, terrified and exhausted, she saw the brick outline of Hollywood High loom up in the darkness. For some reason, it beckoned to her as a place of safety and comfort. She approached it slowly and seated herself on the stairway, much as she had done so many times with her school friends back home, on the steps of Northern High. She rested her elbows on the stone, her fair head dropped forward, and she fell into a dreamless sleep in the shadow of a sign which read "Achieve the Honorable."

She was awakened around three in the morning by the touch of a cold, clammy hand stroking her neck, and the whisper of a low masculine voice in her ear. "Hey! You can't sleep here; you'll get busted."

She looked up into the face of a young man not much older than herself. He wore his hair shaven very close to his head like her dad had in his Marine days, except that this guy's hair was bleached platinum blond. In one ear he wore a diamond stud earring. The other was pierced by an enormous safety pin. Around his white neck were suspended a gilt razor blade and an enormous crucifix. He wore an open sleeveless black leather jacket with a bewildering number of zippers over his bare chest; tight-fitting, leopard-printed jeans seemed pasted to his rake-thin legs. He grinned broadly, displaying a jagged set of yellow teeth. Then he leaned forward and ran a thin finger from Lucinda's throat down to the cleavage of her pink dress.

"Hey! Where'd you get that dress? Oklahoma?" he

laughed. "I think that's what I'm gonna call you—Oklahoma! C'mon, Oklahoma, move your sweet ass. School's out." With that, he gripped her firmly and dragged her to her feet. Tears stood in her eyes. She was too paralyzed with fear to cry out. Sensing this, he touched a cold hand to her flushed cheek. "Shit, Oklahoma, I ain't gonna hurt you none. I just wanna be your friend. You're new here, right?" She nodded assent. "OK, then, you need a friend, right? Let's have a look at you. Shit, you're pretty . . . real pretty. What are you, some kinda model or actress or like that?"

Lucinda nodded again, she even smiled a little and asked his name.

"Name?" laughed the stranger. "I ain't got no name. But you can call me the Angel of Death."

Lucinda's eyes widened in terror. She struggled to pull free of his grasp, only to find that he let her go immediately, laughing at her reaction. "Shit, baby, if you don't like that name, we'll find another. How's Ziggy? Ziggy Stardust the Second."

Zig Two, as Lucinda decided to call her new protector, had a '68 Mustang convertible with a badly slashed top— painted hot-pink—and some kind of soiled fur fabric over the seats that was meant to look like zebra. There was an electric guitar in the back, along with some pointy-toed boots and what appeared to be a pile of underwear.

They drove downtown to Tommy's for greasy burgers, then, as dawn began to break over the smog-laden city, Zig murmured "gotta score" and drove up to a ramshackle house on Olive Street, where the door was opened for him by a rumpled Latin man with an enormous belly and a torn undershirt. Lucinda watched from the car as he and Ziggy haggled over the contents of a small brown paper parcel. She became frightened for a moment when the Latin man appeared to be yelling, but then he calmed down and Ziggy came back to the Mustang grinning. "C'mon, Oklahoma, we're gonna fix you up real pretty!"

It was morning by the time they passed the Golden Age Retirement Home and screeched to a halt in the parking lot of A&D Liquor. "Shops ain't open yet. I'll get us some breakfast." He emerged minutes later with a bottle of tequila, a bag of tortilla chips, and a small box of Morton's salt.

"Bet they never learned you how to drink tequila in Oklahoma, did they? Here, gimme your arm." As a bewildered Lucinda held out her arm, Ziggy poured salt on it, urged her to lick it, then held out the tequila bottle for her to take a swig. This ritual was followed by a handful of tortilla chips. "Good, huh?" the boy grinned, flashing his rotten teeth.

"Beats cornflakes," agreed Lucinda, getting into the spirit of things as Melrose on a Saturday morning began to come to life. Seemingly out of nowhere, there appeared boys and girls her own age sporting an astonishing array of Mohawk hair, rainbow hair, spiky hair, pompadours, pink hair, skinheads, Day-Glo hair, combat boots, motorcycle boots, cowboy boots, pointy boots, bare feet, Hawaiian shirts, Bermuda shorts, mismatched earrings, spiked belts, cartridge belts—every perverse permutation of shock fashion rebellious youth could devise.

"Hot, huh? Bet you never saw shit like this back home."

Lucinda nodded blankly as Ziggy dragged her through a red-doored shop entrance covered in "fuck parents" graffiti. Once inside, he selected an ensemble for her consisting of black fishnet stockings, red pixie boots, a black skirt worn hitched up over them, and a spike-studded leather dog collar with bracelets to match. Zig wanted her to shave the sides of her head too, in a kind of modified Mohawk, but he relented when she burst into tears. He paid cash for the bizarre purchases and made her wear them out of the store. Tillie's ruffled pink dress was flung in the trashcan outside.

"You look real cute now, babe. Of course, you're gonna have to work some now to pay back what you owe me."

Hotel Hell was the name given to a huge building that stood in the heart of Hollywood. Once luxurious, but now decaying and abandoned, it was notorious for the pathetic wretches who called its dank, rat-infested shell home. Many were young people—"children of the night" as one local charity had dubbed them—whose own homes had somehow been so terrifying as to make this nightmarish void, where rapes and stabbings were as much a commonplace as the absence of plumbing and heat, seem a refuge.

Periodically, usually at Thanksgiving or Christmas, some pert newsperson on the local news program would draw attention to the plight of these outcasts. Well-meaning citizens would be called upon to open their hearts with gifts of food or alternative housing, a plea typically answered with a warm response. Still, weeks later, warm bodies were again to be found huddled together on the rank floors of the Hotel Hell. Some were new arrivals, but many simply drifted back.

And it was here, when they weren't cruising Hollywood Boulevard in the hot-pink Mustang, or Cindy wasn't "paying back" her debt to Zig by turning tricks for him up on the strip, that Zig Two would bring Oklahoma in the wee hours of the stale night, and fall asleep in her arms.

Most of the time, however, Lucinda's life with her protector wasn't so bad. He was never really mean to her; he never hit her, or anything. It was only the times when they had no money left—like when he had failed to score on some dope deal, or they had blown it all on booze or coke—

that he would ask her to "get out and do her stuff!" By that, he meant finding some "john" to screw for fifty bucks, usually some fat, married guy from Cincinnati, or someplace. Once she'd got a hundred from some guy from Chicago, who got a real bad attack of guilt afterward when he found out how young she was. It seemed he had a daughter the same age as her just starting college. It almost never was fun, but most of the time it wasn't so bad.

"Remember," Zig would tell her, "you don't have to do anything you don't want to do!" He took fairly good care of her too. He had his system, he said, of telling the sad asses from the "bad asses"—crazies who might try something too kinky or try to carve her up. Plus he was always nearby in case she needed him.

Lucinda really didn't mind turning tricks all that much —she only did it maybe two or three times a week, so it wasn't like she was really whoring, or anything like that, she told herself. All she was doing was just helping the two of them get by. Zig was kind of like a brother to her by now; he never touched her, or anything like that. Most of the time they just hung out on the Strip, checking out the new bands at the New Wave clubs, and smoking dope.

One time, she'd even talked Zig into taking her to Disneyland, a place she'd always dreamed about going to ever since she was a little girl. At first his response had been, "You're out of your friggin' mind! What do you want to go to that marshmallow cream-puff shithole for?" But finally she had talked him into it. They smoked a couple of joints first, and finished a whole quart of tequila—knowing they'd never find any once they got inside—then popped a couple of Quaaludes before they went on the rides. They had a good time too! Zig wound up enjoying it just as much as Lucinda. Space Mountain really freaked him out, and he insisted on going back to the Haunted House twice.

"Far out, man! Really far out!" he kept yelling, grinning with his rotten yellow teeth, as, toward the end of the ride, a luminous Death's head popped up in the funereal black cart between him and Lucinda. Lucinda, however, hated that part and tried to cover her eyes. It reminded her too much of Frank!

Zig Two really had a thing about death, even once driving the pink Mustang out to Death Valley. It was late at night when they got there, and at first Lucinda just froze with fear. There was nothing. Complete nothingness. She had never known the sky could be so black, the moon so cold and unrelenting in its glare. There was no sound. No sign posts. She had the impression that there was even no air, and that they had both stopped breathing. She begged Zig to turn back, but it wasn't any use . . . she could see he was having the time of his life! He started telling her every horrible story he could think of: how the Manson family had camped out not far from where they were right now; how some guy and his wife had kidnapped a girl not far from there and kept her as a sex slave, locking her up in an orange crate at nights. That story made her think of the trailer and Frank, and the blood froze in her veins.

Finally at midnight, they had reached Zabriskie Point. After they had stopped and read some bronze plaque about how this was the lowest place on earth below sea level or something like that, they walked together, hand in hand, on a caked white acrid surface that shone in the moonlight. It was unlike any soil she had ever known, and she had to admit it was beautiful. The moon was huge, encircled by a luminous oval ring. It seemed close enough to touch, Lucinda thought. The stars were pieced out so clearly on the black velvet sky that long-forgotten names of constellations that she had learned in school came back to mind.

"Look!" she cried out excitedly, proud to be able to

show Zig something. "Orion! . . . and the Big Dipper!" She drew him to her and kissed him on the mouth. "Thank you for bringing me here. I've never been any place this beautiful!"

Zig drew back from her embrace. He had already told her there couldn't be any of "that" between them.

That night they slept at a clean and nice place called the Furnace Creek Ranch. In the morning they bought a big bag of fresh dates for breakfast at the general store there, and headed for some place Zig had heard about called Scotty's Castle. On the way, Lucinda Bayes gaped with wonder as the pink Mustang sped across a desolate lunar landscape pitted with craters; past sand dunes on which one almost expected an Arab caravan of camels to appear; past paintbox-colored cliffs of rock striated pink and orange and purple. They drove for hours, never once passing another car. Never even seeing another soul. Lucinda Bayes felt the best she had in her whole life . . . clean and free and alone!

Scotty's Castle turned out to be a screwball mansion some wealthy and eccentric miner had erected over a hundred years ago on the edge of nowhere. The guy had gone broke and disappeared, leaving behind a baroque gilt organ from Germany and piles of Victorian furniture, leaving it to rot in the middle of the most godforsaken desert in the country. Zig and Lucinda loved the place, and wished together that they could just move in and live the rest of their lives right there. But it wasn't perfect, however; it was all fixed up like a tourist attraction, complete with a snack bar and a number of other tacky attachments.

"You see, babe, I told you," said Zig Two. "In this friggin' country you don't have to go to Disneyland. It comes to you."

They ate in silence, then drove back across the desert toward L.A.

* * *

"M.X. . . . M.X. just want that rocker sex/M.X. M.X. just want that missile sex/Rock it. Rocket. You're gonna miss my love/Miss, I'll miss . . . I'll miss your sex/ M.X. M.X. . . . M.X. Sex . . ."

The band wore black jumpsuits with phosphorescent skeletons outlined on them, the kind kids in the suburbs wear on Halloween to go trick or treating.

The lead singer of The Day After—a punk group made up of guys who only a few years earlier were suburban kids —wore, in addition to one of these Halloween skeleton jump suits, white pancake makeup and electric-green streaked hair. He let out a wild whoop, thrusting his tongue out obscenely from his lipsticked mouth, and goading his young audience at the Club Lingerie on Sunset Strip into shrieks of ecstatic approval.

As the band appeared to leave the stage, Zig Two grabbed Lucinda by the arm and led her toward the backstage area. "C'mon," he said. "The drummer's a friend of mine."

Backstage, Zig and the drummer retreated to a corner where they gestured animatedly, and Zig finally received some money in exchange for a small paper bag. While the transaction was taking place, the lead singer spotted Lucinda standing in the doorway alone, wearing black. He watched her in the reflection of the brightly lit mirror as he swept streaks of grease paint from his young face. He was surprised that she seemed so quiet, that she made no effort to get to know him or any of the other members of the band. She was definitely unlike the pretty girls who usually came backstage, all eager to bed down with any of the boys who chose to give them a tumble.

"Hey, you," he called out to her, "Whatsa matter, didn't ya like the show?"

He had a funny voice, Lucinda thought, the kind she'd never heard before except on television. It sounded English or Australian, or something.

"Me? You speaking to me? I loved it . . . I mean, it was real great."

"So what are you standing over there for?"

Lucinda approached the mirrored dressing table and let the boy, whose name turned out to be Nick, hug her.

"That's better!" he whispered, running his hands slowly over her boobs, making imaginary circles around her nipples with his bony fingers. "What's your name?"

"They call me Oklahoma."

" 'Oklahoma, where the wind goes sweeping down the plain . . .' " sang Nick gleefully in a falsetto cockney voice. "I love it! Hey, you and me are splitting . . . OK? We're going to a party, OK?"

Lucinda nodded approval.

"Great!" said Nick as he grabbed her hand and led her out into the night, singing, " 'We're doin' fine, Oklahoma/ Oklahoma, OK!' "

They drove to what seemed to be a pink palace bathed in light. Its cuppolas were halos of blue. At its entrance was a vast red carpet. Ladies in mink stared disapprovingly at the young couple as they crossed the elegant lobby with its cozy fire crackling in an August hearth, and a snotty young clerk with a mincing voice called out, "Can I help you?" in a tone which indicated that nothing could be further from his intention. But Nick replied, "Bungalow 9, they're expecting us!" and headed toward a sign in green scroll that read POLO LOUNGE, then made a right through the door that led them outside again into a wondrous perfumed garden of oleander and hibiscus. The desk clerk at the Beverly Hills Hotel shrugged contemptuously. Rock stars! he thought. You never know who they'll drag in next.

Lucinda immediately liked the guy who opened the door of bungalow 9. He was small and well muscled and wore his dark hair curly and long. He could have been any age from eighteen to forty-five, and it turned out he was a rock star—not one you'd recognize right away like Bowie or Rod Stewart, but he really had played in some famous bands, heavy metal mostly, and Nick said he was worth a bundle. He had two houses in Hawaii—one on Diamond Head and one on Kaui—a Learjet, two smaller planes, a castle in Ireland, an island off Bali, and a string of Arabian horses. Plus, according to Nick, he was "a neat guy."

His name was Robby, and he wore no shirt, just jeans with a big, silver Navajo belt studded with turquoise; in his right hand he carried a bottle of '71 Château Latour from which he took periodic gulps as if it were a can of Coors. He handed the bottle to Nick, who took a couple of swigs and passed it on to Lucinda.

"Stuff costs one hundred seventy-five dollars a bottle. I got four cases, and they're sendin' over some more, so help yourself . . ." said the rock star as he flashed Cindy a white-toothed smile, then rejoined the crowd in the living room. Cindy gaped openly as they inched their way through an extremely heterogenous group of people, all of whom in one way or another seemed to be orbiting around Robby and competing for his attention.

There was a big guy weighing at least four hundred pounds in a leather jacket that said Hell's Angels. There were some guys swathed in what looked like bandages from head to toe, with tall white turbans on their heads. Some black dudes with dreadlocks stood in a corner passing around reefers, which filled the warm air with their rich, potent scent. And there were girls, lots of them, most of them pretty, all trying in one way or another to catch Robby's eye.

Nick and Cindy finally worked their way close enough to him to discover that he was engaged in some kind of discussion about karma or rebirth, or something, with one of the turbaned guys who had a beard and was nodding his head in appreciation. But there was too much noise for Lucinda to catch most of the conversation, or to tell if it made any kind of sense. Some girl wearing a long, pink Indianlike robe and lots of black eyeliner grabbed Nick by the arm and whispered something to him. He followed her into another room—a bedroom, Cindy guessed—and she was left on her own.

A skinny girl with a sharp nose introduced herself as Dahlia and started talking about how she worked in an obscene cake bakery but studied belly dancing in the evenings. She had also found total inner peace with this older guy who called himself "the Seer," who had been to Tibet and knew more about the meaning of life than Maharishi or Rajneesh, or any of those guys. She seemed to get really worked up about it. She said she'd been reborn, and everything, and promised to introduce Lucinda to the Seer. When she talked about rebirth, her nose got red and her eyes seemed watery. Cindy wandered away though because a muscle-bound guy, like a weight lifter, came over and said the skinny girl was full of shit, and Jesus was the answer; and Lucinda didn't want to get involved in the discussion.

She tried to get back to where Robby was standing, but the crowd jostled her into another room, where a black man was fucking a white girl, and some people were standing around snorting coke. She started thinking about Zig Two and how she'd been crazy to leave him because now she had nowhere to go. Suddenly panic-stricken, she made her way through room after crowded room of the sprawling bungalow until she came upon a huge bedroom, one that was almost empty. The only people there were a girl, who was lying face-down on the floor, and Robby, who knelt over her, not fucking her or anything, rather just giving her some kind of massage. He looked up when he saw her come in, and said, "Oh, good. I'm glad it's you. You're next."

Lucinda watched the brown muscles of the rock star's arms quiver as he gently eased the tension from the girl's shoulders. She waited for what seemed like an eternity till he sent the other girl away and motioned her to his side. He stroked her hair gently and asked her name. He had a warm, low voice, rich and kind. Lucinda was glad she had come after all. She liked Robby a lot.

"You don't know who the fuck I am, do you, Lucinda?" asked the rock star, grabbing another bottle of vintage wine from the dresser and opening it with his sinewy hands.

She nodded gravely.

"But you like me anyway, don't ya? That's far out. I'm gonna tell you something about me, Lucinda. I ain't never fucked a man, and I ain't never been a pimp. Everything else, I've done. You get me . . . everything." He held out to her a glass of the blood-red wine. She saw the needle tracks deep in his sunburnt flesh.

"That don't matter," said Lucinda. "I've done some bad things too, but you're a good person. I can tell."

"You and me . . . we're old souls, baby. We've passed this way before . . ."

Robby made love to her with devouring fervor, sinking his sharp teeth into her shoulders, biting the nipples of her rich, abundant breasts, his lean, compact body bathed in sweat. At last, as she lay beneath him, trembling with pleasure, he murmured in a hoarse whisper, "You know me now. We met in another life. Your name then was Mary Magdalen."

When morning came, the air of bungalow 9 was stale

with the fumes of last night's pot, cigarettes, and wine. Room service had brought bacon and eggs and coffee into the dining room, and a bleary-eyed and bedraggled Lucinda dressed and wandered in to find Robby seated at the breakfast table with his business manager and the most beautiful girl Lucinda had ever seen, an ice-cream blonde in skintight, white leather trousers and an angora sweater, who surveyed Lucinda's smeared makeup and shabby black dress with an almost palpable derision.

"Oh, hey, Matty, Suzanne, this is Lucinda . . . I'm thinking about taking her along with us to Hawaii."

Matty, a three-hundred-pound young man with an impeccably-groomed black beard and his own weight in gold chains around his bull-like neck, gaped at Robby in open incredulity, as if to say: "You gotta be joking."

Suzanne merely laughed quietly, as she delicately buttered an English muffin and slipped a morsel between her rosebud lips.

"No, listen, you guys, I'm serious. She's got something. C'mon, Matty, don't you think she looks like a young Jackie Bisset, around the eyes, I mean?"

This comparison provoked such an outburst of mirth in Suzanne that the young beauty nearly choked on her muffin.

Matty drew his burly arm around Robby's shoulder and began to whisper earnestly in his ear. Lucinda's lover first frowned, then looked at her appraisingly, then laughed aloud. When Matty joined the laughter, she knew it was all over for her.

When Matty stuffed a hundred dollar bill down the front of her dress, however, and began marching her toward the door of the bungalow, she drew the money out, crumpled it into a ball, and hurled it straight at the breakfast table, where Suzanne continued to butter muffins languidly. The crumpled bill hit the young beauty squarely in the eye.

"You think I'm dirt, don't you? Well, you can shove your fucking money! I don't need it! I'll show you mother-fuckers who's dirt around here!"

She ran, sobbing hysterically, from the bungalow, her tears running in black-mascaraed rivulets down her young face. She must have been out of her mind, she reflected, once she had stopped for breath, ever to have thrown away that much money! Hell, she had never even held a hundred-dollar bill in her hands before, much less thrown one away! Fuck it, though. Robby had been the first guy she had ever made it with whom she had really liked—and he had liked her too, she knew it. That is, he had liked her until those smartass motherfuckers had opened their goddam mouths. She didn't want him to think that she was just another cheap little tramp, not after he had talked about taking her to Hawaii. She would make it to Hawaii yet!

She would show them! Hadn't she come a long way already from that cramped, dingy trailer where she froze her butt in winter, and sweated to death in summer; where she went to bed without saying "good night" and got up with-out saying "good morning"; away from the Christmases without toys; from a monotonous silence broken only by the hum of the TV or the shouts of her parents' quarreling; from the laughter of the other children because she never had any decent clothes to wear; from the times she went to bed hun-gry because Frank had spent every cent there was on booze. Yes, Lucinda Bayes had come a long way already, and she wasn't going back—no matter what it took.

Merle Greene was in an upbeat mood as she descended the winding path to the Beverly Hills pool. Melissa had been taken to Disneyland for the day. Sinclair would be at the studio until early evening. She would have cabana 5 all to herself for the rest of the day—small vacation, but the first she had had in years. For that reason, she had risen early, breakfasted at the coffee shop counter, and would arrive at the pool entrance within a few minutes of its ten-o'clock opening. In fact, she saw to her dismay that the white entrance gates were still shut. As she began to pace impatiently, she also noticed what appeared to be a black bundle of used clothing lying on the grassy knoll overlooking the pathway.

"How shocking," she thought. She simply could not believe such shabby maintenance in a hotel of this caliber. She would point out the disgrace to Sven immediately. Then an odd thing happened. The bundle began to stir, developing a head of blond hair in the process. Merle, curious, decided to approach and investigate. The bundle turned out to be a girl in her late teens with torn black stockings, runny mascara, and a pretty face blotchy and puffed with weeping. Merle delved into her Gucci beach bag for Kleenex, and helped the girl dry her eyes. She said that her name was Oklahoma and that she had nowhere to go.

Merle was very gentle and comforting, patting the girl's head, and helping her to wipe the streaked makeup from her cheeks. Lucinda thought the lady had the loveliest voice she had ever heard, and that she must be the wife of some very rich man.

"Come along with me," Merle said suddenly, a glint of determination in her gray cat eyes.

"Where are we going?" cried Oklahoma, *née* Lucinda Bayes, still choking back sobs.

"To my room. We're going to clean you up and get you something decent to wear, and then . . . we shall see."

Less than half an hour later, Merle Greene was once again descending the path to the swimming pool, this time with Lucinda Bayes by her side. She had lent the girl a two-piece powder-blue swimsuit, which she had gained a little too much weight to wear—but had brought along anyway, just in case—and a long, matching T-shirt to cover it. With last night's makeup scrubbed from her face, the girl looked quite presentable, very pretty, in fact, and Merle was flattered by the way Lucinda seemed to be in awe of her.

Lucinda had been dumbstruck by the beauty of Merle's wardrobe. She had never seen anything so "delicate," the girl had said. When Lucinda learned that she was the personal friend of a Broadway producer, her attitude was positively worshipful. Merle found it uniquely satisfactory that after months and years of fawning on others, she had this girl dancing attendance on her. What was even more appealing, her admiration actually seemed quite genuine.

As Swen arranged yellow towels on the chaise lounges in Sinclair's cabana, and Lucinda pulled the T-shirt over her head, Merle became intensely aware of the gaze of the men at poolside, how their eyes were riveted on her young companion. The girl was built superbly, there was no doubt of that, and Merle Greene was a connoisseur of the female, as well as of the male, form. As her dearest friend, Rosemary Smythe-Hutchison—the first to introduce Merle to the delights of the sapphic persuasion—had once remarked, "Let's face it, darling. You can't always get what you want, but sometimes, if you try real hard, you get what you need!"

The thought of her friend Rosemary brought to her mind another conversation. Her gray cat eyes narrowed to slits, and she began to scrutinize her new companion very closely indeed. The resemblance was not as great as Ingrid's. She did not have the aristocratic cheekbones or the elegant carriage of the head . . . still, the features were regular, and her alabaster skin was a marvel . . . and her youth . . . surely, she was not yet twenty. If her character proved malleable, the girl had definite potential. In fact, she would telephone Rosemary and ask her opinion.

They had remained in the cabana until after lunchtime, and then both had gone for a brief swim. Merle then suggested they shower and go shopping—perhaps even to Rodeo Drive. Merle's gray eyes tracked Lucinda hungrily as the young girl undressed and entered the shower. She watched as the rushing spray of water cascaded down the girl's magnificent body, over her soft, round breasts with their prominent rosy nipples. Within moments, Merle had slipped out of her own clothing, deftly unfastening the hook which held her own brassiere in front, releasing her own heavy breasts. Without a word, she joined the girl in the bath enclosure, and with one movement grasped Lucinda firmly around the waist and enveloped one nipple with her ravenous mouth. Lucinda stiffened at first, but then made no protest, so an emboldened Merle guided her tongue relentlessly into the innermost reaches of the girl's body, stabbing with incredible agility between Lucinda's legs.

Afterward, as the two women lay drained and exhausted by the frenzy of their lovemaking, entwined on the bed, Merle ran her fingers searchingly over the contours of Lucinda Bayes's profile, musing aloud: "I wonder, dear. You say you have nowhere to go, no family, no one?" Merle's sweet voice throbbed with concern as she stroked the girl's silken skin.

"No one."

"Then how would you like me to be your auntie?"

Something in the impish sparkle of Merle's gray eyes when she spoke these words caused Lucinda Bayes to clasp the older woman's white hand and smile a conspiratorial smile.

"Good!" exclaimed Merle, clapping her hands together excitedly like a little girl blowing out the candles on a birthday cake. "In that case, there's someone I'd like you to meet. But first, there are preparations to be made . . ."

Lucinda's heart was pounding with excitement. She had no idea who this woman was who had taken her in hand or what the nature of her plans might be, but she did know that her long journey was, somehow, nearing an end. At last, that door to a new world was opening for her. She would never have to go home now.

For some reason, the Côterie restaurant of the Beverly Hills Hotel, despite extensive redecoration, had never really shared the popularity of the rest of the establishment. It has failed—in a city which is rigidly structured not only in what restaurants it is fashionable to be seen in, but on what nights (Spago on Thursdays, Mr. Chow on Wednesdays, Morton's on Fridays)—to achieve the status of an "in" place.

As a result, the Côterie derived its clientele mostly from hotel guests traveling on their own, or from misguided couples from the Middle West who had never been to L.A. before. It was not that the service was less than impeccable, nor that the food was much different from that served in the Polo Lounge, where it was impossible to get a table at lunchtime, but, somehow, the atmosphere remained stuffy and uncongenial. However, it was here, at one of the few occupied tables in the dining room, that Martin Sinclair, sitting in absolute silence with his little daughter, was to be found every evening of his stay in Los Angeles. And it was to this table that Merle Greene led Lucinda Bayes.

Lucinda had been taken first, of course, to the hotel beauty parlor, where, under Merle's careful supervision, her hair had been bleached to an even lighter, nearly flaxen shade of blond, then drawn back severely from her forehead. In the fashionable shop upstairs, Linda Lee, Merle had selected and charged to Martin Sinclair's account a white linen Krizia ensemble with a high neckline, accompanied by a single strand of pearls. When Lucinda emerged from the dressing room the effect was startling. The outfit gave the girl a poise and sophistication far beyond her years.

"Martin," Merle said, addressing the grim-faced old man at the table, "I want you to meet my niece, Lucinda. Lucinda has been dying to meet you for the longest time!"

During the course of the dinner which followed, scarcely a word was exchanged (and much of what was said was baby talk addressed by Merle to little Melissa, telling her to finish her carrots). Merle Greene observed Martin Sinclair closely. As she had anticipated, the old man's hooded eyes barely strayed from Lucinda Bayes all evening. The girl played her part well. Acting on Merle's instructions, she spoke little and then only in a low voice, repeating several acute observations—taught to her by her protectress —about the current Broadway season.

On the following morning, Merle made two moves. The first was to place a telephone call to her longtime beau, Arthur Eckstein, who had stayed in New York but remained, nevertheless, a silent partner (as he had been on almost every Martin Sinclair production for twenty years) on the *Moonshadows* project.

"Sweetheart!" cooed Merle. "Oh, I miss you so much! Darling, you remember my niece, Lucinda, don't you?"

"Niece! You're an only child! I wasn't aware you had a niece!" responded Eckstein grumpily. He didn't know what the hell this was about, but he knew Merle, and it was bound to cost him money.

"Well, technically speaking, she's not my niece, of course; she's David's, my ex-husband's niece, but we've always been very close—more like sisters, actually."

"Well what does this niece and/or sister of yours want?"

Merle giggled. "Oh, sweetheart, you're such fun!

Lucinda's a very talented girl—you remember I told you she was majoring in theater arts at NYU?—well, she's done wonderfully well there, and I thought she'd be perfect for the part of Daphne, Leonora Sheldrake's daughter, in *Moonshadows*. It's a small part, and almost any pretty girl of twenty could handle it, so why not my niece? I thought you could ask Martin for me."

Eckstein relaxed somewhat. At least it wasn't going to cost money, but still he smelled a rat. He certainly didn't remember a thing about any niece at NYU. "Why don't you ask him yourself? He's right there with you."

"Oh, sweetheart. You know what a misanthrope he is. Besides, if I ask, he'll say no just to spite me!"

"It's not much of a part, you say."

"Just two or three lines. The rest is mostly screaming. Honestly, anyone could do it."

"All right. I'll speak to Martin and tell him I've promised to cast her as a favor to you. There won't be any trouble about it."

"Oh, thank you, sweetheart." Merle let a suggestive whisper come into her rich voice: "You know, I really miss you. It's been too long."

Eckstein softened. "I miss you too. I'll fly down and join you in the South of France as soon as I can get away."

Merle's second move was to take Lucinda Bayes with her to a lawyer's office on Wilshire Boulevard and draw up a sort of contract between them.

"The main thing to remember about Martin Sinclair," said Merle Greene to her lovely young protegée, after the documents had been signed, "is that, despite his cynicism, even his cruelty, at heart he remains a true romantic. I don't mean 'romantic' in the sense people use it nowadays for anyone who buys a box of chocolates or fucks the same girl twice. . . . I mean a man of dark, turbulent passions. A 'true romantic.' "

The document signed by Lucinda Bayes in the attorney's office was a very curious one indeed, considering the young girl's penniless state. It was a promissory note in the amount of one hundred thousand dollars, which she undertook to pay Merle Greene exactly one year from the date of signature in return for what were described as "managerial services." Lucinda had signed without a moment's hesitation, as readily as if she had been signing away her rights to the Brooklyn Bridge. After all, she had nothing, so how could anyone take anything from her, she reasoned. Moreover, to Lucinda, her new lover-aunt was the personification of elegance and refinement, a charmed inhabitant of a world the girl had scarcely known existed, much less dreamed of belonging to. She would never have dreamed of going against her wishes. Submitting to Merle, while not exactly her preferred option, was a very small entrance fee to that world.

As for Merle Greene, a trivial incident occurred on the return journey from the attorney's Century City office, which confirmed her instinctive belief that in her mysterious new playmate she had "adopted" the perfect "niece" to further her own ambitions with regard to Martin Sinclair.

Merle and Lucinda had been driving north along Rodeo Drive in the direction of the hotel, when a blue chiffon gown in Giorgio's window caught the older woman's eye. In a buoyant mood, Merle impulsively decided to try the dress on just for fun. After all, who knew? She might shortly be in a position to become a Giorgio's customer once again. She swung the car into an abrupt U-turn, drawing up at the curb directly in front of the exclusive boutique, only to find the helmeted head of an L.A.P.D. motorcycle officer thrust itself into the car's window and demand to see her I.D.

The incident passed lightly. In her most cooing voice Merle had managed to convince the officer that she was a visitor from the East accompanying the famous producer, Martin Sinclair, and she had had no idea U-turns were illegal in L.A. The policeman had decided to let her off with a warning, neglecting as he did so to notice something Merle's gray cat eyes had not failed to observe. The young girl beside her in the passenger seat had turned as white as a ghost at the sight of the police motorcycle. Her forehead was bathed in perspiration; her limbs trembled violently.

So, thought Merle Greene, watching as the speck of the officer's motorbike disappeared along Wilshire, our little friend has a secret, has she? So much the better.

As her hand brushed lightly across Lucinda's lap, Merle Greene's smile drew imperceptibly upward at the left corner of the mouth. Merle Greene knew herself to be a woman from whom one would have great difficulty in keeping a secret.

14

Angela Armstrong was getting pissed off! It seemed that, like a jet approaching JFK, her career was always going into a "holding pattern" for some damn reason or another. Although she had lost the Emmy to Ann-Margaret, she was still getting plenty of good offers for television work. She was still unable, however, to manage the all-important transition to the "big screen." Sheinberg kept stalling, saying he was looking for the "right vehicle."

Increasingly, Angela Armstrong began to worry that her liaison with Sheinberg (whose reputation was that of a shrewd hustler, not a person by any means within the first rank of the industry) was lowering her prestige. They were never on the "A" list for parties (Marci Sheinberg was, having remarried a prominent entertainment attorney. In fact, in some Hollywood circles, Nat and Angela were considered barely a notch above Pia Zadora and Menashulem Riklis!

And there was another problem. That "Oreo" porn flick she had made in the days with Gino had resurfaced, causing her further anguish. Many scurrilous jokes at her expense were circulating around town, all of them dutifully reported back to her by her dearest friends.

Her new nickname, it seemed, was Angela Almost—

always *almost* a star! She decided she would show them, just as she had shown Ken's relatives and friends back in Tulsa! She was only beginning her climb to stardom. She told Sheinberg she "needed more space," and insisted he move out of the Wilshire condo he had shared with her since moving out on Marci (despite the fact that he had been making Angela's mortgage payments). The forlorn little man moved back into the Beverly Wilshire and changed psychiatrists. "They could still be friends," Angela assured him, and, indeed, their affair did continue on a fairly regular basis, for Angela was still uncertain of what her next move might be. She decided, for once, to be mindful of her mother's favorite proverb, "Don't throw out dirty water until you've found clean!"

And finally Angela Armstrong got her inspiration. It came while watching *Entertainment Tonight,* followed by Dan Rather on the nightly news. *E.T.* had a piece about Stephanie Powers and the Celebrity Polo Tournament she organized annually at the Griffith Park Equestrian Center in aid of the William Holden Wildlife Preservation Fund. At first, Angela's reaction had been merely one of envy and frustration, since she had not been one of the celebrities invited to participate in the parade of show horses prior to the polo match. *She* could ride a horse! She had ridden as a little girl in Tulsa! What made that damn Stephanie Powers think she was so superior? And Pamela Sue Martin (the other female player on the polo team) couldn't ride to save her life!

These and similar reflections were still simmering in Angela Armstrong's brain when the *CBS Evening News* began. The preoccupied actress glanced up to find that the images on the screen had shifted from those of the "Beautiful People at play on horseback," to the latest footage of hideous starvation in famine-plagued Ethiopia. Angela was about to flick the dial, feeling that her sensitivity would make it unbearable for her to watch these scenes of suffering. "Besides," she reasoned, "what good did it do to worry about it? There was nothing you could do; people had been starving somewhere since the world began." Moments before her long red fingernail hit the remote-control button, however, a light went on in Angela's brain. She could ride. She could learn to play polo—as well as Pamela Sue Martin, anyway—in, at most, a couple of weeks. That was it! She would beat Stephanie Powers at her own game by holding her own polo tournament! The Angela Armstrong Aid to Ethiopia Polo Tournament!!

She would invite Hollywood's highest and mightiest to participate. No one, but no one, however inflated their self-esteem, would publicly snub such a worthy cause! The publicity value would be enormous, to say nothing of the social status and respect she would earn herself by publicly becoming a benefactress to starving African children.

But where would she hold the match? That was the question. It couldn't be held at the same place as Stephanie Powers' tournament. Suddenly she had it! Santa Barbara! That was where many of the big stars who were "into" horses had their ranches. Who could tell? Maybe even the President himself or Nancy might attend. She would show them this time!

Of course this would mean that Nat Sheinberg would have to go! The little producer had been (in Angela's estimation) jerking off for a couple of months now with some idea for a re-remake of Rider Haggard's *She* as a vehicle for Angela to be filmed with below-the-line financing in Yugoslavia. Angela had decided that this project wasn't ever going to happen, plus she wasn't so sure it was such a hot idea even if it did. She was tired of just being a sex symbol. After

"Mildred . . . Portrait of a Massage Parlor Hostess," she felt entitled to regard herself as a "serious actress." Besides, Nat Sheinberg was a loser, and coarse. He just wouldn't fit into the exclusive world of polo.

She picked up the phone immediately and rang her old boss, Irving Samuels. He would know all about purchasing horses, and about obtaining the best riding instruction.

Angela duly began her riding lessons. She soon acquired a string of five polo ponies (each of whom knew the game well enough to practically play without a rider), leased a ranch outside Santa Barbara, and tearfully informed Nat Sheinberg that, ". . . although she was still in love with him, she needed more time to be alone in order to find herself as a person, and didn't think they should see each other for a while."

After months of therapy with a new psychiatrist, Nat Sheinberg finally decided he was secretly relieved to be rid of the Amazon Queen. The success of "Mildred . . . Portrait of a Massage Parlor Hostess," had never really paid him back for the initial outlay it had taken to build Angela up in the first place. Her beauty book, as he had predicted, was a fiasco. And demanding!!! Lately she had been starting to make his ex-wife, Marci, look like Rebecca of Sunnybrook Farm!

Nat took a trip to Vegas, won forty thousand dollars in one night at craps, and met and married an Oriental cocktail waitress named Li-Shiu at the Golden Nugget.

It looked as though the Angela Armstrong Aid to Ethiopia Polo Tournament was going to be a rousing success. Not a single invited star (except for those who would be filming on the proposed date of the match) had refused to participate, either on one of the teams or in the celebrity parade to precede the tournament itself. This "parade" would simply consist of stars riding around the arena, dressed according to their individual fancy, on their own horses or on the prize animals of a high-stepping drill team, which had been specially lent for the occasion.

The affair had received wide publicity, for the cause was one that had touched the hearts of millions of Americans. Tickets (which were then still tax-deductible) sold for either one hundred twenty-five dollars (these tickets included a buffet dinner in a tent which had been set up next to the playing field) or fifteen dollars (seating only). In addition, there were T-shirts for sale emblazoned "ANGELA—ETHIOPIA," with a portrait of the star in the center, proceeds, of course, to benefit the hungry.

Moreover, Angela announced that henceforth a percentage (no one was sure exactly how much, but it was rumored to be substantial) of the royalties from her *Angela Armstrong Inner and Outer Awareness Beauty Concept Book* would go toward feeding starving African children. Sales of that book, which had been, to put it mildly, sluggish in an over-saturated marketplace, suddenly shot up, almost making some of the lists.

Everything was going well, but there was one minor hitch: After months of instruction, Angela remained hopeless at the sport of polo. Her experience as a horsewoman had been limited to leisurely trail horses as a child in Tulsa, using a western saddle on a docile horse. In truth, this game of thundering hooves and whirling mallets scared her to death.

Still, in her skintight, white riding breeches and white T-shirt pulled over the famous boobs, with her handmade English riding boots burnished to a sheen, her golden hair flowing from beneath her riding helmet, Angela Armstrong looked fantastic as she posed for photographers, holding

aloft the ornate silver trophy that was to be awarded to the
winning team.

Despite early morning showers, there were blue skies
over Santa Barbara in time for the celebrity parade. The
stands were packed with the social élite of Santa Barbara
and Montecito, as well as Beverly Hills, and—most important—there were throngs of representatives of the press.

Unfortunately, neither President nor Mrs. Reagan was
able to attend, but both Wallis Annenberg and Betsy Bloomingdale (in Carolina Herrerra and Adolfo, respectively),
were in attendance, as was Barbara Sinatra. Unquestionably, Angela's polo party was a social event of the highest
order.

Among those showing off their equestrian skills were
Charleston Heston, Linda Evans (breathtaking in a white
fringed cowgirl outfit on a white Arabian mare), William
Shatner, Lorne Greene, Zsa Zsa Gabor, Tom Selleck . . .
the list was endless!

Excitement mounted as the parade ended and the polo
match itself was about to begin. For the first three chukkers
the onlookers were treated to a fast-moving, if somewhat
less than professional style of play.

Then, suddenly, in the fourth chukker, disaster struck!
Angela had hitherto contributed little to the game. Her well-
trained ponies had galloped gamely after those of her teammates, and she had swung out feebly once or twice with her
mallet in what she had hoped, rather than perceived, to be
the direction of the ball. Still, since the other three players
on her team were stronger than those of her opponents'
(captained by Stacy Keach), the game was fairly evenly
matched, and the score was tied at three goals each.

Then, on a wet and slippery field, as the opposing team
made a determined foray for the goal, Angela Armstrong's
horse, a palomino named Sheba, suddenly wheeled about of

its own accord and began chasing the other ponies. Accidentally, it collided with one of her teammates' horses, and Angela was thrown violently to the ground. Her frightened animal reared up on its hind legs, and it was only by rolling away in the mud that Angela saved herself from probable dire injury.

One of the other players leapt instantly from his saddle and managed to restrain her horse, allowing Angela Armstrong—bespattered, bleeding, her white riding costume covered in mud—to be led, sobbing incoherently, from the field of play. It was said later that her pony, Sheba, must have lamed herself or broken a leg during that accident, or something, for Angela had the animal put to sleep the following day.

Despite her near-disastrous accident on the playing field, Angela's polo match for Ethiopian relief was a huge financial success and greatly enhanced her prestige in the Hollywood community. The quality of her party invitations increased, as did the caliber of the roles she was offered. The polo match also brought Angela a new beau in the person of one Alan Kaufman, a wealthy young entertainment attorney who had worked at Fox under Melnick, and was now, it was said, rapidly rising to become a major power in his new studio. The studio's balance sheet looked poor, however, and rumors were rife that the fate of the current management was riding on the success or failure of just one major production. Kaufman was ideally situated to become the new studio head in the event of any shake up, and, since word was out that the picture was going to be a bomb, betting around town was that such a shake up was imminent. The picture, on which by now many fortunes were riding, was *Moonshadows.*

15

As Josh Woodard and Pandora Ashley stepped off their plane into the bright Nice sunshine, they were blinded momentarily by the flickering lights of dozens of flashbulbs. A throng of reporters and photographers swarmed like bees around the star and her famous husband, thrusting microphones in their faces, all the while shouting unintelligible questions in a mixture of French and garbled English.

A perspiring young publicity person sent by the studio elbowed his way bravely through the throng, holding above his head an enormous bouquet of red roses intended for Pandora. Reaching the besieged couple, he held up his hands imploringly in an attempt to restore some semblance of order. Pandora was ashen with confusion; Josh was livid with anger.

"Now, gentlemen," said the young advance man, shielding the film star, "if you'll just follow me into the lounge, I'm sure Miss Ashley will be gracious enough to answer one or two of your questions." He led Josh and Pandora, followed by the horde of *paparazzi,* into a small lounge on which a long table equipped with several microphones had been set up facing several rows of folding chairs. Pandora only shrugged when her furious husband asked her if she had had any advance warning that there might be a scene like this awaiting them.

"You can ask Miss Ashley your questions now, gentlemen," said the publicity man.

"Would you tell us a little about *Moonshadows*, Miss Ashley? What is the film about, and, also, who is the character you will be portraying?"

"As you know, *Moonshadows* is based on the bestselling book of the same name by Eric Haas. It is a very contemporary story dealing with a terrorist attack, in the course of which the wealthy guests of a luxury hotel are held hostage. I play Isabel, the spoiled wife of a British cabinet minister, who falls in love with the leader of the terrorists and joins their conspiracy."

"How does it feel to be famous, Miss Ashley?"

"Your husband, Mr. Woodard directed you in *Pavlova*, Miss Ashley—will he be directing this film also?"

"No. *Moonshadows* will be directed by an extremely talented young English director, Anthony Holland."

"Miss Ashley, I am sure you will agree that many of the films in the past dealing with terrorist attacks have been bland and unconvincing. Why, in your opinion, will *Moonshadows* be any different?"

Josh Woodard fidgeted angrily. Only Pandora's hand on his thigh prevented him from rising and putting an end to this ridiculous press conference.

"Monsieur, when I like a script enough to agree to act in it, I can only hope that the audience will share my opinion."

"Madame Ashley, there were many rumors that there was a very bad atmosphere during the making of your last film, *Pavlova*. Do you think that *Moonshadows* will be a happier experience?"

Josh Woodard had had enough. He rose quickly to his

feet, dragging Pandora with him. "That will be all, gentle-men! *Ça suffit!*"

Anthony Holland's heart was as light and buoyant as the motion of the Riva St. Tropez speedboat, in which he skimmed across the cobalt waters of the Mediterranean. At his side were Dennis Jaeger, the director of photography on *Moonshadows,* and Willy Howard, the production manager, an old-timer who, in his cups (and that was often enough), could regale all listeners with stories of the tensions between Bogart and Ava Gardner on *The Barefoot Contessa,* of how, as a youngster, he had personally helped to carry a sodden Errol Flynn to work on *The Roots of Heaven,* of Cimino's monomaniacal perfectionism and the giant tree which was taken apart, shipped across the Atlantic, and reassembled like a jigsaw puzzle on *Heaven's Gate.*

Willy had spent over forty years in the business, and, despite the disasters and the life-threatening glamour of it all, it had been an experience he would trade for no other. He was fond of quoting François Truffaut's remark about movie-making, and did so now to Tony Holland: "Shooting a film is exactly like crossing the Old West in a stagecoach. At first you hope to have a good trip. But very soon, you start wondering if you'll ever reach your destination."

A broad smile crossed Tony Holland's face as the sea breeze ruffled his flaxen hair. He clapped Willy on the back, and pointed toward shore. "There . . . there's our opening shot!"

Across the expanse of blue sea, rising from sheer cliffs of rock, the jetty and pavilion of the Eden Roc came into view. Beyond it, one could also make out from this angle the long, broad gravel path leading through a carefully mani-cured grove of trees to the palatial structure of the main building of the Hôtel du Cap d'Antibes.

"This is what César and his terrorists would see as they approach from the sea. From this, we'll pull back so they can see it's the helicopter shot, pinpointing the geography of the restaurant and pool area and its relation to the rest of the hotel and the surrounding area. The audience has got to be made to understand, visually, just how and why the terrorists are able to lay siege to the pavilion and cut it off so successfully from assaults by the police. If they don't grasp that premise, the whole picture falls apart."

"We'll need the Mobius for the aerial work," mumbled Dennis.

"And I want the anamorphic lenses . . ." Holland reminded him.

Willy Howard groaned. "The damn things cost a fortune."

"The look is worth it . . . a tremendous panaromic look. Right, mates, what's next?"

"Yachts," mumbled Willy Howard.

"Yes. Today's the day we find our *Moonshadows*. Which ones are we looking at today, Willy?"

"There's the *Cristalle IV, Anaconda*—I've seen that one already; it's a bit run-down but it's the cheapest—the *Delta Queen*, and, for some screwball reason, we're also looking at Khashoggi's yacht. Sinclair set it up. It beats me why, though. That thing costs more to run per hour than the entire fucking budget of this picture. We're doing that one last, at five o'clock. Let's start with the *Anaconda*, over in Port Gallice and work our way up."

"Agreed," said Tony Holland, taking a deep breath of the salt air over which wafted a slight perfume of eucalyptus. As they approached the harbor, where graceful white boats were heaped like shells upon the beach, Tony's heart leapt with pride and happiness. The film was going to be a tremendous success. He could feel it in his bones.

* * *

Pandora Ashley arrived at the Colombe d'Or in St.-Paul-de-Vence in a foul mood. Josh had been ridiculous and insisted on hiring a dinky little car, a Renault or some such. Not only was this embarrassing, it was also absurd: Since not even half of Pandora's Vuitton cases would fit inside the damn thing, a publicity man had to follow them in a baggage-laden Mercedes through the winding roads of the hills above Cannes. Not even the breathtaking sight of the medieval city rising like a crown from the verdant hillside distracted the actress from her irritable frame of mind. The red roses she still held in her lap were crushed and wilting. The little car was stifling—it wasn't even air-conditioned. And Josh, as usual, was a hopeless driver and had taken the wrong turn twice. She didn't understand why they had to stay in this out-of-the-way place anyway. If Josh wanted to be away from the rest of the company until the screenplay was finished, why couldn't he get away from them at the Hôtel de Paris in Monaco, or the Majestic in Cannes? At least then she could shop along the Croisette.

It was already the first week of September, and this little village in the hills was sure to be dead. That, of course, did not bother Josh. He was in ecstasies throughout the journey, babbling on about the Fondation Maeght and Miro, the ancient medieval city, and the incredible Léger mural in the restaurant of the hotel where they were staying. "The most romantic spot on earth," he called it, taking a hand off the steering wheel to reach out and touch her thigh.

It was all very well, thought Pandora. She was no philistine, certainly; in fact, she had spent rather a lot of money at Sotheby's over the years. But one didn't come to the South of France to look at pictures, and, even if the Colombe d'Or was the most romantic place on earth, her

husband was, at that moment, the last person on earth with
whom she would have chosen to share it.

It was such a bore. If they had been at the Hôtel du
Cap, it would have been child's play to find opportunities to
be alone with Tony while her husband was writing. As it
was, she would be faced with finding pretexts to shuttle back
and forth, up and down the bloody coast in a bloody stinking Renault.

Her mood softened considerably that evening, however.
They had finally arrived in time to dine on a starlit terrace
beside the Léger. The night was alive with the first scent of
autumn on the Provençal breeze. Pandora sipped cham-
pagne-framboise and laughed delightedly at Josh's mischievous stories about Hollywood, especially those involving
Nat Sheinberg and Angela Armstrong. There was an exquisite succession of dishes—steaming *moules marinières,* suc-
culent rack of lamb, a bewildering array of cheeses, gigantic
peaches, and ripe black cherries were brought to their table.
As they lifted their glasses of the slightly sweet local rosé to
toast *Moonshadows* for the twelfth time, unmistakable affection for her husband shone in the actress's emerald eyes.
Later, in their room, where luxury and rustic charm were
blended with the subtlety only the French can achieve, she
was not at all reluctant to respond to his embraces. Besides,
it was foolish to be annoyed. The production company
would surely supply a limo. She'd ring first thing in the
morning.

For the first few days the screenplay went well. Josh
Woodard was a disciplined writer who had built up good
work habits over a lifetime. He was content to sit in his
hotel room hunched over a typewriter, the shades drawn
tight against the warm sunshine of Provence, lest it prove
too distracting, while his beautiful wife lay out by the small

pool in only the bottom half of a minuscule bikini, oiling her shapely breasts and sipping Campari. But with Pandora's mounting boredom, her commandeering of a Mercedes limo with driver from the production company, her more and more frequent forays from St.-Paul-de-Vence, and the ever-increasing lateness of her returns in the evening, Woodard began to lose his momentum on the *Moonshadows* script.

On the fifth day of their stay, Woodard tried to work in the morning and failed, then drank too much with his room-service lunch so that the afternoon was wasted. He could not free himself from the awful suspicion that the pattern of Pandora's infidelities on *Pavlova* was beginning again. But when she returned that night, laden with a shopping basket brimful of his favorite delicacies purchased in an outdoor market—*Reblochon, Chevret, pâté de campagne,* grapes, apricots—he cursed himself for being an imbecile. Still, in the morning she was gone again and he could not, try as he would, rid himself of the horrible premonition that his love was doomed. On the blank page before him was inscribed the indelible image of Pandora in the arms of a faceless stranger, kissing him in her own particular way, arching herself in the act of sex, crying out with wanton abandonment.

"You look exactly like 'stout Cortez when with' . . . something, something . . . he stared upon the . . . something, something . . ." laughed Pandora Ashley.

"Pacific. He stared upon the Pacific. This is the Mediterranean, and I'm not stout!" beamed Tony Holland, his blue eyes radiating happiness.

They stood on the terraced hillside overlooking the Old Beach Hotel and the bay of Monte Carlo. Below them, white skiffs danced dizzily on the blue waves. Behind them, waiters scurried amid a breaking of china as the wind attacked the yellow-parasoled tables of the restaurant, La Vigie. Tony and Pandora embraced and clung together as a sudden gust blew over them. Wind whipped and snapped through the bright parasols. Tablecloths billowed and blew around the chairs like live things, as the late sun glinted on the sea below.

"How happy you are . . ." whispered Pandora with sudden seriousness, scrutinizing the handsome face of her lover as if to pry out the secret of some riddle. "I shall never know such pure happiness."

"But why?" Holland was somber, staring into her emerald eyes. "Surely you have everything a woman could ask for . . . beauty, wealth, fame . . . my love . . ."

"Ah, your love . . . that's something. As for the rest . . . I don't know. Perhaps some people need more to be happy than others. I don't think you know what anguish means." Abruptly her mood changed, shifting like the winds which blew around them. "Come on, let's go for a swim . . . out to that raft down there! I'm wearing a bikini under this."

"You're mad!" laughed Tony. "Can't you see there's a storm coming up? Look, everyone else is leaving the pool." He pointed to the Olympic-size pool of the Monte Carlo Beach Club below them, where the few guests remaining so late in the season were scurrying to pack up their belongings and get back into town before the rain came. "Besides, I'm not so practical as you are . . . I haven't got a suit with me."

"That shop down there will be open. They'll sell you one. I'll wait for you here." Tony saw at once that to resist was futile.

Moments later, they descended the swaying rope ladder which led from the cliffs of La Vigie into the swirling green waters of the sea, and sliced their way through the rough waves to the small wooden raft which bobbed dizzily on the surging waters. Climbing aboard, they fell laughing into each other's arms, and on that tiny wooden platform in the swirling sea, they made passionate love.

"You're right," whispered Tony, peeling away the thin triangle of her bikini, and stroking the silken skin between her thighs, "I am like Cortez. I am discovering a new world."

16

Having agreed to Leonora Sheldrake's suggestion and acceded to Sean's demands for a European holiday, George Landau decided that he might as well "go whole hog," as he phrased it, and do the "Grand Tour" with the boy. He booked his regular suite at Claridges, and organized the rest of the journey through Venice via the Orient Express, then on to Monte Carlo, and, lastly, to the Hôtel du Cap, where the film company, or rather the important luminaries of it would be staying during the filming of *Moonshadows.*

All went extremely well in London. Sean was outfitted like a young prince in the finest Savile Row had to offer. Then he was feasted in what remained of the garish splendor of the Café Royal, where he was regaled by Landau with stories of the ghosts of Oscar Wilde and Bosie who lingered there, ghosts of a bygone day when ways were simpler, when there still was such a thing as a love that "dared not speak its name."

On the train journey, however, George noticed that the eyes of his handsome companion had lost some of their wondrous luster. Beneath his suntan his cheeks were drained of color; he also seemed to be losing weight. He had developed a cough; his whole body and spirit seemed to

have taken on an ashen listlessness. Even that most glorious
of sights, the city of Venice approached via gondola, failed
to stir the beautiful young man. Landau thought he seemed
pale as marble as he leaned back indolently in the dull black
upholstered seat of the boat, his gazellelike eyes closed, their
long dark lashes grazing his cheek.

Matters did not improve during their stay at the Royal
Danieli. Sean seemed absent and in a weakened, neuras-
thenic state, unable to respond to the beauty around him.
Alarmed, Landau decided to cut short their stay and proceed directly to Antibes. Surely sand and sea would restore
the boy. Besides, George had more faith in French physicians than in the Italians—should one prove necessary. For
that matter, the film company could summon his own doctor from the States if Sean did not improve.

In the chauffeured Mercedes which met them at the
railway station in Nice, the boy's spirits seemed to recover
somewhat. During the drive to Antibes he asked George
many questions about the forthcoming production. He
seemed particularly anxious to know whether Leonora Sheldrake and Rod Ward would have arrived as yet.

Rod Ward and Leonora Sheldrake had flown to Milan
en route to Antibes, where they had taken delivery on the
custom red Maserati Quattroporto Leonora had ordered as
a gift for Rod. "It handles like a dream . . . just like you,
babe," enthused the actor, as they drove across the frontier
into France. Leonora wanted to stop over at the Hôtel de
Paris in Monaco for a few days of gambling, since filming
would not begin for a week. But when Rod telephoned
ahead and found that George Landau and Sean had already
checked into the Hôtel du Cap, he insisted on proceeding
directly to Antibes. "After all," he reasoned, "in this thing,
it's only a half-hour's drive to Monte Carlo, so we can go to

the casino anytime. We might as well get settled in first, plus I want to go over my part with George."

Rod had also vetoed Leonora's suggestion that they share a suite, opting instead for connecting rooms. His explanation: The role of César was a challenging one, and he would need "his own space."

Immediately upon checking in, without even pausing to shower, Ward lifted the phone in his hotel room and asked to be connected with Mr. Landau's suite. Upon being told Mr. Landau was at the pool, Ward descended in the elevator, crossed the elegant lobby hung with tapestries, and strode eagerly through the beautifully manicured grove of olive and cedar trees which led down to the Eden Roc pavilion and the pool. At the entrance to the building was a long desk where Rod signed the guest register and obtained towels and a mattress from a pool attendant. To the right was a magnificent restaurant where luncheon was in progress, its windows giving out on an incomparable panorama of the sea below. To the left—and this is the direction Ward now took —was the sundeck and pool area, an oasis of luxury carved out of the jagged rock.

Rod, however, was quite oblivious to the beauty of the scene; his piercing eyes scanned the pool with but one objective. Presently he found George Landau, more deeply tanned than ever, sipping Campari and playing backgammon with a handsome youth of eighteen or thereabouts. The pair were chatting away gaily in Italian, which seemed to be the boy's native tongue.

"Oh, Rod! Good to see you. I had no idea you'd arrived already. This is my friend, Emilio!" As the slim dark boy extended his hand, Rod noticed around his neck a gold intaglio of the god Osiris, identical to Landau's.

"Where's Sean?" he asked, making no effort to disguise the urgency in his voice.

"Oh . . . he's up in the room. There's something the matter with him," Landau said vaguely, as a cloud of distaste passed across his refined face. "He just hasn't been himself since Venice. Frankly, between you and me, it's becoming a bit of a bore."

"Where is he? What room are you in?" demanded Ward.

"My dear boy, there's no need to shout," responded Landau, sliding a black chip across the board. "Room 226." He rolled his tongue in his shriveled cheek. "I've no doubt he'll be delighted to see you."

Rod Ward could not conceal his shock at Sean's appearance when he opened the door of room 226. His lover lay in bed, pale and immobile, his cheeks sunken and hollow, his eyes feverish. Seeing the boy's obvious delight at his arrival, however, the actor tried to affect an air of nonchalance as he approached the bed.

"Hey, pal, what hit you? It doesn't look as if the European climate agrees with you."

"It's nothing. Maybe I've been doing too much coke or something. I just feel kind of wiped out. I'll be better now that you're here though, I promise." The boy reached out his shrunken arm from beneath the sheets and drew his idol on the bed, urgently seeking Ward's lips with his own eager mouth.

Sean's body seemed frail and hot beneath Rod, his lips dry and hard. The boy's need was suddenly terrifying to Rod, more terrifying than Leonora's. They were both using him! Using him to fight off the specter of death! He broke away from the shivering boy, and fled panic-stricken from the room.

17

By a morbid coincidence, Martin Sinclair's Concorde landed at Charles de Gaulle on the very day his first wife was buried in an obscure grave at Père Lachaise, her only mourners Jean-Claude, the waiter (who had paid for the funeral himself, disdaining to ask the great Martin Sinclair for anything further), his niece, Claudine, who had played her little part so bravely, and the good Dr. Le Maire.

If this circumstance was to be an ill omen for the start of his production, Sinclair was blithely oblivious to the fact as he and his entourage—which included Merle Greene, her niece, Lucinda, and his little daughter, Melissa—whisked through customs and boarded their connecting Air France jet to Nice. There seemed to be a subtle alteration in the old man's appearance. He had brightened his dress somewhat with a smart tie and handkerchief, and added a discreet cologne. His hair was more carefully arranged than usual and seemed a trifle darker.

"What a shame we can't stop here for a few days!" sighed Lucinda. "I would love to see Paris!"

"So you shall, my dear," replied the producer, "as soon as filming on *Moonshadows* is completed."

Ironically, it was only on his arrival at the Hôtel du

Cap that Martin learned of Madelaine's death. A telegram
bearing this information awaited him at the reception desk,
having crossed the Atlantic twice before reaching him. Sent
first to his New York office, then on to Beverly Hills, it was
finally forwarded to this hotel. He waited to read it till he
reached his suite, a magnificent series of pastel-hued rooms
overlooking the terra cotta roofs, green cypresses, and turquoise water. The terse words of mortality struck the old
man with the force of a curse.

He remembered the lines of a Keats poem he had used
to court her:

"My Madelaine! Sweet dreamer! Lovely bride!
Say, may I be for aye thy vassal blest?
Thy beauty's shield, heart-shap'd and vermeil dyed?
Ah, silver shrine, here will I take my rest,
After so many hours of toil and quest,
A famish'd pilgrim—saved by miracle."

For a moment he forgot the years which had inter-
vened, remembering his dead wife only as the pale, lovely
girl he had worshipped in the days after he first met her,
before she had given birth to that misshapen monster, who
became for him the physical embodiment of the black defor-
mity he feared within his own soul. For a moment, the mask
of scornful pride fell from his features, and he buried his
face in his hands and wept shamelessly.

High above Central Park, a meeting of the corporate
officers of G.R.W. was in progress. G.R.W. was a multi-
national conglomerate with tentacles spreading into almost
every aspect of American life: soft drinks, laser technology
for nuclear weapons, pantyhose, data processors, communications systems, running shoes, breweries, yogurt, book pub-

lishing, oil drilling, acrylic floor covering, cake mixes—and a motion picture studio, at present headed by Lawrence J. Rifkind, whose balance sheet for the fiscal year was the reason for the meeting.

The balance sheet of the film-making division in question was not a healthy one. During the previous operating year, the first of Rifkind's tenure, the studio had lost 42.6 million dollars after taxes. There had been more than a few miscalculations. *Ecstatic,* a film the studio had rushed out in an attempt to cash in on the *Flashdance* craze, had fallen flat, failing even to recoup its investment. "Too little, too late" had been the general consensus. *The Wind in the Willows,* a lavish, big-budget musical based on the children's classic, died a similar death. "The kids out there want *Rambo XII,* not goddam singing frogs," had proven to be the correct—but sadly unheeded—judgment of one executive.

The Dudley Moore picture was doing fine, and it looked as though they would have another hit on their hands with the Redford picture which would be ready for Christmas release, but the twenty million they had given to that meglomaniac who was married to one of the town's most ravishing sex symbols and insisted on directing her himself was a total write-off—an unreleaseable embarrassment. And what was with this twenty-five-million-dollar budget Rifkin and Sinclair had now come up with on *Moonshadows?* The mood in the board room was palpably grim.

On the day following this meeting, a three-paragraph announcement appeared in both *Variety* and *The Hollywood Reporter,* stating that Lawrence J. Rifkind had resigned from his position as studio head to pursue independent production activities. The parting was said to be "amicable" and was felt to be "mutually beneficial" by all parties. Rifkind's duties would be taken over by Alan Kaufman, at thirty-one the senior vice-president in charge of production and an all-around *wunderkind.*

Anthony Holland, Willy Howard, and Martin Sinclair inspected some half-dozen yachts available for charter before they settled on one to portray *Moonshadows,* the vessel which, in the book, is seized by terrorists when they make their escape. They chose the *Anaconda,* a sleek, trim ninety-foot-plus craft valued at well over a million dollars. It was by no means the grandest of the boats they had inspected, but it would photograph beautifully, and at five thousand dollars a week Sinclair reckoned they'd got a bargain.

Already the call sheet for the first day's shooting had been drawn up. The first scene to be shot would be one in which Lady Isabel Dunsmere (as played by Pandora Ashley) is accused by her husband of infidelity following a party on the yacht. There was only one problem: No actor had as yet been engaged to play Lord Dunsmere. Finney and O'Toole had rejected the part. Sinclair adamantly refused to pay the fee Christopher Plummer's agent was demanding. The part was, admittedly, not a large one, but Sinclair stubbornly insisted on a "name." While reluctant to come up with the kind of money that kind of name entailed. Still, the call sheet was there, and crew members were already painting out the lettering on the elegant craft. The *Anaconda,* out of Panama, was no more. In her place, gleaming in the white light by the green shore, stood the *Moonshadows.*

"We've got to go with Ian Harrison for Dunsmere," said Martin Sinclair to Anthony Holland. They were seated for dinner in the magnificent dining room of the Eden Roc pavilion, the location of choice for much of the action of *Moonshadows.* Stars were showered like confetti against the night sky, while streams of light from the port of Antibes reflected on the rippled water below.

"If only they could capture the magic of this atmosphere on camera," Tony Holland mused as he sipped his Château Margaux. Then, with only a touch of calculation, he allowed his frustration to surface. "Surely not Ian Harrison! Bloody Firefrorefiddle, the Fiend of the Fell, they call him in the West End! You can't be serious!"

"I am dead serious," Sinclair said evenly, and certainly he looked it, with his dark, brooding eyes and tightly compressed lips. "He's already been signed. Why the nickname?"

"From the lyric in *Cats*." Anthony Holland began to sing softly in a rich, pleasant voice:

"Then, if someone will give him a toothful of gin,
He will tell how he once played a part in East
    Lynne . . .
Well, the theatre's certainly not what it was.
These modern productions are all very well,
But there's nothing to equal, from what I hear tell,
    That moment of mystery
    When I made history
As Firefrorefiddle, the Fiend of the Fell."

Holland finished his song with an appropriate flourish, even earning a smile from Sinclair. "Martin, the man's been an alcoholic for years, but he's become a total basket case since his wife left him. I have friends at the Beeb who had to work with him on *Wellington*. They went through hell with him."

"Hell," repeated Sinclair with an odd, bitter laugh, raising his glass to his lips, and staring malevolently at the handsome young man opposite him. "What would you know of hell, Mr. Holland?" The producer's face seemed drained and waxen. In his dark eyes was the unmistakable glint of hatred.

Tony Holland shuddered involuntarily. The man was drunk. He had to be.

"What do you know of the 'lusts of Hell' . . . of damnation, Mr. Holland? The damned have not only torment, but also mockery and shame to bear—a monstrous combination of suffering and derision, unendurable, but to be endured, world without end."

"I'm sorry . . ." Holland felt not only acute pity, but embarrassment and anxiety. He wanted to be with Pandora. He wanted to be anywhere but there.

"Thomas Mann," said Sinclair quietly, in explanation. *"Doctor Faustus."* Seeing the way in which Holland continued to stare at him, he added sarcastically, "Have no fear, Tony, I am not that far gone yet; I can still tell a hawk from a handsaw. You just worry about your camera angles."

Then, lowering his voice so that his words came out in a lethal whisper, "The money clock is ticking. We go with Ian Harrison."

The tension at the table was broken by the sudden appearance of Josh Woodard, approaching them with a thick manuscript under his arm, which, with great ceremony, he deposited in the center of the table. "Hot off the presses, gentlemen! I give you *Moonshadows."*

The three men parted, the director and producer each taking copies of the screenplay, each promising to call Woodard tomorrow.

Martin Sinclair, however, did not wait until morning to call.

Josh Woodard was awakened from his sleep beside Pandora by the insistent ringing of the telephone. Martin Sinclair's angry voice came over the line, not a shout, but a lethal whisper. "You no-good son of a bitch!" he kept repeating. "You've betrayed me."

"Look here," said a shocked Woodard, "I'm afraid I cannot allow you to speak to me in that way. I'm putting the phone down, and I suggest you ring back when and if you are coherent enough to tell me what the problem is."

There was a sharp intake of breath on the other end of the line. "Coherent! That's good coming from you when you've just presented me with one hundred thirty-five pages of incoherent drivel. Where is the suspense? Where is the action? All we have are endless shots of people—principally your wife, by the way—mouthing flowery dialogue!"

"Look, I'll be happy to discuss this with you in the morning . . ."

"You're damned right you'll discuss it with me in the morning, and the two of you had better move over here immediately so that we can try and salvage something from this ungodly mess. I'll see you in my suite at six-thirty sharp!"

The night he first learned of Madelaine's death had begun for Martin Sinclair a pattern of tormented sleeplessness. He lay awake, shivering as though on the edge of an abyss, reliving without end all that he might have been and done. The horror of his wasted life, of his shriveled emotions, swept over him like a storm. He need not have hurt her like that. Loss, sorrow, despair . . . what if this should be the last night of his life? He was aware of a sharp, stabbing pain in his chest.

The road before him could only be a steep, barren descent into bitter and solitary old age. There was nothing but the baseness and viciousness of his desire to exert power over others to drive him forward, to seize power in this corrupt world. And yet it could not be that there was no choice, no road, no hope. He was not like other men. He was Martin Sinclair, a man who had built an empire from nothing with his own hands.

He could begin again. He was not too old. Was this a delusion? Very well. If it were, he would bear the consequences. He closed his eyes finally, his mind embracing a dim feeling of happiness, yet not relieved from a dark foreboding of coming disaster. He dreamed of young lovely girls, with big blue eyes and yellow hair. Their faces were those of Madelaine and Lucinda Bayes.

18

Despite the insignificance of her status on the production, Lucinda Bayes found that she had been booked into her own room at the Hôtel du Cap. She also found a huge bouquet of yellow roses awaiting her on arrival.

Slowly but surely, just as Merle Greene had hoped, the signs of Martin's attraction to her protégée were becoming unmistakable, even though his bearing in her presence remained stiff, even courtly, and he had as yet made no overt move toward her.

Lucinda's own fear of Sinclair diminished considerably when it suddenly dawned on her that this immensely powerful, successful man was himself very much afraid of her . . . of the inherent power with which she was invested, the power of her youth and beauty, the power to scorn or reject him. She found him almost repulsive in a way, yet oddly fascinating as well. A dark cloud of melancholy seemed perpetually to hang over him. Even here in the blazing Riviera sunlight, as he sat muffled in his tweed jacket and Turnbull and Asser cravat, he was still not able to unbend his rigid manner toward Melissa, the scampering child he obviously worshipped.

In Lucinda's mind, the idea of becoming the wife of one

of the world's wealthiest and most influential producers, moved from the impossible to the inevitable. She threw herself wholeheartedly into the role Merle Greene was coaching her to perform, that of Martin's "lost love" returned, his last chance at happiness realized.

There was even a part of the girl that genuinely hungered to win the old man's heart. It would be a means of proving her own worth. After all, never before had she represented anyone's fantasy! Martin Sinclair might be able to give her the closest thing to a father's love she had yet experienced.

As always, the thought of her real father sent an involuntary chill down Lucinda's spine, and she began to worry if she had done the right thing in telling Merle about that horrible night back at the trailer park. Still, she had no choice; there was no way she could have applied for a passport in her own name, and Merle was able to fix things for her. Lucinda took a deep breath, inhaling the delicate scent of the yellow roses blended with the soft sea tang of the Mediterranean air. Surely, it didn't matter, now that she was in France, she reasoned. She was as good as a million miles from the Oregon police! Besides, she was being foolish. She owed everything to Merle Greene!

Lucinda Bayes had known for a long time that the moment would come, had waited for it even, had hoped for it, in a way, ever since that awful evening at dinner when Martin Sinclair had stared at her with his dark eyes, stared at her uninterruptedly until she thought the flesh would sear from her body with the intensity of his gaze. Since that night she had known what would happen, and what her response would be.

Yet these weeks before filming again had been a respite. The old man never approached her, or tried to lay a hand on her, but often she could feel his eyes . . . watching. Watching, watching with the familiar hunger she had known in her father's feral green eyes on the scalding hot day he had torn the silk shirt from her body.

The crisp green sea and cloudless azure horizon darkened for an instant and swam before her eyes in a blood-red haze, tinged scarlet by the memory of the dark blood that had welled from the gash in Frank Bayes's forehead. For a moment she stood immobile, shivering in the hot Antibes sun; then the pall of the painful memory lifted, and Lucinda refocused on the gilded world of luxury surrounding her. The past, she reflected, was, after all, far away. Surely she was safe now. It could never reclaim her.

Merle Greene had instructed Lucinda to wear a modest, white one-piece maillot swimsuit (unlike the skimpy G-strings the other girls were wearing) and to pass Martin Sinclair's chair as often as possible, frequently taking little Melissa by the hand for her poolside stroll.

At first Lucinda had thought the old-fashioned bathing suit ridiculous. She could sense the old man's hooded eyes peeling her flesh bare of every stitch of fabric anyway, but she made no objection. Merle warned her to speak very little if Sinclair should address her (which he never did) and to keep her voice lowered to a breathy whisper. Though she dreaded it, she wished he would go ahead and make his move. This waiting was worse than anything, not knowing for certain that he wanted her, that this new life of hers would last. So what if he was an old guy and not much to look at? She had seen worse up on the Strip turning tricks for Zig, and innocence had always been just one more luxury Lucinda Bayes could never afford.

Although she had known the feel of a man's cock inside her since she was seven, she had never in her life been out on a real date, with dinner or flowers or movies or high school proms—those had always been for the "nice" girls, not for "cheap tramps" like her. She had been called a dirty little tramp so often and so early by Frank, by Tillie, by her snotty classmates up at the High, that it had never really occurred to her that it might be anything but true. Suddenly she laughed out loud. She'd just like that flat-chested cunt Maureen to see her now! But still she waited for Martin Sinclair to make his move.

Finally, late one afternoon, after a day of swimming and basking in the Riviera sun, she returned to her hotel room to find an exquisite, silver lamé evening dress in a Christian Dior package open on the bed. There were also exquisite, silver evening sandals, a beaded silver evening bag, and delicate underthings in dove-gray lace. She also found a note from Sinclair requesting that she join him on the terrace wearing this ensemble for dinner at eight.

When she slipped on the delicate silver lamé Dior, Lucinda Bayes was thrilled to find that it fit her perfectly. The dress, she noticed, although incredibly beautiful and of the loveliest fabric imaginable, seemed in its design to belong to another era, the sort of dress she had seen Grace Kelly or Angie Dickinson wear on *The Late Late Show*. Still, stylish or not, it was sure as hell a knockout on her, no question about that. She surveyed her reflection in the mirror, impulsively adding a heavy choker of jet and crystal beads, which she and Merle had purchased together in Giorgio's before their departure from Beverly Hills. Finally satisfied, she swept down the long corridor that led to Martin Sinclair's suite. It was precisely eight o'clock.

The suite was illuminated only by a myriad of candles, which had been placed in numerous ornate candelabras throughout the opulent room. Everywhere, massive vases of yellow roses diffused their sweet perfume in the soft night air. There was music playing . . . strange, old-fashioned music Lucinda thought it . . . "A Nightingale Sang in Berkeley Square." Sinclair greeted her wordlessly. He wore a burgundy velvet smoking jacket, with a silken ascot knotted carefully around his shriveled neck. His dark eyes seemed to glow with pleasure as they thirstily drank in every detail of Lucinda's appearance, then clouded over with a fierce displeasure as they lighted on the gaudy necklace at her throat. "That's wrong!" he snarled. "All wrong! Take it off at once!" She did as she was told, and the old man's mood mellowed instantly.

An elaborate dinner had already been laid out on a table facing the moonlit sea. Sinclair seemed to lapse into a deep reverie. "Do you remember," he asked in a voice so gentle it surprised her, "how the fireflies in Jamaica used to gather around whenever we were eating? Do you remember those sunsets? You do remember, don't you, Madelaine?"

"I have no hesitation in telling you," said Harry Schatzberg, withdrawing a document from his Mark Cross briefcase and handing it across the table at "21" to his luncheon companion, "that this will definitely be my client's final offer."

Arthur Gershon studied the document carefully for several moments, nervously shoving the food on his plate into geometric patterns as he did so. "A quarter of a million, in return for which she renounces all further claims upon him and leaves his support of the child to his discretion." He shook his head gravely. "You know as well as I do I can't, in any conscience, advise my client to accept this. We'll try the case."

Schatzberg swallowed a mouthful of Dover sole. "Arthur, you haven't got a case. This de Lisle business is a horse that won't run. Confidentially, I'll tell you why my client has decided to be generous . . . he's thinking of remarrying."

19

By five in the morning there were already signs of activity around the berth of the *Anaconda*, aka. *Moonshadows*. Tony Holland wanted to catch the dawn light, feeling that it would be most effective if Lord Dunsmere caught his wife returning from her lover's arms just as light was breaking. Men in blue nylon anoraks moved cables and huge lights on wheeled tripods. Pandora's dresser made last-minute adjustments to the star's costume, a breathtaking creation of emerald-green sequins. A security guard from Van Cleef and Arpels, armed to the teeth, stood by while nearly a million dollars worth of jewelry on loan to the production was placed around Pandora's delicate neck.

"Where's Ian Harrison, for christsake?" cried out Brian Chalmers, the first assistant director.

Grips were laying dolly track, setting up quartz lamps.

Josh Woodard walked over to Pandora, whispered something in her ear, then kissed her tenderly on the back of the neck. *"Merde,"* he whispered.

At that moment a white Corniche convertible, its top down, screeched to a halt by the dock, and a large man in white denims and Porsche sunglasses sauntered toward the yacht, accompanied by a clinging brunette.

"Firefrorefiddle's just made an entrance, stage left," mumbled Brian in Anthony Holland's ear.

"Makes you bloody sick," muttered George O'Shaunessey, the second A.D. "Turning up bloody late, disrupting everything."

"It's a bloody miracle he's here at all. Now we're in for half an hour of bowing and scraping while everyone rushes around greeting his Lordship."

This prediction of Brian's seemed to be not without accuracy, for Martin Sinclair had rushed over to the actor's side and had his arm around his shoulder, chatting amicably.

"We're going to lose the light," whispered Tony to Brian Chalmers. "I want everyone ready for a rehearsal in fifteen minutes."

"Attention, everybody!" called Brian. "Rehearsal on deck in fifteen minutes! Celia, get Ian Harrison made up, for God's sake!"

More C.S.I. lamps were lit. Dennis Jaeger, the director of photography, dashed around with a light meter, taking readings. "Places, everyone!" called Brian. "We're going for a rehearsal!" Ian Harrison, now attired in blue silk pajamas, his belly protruding above the waistband, was summoned on deck, as was Pandora Ashley. Without the Porsche sunglasses, Harrison's eyes were bloodshot, and there were heavy pouches underneath them.

"Right, Ian, Pandora!" said Tony in a soft but authoritative voice. "I'd like us to just run over the scene once or twice. Now I intend to do this whole bit in one long unbroken take. I feel that would be the most effective way. Questions? Problems? No. Let's go, then! Quiet on the set!"

The rehearsal sounded disappointingly flat. Ian Harrison's reading, despite his mellifluous, throaty gin-soaked voice, was rather mechanical.

"Can we have a bit more rage, Ian? You're supposed to be at the breaking point," suggested Tony.

"I only got those pages last night, for christsake," snarled Harrison.

"All right. Once more. Then we'll go for a take."

A clapperboard appeared and was clicked briskly shut.

"Moonshadows scene fourteen, take one."

"Speed!"

"Turn over!"

"Where have you been?" growled Ian Harrison, Lord Dunsmere as Pandora/Isabel strutted sultrily toward him from the gangplank, resplendent in green sequins against the dawn sky.

She delivered her line: "What are you doing up?"

"Where have you been?"

"I just went out to get a breath of air."

"You . . . what . . . Sorry. Line, please!"

"Cut! The line is 'You look like hell.' Let's try it again, folks! A bit more energy, Ian."

"Silence, *s'il vous plaît.*"

"Moonshadows, scene fourteen, take two."

"Speed!"

"Turn over!"

"Where have you been?"

"What are you doing up?"

"Where have you been?"

"I just wanted to get a breath of air."

"You did, like hell!"

"What do you want me to say?"

"Where have you been?"

"Cut! The line is 'I want you to tell me where you've been.'"

"What's the frigging difference?" roared Ian.

"All right! Places everyone. Let's try it again."

By take six, it was decided to supply Ian Harrison with cue cards. They printed takes nine and eleven, but by then the light was failing; Pandora had become wooden; and Harrison had never been anything but that to begin with. Between takes, as the makeup girl powdered him down, his brunette girl friend would appear at his side with a silver flask from which he refreshed himself.

As they shifted lights to set up the next shot, a dolly shot of Pandora walking up the gangplank, Josh Woodard saw his lovely wife approach her director, whisper in his ear, and, with a gesture somehow conclusive in its relaxed intimacy, run her fingers through his flaxen hair. The smile Holland gave her in response confirmed Josh's worst fears. The bitter irony of having watched for three hours while his unfaithful wife read out the dialogue he had written for her to speak in her role as an unfaithful wife filled him with a terrible rage, unlike any he had ever known. Never had he felt so small, so foolish, so humiliated. He felt as if every member of the crew were staring at him, whispering already behind his back as they had done on *Pavlova*. And with Tony Holland! A man whom he had instantly trusted and admired. Well, this time he had no intention of playing the fool! He would fly back to London that very evening. He'd already seen more than enough of *Moonshadows!*

The dolly tracks were in place; the lights had been repositioned; and all was in readiness for Pandora, a vision of poise and elegance. As she began her march up the ramp, out of the corner of her eye she noticed her husband pushing crew and bystanders out of his way, running frantically to his little Renault. Breaking off in the middle of the scene, she cried out, "Josh! Josh!" But he was gone.

Martin Sinclair and Tony Holland sat facing two men dressed in nearly identical charcoal-gray pinstriped suits.

On a large table between them was a model, accurate to the most minute detail, of the yacht *Anaconda,* constructed by the *Moonshadows'* special effects unit. Holland was endeavoring to explain to the man how they would set up one of the climactic scenes of the film in which the terrorists blow up the boat with several hostages on board, while conducting a battle with police helicopters hovering overhead.

"You see, gentlemen, we will set up a small and carefully controlled explosion near the rear of the boat which is, in my opinion, absolutely vital to achieving believability. We must see the impact of the blast register on the victims' faces. We will do this by erecting an extension of approximately four feet towards the rear of the vessel—that is the only area affected; we will film this sequence from a helicopter, showing the yacht from the aerial P.O.V. We then cut to the shot of this little beauty," he said, lovingly stroking the trim model, "being blown to bits. It is only by clever intercutting of the two explosions that we can convince the audience that what they are seeing is, in fact, the real boat going down in flames."

"We are not questioning your aesthetic judgments, Mr. Holland," said one of the insurance brokers, (for that was indeed the nature of the pinstriped gentlemen's calling, "but you must appreciate that, from our point of view, the mere fact of harboring explosives on board a yacht valued at well over a million dollars represents a considerable risk."

"There is also the question of liability," reminded the second broker. "What if some person or persons involved in the filming should be accidentally injured in such a blast?"

"Even so," remonstrated Sinclair, "the figures you are quoting are outrageous . . . astronomical!"

"That may be," responded one of the gentlemen dryly. "You are, of course, perfectly welcome to obtain other quotations. . . . However, to be candid, I very much doubt if you will find another firm willing to take on this risk at any price."

"That will not be necessary," grumbled the producer. "Your terms are accepted."

George Landau, a magisterial éminence grise, had installed himself in a director's chair emblazoned with his name. In deference to Holland, however, he remained on the periphery of the set. Both Leonora Sheldrake and—even more particularly—Rod Ward deferred to him almost exclusively, keeping their distance from Tony Holland, going over their lines with the old man and insisting on his approval before any of the scenes they were involved in were shot. By the third day of shooting, this routine had, naturally enough, created deep division and tension, to say nothing of delay. The inevitable clash between Holland and Ward finally came, and in the minds of many of the young director's loyal crew it was long overdue.

The scene being shot was a relatively simple one in which César (Ward), the terrorist, holds a knife to the throat of Daphne (Lucinda Bayes) and threatens to slit her throat in front of her mother, Joanna (Leonora Sheldrake, who was already heavily primed for the scene with several glasses of champagne kept ready for her in an ice bucket off-camera by her personal dresser). The shot was set up at the poolside area, where César was to threaten to drop the struggling but helpless girl down to the crashing surf beneath the rocky cliff.

They were on take twelve, several takes having been ruined by Leonora going up on her lines. ("Between her and Ian Harrison, it's like a bloody meeting of Alcoholics Unanimous 'round 'ere," muttered Brian Chalmers.) Still other takes were spoiled by Rod Ward's incessant habit of glancing over to his mentor, George Landau, for reassurance in the middle of a take. He did this once again during take twelve, ruining it as well.

"May I respectfully remind you, Mr. Ward, that the camera is over here. If you are seeking inspiration, I advise you to do so during Sunday prayer," said Tony Holland quietly.

Ward had hated that Holland's guts on sight. Now the tittering of the crew only increased his fury. He lashed out venomously: "I need some direction here, and I sure as hell ain't getting any from you. I can't say these goddam lines. They just don't feel right for my character. César wouldn't speak that way in this kind of a situation. It just doesn't feel right. I mean, what's my goddam motivation?"

Ignoring this loud tirade, Holland spoke even more quietly. "Your motivation, Mr. Ward, is *the light*. We are going to get this childishly simple scene over in the fifteen minutes remaining before we lose our daylight. If, of course, that is satisfactory to Mr. Landau?" He made a sweeping gesture of mock deference to the old man, who winced but nodded agreement. "Good! Then, Mr. Ward, I take it we may proceed."

They printed take fifteen. Tony Holland's health was heartily drunk to in the bar of the Hôtel Flore where the *Moonshadows* crew were lodged.

"I don't know anything about Sinclair, mate," said Brian, the first assistant, "but I do know Tony Holland. He's first-rate. You mark my words, he'll pull this off yet."

The *Moonshadows* cast and crew were on location for the day's shoot in Monte Carlo, *Principauté de Monaco*. The scenes to be filmed involved the recreation on-camera of the spectacular Croix-Rouge de Monaco Gala ball, the jewel in the crown of the Riviera summer social season. The ball sequence would occur quite early in the film, illustrating the

glittering life-styles of those who are about to become the
terrorists' victims. The location for the day was the Sporting
Club d'Été, a vast, pink conchlike structure which perched
dizzily out over the Mediterranean, and which housed an
ultramodern and elegant casino, as well as the Salle des Ga-
las where the Ball itself would be reenacted. Régine's disco
and a Polynesian-Brazilian restaurant and nightclub were
also part of the complex.

It was imperative that the *Moonshadows* filming proceed on schedule since the location work involved considerable expenditure. Should the company be forced, for whatever reason, to return the following day for additional work,
it would be financially ruinous. The Sporting Club d'Été (as
the name indicates) was normally closed during the off-season winter months, and it had cost Martin Sinclair a great
deal of money to have it specially reopened for the *Moonshadows* production. Hundreds of extras, each costumed in
expensive finery, had been engaged for the day to portray
the well-heeled partygoers. It was planned to shoot their
arrival at the gala "day for night," as overtime night shooting could run into a fortune.

Most importantly, the afternoon, from three to five
P.M., had been set aside to film the "receiving line" sequence, in which His Royal Highness, Prince Rainier, and
his daughter, Princess Stephanie, had graciously consented
to make "a cameo appearance." This was all-important,
since any depiction of this gala social event without Their
Highnesses' presence would have been deficient, not to say
wholly unconvincing. Leonora Sheldrake, who had been a
close friend of the late Princess Grace in the latter's Hollywood days, claimed partial credit for this coup. She herself
was to be absent from filming from noon to three, as Prince
Rainier had invited her to be his personal luncheon guest at
the Royal Palace.

Martin Sinclair fidgeted like a cat on hot bricks, as Tony Holland and Dennis Jaeger patiently worked out the lighting for a crane shot of dancers gliding across the ballroom floor. An agitated Brian Chalmers, the first assistant director, darted frantically through the crowd of milling extras, waiting for their call, and, his face ashen with obvious worry, made his way toward Tony.

"It's no use, guv!" wailed Brian. "We can't find fucking Firefrorefiddle anywhere!"

"What!" yelped a stricken Martin Sinclair.

"He gave his driver the slip over an hour ago. Sent the poor bugger off to get some ciggies and when he came back, he was short one Ian Harrison."

Tony Holland gritted his teeth in cold fury. He had warned Sinclair, right from the beginning, of Ian Harrison's notorious unreliability. Trust the bastard to pull a stunt like this on the single day it would be least possible and most expensive to shoot around him! "All right, Brian. It's not your fault," he told his assistant in a level voice, and looking directly at Sinclair with his piercing blue eyes, "Get some of the boys and check out the neighboring bars!"

Martin's face flushed purple with rage. He clenched and unclenched his fists in apoplectic fury. "Shoot around him!"

"We can't. We must get the quarrel between him and Pandora on the ballroom floor this morning. The afternoon will be taken up with the Rainier work. Besides, whenever we do shoot that quarrel scene, it will mean calling back the whole lot of extras."

At this, the producer's face assumed an expression which shook Tony Holland profoundly, This, the young man recognized with shock, was no ordinary display of temper. Martin's hooded eyes darted frantically. His mouth was twitching uncontrollably. The man was obviously on the brink of madness. Just at that moment, however, a triumphant and grinning Brian Chalmers, the color restored to his cheeks, reentered with a crumpled Ian Harrison draped around his shoulders like a pile of rags.

"You were dead right, guv," he beamed at his director, "Willie and Derek found him at Tip-Top over the way, soaking up Guinness and champagne. Found him just in the nick of time too. He'd already smashed up a slot machine when he didn't win on it, and the bartender was just about to call in the *flics.* Willie bunged him a thousand francs and saw to it he'll keep stumm."

Unable to vent his fury on Tony Holland, and with Ian Harrison too near comatose to understand, a livid Martin Sinclair directed the full force of his wrath against Brian Chalmers. "You incompetent fool! It's your responsibility to see that nothing of this kind happens, that the actors get here on time!"

The first assistant director stood silent, quaking with a mixture of fear and repressed indignation.

"Sinclair!" said Tony Holland in a voice so low as to be almost inaudible, yet which silenced the producer more effectively than a blow, "Brian here is a first-class A.D. It's no part of his duties to play nursemaid to has-been alcoholic hams. If you will recall, I myself specifically warned you against hiring Harrison, who is well known for this sort of trick. You felt, however, he would be a bargain. Very well, you've got your bargain. It's my job to get a performance out of him, and with Brian's help, I bloody well am going to do so. Brian . . . get some black coffee into the bastard, and sober him up!"

Ian Harrison, who had hitherto been speechless, was apparently sufficiently sober to take umbrage at the director's remarks, and now, still supported by Brian, began to wave his fists at Tony and spew out a torrent of obscenities as he was led away. No sooner had Firefrorefiddle been dealt with than an overwrought Leonora Sheldrake, dripping Harry Winston diamonds, and clad in a breathtaking one-shouldered white jersey evening gown, strode purposefully into their midst, with George Landau and an agitated Yves Dupuytout, the film's costume designer, trailing in her wake. The star was obviously in a high temper.

"Martin! Mr. Holland!" she seethed, "I just wanted you both to see this . . . this atrocity" (here she tore at her exquisite dress with a gesture of infinite disgust) ". . . before I take it off! You don't suppose for one minute that I, Leonora Sheldrake, am going to allow myself to be photographed in these rags, do you?"

"Rags!" blurted an incredulous Martin Sinclair, "That dress cost thousands!"

"You saw the sketches and approved them, Miss Sheldrake," Tony pointed out firmly, ". . . and, if I may say so, you look exquisite."

"Exquisite! Hah!" she exploded. "I cannot play the scene in this dress. My character would *never* attend the most important social event of the year, and be presented to royalty, in this . . . this travesty of a gown."

Much of Leonora's tirade was, unfortunately, rendered unintelligible by the fact of its coinciding with an equally vociferous outburst unleashed (in French) by the much maligned Monsieur Dupuytout.

At this point, George Landau found the moment opportune to inject himself into the proceedings.

"Miss Sheldrake is absolutely right," he opined, "It is imperative that she wear something appropriately splendid in order to capture the mood of the scene."

"*Nom d'un nom! Jamais de ma vie . . .*" wailed Yves Dupuytout.

"May I remind you . . ." sneered Tony Holland,

"Miss Sheldrake has precisely one line in this scene: 'Charmed, Your Grace!' "

"It is out of the question, Leonora!" stormed Sinclair. "Besides, where the devil would we get another dress at this hour, even if we wanted to?"

"Dior!" announced Leonora Sheldrake triumphantly. "They have a branch here behind the Hôtel de Paris. I've already noticed that they have the perfect gown on display in their window. It is white taffeta, and I've already checked —it's my size. I shall now return to my trailer and take off these rags! You may deliver my costume to me there!" With that, the star turned on her heel, prepared to sweep off, but was halted by Anthony Holland's hand on her arm.

Holland's voice was gentle, yet firm. "I will not have such prima donna tactics on my set, Miss Sheldrake. As far as I'm concerned, you may remain in your trailer. We will use the dress you are wearing on your stand-in, and shoot over her shoulder. We can, in short, dispense with your services today."

"Not so fast, buster!" the actress wheeled around in fury. Every year of her true age was betrayed by the venom which now distorted her features. "If I don't appear in this scene, neither do Prince Rainier nor his daughter! They have only agreed to do so out of personal friendship to me, Leonora Sheldrake! May I remind you that I shall be lunching with their Royal Highnesses today!"

"She's got us by the balls, Holland," muttered a defeated Sinclair. "All right, Leonora, you've got your Dior!"

Leonora and George Landau flounced off majestically, Landau darting a smirk of malicious triumph over his shoulder at the handsome young director.

"Jesus wept!" moaned Tony Holland. "All right! Someone see if Firefrorefiddle is coherent yet, and let's get fucking rolling!"

* * *

Josh Woodard had written and rewritten the imaginary confrontation scene over and over in his mind. In some versions, he was the man of action, punching Tony Holland squarely in the jaw while Pandora whimpered pitifully in the background, imploring his forgiveness. In others he reeled off urbane West End dialogue, devastating in its sarcasm; in yet other versions, he pleaded with Pandora for another chance; surely she knew that she was all he had in life, that this betrayal would kill him. There were these scenes and an infinite number of variations along the same lines.

In the end, Josh knew that he could deliver none of them. For in all of them he knew Pandora would inevitably utter the one line of dialogue that he could never bear to hear her speak. Without another word to anyone, without so much as a stop by their hotel room to collect his possessions, Josh Woodard had gotten into the tiny Renault his wife had despised so bitterly and driven straight for Nice airport. He would return to Wandsworth House and wait. The day would come when Pandora would have need of him, so he would wait. And if he stayed away long enough, maybe he would never hear those dreaded words: "I'm sorry, Josh. It's no use. I love him."

When Martin Sinclair learned that Josh Woodard had flown back to England, his rage was apoplectic. "You son of a bitch," he thundered at Josh through the telephone. "You're destroying me. You leave me here with a script I can't shoot. You listen to me, you bastard! You're finished! I've got a contract with you . . . I'll see to it you never do a major picture again . . . !"

"Martin . . ." Josh's voice was very subdued and tired. "Believe me, I'm not proud of walking out that way. I don't blame you for your anger. I've let you down, I know that . . . but it was no good. I'm not in a fit state to write the screenplay at this moment in my life. I'll be happy to pay you back in full every cent you've paid me. It's not a question of money or career or anything now. They're suddenly not very important."

"Not important," sneered Sinclair. "Since I've already paid you close to two hundred thousand unimportant dollars, perhaps you'd be good enough to tell me just exactly what the fuck is so important?"

"My wife . . . Pandora . . . my wife and Tony Holland!"

20

George Landau's initial reaction to Sean's illness had been little more than pique and irritation at having their holiday together spoiled. It had never really occurred to him that there could be anything more seriously wrong with the youth than a bout of flu or some such thing. But weeks had passed since their arrival on the Continent, and—far from improving—the boy's condition had deteriorated with alarming rapidity.

Horrible sores were now beginning to appear on Sean's once flawless skin, and he continued to lose weight. The hotel doctor confessed himself baffled. Landau was by now in a state approaching hysteria himself. His daily intake of cocaine, always heavy, had now doubled. After a long discussion with Leonora Sheldrake and Rod Ward, it was decided to fly in one of the most respected physicians in Beverly Hills, a Dr. Silver, without any further delay.

Dr. Silver was a polished, deeply suntanned man whose silk Cerruti suit and gold Rolex belied his professional acumen. It took him less than five minutes at Sean's bedside to diagnose the nature of the illness which had baffled the hotel's doctor, but then, perhaps, this particular affliction was not one yet so casually brought into the realms of the Riviera rich and beautiful people. It was the ignorance of Landau and the other Californians he couldn't comprehend. Apparently this was something that only happened to "other people."

He took a sharp intake of breath, smiled broadly at the patient, and said "We'll have you out surfing in no time, lad." Then he drew the hushed group, George Landau, Rod Ward, and Leonora Sheldrake, into the sitting room of the luxurious suite.

"What is it, Doctor?" intoned Leonora Sheldrake with precisely the same measured throb in the voice she had used on that same line of dialogue in at least eight pictures.

The shock she and the others registered when the physician spoke, though, was totally unaffected. He spoke only one word, but that word was enough to freeze the blood in their veins.

"AIDS."

"Have you seen this?" hissed Martin Sinclair, waving a telegram under Tony Holland's nose as they sat in a darkened screening room at the Studio Victoune, waiting to go over the day's rushes. "It's a memo from the studio, from Alan Kaufman. He demands to know why, after a week's shooting, we are already a week behind schedule. His words include 'extravagance . . . waste . . . reminiscent of Von Stroheim!'" Sinclair paused: "Well, what do you have to say?"

"I'm flattered by the comparison to Von Stroheim. Look, seriously, considering that we have no script, and a cast including two alcoholics and a psychopath, I think we're doing fairly well."

"You're wasting too much time on these long, complicated scenes that you're staging with those short focal lenses. George Landau tells me you'd save a lot of time and effort in placing the camera and actors by shooting with longer focals from farther away. And the actors are complaining about these long scenes you shoot in one take without a break: Something goes wrong in the last few seconds of a ten-minute take and the whole shot's fucked!"

"Look! I'm not at USC film school here, and I'm not prepared to listen to George Landau's Cinema 1 lecture. If you want that doddering old queen to run the show, that's fine! If you want me to shoot twenty pages a day, fine! I just hope you like what you get. Either way, I suggest you let me get on with it!"

Martin Sinclair was silent.

"And," continued Tony Holland, "as long as I am directing this film, I do not want George Landau in this screening room watching dailies!"

"Agreed!" nodded Sinclair.

Suddenly the door banged open.

"What is this? Just what *is* this? I demand to know." Pandora Ashley stormed into the screening room like a Fury, brandishing pink pages. Tony was momentarily taken aback by the transformation. Her green eyes blazed fire. Her mouth was drawn tight, imparting a hardened look to her countenance. There were dark circles under her eyes, as if the drama with Josh were taking its toll.

"All of a sudden, it seems everyone around here has developed a mania for waving around bits of paper." He placed a soothing hand on Pandora's shoulder. "Calm down, my love. I know it's not been easy for you."

"We've gone back to the McAlastair script on that scene," said Sinclair. "It just didn't play the way your husband wrote it. It was just too talky . . . talk . . . talk. The important thing is they wind up in bed. The talk just slows it down."

"But it doesn't!" argued Pandora. "That scene is critical to the whole development of my character. It shows why and how she is attracted to César. It's the focal point of the whole film for her. It would be like doing a film about Patty Hearst and not bothering to show how she was won over by her captors!" Her huge eyes widened beseechingly at Tony. "Look, can't you shoot it both ways, then choose the best?"

"It's simple male-female chemistry. When the audience feels the heat between you and Rod Ward, they'll accept gladly that you're willing to do anything for him," argued Sinclair.

"But it's more than that!" pleaded Pandora. "We have to feel the boredom, the stultification of her society marriage to this rich man . . . otherwise, she's just a whore and no one will care a damn about her—or anything else, for that matter!"

Tony Holland listened thoughtfully. "She may be right, Martin. After all, that was your initial response to the McAlastair version. It may be worth shooting it both ways."

Martin Sinclair looked from the handsome man to the beautiful woman, then nodded gravely. "All right. Just this once. We'll try it."

"We're ready now, sir," called out a voice from the projection booth.

"Go ahead," called Sinclair. And as the lights dimmed on the tiny screen before them, in a rough print with the color still unbalanced, the images of the day's disappointments and frustrations flickered before them mockingly.

At three A.M. Rod Ward answered a knock at the door of his hotel suite and opened it to find Leonora Sheldrake dressed in a white satin robe trimmed with maribou feathers and carrying a bottle of Perrier-Jouet. "May I come in?" she whispered throatily. He flung the door open, but without a word turned abruptly away from her, striding toward the balcony which overlooked the dark sea. "Darling," she said, following him, and placing her jeweled hands on the back of his shoulders, "why have you been avoiding me? You know I can't live without you."

He brushed her away as though she were some loathsome insect. "You've been drinking! You know I can't stand drunken broads!"

Leonora was abject. Tears welled in her beautiful eyes. She looked childlike, defenseless. Her voice, when she found it, emerged as a babyish whine. "It's not my fault! When you're not there, I get lonely . . . so I drink!"

"Ha! You were drinking on the set yesterday. You damn near fucked up my scene. Was that because you were lonely?" Rod sneered, mimicking her little girl voice.

"I won't do it anymore, I promise," said the actress, sliding her hands around his slim hips and grasping for his crotch. "Just hold me."

Rod Ward whirled around and thrust her from him roughly, using all his strength. She fell to the ground near the foot of the bed, shivering with suppressed anguish.

"Now get out. I've got an early call."

Leonora rose to her knees and stretched out her arms to him imploringly. "I know what it is. You're upset about the boy! Darling, you should have told me . . . I'd have understood . . . I forgive you . . ."

"You! Forgive me?" sneered the actor. "That's a good one! That really is. Look, old lady, just get out of here. You revolt me."

Leonora's hysterical screams awakened many guests as she rushed down the corridor to her room. Some even complained to the management, but moments later all was calm. Happy silence reigned once more in the grand hotel.

Rod Ward stood on his balcony in the cool night air,

staring fixedly at the black sea. In his imagination, a white stallion, riderless, pranced triumphantly upon the strand.

Merle Greene lay basking like a cat in the Riviera sun. She drew down the brim of her big straw hat to protect her delicate complexion, but removed the black overshirt she wore over her swimming suit, and rubbed lotion on her thighs. On the chaise beside her, patches of pink appearing on her little tummy, lay Melissa. Beside her was an untouched Smurf coloring book and wax crayons, melting in the sun. The child seemed bored and fidgety. She reached repeatedly for Merle's hand, but was told to color her Smurf book. Auntie Merle was resting.

"Auntie Merle! Auntie Merle! Where's my mommy? When am I going home?"

Something in the child's question, far from annoying Merle, appeared to give her satisfaction, for she smiled her peculiar smile. "Your mother has gone to spend some time in a place called Reno."

"What's that? Why didn't she take me with her?"

"Because, sweetheart," cooed Merle Greene, "your daddy loves you very much. He wanted you to be with him. Don't you love your daddy?"

The child hesitated. "Yes," she said solemnly, after a long pause, "but he's so awfully sad all the time. I want my mother. My mother is very beautiful. Why did she go to Reno?"

"That's a place where grown-ups go when they don't want to be married anymore. Your mommy and daddy don't want to be married anymore, and that is why your mommy has gone to Reno—to fix things," Merle explained with sweet patience.

"But when will I see her? When? When?" cried the uncomprehending child.

Merle, tiring of this game, suddenly became very strict. "Don't you raise your voice to me, Melissa! Now you go color your Smurf book. Your Auntie Merle is resting."

That night Tony Holland and Pandora Ashley drove to the African Queen in Villefranche to eat bouillabaisse and watch the street lamps shimmer on the black harbor. In the tiny port, the rocking masts of the boats pointed at the multitudes of stars. The mood of the couple, considering the beauty of the scene, was oddly subdued. A hard, spiteful look, quite unfamiliar to Tony, had subtly stolen over Pandora's beautiful features.

He spoke, softly, in a voice charged with deep feeling: "Darling, as God is my witness, I've never loved a woman as I love you . . . and I always shall. But I thought it was understood—you know I've never lied to you. We never spoke of marriage."

Pandora shredded a napkin with her long fingernails. Her green eyes darted fire. "Yes, but that was before! Now Josh says he's filing for divorce!"

"He'll make it up with you! He worships you."

"My husband does not make idle threats. And what about you? Do you 'worship' that prissy wife of yours, Christine, or whatever her stupid name is?" sneered Pandora.

"Don't speak that way. Don't be vicious. You're not like that. I know you're not. I love you. I just can't leave my daughters. I cannot. You knew that from the beginning. Jesus, don't you think I've thought about leaving my family? Agonized over it? But we can't just run away like a pair of carefree schoolchildren.

"The pain we'd inflict on Christine and Josh and my daughters would always be there on our consciences, poisoning any chance we may have had at happiness. Not right away perhaps, but inevitably we'd come to feel guilty and miserable and blame one another. Come, Pandora, in your heart you know I'm right. Deep down, you don't really want to hurt Josh any more than I want to hurt my children.

"Look, darling, nothing has changed. We can go on as we are. We belong to each other. What difference does it make if we're married or not?" He reached across the table and stroked her dark hair tenderly. Her green eyes filled with tears.

"We'll go on then," she whispered in a small voice, "As we are . . ."

Both versions of the César-Isabel love scene were to be filmed that morning in the main bedroom of the yacht. Against Tony Holland's objections, the scene was to be shot "day for night," thereby cutting down on overtime payments to the crew, and negating the need for turnaround days off between night shooting. Holland had argued with Sinclair that the results were never as effective, but Martin had remained adamant. Plywood sheets were slid through the window for dollying, cables snaked their way along the floor, prop men carried in machine guns and crates of live ammunition which Rod Ward, as César, was to convince his mistress, Isabel (Pandora), to hide on board her husband's yacht. The sound man was forced by the cramped quarters to set up his mixer in the adjoining bathroom of the cabin.

Pandora, clad only in an emerald silk kimono, beneath which she was naked except for a pair of bikini panties, puffed nervously at a cigarette while a hairdresser adjusted a strand of her raven hair. Rod Ward, his muscular torso deeply suntanned, and wearing only Jockey shorts, huddled in a corner with George Landau, who appeared to be going over a reading on one of his lines.

Pandora could not help glancing from the actor to her lover, Tony, as he stood, going over the lighting of the shot with his D.P., Dennis Jaeger. She compared the relative merits of their very different forms of masculine beauty: Tony, with his flaxen hair, frank blue eyes, his easy grace and innate refinement; Rod Ward, his arrogant hazel eyes exuding animal menace, every gesture charged with raw sexuality. As Brian Chalmers called out, "Places for a rehearsal, everybody, if you please," and she peeled off her green silk robe and slid between the sheets, Pandora thought that it might be interesting to pursue the comparison still further.

"By the way," mumbled George O'Shaugnessy to Brian Chalmers, "not that I miss him, but where's Martin Sinclair? I haven't seen the old boy this morning."

"You wouldn't believe me if I told you, mate!"

"Go on!"

"It's his fucking wedding day and all, isn't it? He's getting himself spliced to Lucinda, that little bird that's playing Daphne."

"Jesus Christ Almighty! That sweet little thing? Why, she could be his granddaughter! If that don't beat all! Fuck me, as the duchess said, more in hope than anger!"

"I told you you wouldn't believe me! Right, places please! Quiet on the set!"

"Let's just have a run through of the Woodard version first, please. Give me some passion, please!" called Tony Holland.

Rod Ward slid under the covers beside Pandora. Margo, the costume woman, stood by the bed, draping the sheets so that they would flatteringly expose Pandora's bare breasts and Rod Ward's muscular back. Nicole, the continuity girl, whispered in Tony's ear. "We can still see his shorts."

"Look, Margo, can't you get him some flesh-colored shorts that won't show up on-camera?" asked Tony patiently.

"I'm sorry," said the flustered woman. "I have some ready. I forgot . . . I'll get them right away!"

"Don't bother!" called out Ward, writhing out of his shorts and discarding them by the side of the bed. "I don't need them." Turning to Pandora, he added suggestively, "Do I?"

"Look here, Ward!" shouted Tony furiously, "I've had just about enough from you!"

"It's all right, Tony," Pandora Ashley said soothingly. "I couldn't care less what Mr. Ward is or isn't wearing. Can we just try the scene, please?"

"Right! *Moonshadows,* scene twenty-eight. This is a rehearsal. Quiet, everybody!"

That evening the Eden Roc pavilion of the Hôtel du Cap was given over to a party in celebration of Martin Sinclair's marriage to Miss Lucinda Bayes. (The wedding had been a simple ceremony in the registry office of Nice earlier in the day.) The bride was radiant in silver lace, and a gigantic diamond from Fred graced her lovely hand. Beside her, in flounces of pale blue chiffon, was her "Aunt" Merle Greene, beaming almost as serenely as if she herself had been the bride.

Sinclair had hired a small orchestra to enliven the festivities, and violins scraped the scores of his past Broadway successes, as spotlights swept the floor, glinting off an enormous bar where dark bottles and crystal goblets gleamed.

Crew members as well as cast had assembled for the celebration, and as they piled their plates with lobster, pâté and other delicacies from the lavish buffet spread out in the exquisite room with its panoramic vista of the Mediterranean, the mood of futility which had settled upon the production of *Moonshadows* appeared, temporarily, at least, to have been dispelled. Only two people were absent from the festivities—Josh Woodard, who, of course, had flown back to England, and Leonora Sheldrake, who had had no scenes to shoot and had not, apparently, left her hotel room all day.

Brandon, Sheldrake's secretary, approached Rod Ward, who was discussing the day's work with George Landau, and asked the actor if he had seen Leonora. When Ward responded in the negative, Brandon said, "That's odd. I've been calling her room and there's no answer. You'd better come with me and see if anything's happened to her."

"Nothing's happened," scoffed Ward. "She's just sulking."

Brandon then approached Tony Holland who instantly agreed to accompany him to the actress' room. They enlisted the help of the hotel's assistant manager in entering the star's lavish suite. They found her dressed in a robe of white satin, crumpled like a doll on the floor in front of a full-length mirror. In her jewelled hand was clutched an empty bottle of sleeping pills.

Tony grabbed her to her feet and began shaking her. "For God's sake!" he cried, "get an ambulance! Quickly! She's still breathing!"

The mood in the screening room was grim. The delays in production caused by Leonora Sheldrake's suicide attempt were causing production costs to escalate out of control. Replacing the legendary actress was, by now, out of the question, since too much complicated and expensive footage would have to be reshot. There was nothing to do but to reschedule, to work around her and wait for her recovery, which according to the doctors would take a minimum of ten days. It meant holding on to not only the *Anaconda,* but also the Hôtel du Cap, for a minimum of ten days extra, an expensive proposition, even with taking into account the overtime for cast and crew.

The *Moonshadows* situation was considered sufficiently grave at G.R.W. for Alan Kaufman—in one of his first acts as studio chief—to make an immediate visit to the South of France to attempt to bring this "runaway" production under control. It also offered him an opportunity to get a few days' vacation with his new lady love, rising star, Angela Armstrong. Privately, Kaufman had already stated that he regarded *Moonshadows,* a holdover from the previous régime, as a "dog," and Martin Sinclair as a "throwback." Still, the studio had already tied up fifteen million in the picture—too much money to write off as a loss.

Kaufman, dressed in navy cashmere jacket and neatly pressed jeans, regarded the flickering images on the screen while gnawing the fingernails of one hand; the other rested on Angela Armstrong's silken knee. He watched the *Moonshadows* rushes with the clinical detachment of a physician watching a geriatric patient on life-support systems. He was aching to pull the plug—still, it was a fifteen-million-dollar plug.

Angela whispered a derisory comment in his ear as the footage of the Rod Ward-Pandora Ashley love scene flashed on the small projection room screen. Since her rejection by Pandora's husband, Angela's hatred and envy of the English actress had been growing. Adding to her irritation was the fact that since her arrival in France, Angela had found that word of her own celebrity status had not spread there. In fact, no one had any idea who she was. Pandora Ashley, on the other hand, was clearly considered a superstar. Angela would have liked nothing better than for her new beau to close down the film.

As for Pandora, she sat hunched in her chair, staring at

the screen in a near-catatonic state of gloom. Tony Holland glanced from his director of photography to his editor, Cliff Newsome in mute agony. Only Rod Ward, who leaned back with his feet up on the row of seats in front of him, appeared to derive satisfaction from his performance.

A chasm of silence opened as the screen went dark. Alan Kaufman, pressing the tips of his fingers together carefully was the first to speak. He used a voice so soft it was almost inaudible: "We are prepared to continue financing this picture, but only up to a point. I have had a new schedule and budget drawn up by Grant Stockler, the head of our business affairs department, one that bears some relationship to reality. It allocates twenty more days of shooting at one hundred thousand a day. That is two million dollars.

I want you to bring in a new writer, Jeff Freiberg. I'll have him here on the first plane tomorrow morning."

"Twenty days! It's just not possible! Besides, how can I accept a schedule made by someone who has had no input from me and cannot possibly understand what remains to be done?" complained Tony Holland.

"Gentlemen," said Kaufman, rising to his feet with Angela on his arm. "I am sorely tempted to put us all out of our misery and send everybody home tomorrow morning. Don't push me, Holland!"

As the couple swept from the room, Angela thrust her proud breasts forward and held her lovely head high. She struck a regal pose, marred only by the unmistakable smirk which played at the corner of her mouth.

Kaufman paused at the door and turned to Sinclair, repeating menacingly, "Twenty days. Two million. Jeff Freiberg. Take it or leave it!"

As Martin Sinclair nodded mutely in acquiescence, the full weight of his years seemed to press down upon him as he felt control of his dream project slipping through his fingers. It was only when Kaufman and his mistress were safely out of earshot that the old man's rage vented itself with the force of a volcano on Tony Holland: "This is all your fault! I told you to shoot the McAlastair version! From now on, Mr. Holland, I hope it is perfectly clear to you that I will not allow so much as one single line to be altered, transposed, cut, or changed in any way, shape, or form without my express approval!"

"Wait a minute," yelled Rod Ward. "Sure, it's not perfect, but it's not the script. It's the way he shot it. Can't we get George Landau in here to have a look? Hell, that's one of my best scenes in the whole fucking script . . ."

Dennis and Cliff had to restrain Tony Holland from going for Ward physically. The very sight of the man, sitting here wanking over his own image while a woman who had tried to end her life on his account lay in the hospital, had incensed the young director beyond endurance . . . and now this! "If that old queen so much as sets foot in this screening room, I'm off the picture! There is only one director on this film, Mr. Ward. The sooner your feeble brain can absorb that information, the happier we will all be. There will be no visitors on my set as of tomorrow. By visitors, I specifically mean Mr. George Landau, who is *not* employed by this production, and whose services have, I understand, been paid for by your friend Leonora Sheldrake. I suggest to you that his time would be more profitably spent visiting that poor woman in the hospital where you put her."

"I don't have to take this kind of shit from you, you fuck! You're not through with me yet!" shouted the actor at the top of his lungs as he stormed from the room.

"I told you, Martin, the man's a psychopath!"

"But surely the scene can be saved," interjected Pandora. "In the editing, perhaps? I agree, some of it didn't work, but parts of it were very good . . . my long speech for instance."

"This is a movie. *I.e.,* movement is implied. We don't want long speeches. I'm afraid, darling, that what I said to Ward is true for you also. We can't have this film directed by a committee. I did listen to your point of view. You must admit that. It just didn't work."

"Tony is right, Miss Ashley. The scene is out. It's no use having any further discussion about it." Martin Sinclair's gruff voice silenced the actress, but the look in her emerald eyes spoke volumes.

Lucinda Bayes had taken it for granted that, with her marriage to Martin Sinclair, Merle Greene's unwelcome sexual attentions would cease. Merle, however, soon let it be known that this was far from being the case. It was quite the opposite, in fact. Now that Lucinda was Martin Sinclair's bride, Merle's sexual demands on her became increasingly voracious and peremptory. Often, she made a particular point of insisting Lucinda come directly from Martin's bed to her own, relishing the idea of enjoying the girl's body directly after the producer had made love to his new bride. Only in this way, did Merle Greene feel complete in her triumphant mockery over the man who had scorned her.

When Lucinda Sinclair, counting on her new-found importance as the producer's wife, sought to rebel against this degradation by suggesting to the older woman that perhaps for the time being they should cease their "affaire"—it was too "risky" now—the older woman lost no time in reminding the girl exactly how precarious her position remained. "But, sweetheart," she purred, "we don't want any unpleasantness to interrupt our honeymoon, do we? Just remember, your Auntie Merle knows what's best. She'll never let the past harm you!"

21

"**R**ight," called Brian Chalmers. "We're going for a take on this one! Quiet please!"

Once again, Pandora Ashley, naked except for her brief panties, lay beneath the sheets beside Ron Ward in the bedroom of the yacht.

"Tony," she protested, "I still don't feel comfortable with this scene! It doesn't make any sense this way! Can't we at least put back the speech where Isabel says, 'My life is suffocating me . . . sometimes I feel I just can't breathe'?"

"Pandora, we've been through this a hundred times, and frankly it's beginning to be rather boring for all concerned. It looked fine just now the way you rehearsed it. Now we're going to shoot it," responded Tony Holland, patiently but firmly, as though addressing a recalcitrant child.

"*Moonshadows,* scene twenty-eight, take one."

"Speed!"

"Turn over!"

The scene called for the couple to mimic the act of love. As Ward crouched over her with his tan athletic body, Pandora felt the electric tension emanating from his warm flesh. The proximity of his masculinity, combined with her anger at Tony's stubbornness, carried her emotions to an almost fever pitch. She could feel the pressure of Ward's enormous penis against her thigh, and there was a teasing mockery in his hazel eyes, as if daring her to respond, which only provoked her further.

"Cut! There's too much motion! The sheets are flapping around too much!"

"Right! Nicole! George! You two go over and hold down the sheets on either side of the bed, will you?"

The two assistants then crouched down low, each one grabbing hold of the sheets so that the "lovemaking" could continue.

"A little lower, George. You're still in camera range!"

"Where's Anne? Anne, touch up Miss Ashley's hair please!"

"Right!"

"Moonshadows, scene twenty-eight, take two!"

"Speed!"

"Turn over!"

Once again, the actors' perfect bodies twisted photogenically in an embrace which Pandora began increasingly to wish was not merely simulated. She felt once again his genitals rub against her, felt the excitement surge within his body. She wanted him to enter her there . . . that very minute . . . in front of everyone . . . with lights and camera rolling. In front of everyone . . . especially Tony Holland.

"You will help us, then, Isabel? You will help the cause?"

"Yes. I will help the cause!"

"I welcome it. My life is suffocating me . . . sometimes I feel as if I can't breathe."

"Cut!" Tony Holland was shouting. His anger was icy, controlled, but very, very real. "Miss Ashley! As you are doubtless aware, that line has been cut! Your line is, 'I welcome it.' Period! Finish! End of sentence! Is that clear, Pandora?"

"Yes, Tony," Pandora hissed. "It's quite clear."

"Bloody marvelous!" cried Tony in mock exultation. "And while we're 'bout it, Mr. Ward, could you, perhaps, favor us with fewer grimaces. You are making love to a lady, not perpetrating the Texas Chainsaw Massacre, right?"

"Moonshadows, scene twenty-eight, take three."

"Speed!"

"Turn over!"

As Rod Ward once again cradled Pandora in his powerful arms, he whispered softly, almost inaudibly in her ear, "Meet me! Here! Tomorrow at midnight!" Her green eyes flashed assent.

"You will help me then, Isabel? You will help the cause?"

"Yes. I will help the cause!"

"You know you will be running a great risk?"

"I welcome it."

It was dawn, and Tony Holland, his frank blue eyes as clear and crisp as the sea, stood alone on a rocky, deserted strip of beach past Juan-Les-Pins, staring moodily out at the Mediterranean. He had risen from Pandora's bed and driven restlessly for miles up and down the coast before settling on this dreary spot, for he needed desperately to be alone with his thoughts, away from the intoxicating scent of his mistress, and the rich, warm curves of her tantalizing flesh.

He was convinced he knew Pandora's weaknesses, knew all about her childish willfulness, her sexual amorality, her insatiable hunger for love. He knew all this. He knew too of her callous treatment of Josh Woodard. All this he weighed carefully in the balance sheet of his mind.

On the positive side, there was an equally firm knowledge that the two of them—he and Pandora—had found something together that neither had known before or would ever know again, some rare and wonderful alchemy of lust and affection. He took a certain manly pride in his realization that his mistress, who, with so many others, had been a heartless vixen, should have softened, blossomed under his touch. He felt the pride of a man who has at last broken the wild horse who has thrown so many riders before him.

Still, he was under no illusions that he had tamed her. He could not make Woodard's mistake of letting Pandora presume too much on his tenderness. Love is, at the best of times, the most fragile and ephemeral of man's possessions; the slightest loss of respect—either Tony's for Pandora, or hers for him—could strike their love stone-cold dead without murmur. Now these insufferable tantrums of hers about a verbose, unactable scene! Was she really such a fool as to think that her sexual power could exert itself over him on the set? At whatever cost, the lady would find herself sorely mistaken.

Holland picked up a pebble from the beach and hurled it, moodily, out to sea. A flock of gulls started in fright, then fluttered skyward, berating him with hoarse cries for disturbing their repose. *Moonshadows!* What high hopes he had held for it such a short time ago! Now it would try his resolve, his expertise, his spirit to the utmost merely to see it through to the end. He had been warned by several of his colleagues before accepting the directorial assignment of what they had termed the "Martin Sinclair Golden Rule— Divide and Conquer!" He had learned the bitter accuracy of this description of the producer's policy at first hand.

Tony had found his authority systematically undermined by George Landau's presence on the set, yet Sinclair had persistently refused to bar the older man. The producer seemed to delight in the rivalry between the two men and to encourage the cliques of supporters which had inevitably formed around them. It seemed to be his way of assuring that he, Sinclair, should always have the last word, that his own judgment should be paramount.

Now, moreover, with the producer's marriage to Lucinda Bayes, the old queen Landau—having been known in his heyday, some fifty years earlier, as a "woman's director" —had more or less been enlisted as the new bride's drama coach, and he, Tony, was powerless to prevent it. After all, he had enough on his plate without giving crash courses in drama to nubile adolescents! Good or ill, Lucinda was in the film, and his name was going up on the screen with hers!

A reddish ball of fire glowed crimson in the eastern horizon over the azure waters of the Mediterranean, and Anthony Holland turned his steps back across the sands toward his Peugeot and another day of shooting.

"By God!" he thought to himself, "I'll make a fine picture of bloody *Moonshadows* yet, in spite of Pandora, Rod Ward, George Landau, Lucinda, Martin Sinclair, and the devil himself! I'll turn this pile of shit into something I can be proud of, if it's the last thing I do!"

The departure of Josh Woodard followed by Leonora's suicide attempt had thrown a pall over the *Moonshadows* shoot. Pandora Ashley had become like a cat on hot bricks, all frayed nerve endings and near hysterical shifts of mood. Since the arrival of Jeff Freiberg, fresh out of USC film school, Pandora had been appalled to find that the role of Lady Isabel was appearing on fewer and fewer of the pink pages which replaced the original scenes. Imperceptibly, the role of Daphne, as played by Lucinda Sinclair, was burgeoning out of all control. So now there were three scripts on the floor of her room, all for a film it now looked might

never even be completed. In bed, as she expertly fondled
Tony's balls with her deft fingers or arched her perfect body
into the most erotic poses, Pandora would complain "they"
were destroying the film by cutting her part, and it was up
to Tony to fight for it.

In reply, though, he had only stroked her hair gently,
as he might a wayward kitten, and explained that she would
be her best by being in the best film possible, and that was
what he intended to make. Hadn't she told him a thousand
times that the ambition of being a movie star had all been
Josh's idea, that her only dream was to be a fine actress? She
could only nod forlornly at his comments and fall asleep,
cradled in his strong arms.

The following morning she sat moodily in the poolside
area of the Eden Roc. Her hairdresser put the final touches
on her raven locks, and Wardrobe fiddled with the cleavage
of the bronze Lurex bikini, which was to be her only costume for the morning's shooting. George O'Shaughnessey,
the second A.D., sweated profusely as he timidly approached her chair, for by now one and all among the crew
were more than accustomed to sharp outbursts of temper
from Milady—as they had nicknamed her.

From the look in Pandora's emerald eyes as they surveyed the new lines of dialogue written for her by Jeff Freiberg, O'Shaughnessey had acted wisely in sprinting out of
her way with as much speed as possible. Raising her eyes
from the printed page where the word *Isabel* appeared no
more than twice, and many of her best lines had been transferred to the character of *Daphne,* she shifted her lazer beam
gaze to the canvas chair opposite, where the name "Lucinda
Sinclair" had so recently been printed.

The young lady in question sat like an infanta, surrounded by a newly acquired entourage, which fussed like
mother hens over every minuscule detail of her toilette and

makeup. She had been given a long white robe trimmed with silver over a revealing, white and silver bathing costume to wear in the scene, and appeared to be listening intently as George Landau bent over her shoulder, whispering direction in her ear as she read through her new lines.

A furious Pandora Ashley yanked the hairbrush out of the hand of the hairdresser who was attempting to arrange her coiffure, and strode purposefully to where Tony Holland and Dennis Jaeger, the director of photography, were painstakingly arranging the complicated lighting for the morning's first set-up. Tony obviously failed to note the look on his lady love's face as she approached, for he merely put an arm around her genially and said, "Sorry, love, no time to talk now . . ."

The tone of Pandora's voice, however—pitched in a hissing whisper which could easily have carried to the back row of any amphitheater—soon alerted him (and anyone else within a hundred-yard radius) that he had a problem. Brandishing pink pages under his handsome nose, she shrieked, "You don't mean to stand there and tell me you seriously propose to shoot this pile of shit!"

Clutching her firmly by the wrist, he yanked her away from the others and spoke in a low, firm voice in which velvet covered steel: "If you are referring, Pandora, to the new scene fifteen, we *are* going to shoot it, and we will *all* play our parts."

Gesticulating wildly, she pointed over to where Lucinda Sinclair and George Landau still sat, huddled together in conference over the new version of the scene, and protested, "You bloody fool! Can't you see what's happening? They're taking over the whole picture! You bloody fool! First, they'll push me out . . . next, it will be you!"

"Pandora," he began, his voice gentle yet authoritative, his speech emphasized by a pause between every word, "you are mistaken. I am *nobody's* fool. We are shooting the scene this way for exactly three reasons. Number one: Leonora Sheldrake is still too ill to work; therefore, the burden of her role must fall on someone's shoulders. In this case, those of her daughter, Daphne, as played—it so happens—by the new Mrs. Martin Sinclair. It also happens, unfortunately for us, that the new Mrs. Sinclair, while undoubtedly a very pretty girl, is a very inexperienced actress. Therefore, if our dear friend, Mr. George Landau, should choose, out of the goodness of his heart, to coach her into giving a better performance . . . who am I to argue? Number two: If you even troubled to read any further than your own lines of dialogue, Miss Ashley, you would see that *the scene works!* Number three: *I* am the director on this picture."

With that, Pandora raised her arm as if to strike him, but instead merely flung the sheaf of papers she was carrying over the cliff into the foaming sea beneath, where they fluttered gently like so many petals from a dying flower.

"George!" said Tony Holland calmly, addressing his second assistant. "See to it that Miss Ashley gets another copy of the scene, will you!"

Lucinda Bayes Sinclair had observed the scene between Tony and Pandora from a distance, that distance made even greater by her new status as the producer's wife. Now she knew exactly what was meant by that old song about being a bird in a fucking gilded cage. Just when it seemed she had everything she wanted in the world in the palm of her hand, the old man wouldn't let her enjoy any of it!

In the few short weeks of her marriage, Lucinda had adjusted very well indeed to her new status in the spotlight, almost to the point of believing the flattering assessments—directed, of course, to the new Mrs. Sinclair—of her surpassing beauty and talent, delivered, of course, by a bevy of her husband's toadies and sycophants, headed by George

Landau. She knew it would be so easy to dismiss her earlier, sordid life as an aberration, to proclaim that her new, exalted status was her true destiny.

After all, hadn't she known deep down, way back when she sent off to Saks for that red silk blouse, that she was somebody special? Hadn't she been chosen the winner in the "Madonna Wanna-Be" contest out of dozens of other pretty girls because hers was a special destiny? No. Despite all the fawning attention of these people, who a few months ago would not even have acknowledged her existence, she knew deep down it just was not so.

And now Martin Sinclair wouldn't let her enjoy the pretense of her new status. The embers of resentment against her new husband were fueled by the bitterness of her discovery that ultimately she, Lucinda Bayes, held no interest, no existence, for him as a human being. Nothing whatsoever! He didn't love *her;* he didn't desire *her.* Martin Sinclair wanted nothing from her that was not Madelaine. He would offer her no comfort, nor would he accept any from her. Each time he held her, he made love to a ghost.

Here she was, light-years away from her hateful past, and *still* she was only a thing for others to use. *Still* she was not her own person. And so Lucinda had already learned both to fear and despise her new husband. She despised him for the way he had lain trembling in her arms the first night she had let him make love to her. He had called her "Madelaine," begging her forgiveness over and over in a quavering voice, full of remorse. And even though it was dark in the room, Lucinda could have sworn there were tears in his eyes.

Nor was that all. His madness had a second, darker face, for at times Martin became a wild man. Once he had lit a fire in the grate of the hotel suite and had forced her to make love to him right on the floor, so close to the flames she could feel their scorching heat. He had made love to her brutally, as if exacting vengeance, calling her filthy, horrible names, slapping her around roughly. When his wife looked up at him afterward with tear-filled, frightened eyes, he had told her she was "foolish." It was "only a game," he had said, but she could see shame in his eyes, and he had left her to sleep alone while he made a bed on the sofa in the den.

The next morning he had given her an incredible diamond and platinum bracelet from Van Cleef and Arpels as a peace offering—a reward exacted at an awful price. And Lucinda remained afraid of him, of his moods and his terrible jealousy. If she so much as looked at another man . . . God help her! She had no freedom at all. Martin saw to it that she never had a cent in cash on her, so there was no way she could go off on her own for any length of time. Naturally, she had no credit cards in her name either. Furthermore, she divined that Sinclair's chauffeur had received instructions to report her every movement to his boss. So if her husband wasn't watching her, there was always someone else. It was a rare moment indeed when she found herself away from the watchful eyes of either Merle Greene or George Landau, both of whom had been assigned to keep tabs on her movements.

Naturally, Merle got a great kick out of her position as watchdog over Lucinda's honor. Overwhelmed by the perversity and the irony of it all, Lucinda, for the first time, began to abandon herself in bed with the older woman. In spite of herself, it began to turn her on, being able to outsmart Martin, to cheat on him in spite of his insane precautions—even if it was with the likes of Merle Greene. Too bad both Landau and the chauffeur were gay!

And then, of course, there was Rod Ward. It seemed millions of years ago when she had watched him on that television awards show. Now here she was, actually making a movie with the gorgeous hunk, and of course she couldn't say two words to him that were not a part of the script. Lucinda had always been crazy about Rod Ward, had even hung a poster of him—all glistening with sweat in cut-offs and no shirt—in her tiny bedroom back at the Shady Lane trailer park.

Oh, yes, here she was, imprisoned by Martin Sinclair as surely as she had been imprisoned by her father. Why couldn't she ever be like Pandora Ashley? That English bitch had all the luck! All the guys, including Tony Holland (who was a dreamboat, Lucinda had to admit, even if he wasn't exactly her type), clustered around Pandora like flies, and now it looked like Rod Ward had started coming on to her. Maybe that was why he had dumped Leonora Sheldrake. Pandora could just sit there like an empress, like goddam Catherine the Great, or something, while Lucinda was stuck acting out the demented fantasies of a lunatic old man.

One time Lucinda and Ward had filmed a scene together, the one where he, as César, the terrorist, grabs her from behind, holding a knife to her throat and threatening to throw her off the cliff at Eden Roc. All that was required of her in the scene was that she look terrified and scream on cue. It had sounded so simple, but when they started filming, all she could think of was this hunk, Rod Ward, with his arms around her. She could even feel the prodigious bulge of his crotch pressed up against her rear. It was incredible! She wanted to scream, all right, but for all the wrong reasons. They had to do six takes before they managed to get a decent scream out of her. In between shots she had kind of wiggled up against Ward and smiled, but he had pretended not to notice what she was doing. Lucinda figured it must be because she was the producer's wife, and even Rod Ward would be scared to start any trouble with her husband.

And then there was the matter of her appearance. Every single thing she wore had to be handpicked for her by Sinclair, from her shoes to her eyeshadow. It didn't matter that they were rich. Invariably, if Lucinda saw something she liked, whether on another girl or in a shop window, Martin always said it was "vulgar" or "unsuitable," and would refuse to buy it for her. She felt like some dummy in a waxworks with all the blood and youth drained out of her. She couldn't even change her hairstyle and wear it loose, the way she liked it. Oh no! It always had to be swept back because—so Merle had told her—that snooty, dead wife of his used to wear it that way twenty years ago! Lucinda was becoming sick and tired of pretending to be a dead woman.

But Lucinda, despite much of her coarseness and her lack of proper education, was not stupid. And, as she was coming to realize, she was a good actress. Very good, in fact, and she was learning all the time. There was one very important thing she had learned from Merle Greene. She had learned to hide her emotions—to smile and to wait.

And so she smiled. And she waited.

Oh, how she waited!

The room was dark and in total silence, except for the haunting sound of the wind blowing in gusts outside, hurtling the waves against the rock below. Martin Sinclair could feel his young bride's presence beside him, but he did not reach out to touch her. He could feel the gentle heaving of her breasts, sense the faint smell of her soft perfume in the cool night air. She had submitted to him tonight, as before. She had once again allowed him to make love to her because she was his wife. She had lain beneath him, unmoving, staring at him fixedly with her wide, terrified eyes. He sensed darkness flowing between them, almost a palpable living thing.

No, surely he was wrong. He was imagining it, he told himself. She *did* feel real affection for him. She had shown it plainly; in fact, she was always highly demonstrative. In public, at least. It was only that she was very young and frightened and inexperienced. In time she would come to love him; he was sure of that.

He continued to sit erect and motionless, staring at the strip of light under the door. The sudden shrill ringing of the phone jolted him from his somber reverie. Lucinda stirred restlessly beside him.

"Yes! What is it?"

"Un instant, Monsieur Sinclair, J'ai New-York en ligne!"

Suddenly Ingrid Sinclair's agitated voice was on the phone. "Martin, Martin! Oh, thank God I've found you in. Something terrible has happened!"

"Sweet Jesus! There's nothing you and I have to say to each other. It's three-thirty in the morning here. Are you out of your mind? Call my lawyers!"

"You don't understand. It's Alison, Martin! They called me from the institution because they didn't know how to get in touch with you!"

"Well! What's wrong with her? Is she ill? Dead?" Sinclair's voice was gruff and unconcerned, betraying no suggestion of anxiety at either of these possibilities.

"No, no she's unharmed but . . ."

"Then why the devil are you bothering me?"

"She's set fire to Clover Hill. Somehow she got hold of some old rags and set them ablaze, and then made her escape out a window. The blaze destroyed over half the building before they were able to extinguish it. It was just before dawn . . . most of the poor children were sleeping . . ." Ingrid collapsed sobbing, for a moment unable to continue. "It was horrible, Martin! Nine children were burned alive.

Many more were injured . . . they don't know yet if all of them will pull through."

"God Almighty . . . God save me!" stammered Sinclair. Blood pounded in his brain. He felt a sharp, stabbing pain in his chest. He seemed to see Alison before him, yelping her wild animal laugh, dancing in a sea of flames which swept over continents to devour him. He clutched at his heart, doubling up in pain. "Quick!" he shouted at Lucinda, "my tablets . . . on the bathroom shelf! Hurry!"

A doctor had been summoned immediately to the producer's bedside. It was a very mild stroke. There was no immediate cause for concern. Sinclair must simply rest comfortably for a day or so. He must have no further aggravation, the physician told the young bride.

"I'll do what I can, Doctor."

She seems a sweet young thing, thought the doctor. She is genuinely concerned. Old Sinclair is a lucky bastard after all. Not much wrong with him, really; all things considered, he is in pretty good shape for a man his age.

22

At dawn's first light, a bizarre procession of cars and vans snaked its way along the perilous hairpin curves high in the mountains behind Nice at La Vésubie. One side of the scenic road is carved out of the mountain. Only a few stone markers separate the motorist from a steep drop of several hundred feet into the valley below.

The camera had been positioned in the rear of the first vehicle, a truck, and the entire technical crew, led by Tony Holland, huddled as best they could upon its small platform. Spotlights within the truck were carefully positioned to reflect diffused light into the following car, a magnificent yellow and black Rolls-Royce Corniche convertible. The car's top was down, and in the driver's seat sat Ian Harrison portraying Lord Dunsmere.

Next in the line were an assortment of cars bearing the stunt man, makeup artists, script girl, and so forth. Bringing up the rear of the parade was Martin Sinclair's black chauffeured Mercedes.

The scene being filmed was one in which a furious and drunken Lord Dunsmere chases after his unfaithful wife and her terrorist boyfriend, and is killed when his vehicle plunges off a cliff.

"Good, Ian!" called out Tony from the truck to the convertible behind him. "Now reach for the glove compartment, take out your pistol, and lay it on the seat beside you! Good! Well done!"

The scene was looking good so far. The early light reflected eerily off the dark, lowering clouds overhanging La Vésubie, providing an extra touch of drama and foreboding. "Cut! Print! . . . now where's our stunt driver?" called Tony as the procession halted by the roadside near a particularly hazardous bend, where runners had already been laid along the ground so that the Rolls would travel down the cliff by a predetermined route.

Wires had been attached to the car, then doubled back so that when the car reached just the right point in its descent, explosives could be detonated automatically. In addition, another gadget, a sort of plunger in a spring, had been attached to the front of the Rolls-Royce, a mechanism which required great impact to set it off, and would be triggered only when the car hit the ground at the base of the hill. In this way, there would be a dramatic series of explosions, far more spectacular than just one big bang. A second camera was placed halfway down the ravine to record the convertible as it hurtled into space. As the stunt man, François Bessière, dressed in clothing identical to that worn by Ian, seated himself behind the wheel of the magnificent automobile, and came skidding around the curve in a series of practice runs, the company held its collective breath.

"Jesus Christ! Why did it have to be a Rolls?" moaned a sweating Martin Sinclair. "Couldn't we have faked it and sent a cheaper car over the cliff? Do you know what this is gonna cost me if you don't get it on the first shot?"

"What about him?" asked Tony Holland, pointing at the young Frenchman behind the wheel of the car. "Do you know what it could cost him?"

"Bon!" called the young man. "I am ready. *On y va?"*

"Right!" called Brian Chambers. "Places everyone!"

"Moonshadows, scene thirty-two, take one."

Someone muttered under their breath, "Or nothing!"

"Speed!"

Tony Holland hesitated for a moment, paralyzed by the knowledge that for the next few seconds a man's life was in grave danger. If something should go wrong, what would it be for? A strip of celluloid lasting seconds on the screen in a film which he had already begun to fear would be no more than mediocre? God help him! he said to himself, and then aloud, "Turn over!"

The shot went flawlessly. Like a dream. Bessière drove the Rolls as fast as possible, turning and skidding on the hairpin curve, abandoning the wheel at the last possible moment, just before the car went hurtling down into the gorge. Halfway down, there was a small blast, then at the foot of the cliff the second, much larger detonation occurred, and the magnificent machine was an exploding inferno.

"Cut! Print!"

"Hurrah! Bravo!"

Smiling broadly, Holland clapped his director of photography, Dennis Jaeger, on the back, saying, "You better not tell me there was no film in the camera, or you're the next one over the cliff!"

"It's all right, guv, we got it!"

Somewhat shyly, now that the mood of tension had been dispelled, George O'Shaugnessy, the second assistant, approached Tony Holland and asked if he might have a word with him in private.

"Of course, George." He noted the man's troubled expression. "What can I help you with?"

"I dunno, guv. You see, I've been thinking whether to speak to you about this all morning. You know, since that scene on the boat between Miss Ashley and that fucking cowboy . . ."

"Yes . . . go on . . ."

"I don't rightly know how to say this . . . but, well, everyone of us thinks you're first-rate, guv, and none of us likes to see you get screwed around, especially not by that lot . . ."

"Go on, man; for christsake, whatever it is can't be that bad."

"No sir. It's just that . . . you know . . . when I was crouched down by the side of the bed, like, I heard them two talking . . . arranging a meeting, and, knowing how you feel about Miss Ashley, I thought . . . well, you see how it is, sir."

Tony Holland swallowed hard and stared blankly out over the hillside at the still-flaming wreckage in the gorge beneath. Red tongues of flame shot up against the gray sky.

"I'm sorry, guv. Are you all right, then? You aren't angry with me for telling you?"

Tony clasped the man warmly on the arm. "I'll be fine, George. Don't worry about me. You did what you thought was in my best interest, I know that. I'd just like to be by myself for a moment."

The Eden Roc pavilion had been filled with quartz lamps, cables, and nearly a hundred extras for that morning's shooting. Nearly the entire company was, in fact, assembled, since the scene to be shot was one of the major set pieces of *Moonshadows*—the moment when the gang of six terrorists, aided by several accomplices disguised as waiters, and by Isabel, Lady Dunsmere, a guest of the hotel, burst into the Eden Roc during a busy lunch hour at the height of the fashionable season, and take hostage the guests, among whom are numbered some of the world's wealthiest and most influential men and women. The effect of this maneuver is to isolate the pavilion, which has its back to the sea and is separated from the main body of the hotel by an expanse of park. Beneath them—through Isabel's contrivance—the yacht *Moonshadows* lies moored at the dock, waiting to spirit César and his gang away, once his ransom demands have been met.

The logistics of the scene were very complicated, and the entry of Rod Ward and his terrorists had been choreographed as intricately as any ballet. It was feared initially that Leonora Sheldrake would once again that day be unable to work, thereby necessitating another expensive postponement, for her role in the shooting of the scene was central. However, like a true professional, she had left her hospital bed several days early. She was a trooper, everyone agreed.

Cast and crew alike broke into applause when Leonora Sheldrake, along with her entourage of personal hairdresser, personal wardrobe assistant, and two Shih Tzus, swept on to the set. Her bearing was, as always, erect and graceful. She wore a simple, black silk Givenchy shift, adorned only by an enormous platinum cross encrusted with diamonds, which hung as a pendant on her bosom. Her wide brown eyes, with their famous lashes, brimmed with tears at the warmth of her reception.

"Thank you! Thank you all from the bottom of my heart. All you dear, dear people who have helped me through my ordeal. And, most of all, I thank our Lord Jesus Christ, who has brought me back to be with you here today!"

Leonora strode over to Anthony Holland and wrapped her arms around him in a warm embrace. "And last but far from least, I want to thank this lovely man who saved my life. Tony, I was very wrong about you. Can you ever forgive me?" There was another spontaneous burst of applause as Holland hugged her and called her "a great star and a great lady."

Pandora Ashley patted her hands together politely but soundlessly. Only Rod Ward stood apart with his back turned, scowling balefully out at the sea.

Leonora approached him next, extending her graceful hand to him. "God spoke to me, Rod, and asked me to forgive you. Can't we be friends?"

"Look," said the actor, flushing with embarrassment as he gave her a perfunctory handclasp, "is this supposed to be a movie or a revival meeting? Because if you folks are going to stand around here praising the Lord, I'll see you all later."

"For once, incredible as it may seem, Mr. Ward is right," agreed Tony. "All right places for scene seventeen, everybody. Props! Let's see César's gun again!"

"Here it is, guv," said Paul Cowley, the prop man, scurrying over with a tray on which several firearms were neatly set out.

"Which one did we say again?" asked Tony.

"We decided on that one, guv," said Cowley, pointing to a .45 Magnum.

"I still think it's too big. However, Sinclair wants to use it. All right, let's go.

"All right, everyone. Places for a rehearsal, please!"

Paul Cowley handed the huge gun to Rod Ward, who stroked its smooth, gleaming barrel with an appreciation that was almost sensual. "Thanks," he told the prop man. "I've always wanted a gun like this."

It was midnight. Pandora Ashley, wearing a red décolleté St. Laurent cocktail dress and the Cartier neckpiece given her by her husband just before the filming had begun, made her sultry way up the gangplank of the *Moonshadows* yacht, which danced ablaze with light on the dark water. In the main bedroom of the yacht, where so much of the filming had taken place, she found Rod Ward already waiting for her.

He wore skintight jeans and a black silk shirt unbuttoned to the waist, and was seated in an armchair facing the entrance to the cabin, pouring champagne from a bottle of Dom Perignon that was already three-quarters empty. He barely glanced up at her entrance. On the bedstand near him lay a small silver box, along with the .45 he had used in that day's filming. He opened the lid to the silver box, exposing the fine white powder inside; he wet his forefinger with champagne, dipped it in the powder, held it to his nostrils, and inhaled deeply. Then he took another swallow from his glass.

"Hello," whispered Pandora in a dusky voice.

"Hi," Rod mumbled laconically. "Here! You want some of this?"

Pandora nodded, and he poured her a glass of Dom Perignon, emptying the bottle. Then he held out the silver box of cocaine. Holding up the empty bottle, he added, "I got more of this crap in the fridge . . . I'll go open some. Hey," mockery gleamed in his hazel eyes, "what the fuck are you all dressed up for? Did you expect ballroom dancing?"

"Look," snapped Pandora angrily, "if you don't like the way I look, I can leave this minute."

Rod Ward threw back his head and laughed, flashing his magnificent white teeth. "You know what your problem is? All these assholes, like your husband and this Tony Holland, treat you like a lady." He lowered his voice to a rich, suggestive whisper, and put his arms around her: "You and

I both know you're no lady." He drew her toward him and kissed her hard on the mouth.

"Let me go!" she gasped.

"No problem," he said, clasping her small buttocks and pulling her against his body so that she could feel the pressure of his cock through the thin silk of her dress. "You can leave any time you want to . . . but you won't. You want what I got, and you want it bad." He glued his lips to hers once more, but this time, Pandora—trembling, panting—responded with her whole being.

"Take that thing off," he whispered, placing his hot tongue in her ear. The red silk shimmered to the floor around her feet. "That's better. Now . . ." he said, motioning toward the bed, "get over there. I just want to look at you for a while."

Now wearing only her red evening slippers with their delicate diamanté straps, Pandora stretched her lithe, tanned body alluringly on the sheets, holding her arms out toward her new lover. From outside, there came a continual hypnotic noise—bump, bump, bump, as black water lapped against the sides of the boat.

"Not yet," whispered Rod Ward, pouring himself another glass of champagne. "I told you. I want to look at you. Now spread your legs for me, baby. I want you to play with yourself."

He fixed his tigerlike hazel eyes on Pandora with the hunger of a predatory animal as her hands traveled over the hard, firm swell of her breasts, then down into the secret cleft between her thighs. His lips curled in a cruel, sensual smile as he watched her movements, waiting for her climax, waiting for the honey to flow from her.

Pandora's movements were quicker now, frenzied almost to the point of desperation as she spread her beautiful brown legs, begging to be satisfied.

Only then did he crouch over her so that he could enter her with more force. "Beg for it!" he whispered in a voice thick with lust, barbed with contempt.

Her flesh was burning. She wanted to raise her body, to engulf the insolent baton of his swollen sex deep within herself, to abandon herself totally, to find oblivion in excruciating pleasure. "Yes . . . yes . . . I need it," she whimpered almost childishly. "Give it to me, baby."

"Not yet!" taunted the actor. "You're not ready for me yet." He paused above her, touching her mouth briefly with the tip of his penis, then withdrawing it again, then burying his avid mouth in Pandora's sex, his probing tongue darting into the very core of her being as she bloomed under him like some moist, hothouse flower.

Her cries now mounted in their savagery: "Don't stop! Please don't stop!!"

Suddenly, though, like a jungle beast that scents the smell of hunters, he raised his eyes from the writhing woman on the bed and looked toward the doorway. There was a muffled sound of footsteps, and Tony Holland stood before him, rigid with anger. His ice-blue eyes were filled with disgust and loathing as he surveyed the scene before him. With a rapid gesture he tore off the jacket he was wearing and flung it at the woman on the bed.

"Put this on, you slut!" he shouted at Pandora. "You're coming back with me!"

In a split-second, with a violent, merciless lunge, Rod Ward fell upon the intruder, first aiming an expert kick at Tony's groin, then crashing his fist into the director's jaw with deadly, bone-crushing accuracy. Holland could taste the warm blood in his mouth as he lashed out with his right hand against the actor's jaw. The blow connected powerfully. He could feel several teeth break against his knuckles. Ward staggered backward, then lunged forward with a vicious kick at his adversary, connecting with his ribs. Tony fell to his knees, but in a lightning movement, he managed to catch Rod's foot at the ankle and, with a bone-wrenching twist, threw him to the ground. Teeth grinding with rage, he grabbed the prone actor by the shoulders and began to pound his skull against the floor.

Pandora whimpered childishly as Tony's blows dazed Ward with their devastating power. In an instant she realized that he struck Ward not out of revenge for her lost honor, which was beneath contempt, nor even for his own, which was beyond redemption, but for Josh Woodard, and for the fools she had made of all of them. In that instant she knew with horrible certainty that she had lost him irrevocably, and . . . in that instant . . . she grabbed the gun beside her and fired.

Ward cried out as the shot tore through the darkness, and Holland's lifeless body slumped on top of him on the floor. Dark blood welled from a gaping hole in the back of his shirt. Pandora stood over them, her naked brown legs astride her lover's body, his jacket covering her nakedness. Still holding the gun to her bosom, she broke the sudden silence with her hysterical sobs: "I loved him! My God! I really loved him!"

In a second, Rod Ward was on his feet. He swung out, catching the left side of Pandora's face with a stinging blow.

"You no-good, crazy bitch! Don't you know what you've done? You've finished both of us!"

Pandora was shaking uncontrollably. Her face and jaw burned with the force of his blow. "Couldn't we say it was suicide?"

Ward laughed bitterly. "With a slug that size in the center of his back, you dumb, fucking cunt?"

"We can say he tried to rape me. You heard my cries for help and had to shoot to stop him!"

"It's no good. Everybody on the picture knows you were lovers. Besides, with your reputation, who's going to believe in a rape? The minute they see the body, we're dead."

Suddenly Pandora lost all trace of hysteria. She was cool, collected. "Then they mustn't find the body."

"We can't just dump it overboard. It'll take them longer, but they'd find it anyway. Even if we dump it further out, they might dredge for it, or it might wash up on shore. The bastard was a famous director, for God's sake, in the middle of a twenty-five-million-dollar picture. No one's gonna let him just vanish!"

Pandora's voice was icy. "Look, can you run this boat?" she asked.

"Yeah! I think so! But what the fuck good is that going to do us?"

"Don't argue with me. Just put out to sea, and hurry!"

Lucinda leaned provocatively across the dinner table and lit a Havana cigar for her husband. The old man inhaled placidly, staring into his young wife's sparkling eyes. He had recovered almost completely from the shock of the previous evening. The American tabloids had made a fuss over the terrible accident at Alison's "school," but his lawyers—and his money—had managed to quiet the furor, for now, at least.

The day's filming had gone surprisingly well. Leonora Sheldrake had come through for them, and the day's difficult scenes had gone smoothly. Holland had done a fine job. After a rocky start, it looked as though *Moonshadows* was taking shape after all. Praise for his young wife's work was, moreover, unanimous. She had risen splendidly to the challenge of her first role, and, even more remarkably, she had that luminous, elusive quality on screen that makes a star.

Sinclair took a sip of his Rémy Martin, and gazed at the floodlit white outline of the schooner which stood on the shore at La Siesta, its proud masts etched against a starry sky. At first he had resisted Lucinda and Merle's combined entreaties to dine in this garish French "mini-Disneyland" as he called it, with its lily-pond dance floors and miniature go-cart racing, but the two ladies had argued that Melissa would love it, and he was forced to admit that the evening had been a tremendous success.

Merle and Lucinda had taken turns steering the miniature racing cars around the track, with the child beside them, squealing with delight. Then they had dined, not well, but not badly either, on grilled *loup au fenouil* flamed at the table with Pernod. A festive mood had prevailed all evening, and Martin was blissfully unaware when Merle Greene slipped her foot out of her black satin pumps and ran it up the inside of Lucinda's thigh. In the background, a Gilbert Bécaud record, a perennial favorite in the South of France, was blaring as couples swayed together intimately on the floodlit dance floor.

"L'importante, c'est la rose. L'importante c'est la rose! L'importante, c'est la rose . . . crois-moi . . ."

"Daddy! Daddy! Look!" cried little Melissa, clutching her father's arm excitedly and pointing out to sea. "Look! Fireworks!"

It was true. An eerie red glow was reflected on the black, still mirror of the sea.

"My God!" cried Merle Greene, "that's not fireworks! It's something burning! A boat."

The foursome watched transfixed as the night sky ignited with a massive explosion, and the yacht erupted in a bright orange ball of flame, searing the blackness above.

Around them in the restaurant there was momentary

panic and confusion as the customers scrambled excitedly to get a better view.

"*Mon Dieu!*"

"*Qu'est-ce que c'est?*"

"*Qu'est-ce qui se passe?*"

Only Martin Sinclair sat rigid and immobile, his lower lip trembling convulsively, his face the color of ashes. Only he knew what burned upon the waters. It was the *Moonshadows*.

23

Flashbulbs popped like gunshots as a haggard Pandora Ashley wearing a plain black linen suit, and with dark glasses covering her famous eyes, made her way on the arm of her husband, Josh Woodard, through the hostile throng which surged around her like an angry sea. Cameras from the U.S. television networks, as well as from Téléfrance, I.T.N., and the B.B.C., were positioned outside the courtroom in Nice where the coroner's inquest into the death of Anthony Holland was about to begin.

Pandora felt her legs buckling under her. Only Josh's strong hands prevented her from crumpling to the ground like a puppet whose strings have been cut. The outcry against her in the popular press had been strong. Despite the best efforts—and, if truth be told, considerable sums of money—expended by studio publicists to quell them, all sorts of wild rumors were circulating about the exact nature of her involvement in Tony Holland's death. According to some accounts, Rod Ward, her costar in *Moonshadows*, was also implicated, but these rumors were discounted when George Landau swore that he had been with the actor all evening on the night the young director died.

There were certain other unexplained circumstances

which tended to further fuel speculation. What, for instance, had become of the .45 caliber pistol which had vanished from the prop department on the afternoon of Holland's death, and which had last been seen in Rod Ward's possession? How to account for the two life preservers bearing the *Moonshadows* name which had turned up along the beach, miles down the coast from the rest of the debris of the wreck?

In any case, the public fury tended to vent itself more on Pandora, who was viewed as a homewrecker and even a whore. Some middle-aged women in the crowd actually spat in her face, calling out, *"Putain!"* "Murderess!" "Assassin!"

Christine Holland had remained sequestered in England with her children, issuing a statement that she had no reason whatever to believe that her late husband had been guilty of any sort of immoral conduct. She was sure that the explosion on board the yacht would prove to have been merely a terrible accident, connected with improper storage of explosives needed for special effects during filming.

Josh Woodard, inched forward, clearing a path through the forest of microphones thrust in his wife's face. To the barrage of reporters' questions, he finally paused long enough to comment: "Gentlemen, I can only say that my wife's testimony will show her to be not only innocent of all wrongdoing, but, in fact, a victim herself."

In a tiny courtroom packed to the rafters with a restless crowd, Pandora Ashley's story, related in a feeble, trembling voice, was translated into French for the presiding *juge d'instruction.* She told the court how she and the dead man had, briefly, been lovers. How her husband, Josh Woodard, had discovered their affaire and had flown back to England and threatened to divorce her. Overcome with remorse, and realizing too late how much her marriage meant to her, she had confronted Anthony Holland on the evening of his death and told him that it was all over between them, that she could never see him again.

Holland had first become wild with anger, then hopelessly despondent, falling on his knees and pleading with her not to abandon him. When this had failed, he had threatened suicide, and then run out into the night. He had also threatened, she said, to make his death "a spectacle." At the time, she had not known what he meant. She later assumed, however, it referred to setting ablaze the *Moonshadows* loaded with explosives, and turning it into his own funeral pyre.

The judgment of the court was that Anthony Holland had died by his own hand.

Naturally, after Anthony Holland's death, production shut down on *Moonshadows.* For the present there was nothing for the company to do but sit gloomily in a state of shock, drinking in the half-deserted bars and cafés of the off-season resort town, trading stories of other films that had folded. The skies above the Côte d'Azur were laden. Rumors flew. Names of other directors who might be brought in were bandied about—Friedkin, Hal Ashby, even Frankenheimer. The word, though, was that no one would touch this picture with a ten-foot pole. A petition signed by all the English members of the crew and a majority of the French ones was presented to Martin Sinclair, respectfully informing him that none of the signatories, regardless of the consequences, would set foot on the same sound stage as Miss Pandora Ashley. This gesture, they felt, was the least they could do in honor of Tony Holland's memory, for every man among them knew, in some way or other, the bitch was responsible for his death.

With or without this gesture, however, the only thing certain about *Moonshadows* was that Ashley was out. The studio had been bombarded with hate mail against the actress, and all were in agreement that she was "box office poison." Furthermore, the bulk of her scenes would have to be reshot in any case, unless they could find another boat just like the *Moonshadows* so that the previously shot scenes would match with the ones yet to be filmed—assuming, of course, there was to be any further filming—on board that boat. The studio's legal department had, in addition, gone over Pandora's contract and found that it contained a somewhat antiquated, but under the circumstances, highly useful clause enabling them and Sinclair as producer to terminate the actress's services without further compensation, for "reasons of moral turpitude."

Still, the odds in the Flore bar were six to one against *Moonshadows* ever being completed, and there were few takers. Insurance would cover part of the cost overruns, of course—the yacht; Holland's death—but without a minimum transfusion of at least three million additional dollars, the situation was hopeless. It was by now an open secret that around the studio's executive suite the *Moonshadows* set had long been referred to as the "geriatric ward" by Kaufman and his slick young assistants.

Unlike his predecessor, Kaufman was a sharp young ex-entertainment attorney who stood in no awe of the Broadway stage and had no great respect for Martin Sinclair. Any picture that didn't take into account the thirteen-to-twenty-five age group was, to Kaufman's mind, predestined to failure. And who the fuck wanted to know from terrorists, anyway? "You want to see terrorists, you watch Dan Rather." There was only one hope: that the sensationalism attendant upon Tony Holland's death and the attendant hints of scandal had aroused enough curiosity in the public to make them want to see this film. It was this angle that a broken Martin Sinclair hoped to exploit when he decided to make a last-ditch effort to save the picture by flying to Los Angeles to meet with Alan Kaufman.

"They can't do this to me!" shrieked a hysterical Pandora Ashley. "What do they mean, 'moral turpitude'? That went out with Fanny Arbuckle! We'll sue them for a fortune!"

"*We* won't do anything," said her husband, Josh Woodard, opening a drawer in the dresser in their hotel bedroom and flinging an armful of shirts onto the bed. "In fact, *we* do not exist."

"What do you mean, Josh? You don't know what you're saying! I know you've every reason to be upset, but I'll make it up to you. I swear it!"

Josh, ignoring his wife's outburst, flung a Gucci suitcase on the bed and proceeded to fill it with his clothes. Pandora ran toward him and grabbed him by the arms. Tears were streaming down her cheeks.

"You can't leave me now! You can't. I've always loved you! I've been bad, I know, but I've always loved you!"

"Come on, my dear! Surely you can do better than that fourth-rate dialogue. In fact, the whole performance is really rather old hat."

Pandora crumpled to her knees, weeping. "I'll die if you leave me now!"

"A bit better," said Josh, "but not up to your best standards. Not half as good as that show you put on in the courtroom today!" Pandora opened her green eyes wide with genuine alarm. "Come, come," said her husband. "You didn't suppose for one moment that I was such an idiot as to believe that load of rubbish you told them? You really do think me a fool, don't you?" he added sadly.

"But if . . . if you didn't . . ."

"If I didn't believe you, why did I stand by you? That's

what you want to know, isn't it? Because . . . I once loved you very much. I could not face the thought of them trying you for murder."

"Then you do love me! Josh, I beg you, listen to me. We can begin again! I don't care about *Moonshadows*. I don't care about the part! Let's go away together . . . far away! To Rio . . . or the Seychelles . . . anywhere, darling, so long as it's with you."

"There is just one small fact you seem to have overlooked, Pandora."

"What is it? Tell me! Whatever it is, I can put it right."

"You are a murderess. You murdered a kind, decent man, whose only sin was falling in love with you . . . a man, I daresay, very like myself."

Josh Woodard slapped tight the lid of the suitcase and flicked the lock. "Consider yourself lucky, my dear. There are not many people who get away with murder." Josh picked up the case and strode toward the door. "I believe, my dear, your line is, 'What will become of me'? Mine is . . . 'Frankly, my dear, I don't give a damn!' "

By the time Martin Sinclair had seated himself facing Alan Kaufman's desk, he was livid with rage. The young executive had kept him waiting in his outer offices for over thirty minutes. Kaufman, a young, dark man with outsized horn-rimmed glasses and a carefully honed, minuscule nose on which they balanced uneasily, leaned back in his tufted leather chair, pressed the fingertips of his small hands together, and held them up to his mouth.

"As I explained to you over the phone, Mr. Sinclair, I am really not certain about the point of this meeting. We are both very busy men, and I sincerely wish you had not taken the trouble to make this trip. I am afraid I just don't see any possible way this deal can be restructured. I'd like to help you, naturally . . . excuse me a moment, will you, while I

take this call. Hello . . . Freddie, how are you, kiddo?
. . . Yeah, yeah, uh-huh . . . I think the tie-in with the
score here is just gonna be phenomenal. We start airing that
rock video of the title song on MTV about three weeks before we open. I tell you, Pat Benatar's sensational . . .
those kids are gonna piss themselves . . ."

With a sudden movement of surprising agility, Martin
Sinclair shot to his feet, lunged across the expanse of Alan
Kaufman's desk, wrenched the telephone from the stunned
executive's hand, and slammed it back down on its cradle.
He leaned over the desk menacingly, staring at Kaufman
with his deep black eyes, eyeball to eyeball.

"Jesus Christ! What's the matter with you, are you
crazy?" The younger man was clearly frightened.

"Now, punk, allow me to introduce myself. My name is
Martin Sinclair. I have been lighting up Broadway for as
long as you've been alive, and I will continue to do so long
after you've lost your space in the executive parking lot. So I
suggest you show a little more respect. Now I want you to
get on that intercom and inform your secretary that you are
in a very important conference and are not taking any
calls." Sinclair's voice was a lethal whisper.

Kaufman was swift to comply. "Mia . . . I'm not to
be disturbed. No. Don't put any more calls through for a
half hour or so."

"That's better," Sinclair hissed approvingly.

"Mr. Sinclair, look, I apologize if I've been uninten-
tionally rude in any way, but this still does not alter the
fundamental situation. I just cannot see the justification of
our sinking more money into *Moonshadows*. At this stage,
frankly, I feel it would be throwing money down a well."

"When were you last in a supermarket, Mr. Kaufman?"

Kaufman stared at him with a kind of blank panic,

fearing that he was in reality trapped with a dangerous lunatic. He gave an involuntarily start when the old man opened
his briefcase, and reached inside. Rather than a weapon,
however, Sinclair extracted from it a pile of tabloids and
magazines which he proceeded to pile on Kaufman's desk.
Then he began pointing out their headlines.

"Look!" said the producer. " '*MOONSHADOWS* MYS-
TERY! DIRECTOR'S DEATH TRYST' . . . 'PANDORA
ASHLEY'S AGONY' . . . '*MOONSHADOWS* DEATH
TRIANGLE.' Do you have any idea how many millions of
dollars worth of free publicity this represents? You've already got over fifteen million tied up in the film, and now
you're going to throw out a picture that the public is burst-
ing to see, just because of a lousy three million dollars?"

Alan Kaufman surveyed the stack of papers before
him, displaying a degree of increased interest. Nevertheless
he hesitated: "You have a point. Still, there's no guarantee
this scandal can be translated into box-office dollars. After
all, everybody read about *Cleopatra,* and look what a disaster that turned out to be. Besides, you're talking *three* million? For that amount you expect to get a director and a
leading lady and a yacht and another three weeks on location? That sounds to me more like six, eight million. Besides, I hear Streep, even Jackie Bisset, turned you down flat
about taking over Ashley's part."

"We don't need a *new* leading lady."

"I don't know what you're talking about."

"Look. It's Pandora the public is whispering about,
right?"

"Yes, but she's already been released from her contract."

"True enough . . . still, there's nothing that says we
can't use the film we already have on her. All we have to do
is rewrite some of the remaining scenes so that instead of the

Isabel-Pandora character getting mixed up with Rod Ward and the terrorist plot, it becomes Daphne, Leonora Sheldrake's daughter."

"Who just happens to be played by your wife, Lucinda Sinclair."

"My wife, Lucinda Sinclair, will defer her salary . . . and we still have Pandora there for publicity value, which we wouldn't have even if we *could* get the likes of Streep or Bisset."

Alan Kaufman pressed his fingertips together once more; "Go on," he said, "I hear you. What about a director?"

"George Landau."

"You *are* crazy! The man has got to be over a hundred years old. Why, he's senile!"

"George Landau is precisely the same age as the President of the United States and is neither more nor less senile. Holland shot most of the difficult footage; the rest is a piece of cake. Besides, Landau is an enormously wealthy man. He doesn't want much money. He wants to see his name up on the screen again once more before he dies. He too is willing to defer his salary in exchange for points in the picture."

"Go on."

"Now my partner, Arthur Eckstein, has gotten in touch with some of his sources in Hong Kong, and they would be prepared to put up the remainder of financing, the entire three million—more, if necessary—if we can give them distribution rights in Asia and the Far East. It seems Rod Ward is very hot in Japan. His old TV series is rated number one there."

Alan Kaufman pressed his fingers to his lips, leaned back in his chair and paused for a moment. His button eyes blinked nervously behind the thick lenses. "Martin," he said finally, "I'm going to let you run with this. On these conditions: The studio will put up another 1.5 million, and not another cent. We retain world-wide distribution. You will be held personally responsible for any cost overruns. Do we have a deal?"

Martin Sinclair extended his hand for Kaufman to shake. Inwardly, he thanked God. There had been no Asian investors.

George Landau and Leonora Sheldrake were the only mourners to follow Sean's wasted body to his grave in a small cemetery near Long Beach. Rod Ward had been obdurate in his refusal to attend . . . indeed, the very mention of the boy's name was enough to make him break out into a cold sweat.

Tears streamed down George Landau's leathery cheek.

"Who would ever have thought I'd live to bury my beautiful boy?" Leonora put a comforting arm around the old man's shoulder, and walked by his side away from the grave.

"We are survivors, George, you and I."

Angela Armstrong was in an exuberant mood, as she applied the final touch of mascara to her eyelashes and set her makeup with a finishing mist of Évian. "At long last . . ." she thought, "things are beginning to go my way!" She clipped on the gold and diamond seashell-shaped earrings from Fred which she had recently received as a present from her soon-to-be-husband, Alan Kaufman. He had been a spectator at her polo match, and had fallen for her right away, inundating her with bouquets of flowers until he had won her completely. Angela positively glowed as she admired her reflection in the mirror, imagining with relish the power she would wield once she was married to Hollywood's youngest studio chief.

She slipped gingerly out of her pink robe and slithered into the Nolan Miller jersey and sequin creation. It had been designed specially for Angela to wear to tonight's party—a gala charity banquet at the Century Plaza Hotel honoring Frank Sinatra—and she had been to the designer for several fittings to make sure the dress would cling to her like a second skin.

The gown was a molded white silk jersey column, plunging deeply over the bodice which had been carefully cut to display to perfection Angela's famous bosom. On one side, the dress was heavily encrusted with a starburst pattern of gold sequins and beading. This pattern then descended asymmetrically on the bias to the skirt of the dress, which was also lavishly embroidered. Otherwise, the gown was simplicity itself, merely serving to accent each curve of the wearer's body. Smiling with satisfaction, Angela Armstrong zipped herself into the skintight creation, then let out a sudden gasp of horror as she surveyed herself in the mirror! The lovely dress, which had fitted her to perfection a week earlier, now drooped limply at the bodice, loose by a full two inches! Angela Armstrong's boobs were shrinking!

Dr. Harry Slotnick's face wore an expression of grave concern as he ran his practiced fingers over the scars beneath the actress's breasts. He shook his head disconsolately. "As we discussed before performing the implant, Miss Armstrong, there is always a risk with any surgery. The procedure is still, to some extent, an experimental one. We do see excellent results in ninety-nine percent of all cases . . . but in your case . . ."

"But there must be something you can do! Can't you just shove in another pouch of silicone or something?" shrieked Angela hysterically.

Slotnick shook his head ruefully. "As I have explained,

in a tiny number of cases the pouch we insert containing the silicone solution can rupture, gradually releasing its contents. To my mind, performing another operation at this point would only result in further scarring and expose you to the risk of breast cancer. Of course, you are always welcome to seek a second opinion, but I myself would strongly advise against surgery."

"You miserable quack!" screamed the actress. "I'll have your ass for malpractice."

"Miss Armstrong, I must beg you to calm yourself," said Dr. Slotnick soothingly. "If you remember, the procedure was a purely voluntary one—I even advised you against it, remarking that, as you were already a very attractive young lady without the operation, it might be wise to forego it. You were most insistent that I go ahead. Your consent form, signed by you, clearly indicates that you understood the possible risks involved and were prepared to take them."

Angela Armstrong concealed her red-rimmed eyes behind dark Cartier glasses and staggered out into the bright sunlight of Roxbury Drive. Her career was over . . . finished! Just when Kaufman had put together a package on the *She* remake! Her entire wardrobe was to have consisted of little more than leopard skins draped strategically about her hips. She could never star in such a film now! With tears streaming down her cheeks, she got behind the wheel of her new canary-yellow Corniche convertible, whose customized plates read T.N.A.1. However, by the time the luxurious machine pulled through the gates of Bel Air, climbing toward Chalon, Angela had recovered her composure. After all, she was still engaged to Alan Kaufman. She would soon be the wife of the youngest studio head in Hollywood. Fuck it! She was still at the top!

* * *

Lucinda Bayes Sinclair and Merle Greene sat cross-legged on the floor of Lucinda's bedroom in the gorgeous old Beverly Hills mansion Martin Sinclair had bought her upon her completion of *Moonshadows*. They shrieked and squealed with the eagerness of two little girls as they unwrapped the parcels that had arrived from the day's visit to Rodeo Drive. The huge room was strewn with an incredible amount of boxes, tissue paper, and plastic shopping bags bearing the most prestigious names in the world of fashion. Boxes of shoes from Maud Frizon, Andrea Pfister, and Bruno Magli were stacked up like minibricks. Dozens of silk blouses from Saint Laurent and Ungaro, and Hermès scarves in every color in the rainbow were flung about the room like streamers. Enough Chanel chains and pearls to fill a pirate's chest gleamed on the bed.

The mirror-lined doors of the room's several armoires were flung open so that the two ladies could swirl about in their new finery, inspecting their reflections from every angle. Lucinda held a stunning, violet beaded Assaro creation up to her beautiful face and smiled exultantly at what she saw reflected in the mirror. She hugged Merle impulsively, saying, "I have to pinch myself sometimes to remember all this is real! Who would ever believe that it was less than six months ago that you found me sitting by the pool at the Beverly Hills, crying my heart out?"

"You don't regret our bargain, then?" smiled Merle Greene.

At that moment, Martin Sinclair returned home from a triumphantly successful screening of the final act of *Moonshadows* for Kaufman and the other studio biggies. As he passed the partially open door to his wife's bedroom, he heard girlish laughter. Clutching a small blue parcel in his hand—a sapphire ring he had brought back from Tiffany's as a present for his young bride to celebrate the successful completion of *Moonshadows*—he approached the open bedroom door without making a sound. It would be fun to surprise Lucinda.

The mirrored doors of the huge armoires inside were flung open so that he caught his wife's reflection before she was aware of his approach. A burst of light swirled before Martin Sinclair before his world went pitch-black. He clutched convulsively at his throat and, gasping for air, dropped helplessly to his knees, rocking back and forth, uttering a horrible strangled cry, as the dark void closed on him, inexorably.

The mirror had revealed Lucinda, her dress unfastened and in wild disarray, her head flung back, her eyes closed, moaning with sensual abandon as Merle Greene's ravenous mouth sucked greedily at her magnificent breasts.

"This is Gary Franklin, and as you can see, televising live from in front of the Dorothy Chandler Pavilion, where the excitement is really starting to mount. You can hear the crowd going wild behind me as the nominees and many other celebrities file into the auditorium.

"There is Angela Armstrong, Jess. She is with her husband, Alan Kaufman, the head of the studio that produced *Moonshadows,* a film nominated in nine categories tonight. This could be a very big evening for them. Let's just see if we can get a word with Miss Armstrong.

"Allow me to congratulate you, Mr. Kaufman, on the success of *Moonshadows.* Miss Armstrong, are you looking forward to the festivities this evening?"

"Oh, yes, Gary. This is such an exciting evening! We're both just terrifically excited!" Angela posed for a moment, attired in a gold lamé gown with an unusually demure neckline, then she and Alan Kaufman made their way through the gauntlet of binding klieg lights to the Dorothy Chandler Pavilion.

"We can see Al Pacino over there just getting out of his limousine. As I'm sure you know, he's up for Best Actor this year for *Clash;* he's a great popular favorite, but once again he's facing very stiff competition from Dustin Hoffman, who's won before, of course, as well as from Robert De Niro, Michael Caine, and Jeremy Irons.

"Now . . . oh, and you can hear the crowd behind me going crazy as this lady approaches. Now she's a great popular favorite for the Best Actress award, Jess, in spite of the fact that *Moonshadows* was her first role in a film.

Jess Marlow, Gary Franklin's coanchorperson back in the studio, interjected a question: "But, Gary, isn't she up against some rather stiff competition with the likes of Debra Winger and Meryl Streep, just to name two?"

"That's very true, Jess, but, still, you've got to remember, there's been a tremendous outpouring of sympathy for this lady since her husband, producer Martin Sinclair, was so tragically paralyzed by a stroke just when he had so successfully completed several grueling months of filming on *Moonshadows.* And, as you know, Jess, sometimes sentiment can play an important role with Academy voters. But even discounting her personal tragedy, she came through with with what many people feel to be tremendous performance.

"Here she comes now; let's just see if we can try and get a few words with her. Oh . . . and Jess, I can see now as she approaches that Mrs. Sinclair's escort this evening is none other than her costar, Rod Ward. Now although Ward was not nominated, most people feel that he gave an excellent performance, so this is certainly a young man to watch!"

Lucinda Sinclair, accompanied by Merle Greene and Arthur Eckstein, a fabulous ice princess in white silk organza by Valentino, was gracious enough to halt in her royal progress along the red carpet to say a few words to the camera.

"Lucinda Sinclair . . . ladies and gentlemen . . . let me first congratulate you on your wonderful performance and tell you how beautiful you look . . ."

"Oh, thank you so much, Gary. It's just so wonderful to be here."

"Lucinda, if I may, can I just ask you to describe for us some of your thoughts, your emotions, about your Oscar nomination."

"First of all, I just want to say how tremendously honored I feel even to have been nominated in the same category as Meryl Streep, Sissy Spacek, and all those other fabulous ladies. Secondly, I would just like to add how sorry I am that my beloved husband, Martin, who made all this possible for me, is too ill to be here to share this moment with me. If he could speak, I'm sure he would wish to thank all the kind people out there who have sent messages of prayer and good will for his recovery. God bless each and every one of you!"

"Thank you, very much, Lucinda Sinclair, for stopping to talk with us, and we certainly wish you good luck."

"Thank you, Gary."

"And here I see Jack Nicholson with Angelica Huston. Let's just see if we can speak to them for a moment . . ."

"The nominees for Best Actress are . . ." Shirley MacLaine gave her famous pixie grin, as the first clip from the nominated film performance was flashed on the screen behind her.

"Debra Winger . . . in *Clash* . . . Jessica Lange . . . in *Twilight Time* . . . Lucinda Sinclair . . . in *Moonshadows*

. . . Meryl Streep . . . in *The Jazz Age* . . . and Sissy Spacek . . . in *Josie.*"

Shirley MacLaine's fingers shook in mock anxiety as she fumbled momentarily with the envelope, then, with a shrill whoop of excitement, read out the name of the winner.

As soon as she heard the name of Lucinda Sinclair announced, Pandora Ashley hurled the contents of her glass of Scotch at the TV screen in her small Manhattan apartment, and switched the set off in a paroxysm of rage. "That fucking little cheap tramp," she screeched. "That Oscar was mine! Mine!"

"Hey! What did you switch it off for?" asked the young man sprawled out on the bed. "I wanted to watch."

"Oh, you did? Well, this is my place, and you can just get out if you don't like it! Get out! Get out!" she shrieked hysterically.

"My pleasure," said the youth, grabbing his shirt and heading for the door. "Look, lady, I know who you *were* . . . but you ain't nothing but *shit* now . . . a fucking has-been. You're past it!" With that, he slammed the door and was gone.

Shaken and trembling, Pandora staggered into the bathroom where she searched frantically until her hands came to rest on a hypodermic syringe. With it, she found a piece of cord which she wrapped tightly around her forearm. She sought the vein, gasped, then waited for the powerful drug to course through her body, bringing oblivion.

As the seemingly endless stream of limousines swung into the floodlit drive of the Beverly Hilton Hotel for the post-Oscar gala celebration, hundreds of onlookers had gathered, straining to catch a glimpse of their favorite celebrity. There was a momentary scuffle as one man detached himself from the throng and with the agility of a commando thrust his way through the blue-coated security men and past the blue velvet ropes used to hold back the crowds. He was a thin man who appeared to be about forty years of age, dressed in a shabby khaki jacket. He had long sandy hair and wore a small gold earring in one ear.

He might have been considered good-looking, were it not for the black patch which covered his left eye, and the deep, jagged scar which ran down his forehead. His right eye was green and stared straight ahead with an awful fixity of purpose at the entrance to the main ballroom where klieg lights were blazing, and the most glamorous party of the season was in full swing. He roughly shook off the grasp of the guard who tried to restrain him as he strode purposefully toward a dais where the year's winner of the award for Best Actor, Al Pacino, was having his picture taken with the year's award winner as Best Actress. The lovely young woman in white smiled brightly, holding her precious trophy aloft.

Then, in a split second, the smile on her face froze; the precious statuette slipped from her grasp as she swayed unsteadily on her feet.

"What's the matter? What's going on?" cried the alarmed photographers.

"What's the matter, honey?" said Frank Bayes. "Ain't you gonna say hello to your pa?"